HAIL TO THEE, OKOBOJI U!

HAIL TO THEE, OKOBOJI U!

A Humor Anthology
on Higher Education

Selected and Edited by
MARK C. EBERSOLE

FORDHAM UNIVERSITY PRESS
New York

Copyright © 1992 by Fordham University

LC 92-17673

ISBN 0-8232-1383-8

Library of Congress Cataloging-in-Publication Data
Hail to thee, Okoboji U! : a humor anthology on higher education
 / edited by Mark C. Ebersole. — 1st ed.

   p.   cm.
  ISBN 0-8232-1383-8 : $23.95
  1. College wit and humor.   2. Learning and scholarship—United
States—History—Humor.   3. Scholars—United States—Anecdotes.
I. Ebersole, Mark C.
PN6231.C6H35   1992
817.008′355—dc20   92-17673
                                                           CIP

Printed in the United States of America

Copyright acknowledgments begin on page 317

This anthology is dedicated to our sons:

Stephen,
> who bore suffering with courage and spirit

Philip,
> who sustained his brother with sensitivity
> and compassion,

and to the sense of humor both maintained
throughout the ordeal.

Contents

Introduction

"How do you like working on a campus?" I asked my friend recently retired from state politics.

"It's really different from the political arena." A small, somewhat forced smile grudgingly bared itself; he was now a vice-president at a large university. One of my favorite oh-yes-tell-me-more expressions greeted his revelation.

"You're an academic, you should know," he said. "You people take your politics far more seriously than we politicians do. People in the legislature blast each other on the floor, but when it's over they forget about it. They go out and play golf together. They don't take it personally."

"And we do?" I asked knowingly.

"You also answer everything with a question." He shook his head. "And if you academics aren't asking each other questions, you stop talking to each other altogether. Amazing! Half the people in the history department here don't talk to the other half. Look around." We paused and briefly gazed at a few faculty walking across the campus quadrangle. "See that? Everybody's so self-absorbed and solemn, as though they're marching to their execution. Why don't they loosen up?"

"Why do you think?" I asked soberly.

"There you go again." He sighed, without smiling.

It does seem that learned personages of higher education—presidents, administrators, professors alike—are a somber lot. We don't deliberately set out to be that way; it's something that just happens naturally, like tennis elbow or writer's cramp.

Despite our quarreling with each other, society celebrates us as beacons of learning; and, indeed, we begin to see ourselves as superior intellects whose pronouncements are full of deep and memorable truths. And when we speak, we want our listeners to appreciate our extreme profundity. So we take on an exceedingly serious demeanor. After all, we secretly know that a somber presence does wonders: mundane observations translate into the verities of oracles. I remember a professor in a freshman course saying not once, not twice, but three times, "Mortality is an inextricable ingredient of human life," pronouncing this banality with such rising passion that, at his climax, I actually felt weak all over.

Our sage-like visage is conveyed to our adoring audience in other ways—by sitting seriously; by mumbling seriously; by pausing seriously; by putting glasses on and taking them off seriously; by seriously pushing the tongue against cheek while raising the eyebrows; and, of course, by staring vacantly at the ceiling.

Hail to Thee, Okoboji U! focuses on the lives of serious academicians, but this anthology invites all of us to be serious about viewing them more lightly. "What could be more preposterously funny than for a human being to think his knowledge is truth," wrote a wise man. Many famous thinkers echo this sentiment, among them Thomas Aquinas, Karl Barth, and Erasmus. I like especially what Erasmus wrote in *The Praise of Folly*: "But methinks I hear the philosophers . . . saying 'tis a miserable thing for a man to be foolish, to err, mistake, and know nothing truly. Nay, rather, this is to be a man. And why they should call it miserable, I see no reason; forasmuch as we are so born, so instructed, nay such is the common condition of us all."

The materials in *Hail to Thee, Okoboji U!* are the creations of 64 writers and artists. Most are not full-fledged members of the academic community. In that sense, they are outside observers. Many are household names—Woody Allen, Russell Baker, Robert Benchley, Peter De Vries, Max Eastman, Jules Feiffer, Don Marquis, Henry Martin, Ogden Nash, Frank Sullivan, James Thurber, Garry Trudeau, and Mark Twain, to mention a few. Through their wonderful comic sense, they see right through academic façades.

The collegiate world, however, is not without its own humorists. And so this anthology also contains pieces by persons in the academic ranks, such as Jeremy Bernstein, Richard Chait, John Kenneth Galbraith, Madeleine Green, Samuel Pickering, Jr., John Crowe Ransom, David Rein, and Leo Rosten.

The topics these writers and artists pursue deal comprehensively with higher education, ranging from its early history to current admissions procedures, from students and student affairs to professors and faculty meetings; from the academic fields of literature, art, music, history, philosophy, and science to the more mundane pursuits of college presidents and commencement speakers. There is nothing on college trustees, however. Working through innumerable publications on humor, I uncovered only one piece on trustees, and that was of minimal comic value. Apparently trustees are not very funny.

How should one read *Hail to Thee, Okoboji U!*? The anthology begins with an historical sketch and admission procedures, and ends with graduation and alumni affairs. That seems altogether logical, but the logic pretty much ends there. In between, the materials on students, professors, college presidents, and various programs and events could be put in any order. All are equally important and equally splendid subjects for humor (though professors contend that genuine humor reaches its peak in presidents, while presidents hold an identical view about professors). It matters not which essay, verse, or cartoon you turn to. You can leap backward and forward through the book according to your mood and curiosity.

Finally, though, what is most important as you read this anthology is that you allow your sense of humor full play. Let it burst, if it will. Don't bother examining and analyzing; and, above all, don't ask questions—that's a sure way to kill humor. Just let the thing amuse you. Let it "laugh its way" into your bones. That's what the book is about: to make you smile, grin, chuckle and, yes, even hoot, shout, or guffaw—in other words, to make you feel delightfully unacademic.

MARK C. EBERSOLE
Lancaster, Pa.

A Short History of Higher Education

Richard Armour

Prehistoric Times

Little is known about higher education during the Stone Age, which is perhaps just as well.

Because of a weakness in the liberal arts, the B.A. was not offered, and there was only the B.S., or Bachelor of Stones. Laboratory facilities were meager, owing to lack of government contracts and support from private industry, but the stars were readily available on clear nights for those interested in astronomy.

Prehistoric students, being before history, failed to comprehend the fundamentals of the subject, such as its being divided into Ancient, Medieval, and Modern.

There were no college boards.

Nor were there any fraternities. The only clubs on the campus were those carried by the students.

Alumni organizations were in their infancy, where some of them have remained. The Alumni Secretary occupied a small cave, left behind when the Director of Development moved to a larger one. While waiting for contributions to come in, he idly doodled on the wall, completely unaware that art critics would someday mistake his drawings of certain members of the board of trustees for dinosaurs and saber-toothed tigers.

The Alumni Quarterly came out every quarter of a century, and was as eagerly awaited as it is today.

The Classical Period

In ancient Athens everyone knew Greek, and in ancient Rome everyone knew Latin, even small children—which those who have taken Elementary Greek or Elementary Latin will find hard to believe. Universities wishing to teach a language which had little practical use but was good for mental discipline could have offered English if they had thought of it.

1

Buildings were all in the classical style, and what looked like genuine marble was genuine marble.

The professors of the Peripatetic School kept moving from town to town, closely followed by students and creditors. Sometimes lectures were held in the Groves of Academe, where students could munch apples and occasionally cast an anxious eye at birds in the branches overhead.

Under the Caesars, taxation became so burdensome that Romans in the upper brackets found they might as well give money to their Alma Mater instead of letting the State have it. Thus it was that crowds often gathered along the Appian Way to applaud a spirited chariot race between the chairman of the funds drive and the tax collector, each trying to get to a good prospect first.

The word "donor" comes from the Latin *donare*, to give, and is not to be confused with *dunare*, to dun, though it frequently is.

When a prominent alumnus was thrown to the lions, customary procedure in the alumni office was to observe a moment of silence. Then the secretary, wrapping his toga a little more tightly around him, solemnly declared, "Well, we might as well take him off the cultivation list."

The Middle Ages

In the period known as the Dark Ages, or nighthood, higher education survived only because of illuminated manuscripts, which were discovered during a routine burning of a library. It is interesting to reconstruct a typical classroom scene: a group of dedicated students clustered around a glowing piece of parchment, listening to a lecture in Advanced Monasticism, a ten-year course. If some found it hard to concentrate, it was because they were dreaming about quitting before exams and going off on a crusade.

Some left even sooner, before the end of the lecture, having spied a beautiful damsel being pursued by a dragon who had designs on her. The dragon was probably an art student who was out of drawing paper. Damsels, who were invariably in distress, wrought havoc on a young man's grade-point average.

Members of the faculty were better off than previously, because they wore suits of armor. Fully accoutered, and with their visors down, they could summon up enough courage to go into the President's office and ask for a promotion even though they had not published a thing.

At this time the alumni council became more aggressive in its fund drives, using such persuasive devices as the thumbscrew, the knout, the rack, and the wheel. A wealthy alumnus would usually donate generously if a sufficient number of alumni could cross his moat and storm his castle walls. A few could be counted on to survive the rain of stones, arrows, and molten lead. Such a group of alumni, known as "the committee," was customarily conducted to the castle by a troubadour, who led in the singing of the Alma Mater Song the while.

The Renaissance

During the Renaissance, universities sprang up all over Europe. You could go to bed at night, with not a university around, and the next morning there would be two universities right down the street, each with a faculty, student body, campanile, and need for additional endowment.

The first universities were in Italy, where Dante was required reading. Boccaccio was not required but was read anyhow, and in the original Italian, so much being lost in translation. Other institutions soon followed, such as Heidelberg, where a popular elective was Dueling 103a, b, usually taken concurrently with Elementary First Aid. In England there was Oxford, where, by curious coincidence, all of the young instructors were named Don. There was also Cambridge.

The important thing about the Renaissance, which was a time of awakening (even in the classroom), was education of the Whole Man. Previously such vital parts as the elbows and ear lobes had been neglected. The graduate of a university was supposed, above all, to be a Gentleman. This meant that he should know such things as archery, falconry, and fencing (subjects now largely relegated to Physical Education and given only one-half credit per semester), as well as, in the senior year, how to use a knife and fork.

During the Renaissance, the works of Homer, Virgil, and other classical writers were rediscovered, much to the annoyance of students.

Alumni officials concentrated their efforts on securing a patron: someone rich like Lorenzo de' Medici, someone clever like Machiavelli, or (if they wished to get rid of a troublesome member of the administration) someone really useful like Lucrezia Borgia.

Colonial America

The first universities in America were founded by the Puritans. This explains the strict regulations about Late Hours, Compulsory Chapel, and No Liquor on the Campus which still exist at many institutions.

Some crafts were taught, but witchcraft was an extracurricular activity. Witch-burning, on the other hand, was the seventeenth-century equivalent of hanging a football coach in effigy at the end of a bad season. Though deplored, it was passed off by the authorities as attributable to "youthful exuberance."

Harvard set the example for naming colleges after donors. William and Mary, though making a good try, failed to start a trend for using first names. It was more successful, however, in starting Phi Beta Kappa, a fraternity which permitted no rough stuff in its initiations. At first the Phi Beta Kappa key was worn on the key ring, but the practice went out with the discovery of the watch chain and vest.

During the Colonial Period, alumni officials limited their fundraising activities to alumni who were securely fastened, hands and legs, in the stocks. In this position they were completely helpless and gave generously, or could be frisked.

Revolutionary America

Higher education came to a virtual standstill during the Revolution—every able-bodied male having enlisted for the duration. Since the ROTC had not yet been established, college men were forced to have other qualifications for a commission, such as money.

General George Washington was given an honorary degree by Harvard, and this helped see him through the difficult winter at Valley Forge. Since he gave no commencement address, it is assumed that he made a substantial contribution to the building fund. Then again, mindful of the reputation he had gained through Parson Weems's cherry tree story, he may have established a chair in Ethics.

Unlike the situation during World War I, when colleges and universities abandoned the teaching of German in order to humiliate the Kaiser, the Colonists waged the Revolutionary War successfully without prohibiting the teaching of English. They did, however, force students to substitute such good old American words as "suspenders" for "braces," and themes were marked down when the spelling "tyre" was used for "tire."

The alumni publication, variously called the Alumni Bulletin, the Alumni Quarterly, and the Alumni Newsletter, was probably invented at this time by Benjamin Franklin, who invented almost everything else, including bifocals and kites. The first such publication was *Poor Alumnus' Almanac,* full of such homely sayings as "Early to bed and early to rise makes a man healthy, wealthy, and wise enough to write his Alma Mater into his will."

Contemporary America

In the nineteenth century, denominational colleges were founded in all parts of the country, especially Ohio. In the smaller of these colleges, money was mostly given in small denominations. A few colleges were not named after John Wesley.

State universities came into being at about the same time, and were tax supported. Every taxpayer was therefore a donor, but without getting his name on a building or being invited to dinner by the President. The taxpayer, in short, was in the same class as the Anonymous Giver, but not because he asked that his name be withheld. It was some of his salary that was withheld.

About the middle of the nineteenth century, women were admitted to college. This was done (1) to relieve men of having to take women's parts in dramatic productions, some women's parts being hard for men to supply, (2) to provide cheer leaders with shapelier legs and therefore more to cheer about, and (3) to recruit members for the Women's Glee Club. It was not realized, when they were admitted, that women would get most of the high marks, especially from professors who graded on curves.

In the twentieth century, important strides were made, such as the distinction which developed between education and Education. Teachers came to be trained in what were at first called Normal Schools. With the detection of certain abnormalities, the name was changed to Teachers Colleges.

John Dewey introduced Progressive Education, whereby students quickly knew more than their teachers and told them so. Robert Hutchins turned the University of Chicago upside down, thereby necessitating a new building program. At St. John's College everyone studied the Great Books, which were more economical because they did not come out each year in a revised edition. Educational television gave college professors an excuse for owning a television set, which they had previously maintained would destroy the reading habit. This made it possible for them to watch Westerns and old movies without losing status.

Of recent years, an increasing number of students spend their junior year abroad. This enables them to get a glimpse of professors who are away on Fulbrights or Guggenheims.

Student government has grown apace, students now not only governing themselves but giving valuable suggestions, in the form of ultimatums, to the President and Dean. In wide use is the Honor System, which makes the professor leave the room during an examination because he is not to be trusted.

Along with these improvements in education has come a subtle change in the American alumnus. No longer interested only in the record of his college's football team, he is likely to appear at his class reunion full of such penetrating questions as "Why is the tuition higher than it was in 1934?" "Is it true that 85 per cent of the faculty are Communists?" and "How can I get my son (or daughter) in?"

Alumni magazines have kept pace with such advances. The writing has improved, thanks to schools of journalism, until there is excitement and suspense even in the obituary column. Expression has reached such a high point of originality that a request for funds may appear, at first reading, to be a gift offer.

All in all, higher education has reached these heights of attainment:

Despite their questionable contribution to earning a living, the liberal arts are accepted as an excellent means of keeping young people off the streets for four years.

Young people, in turn, are continuing their studies longer and longer, having discovered this an excellent means of keeping out of the Army.

Faculty members, publishing more voluminously than ever, are making an important contribution to the national economy, especially to the pulp and paper industry.

The government is helping students with scholarships and professors with research grants, thereby enabling more and more students to go to college, where more and more professors are too busy with research grants to teach them.

Solemnity, Gloom
and the Academic Style:
A Reflection

John Kenneth Galbraith

In 1976, following my retirement from active teaching, The Harvard Lampoon, *a magazine of good cheer, called forth in Boston a major convocation of its editors, former editors, readers, intended readers and friends and presented me with a purple and gold Cadillac Eldorado convertible, a check for $10,000 and the offer of a free vacation in Las Vegas, which my wife and I did not accept. The car, which unhappily would not fit in our driveway, let alone our garage, we did accept and put into storage. Then, with the permission of the donors, we allowed it to be sold for the benefit of WGBH (public television station) at its auction a year later. All this largesse from* The Lampoon *was not a reward for the economic knowledge I had conveyed over the years; it was, I was told, because I had done something to lighten the tedium of college life. I was required, in turn, to describe to the audience of nostalgic* Lampoon *alumni the academic style at Harvard, as I do in this essay derived from my speech.*

In these last years I have been led to reflect on the extreme solemnity that has become the modern academic style—and not least at Harvard. I do not suppose that universities were ever joyously amusing places; certainly professors were always expected to take themselves rather seriously. Still, as I move about the university's purlieus and attend its meetings, social exercises and other rituals, I cannot but think that we have become exceptionally grave these days, given even to an ostentatious gloom. That is now the academic style. Perhaps the reasons should be examined.

Partly, of course, solemnity derives from what we are compelled to teach. This, on occasion, is so funny that to relax even for a moment would be fatal. In economics we dutifully explain that a country can have inflation or it can have recession, but it can never have both at the same time. And all this while it does. As we proceed into more advanced and theoretically more refined instruction, we cease to discuss corporations of any puissance, trade unions of any power or the existence of intercourse, in the platonic sense, between these and the government. There is no independent exercise of power; all and everyone are subordinate to market forces. Were we even to smile as we thus lectured, brighter students, if any, might catch on.

7

The professors of government must be equally on guard against levity. This is a democracy, and its citizens, like its consumers, are sovereign. Subsidies to politicians, whether emanating from Nelson Rockefeller, Northrop or Gulf Oil, are not meant to affect the distribution of power; they serve only to affirm the deeply philanthropic instincts of the American people. Power remains with the White House and the Congress; perish the thought that it should have passed to the Pentagon.

Even greater solemnity is required of those who teach the law. Some weeks ago the dean of the Harvard Law School is believed to have issued a ukase against laughter to all professors concerned with the subject of legal ethics. It was on the day after the former dean of the University of Chicago Law School, Mr. Edward Levi, presided over the unveiling of the portrait of former Attorney General Richard Kleindienst on the walls of the Department of Justice. There would, he said, be no chuckles, no mention of G. Gordon Liddy, Watergate or the legal inhibitions on perjury. One presumes that he reminded all students attending that John Mitchell's portrait would, sometime in the future, also be unveiled, but only by the dean of a medium-grade correspondence school.

The historians are the gloomiest case of all. Although they have no current conflict between scholarship and reality, they, too, must reflect on what they teach. In this year of bicentennial self-congratulation they must consider (as I believe Eugene McCarthy first said) that in these last two hundred years we've moved on from George Washington to Richard Nixon, from John Adams to Spiro Agnew, from John Jay to John Mitchell and from Alexander Hamilton to John B. Connally. Understandably, the more sensitive come into the Faculty Club, after a lecture, distraught with grief.

The subject matter we teach is not the only cause of our solemnity. Once, Harvard professors were judged by the president of the university and in theory, if not in fact, by the genial Harvard graduates who served on the Board of Overseers and the Visiting Committees. Those who made the evaluations were safely at a distance. One could enjoy an occasional laugh in classrooms, department meetings or in public, confident in the knowledge that no one vital to one's career was watching. Now professors are judged by their peers; that means we can never relax.

(1976)

When I returned to Harvard after World War II, the chief auditor of our virtue in the economics department was Sinclair Weeks, sometime senator from Massachusetts and later President Eisenhower's secretary of commerce. Three generations of Weekses had served the Massachusetts citizenry with no trace of a generation gap; all had rigorously identified the public interest with that of the rich. Shortly after Sinclair took over at Commerce, he fired the head of the Bureau of Standards for finding, against the wishes of a West Coast entrepreneur, that Glauber's salt—sodium sulfate—was worthless as a battery additive. The scientists protested violently. Bernard DeVoto came to Weeks's defense, saying that he was the first politician so brave as to stake his career on the proposition that a battery could be improved by giving it a laxative. It was a joyous moment. But one cannot afford such fun with one's academic colleagues. They may not like your laughter and will one day hold it against you.

There are other reasons for our style. Since we are Harvard professors, we know, uniquely among American parents, that our offspring will never be as brilliant as we are. They may end up teaching at some lesser Ivy League school or, God forbid, some agriculturally oriented academy in the Farm Belt. That is a grim thing on which to reflect. Those of us who are older also observe with grief the kind of Harvard professor who now gets selected for public service. We can hardly avoid showing our sorrow as we think how much better material there used to be in our time, how much wiser the appointments that included us.

An aspect of grave harassment also suggests deep devotion to one's work; this, indeed, has long been so. A propensity to amusement, in contrast, could be thought to imply idleness. This is now especially important, because Harvard may be the only considerable community in the world, the Pentagon possibly excepted, where the effort to simulate effort can exceed the effort itself. After three months' vacation in the summer, a professor may feel obliged to take a sabbatical leave in the autumn so that he will be rested and ready for a winter committed to a course on the work ethic.

Such are the sources of the modern academic style. It has been said of sexual congress—as I was brought up to call it—that the pleasure is momentary, the position is ridiculous and the expense is damnable. Considering what laughter does to our dignity, to our reputation and thus to our academic income, our attitude must inevitably be the same toward any lapse from solemnity. In my youth I tried hard to master the Harvard academic style and often believed I had succeeded. You tell me today that, sadly, I did not. It is nice sometimes to be rewarded for failure.

How to Get In

Richard Armour

Let us assume that the prospective student has read the catalogue and, naively accepting all of its statements as true, has decided, "This is the college for me." Let us also assume, though it is usually my practice to be quite unassuming, that the prospective student has filled out all the blanks and paid the necessary deposit. What then?

A curious thing about college admissions is that while students are trying to get in, colleges are trying to get students. The reason for this is that the colleges the students are trying to get into and the students the colleges are trying to get often don't match.

"I'd give everything I have," says Bert Smathers, "to get into Harvard."

But what does young Smathers have? An average of not quite C during his last two years at Central High, a CEEB verbal score of 367, no athletic ability, and a personality that won him his only award in high school, that of being voted Creep of the Year. Moreover, having no financial resources, he will need a scholarship sufficient to cover at least such essentials as room, board, and tuition.

"I think I'll go to a state university in the Middle West," says H. Saltonstall Lowell. "I detest the snobbishness and provincialism of places like Harvard."

Young Lowell graduated first in his class at Choate, racked up a CEEB verbal score of 800 and a math score of 790, captained the undefeated tennis team, set track records for the 100 and 220, and was president of the student body. Since his father, a member of the Harvard Board of Overseers, is a major stockholder in General Pneumatics, he would not require financial assistance.

As a Dean of Admissions said, when told of the above cases, "That's the way the cooky crumbles." He appeared fatalistic, even nonchalant, but he was unable to control the tear that rolled down his cheek.

To find and persuade students like H. Saltonstall Lowell, most colleges have a Field Representative, constantly prowling the countryside. Seen on a train or airplane, he could not be distinguished from an insurance salesman or a manufacturer's representative, except for his constantly humming the Alma Mater. At the schools he visits, appointments are set up with any students interested in the college he represents, and since this means a great deal to some students, such as getting out of class, he usually has a full day of interviews.

When the Field Representative has tracked down a student who would be a real catch, one who would make both Phi Beta Kappa and the All-Conference football team, the interview goes something like this:

STUDENT: What's so special about your college?

FIELD REPRESENTATIVE: Well, for one thing, many of the classes are very small. (He doesn't say why they are small. They are small because the professors who teach them are either dull or uninformed. In the extremely small classes they may be both. Nor does he explain the disadvantages of a small class, such as being missed if you are absent.)

STUDENT: What about faculty-student relationships outside of class?

FIELD REPRESENTATIVE: They are close. (This means it is always possible to make an appointment with a professor, and sometimes he will remember to keep it.)

STUDENT: How is the food?

FIELD REPRESENTATIVE: Marvelous. (The Field Representative looks well fed, and no wonder, since he never eats at the college.)

STUDENT: Is liquor allowed on the campus?

FIELD REPRESENTATIVE (Who looks horrified, either because (1) of course it isn't or (2) of course it is. In either case it is a stupid question, and the Field Representative pretends not to have heard it): Well, I think it's time for the next appointment. It's been great talking with you.

STUDENT: Don't I get any samples or anything?

FIELD REPRESENTATIVE: Of course. (He gives him a pennant, copies of several publications, including last year's commencement address, "The Liberal Arts in Transition," and a memorial ash tray, embellished with the college motto, the famous admonition of Publius Ibid, *"Vide supra et vide infra."*)

The Field Representative submits a confidential report to the Dean of Admissions. This report can be very helpful in evaluating an applicant, since it is full of such perceptive remarks as: "Wouldn't fit into our student body. Too intellectual." Or "Weak student and poor citizen, but father owns local brewery and might help with our new chapel." Once a Field Representative, an attractive young man who had graduated only a couple of years before, made the following report on an exceptional find: "This girl has everything—brains, beauty, talent. But she has decided not to go to college. We are getting married."

Now a few pointers for applicants who wish to know on what basis they are likely to be judged. Of course high school grades are important, especially in such solids as English, history, Latin, and chemistry. Grades in liquids such as domestic science (to be distinguished from imported science), music appreciation, and basket weaving fail to impress the authorities unless they are unusually low, say a B. The school, too, makes a difference, some schools having an even poorer reputation than others. Also it means more to be in the first ten in a graduating class of six hundred than in a graduating class of six.

As for College Board scores, these are so mechanical and depend so much on how the student feels on the day of the test that they carry little weight with anyone but admissions officials.

"What chance is there for my son, who made terribly low scores on both the Verbal and Mathematical tests?" a parent is likely to ask, somewhat discouraged.

"Every chance in the world," the Dean of Admissions says reassuringly. "He's probably just a slow maturer."

"What do you advise?"

A slow maturer

"Wait until he matures," the Dean of Admissions says helpfully.

By waiting a few years, the applicant may become mature enough to realize how unnecessary a college education is, by that time being the head of his firm.

It might interest parents and prospective students to know that the Dean of Admissions is assisted by a faculty committee which has no confidence whatsoever in the judgment of the Dean of Admissions.

"He hasn't a Ph.D.," one member of the committee says, his upper lip curling derisively.

"And he hasn't published a line, not so much as a book review," says another.

"He's not even a member of Phi Beta Kappa, just some Education fraternity," adds a third, making a thumbs-down motion with one hand while twirling his Phi Beta Kappa key with the other.

If it were not for the members of the faculty committee, someone who is not a "brain" but has character, drive, originality, and high qualities of leadership might slip in and become president of the student body. The faculty is concerned about academic excellence, hoping to admit so many students of intellectual brilliance that a fair percentage will go on to win Fulbrights and Woodrow Wilsons, no matter how poorly they are taught.

Students are advised to apply to several colleges, not merely the college of their choice. This is because each application must be accompanied by a fee, which is non-returnable, and every little bit helps when the budget is tight. Students who are afraid they will not get into any college are advised to submit their names to a central organization which keeps a list of colleges which are not well known, because they are unable to afford a football coach, or even a football. Then again, their moral standards may be so high that they have failed to gain national attention through headlines such as STUDENT CUT BY BUSTED BOTTLE DURING BEER BUST or COLLEGE PREXY ADMITS KEEPING DEAN OF WOMEN IN LOVE NEST. But students can learn a great deal at such colleges, even when they are church-connected, if there is a large city nearby.

Outstanding students are given Honors at Entrance. If they continue to do well for four years, they are given Honors at Exit.

Inquiries should be addressed to the Dean of Admissions, who hopes there will not be too many, at least until the new secretary, the third this year, learns to type.

The Rich Scholar

Teresa Bloomingdale

"Hey, Mom," asked our son Dan as he was filling out a questionnaire, "what class are we?"

I thought for a moment. What class?

"Seniors," I said sophomorically. "Or shall we be juniors? Which class has more fun?"

"Aw, Mom, be serious," said Dan. "I gotta know; what class are we? Upper? Middle? Lower?"

"I suppose that would depend on who's doing the classifying," I told him truthfully. "Our uppity neighbor has always been sure we are 'lower,' but your grandmother insists that we are 'upper.' Those who are in-the-know, however, would probably place us in the Great American Middle."

"Who are those in-the-know?" he asked.

"The IRS," I said. "Who else? What are you filling out, anyway?"

"A financial-aid request," he replied. "I'm applying for a college scholarship."

"In that case, go with the neighbors," I said emphatically. "Check 'lower.' And underline it. But do it in pencil; if they think you can afford a pen, they'll shove you into 'upper middle' and tell you to go paddle your own canoe."

I didn't have the heart to tell him he was wasting his time. I know. I have been this route before.

When our first son was preparing for college, he applied for financial aid and was told there should be no problem, as there were over 8,000 various types of scholarships available. That may be true; but what they failed to tell him was, at least 7,975 of them are limited to athletes, and the rest are parceled out to academically superior students who can prove financial need. Since his high school athletics had been pretty much limited to intramural wrestling (the coed variety), he could hardly qualify as an athlete (though he did earn the coveted Octopus award given annually by the Girls Pep Club.) He didn't even try to prove financial need, for he knew he would never be able to prove "academic superiority" with a report card that had seldom seen an A.

Our second son had plenty of A's but he, too, failed to qualify for a scholarship because, despite his close relationship to (as well as often being the cause of) my always in-the-red budget, he could not prove financial need. It seems that eighteen years earlier his godfather had bestowed upon him a small baptismal bequest, which we insisted that he not touch until he went to college. Even with accrued interest, the bequest would barely pay for books and fees, but the Office of Financial Aid considered it a "source of income" and denied him any monetary assistance. (A pronouncement which caused him to cry: "See? I told ya you should have let me buy a motorcycle!")

Oddly enough, had he squandered that bequest on a motorcycle, or even on booze, he might have been eligible for financial aid, as we discovered when our third son (a straight-A student lacking a baptismal bequest or any other source of income) submitted his request for a scholarship. Alas, despite his good grades and indigent status, he too was denied financial aid because he was burdened with an even greater albatross than a baptismal bequest. He had parents.

"What have my parents got to do with this?" he asked the clerk in the Financial Aid Office, where he had been practically camped out all summer, like Lazarus begging for a crumb. "My parents aren't the ones going to college! I am!"

"Yes," replied the clerk, "but we expect parents, whenever possible, to pick up the tab for their children's tuition."

"You just spoke the magic phrase," said my son cheerfully. "When and if it's ever possible, I am sure my parents will gladly fork over the ten grand I will need to get my degree. Right now they have nine other kids, all of whom consider their meals more important than my education."

"I am not responsible for your siblings!" said the clerk firmly (a fact to which I will certainly attest). "Our decision was not based so much on your father's salary as it was on the fact that your family has a savings account."

"We do?" asked our son in surprise. "I didn't know that. Say, how come *you* know that?"

"We have our methods," said the clerk proudly. "In any event, we feel that in light of this cash asset, you do not qualify for financial aid."

When our son related this conversation to me, I couldn't believe it. The next morning I called the Financial Aid Office myself.

"That's correct, Mrs. Bloomingdale," the clerk said in response to my inquiry. "The fact that you have that savings account indicates you can afford to pay your son's tuition."

"Look," I said sincerely, "that savings account isn't really a savings account; it's my station wagon fund. For years I have needed a new station wagon but I cannot afford to pay for a station wagon and finance charges as well, so I have been struggling along with this ten-year-old lemon and in another three hundred dollars I will have my new station wagon. You cannot have my new station wagon!"

"I am sorry," said the clerk, "but rules are rules."

"Am I to understand," I asked with sudden inspiration, "that people who have accumulated any assets are not eligible for aid?"

"That's correct," he said.

"Then how come my neighbor's son got a two-thousand-dollar-grant when his parents own three Cadillacs, a motor launch, and a summer cottage on Cape Cod? Explain that to me!"

"Those are not cash assets," sighed the clerk, "and it is very possible that the vehicles and the cottage are heavily mortgaged."

"So that's the secret!" I said. "Give me thirty minutes. In half an hour I can deplete my cash assets and run up all kinds of bills. Give me till noon, and I can probably even declare bankruptcy!"

The clerk was not amused.

"Tell me," I sighed in resignation, "how did you know about that savings account?"

"Clues!" the clerk admitted proudly. "We learn to spot the clues. In your son's case it was the watch he was wearing the first time he came into this office. There are at least seven hundred students who have one exactly like it. Then there was the pen he used when he filled out the second and third applications. But the clincher was the briefcase he brought in here yesterday. That's when we knew for sure about the savings account."

"But I don't understand," I told him. "What do a watch, a pen, and a briefcase have to do with a savings account?"

"They were premiums!" said the clerk triumphantly. "I recognized those premiums. Frankly, I got one of those briefcases, myself. So you see, I not only know which Savings and Loan you use, I can also make a pretty fair guess as to the amount of the last three deposits!"

"I guess you kids are just going to have to work your way through college," my husband said at dinner that night. "We'll help you all we can, but it looks like 'financial aid' is limited to those who go out for sports, or who belong to a minority group, or who are truly in need."

"Well you won't have to worry about me!" said our eleven-year-old Pat as he wolfed down his third hamburger. "I'm gonna be the star quarterback on the college football team!"

"And you probably won't have to worry about me, either," said Tim, our ninth child, "'cause if Pat keeps eatin' like a pig, by the time I get to college all our money will have gone for food!"

"I think I should qualify under all three categories," offered their sister Mary, who had already completed two years in the university's college of Fine Arts.

"How do you figure that?" asked her brother. "You're not in athletics, you're not in a minority group, and you're not in need."

"Oh, but I am," she said. "I just signed up for Fencing, which is not only considered a sport but which definitely places me in a minority group. There aren't many female fencers, I'll wager!"

"How about the 'need' aspect?" badgered her brother.

"Simple," she said with a sigh. "I've been dating three seniors, all of whom once qualified for that Octopus award. Boy, do I need to know Fencing!"

To our surprise and delight, Dan actually did get a scholarship, but it wasn't based on athletics, social status, or even need. It was, in fact, based on his showing in the American College Tests; he landed in the percentile the examiners refer to as "scholars."

Can you believe that? A scholarship granted to a scholar! What is this country coming to?

Off to College

Teresa Bloomingdale

When I went away to college, a generation ago, I took a steamer trunk to hold my clothes and a shopping bag for miscellaneous items such as an alarm clock, an umbrella, a radio, and a tennis racket. I remember my father teasing me about "taking all that stuff to school," and my arguing that these were all "absolute necessities," though I suppose it was a bit much, especially since I was also toting a typewriter, an extra coat, and a huge stuffed animal to which I was not particularly devoted but which was definitely *de rigueur* in a girl's dorm room in that era.

A generation later, when our son John went off to college, things were a bit different. John took a shopping bag to hold his clothes (his entire wardrobe consisting of two pairs of jeans, a couple of T-shirts, and twelve sweat bands) and a U-Haul for his miscellaneous items: refrigerator, recliner, hot plate, sunlamp, television set, full component stereo system, typewriter, tape recorder, ten-speed bike, and numerous boxes of records and books, some of which were expensive college texts that he had managed to purchase secondhand during the summer.

"You can't take all that stuff to school!" I admonished John, with much less humor than my father had shown me twenty-five years before.

To my surprise, John agreed.

"You're right," he said. "I'll never be able to store all this stuff in my dorm room. I'll have to sacrifice something."

And he did. He gave up the textbooks.

Like dutiful parents, we accompanied John to the state university in Lincoln, Nebraska, where he had been assigned a room in Abel Hall. There is an excellent branch of Nebraska University in our own Omaha, but of course John was not about to go there; that would mean living at home for four more years! John wasn't too happy about our "tagging along" ("You didn't take me to kindergarten; why should you take me to college?"), but like all college alums, I was afflicted with "back-to-school fever" and was determined to spend at least a few hours reveling in the nostalgia which would surely be aroused by the familiar aura of a college dorm.

I was first aware of just how drastically things had changed when my husband and I followed John into the elevator of his dormitory. In my old dormitory elevator at Duchesne College, there had been a permanent odor of incense wafting from the nearby chapel, and on weekend evenings the incense mingled pleasantly with the faint fragrance of our perfume.

The "aura" of John's elevator bore the unmistakable "fragrance" of fast food, stale cigarettes, and unwashed sweat socks. But then one could hardly expect a men's dormitory to smell of girl's perfume!

As we stepped off the elevator on the thirteenth floor (we thought it hilariously suitable that John's dorm was one of the few buildings in existence to claim a thirteenth floor), I said:

"Hold it. Wait a minute; something's not right here."

"What's the matter, Ma?" asked John as he juggled books, record albums, and a lamp.

"We're in the wrong building, that's what's the matter," I said, wondering why he couldn't see the obvious.

"No, we're not," he said. "This is Abel Hall; I've got my assignment right here in my pocket."

"But look!" I cried, pointing to the people scurrying up and down the corridors. "This is a girls' dormitory!"

"Oh, Ma," laughed John, "this is a coed dorm. The girls live on the even floors and the boys live on alternate floors."

"Then why are there girls on your alternate floor?" I asked.

"Because the top floor is for 'afterthoughts,' kids who registered late. Both boys and girls live on this floor."

"Do you mean to tell me," I exclaimed in disbelief, "that you are going to share living quarters with girls?"

"We don't share 'living quarters,' Mom," said John with impatience; "we just share the residence, just like I shared our house with Mary, Peggy, and Annie."

"Not like *that*, I hope," quipped his dad. "You'll get arrested for cruel and inhumane harassment."

"Don't panic, Mom," said John. "The girls are all at one end of the floor and the guys are at the other end."

"And the girls never come down to your end, right?" I asked hopefully.

"Only during visiting hours, Ma," said John, and I was tremendously relieved . . . until I found out that visiting hours were from 6 A.M. to 2:30 A.M.

I needn't have worried, for while rumor drifted home to us that John's dorm room was frequently visited by beautiful girls, it was seldom visited by John. Actually, it was not so much rumor, as it was proof positive provided by the telephone company. Whenever I would call John on his room phone (and I could call in the middle of the day or the middle of the night, it made no difference), he was never there, a fact I met with mixed emotions because somebody *was* there and that somebody was almost always of the opposite sex.

When John came home for Christmas I complained that I could never seem to catch him in his room, and he explained that he was spending little time in his dorm room as the dorm was too noisy for either studying or sleeping. (I dared not ask him where he had been sleeping, and I didn't need to ask him where he had been studying, as his report cards indicated he hadn't been too bothered with that particular aspect of college.)

We both concluded that he would be better off living in an apartment, so the next semester he and his former roommate moved into a small apartment in Lincoln.

The following fall, when John's brother Michael registered at the University of Nebraska at Lincoln, I was dismayed to learn that he had asked to be assigned a room in Abel Hall.

"Why do you want to live in a dorm?" I asked. "Why can't you live with John? I can't afford to 'furnish' another dorm room; I thought we would never get all John's stuff moved down to Lincoln."

"Calm down, Mom," said Mike. "Things are different today than they were in John's day." One would have thought he was referring to a generation gap rather than a two-semester time span.

"Different?" I asked suspiciously. "How different?"

"In the first place," said Mike, "I won't be hauling a bunch of miscellaneous stuff down to the dorm. Of course, I will need more luggage than John did. College kids today don't live in jeans and T-shirts anymore. I figure I will need a couple of three-piece suits, some sport coats, slacks, loafers, dress shoes, tennis shoes, and running shoes, half a dozen shirts, some ties, pajamas (pajamas? I didn't even know he *knew* about pajamas!), a robe, socks, underwear, and two tuxedos."

"*Two* tuxedos?" I asked incredulously. (Why do I ask?)

"Sure," he said. "You don't expect me to wear a winter tux to the spring dances, do you?"

Somehow I think I preferred the ridiculous remnants John called clothes. *Those* I could afford.

"At least we won't have to rent a moving van for your miscellaneous stuff," I said to Mike. "What *are* you taking? Should I save a couple of grocery cartons for you to pack things in?"

"Not necessary, Mom," said Mike cheerfully. "My 'miscellany' will fit right here in the old wallet."

"What do you mean?" I asked. (There I go, asking again!) "What kind of miscellany will fit in your billfold?"

"Your MasterCharge card!" said Mike confidently. "That will take care of everything I need. . . . Unless, of course, you'd rather give me cash?"

That noise you hear is my father in heaven, roaring with laughter.

Gather Round, Collegians

Roy Blount, Jr.

Generally my advice to young people is, Don't listen to advice. I say that not only because it is something young people will listen to. I say it also because questionable advice ("Hey, organic chemistry will take care of itself") is always so much more appealing than sound advice ("Worry about everything").

But this year I am a sophomore parent. That is, my daughter Ennis is a sophomore at Stanford. That is, I believe she is. Since Stanford's policy is not to send grades, comportment ratings, or even bills, as such, to parents, her only connection with the university may be that she has a room, a mailing address, and a number of college-age-looking friends there. Of these things I have personal knowledge. (One of the friends, Chuck Gerardo, a gymnast, feels that he has invented a dance step called the Goober, which entails moving exactly counter to the beat. In point of fact I stumbled upon a subtler and rather more complex version of that step myself, quite a few years ago, and by now it has become more or less second nature—give or take a half-sh'boom—to me. You young people today aren't necessarily the first people in history to be hup. Hep.) And every so often I receive word from Ennis that she has made five more A-pluses and needs another $47,000 for gasoline, incidentals, and felt-tip pens. (We didn't have felt-tips in my day. We improvised:

Q-tips and our own blood. We parents want to spare you all that—in fact, *don't bleed.*)

So I know, as surely as I know most things, that I am a sophomore parent. And it may be that there is no one who knows more about anything, aside from a sophomore student about life outside college, than a sophomore parent about life inside college. It may also be that I am being incredibly unassuming and gracious, as parents are, as you will realize when you are parents.

So if you would just stop darting your eyes around for one moment, please.

• Eat pizza. (See, you thought I was going to come down hard. Not at all. Parents do not come down nearly as hard as they have every right to, because parents came *up* hard, and are tired.) Chuck Noll, the head coach of the Pittsburgh Steelers, once told me that pizza contains every element of the human body. For a while this put me off pizza. But the Steelers won the Super Bowl that year, so Noll must have been right: There is no more perfect food. Even *gigot de français* (leg of Frenchman), say, does not contain *every* element of the human body. I don't think. You could check me on that, with your School of Medicine. Or Romance Languages. Oh, the banquet of knowledge that is spread out before you.

• Learn a trade. Even if it is something so highly technical that of course it makes us very proud of you, but perhaps is not the most considerate field you could have gone into, since how can we tell whether you are doing it right? Every moment that you aren't learning a trade, worry about why you aren't. This is known as pure thought. Or "unadulterated" thought, so called because adults cannot afford to indulge in it. By *trade* I mean something that will support aging parents, suitably, before you know it.

• Save mailing tubes. Those cardboard tubes. I tried to buy one recently, in which to mail someone something, and looked all over everywhere. I could have bought an expensive fancy plastic art-supply deal with caps on the ends, suitable for shipping a Caravaggio to the Vatican, but I didn't want that. I wanted just a regular cardboard tube, the kind you receive in the mail with something non-invaluable rolled up in it. I could not buy one for love or money. I had to learn this the hard way. You don't.

• Finish up in four years. Maximum. Every extra day after four years means another three months off your parents' lives. There has been a study on this. By a university. Whose bursar suppressed the findings.

● Don't keep small, gnawing pets, such as hamsters, in your room. Hamsters get loose and eat money. This is why college costs so much. *Why does college cost so much?* Oh, you want to change the subject! You want to know how my generation has managed to run up a $2,000,000,000,000 debt. Well, how else can we send you through college in 100 percent natural-fiber clothes? The natural-fiber money ran out! I'll tell you this: My college roommate insisted on keeping a hamster, and one night it got into my wallet and ate everything. It was a valuable lesson. There are some things we can't control. *But we can do without insidious little animals out there in the darkness gnawing.*

● Cling to eternal verities. This is all recent, you know, all these post-hypen-you-name-it-isms. Post-modernism, post-vandalism, whatever. We didn't have any of them in my day, and we didn't exactly come to town on a load of rutabagas. Mark my words: These things will blow over.

● So will everything else. Except parents. Who will just get pitiful and die. But you let us worry about that. You just worry about how bad you are going to feel—too late.

● If some fad like riding five to a motorcycle backward or watching insect-monster movies for seventy-two hours straight while wearing nothing but feelers arises, hey, you're only young once. But think what it will do to your parents. They are only going to be middle-aged once, which is all they have left, and perhaps not for long. Call your parents. Talk to them—*about something else*—until the urge passes.

● On the other hand, what makes you feel the need to take sixteen courses in accounting? We're sending you to college so you can learn everything there is to know about the bottom line. You want to know about the bottom line? Call your parents.

● *Drugs.* Young people don't need to get high. Young people are already, *qua* young people, higher than they will ever be again, even tomorrow. Wait until you are seventy. There is no one more tickled with himself or herself than a seventy-year-old college graduate who *feels* seventy but who has not yet developed a tolerance for killer Nepalese mushrooms.

● *Politics.* I fully realize that the point of collegiate political activity is to make all the blood drain out of your parents' faces. Fine. Fair enough. But if anything involving explosives ever comes back in style, remember that you will be alumni soon. For every $100,000 in damage done to campus property, you may count on receiving two dozen solicitations to contribute to the building fund. In demolitions, as in economics, there is no such thing as a free boom. On the other hand, before you plunge headlong into your Campus Young Arch-Reactionary Club, stop and think. Shouldn't *some* gratifications be deferred until you can no longer enjoy anything else?

- *Plagiarism.* This above all, to thine own self be true.
- *Extramarital relations.* Never marry your relatives. See? Parents can laugh about these things. As long as we are sure your heads are on straight. Once we realize that they aren't, we can never laugh again.
- Excuse me. Will you please stop doing that with your corneas when I am talking to you? Yes, your corneas. You know what I mean.
- Yes, you do.
- And don't expect to remember any of this, unless you write it all down. Right now. The older you get, the less you remember, even tomorrow.
- Any of what?

Jules Feiffer

Hail to Thee, Okoboji!

Okoboji's football team (The Fighting Phantoms) always wins. No student demonstration has ever ruffled the tranquil campus, and the school refuses to raise tuition. The university's financial resources are awesome: a new Howard Hughes will recently turned up in the salad bowl of a local restaurant, leaving all the billionaire's fortune to the Iowa university. Too good to be true?

Precisely. Six years ago, Herman Richter—who runs a clothing store with his brother in tiny Milford, Iowa—produced a batch of University of Okoboji T shirts as a lark. He then concocted a mythical institution to go along with them. Richter's idea caught on. The school's T shirts have appeared as far away as Saudi Arabia, and Okoboji pennants and car decals are popping up across the U.S. This year, Richter expects to sell $100,000 worth of his university's souvenirs.

Loyal sons of Okoboji actually have formed alumni groups in five cities, and 1,000 people attended a homecoming weekend in July, which featured polka dancing and a marathon around Lake Okoboji (the resort north of Milford that gave the school its name). "The biggest thing we teach is perspective on life and a sense of humor," says Richter, 34, who named himself dean of student affairs. Last week, the hottest selling item in his store was a ticket to the annual Notre Dame game. In another rousing victory, the Fighting Phantoms of Okoboji won, 72–0.

–Newsweek

Wherefore Art Thou Nittany?

Calvin Trillin

January 12, 1987

"Daddy, why is the Penn State football team called the Nittany Lions? What's a nittany?"

"I thought girls were supposed to know all about football these days."

"Does that mean you aren't sure what a nittany is, Daddy?"

"Let me just give you the cereal choices for this morning: we have the kind with enough riboflavin to power the entire Southwestern Conference through the next three recruiting scandals and we have the kind that tends to get stuck in your teeth."

"That's all right, Daddy: I can just ask Mr. Hopkinson at school. He knows all about football. I'll have the kind with the riboflavin."

"Hopkinson's a blowhard. That man's got no historical perspective."

"You're not going to recite the starting line-up of the 1947 Kansas City Blues again, are you, Daddy?"

"I do know that it's lovely around Penn State in the autumn, undergraduates strolling hand in hand along the banks of the flowing Nittany."

"There isn't any Nittany River, Daddy. I looked it up in the atlas."

"It's ironic, of course, that Penn State is so famous for football, because classicists know it as the place where, some years ago, a group of brilliant undergraduate pranksters managed to fool half the scholars in the world with a bogus manuscript in ancient Greek that included a mythical mythical beast, the Nittany, and a scene in which Zeus asked Hera to return a token of his affection that seemed very much like a modern fraternity pin. I'll never forget the closing couplet: 'She nearly had a fit, and he / Rode off on a Nittany.'"

"No, Daddy. Not a mythical mythical beast."

"No?"

"Definitely not."

"Why can't you be interested in something like how the Georgetown Hoyas got their name?"

"Because Penn State's number one, Daddy."

"Well, you might take into consideration that a hundred years ago, when football began at Penn State, the area was known for its nittany mines. That semiprecious stone was in its heyday then. Sure, it later disappeared from jewelry stores almost overnight after the introduction of the artificial zircon, but at that time it was so important to the economy of the region that naming the Penn State football team in its honor seemed natural. But then the players complained to the coach. They said—"

"I know, Daddy: they said, 'We don't like being called the Penn State Semiprecious Stones, Coach.'"

"Right. Also, the cheerleaders complained that it just didn't sound right when they yelled, 'Go, go, Semiprecious Stones!'"

"Daddy, I think the kind with the riboflavin and the kind that tends to get stuck in your teeth are the same kind."

"In those early days of Penn State, of course, the mountain lion was quite prevalent in the region. People in Pennsylvania, being very orderly, categorized the various mountain lions according to which mountains they could usually be found in. The Pocono Mountains were actually the closest mountains to Penn State. But even then the Poconos were a resort area, so if the team had been called the Penn State Pocono Lions, people might expect them to come out on the field, do five minutes of stand-up comedy, and then announce that the special luau would be held by the pool at seven-thirty. So they compromised on Nittany Lions."

"Daddy, I think I'm going to be late for school."

"Of course, it could hardly be a coincidence that the first coach at Penn State, a hundred years ago, was the beloved Alonzo Nittan."

"Nittan, Daddy? That's a name?"

"That's right. Good Pennsylvania Dutch name, Nittan. The team was just called the Lions then. They had to play the University of Miami, which had a quarterback who could throw the bomb so well that he had been drafted by both the Union and the Confederacy."

"The forward pass came years later, Daddy. So did the University of Miami. And the Civil War was already over."

"Penn State was the underdog, and when they took the field a cynical local sportswriter said, 'Those lions look a little kitteny.' To which a Penn State supporter is said to have replied, 'I think you'll find them rather Nittany.' And sure enough, they wiped up the field with the University of Miami."

"O.K., Daddy. I give up. How did the Georgetown Hoyas get their name?"

"I'd rather not say."

"I really have to get to school, Daddy. I'll let you know tonight what Mr. Hopkinson says about the Nittany Lions."

"On the other hand, I'm perfectly willing to reveal the line-up of the 1947 Kansas City Blues. They had Cliff Mapes in center field, of course. And in left, Hank Bauer, always referred to as 'rugged ex-Marine Hank Bauer.' And Eddie Stewart in right. Good old Eddie Stewart . . .' "

University Days

James Thurber

I passed all the other courses that I took at my University, but I could never pass botany. This was because all botany students had to spend several hours a week in a laboratory looking through a microscope at plant cells, and I could never see through a microscope. I never once saw a cell through a microscope. This used to enrage my instructor. He would wander around the laboratory pleased with the progress all the students were making in drawing the involved and, so I am told, interesting structure of flower cells, until he came to me. I would just be standing there. "I can't see anything," I would say. He would begin patiently enough, explaining how anybody can see through a microscope, but he would always end up in a fury, claiming that I could *too* see through a microscope but just pretended that I couldn't. "It takes away from the beauty of flowers anyway," I used to tell him. "We are not concerned with beauty in this course," he would say. "We are concerned solely with what I may call the *mechanics* of flars." "Well," I'd say, "I can't see anything." "Try it just once again," he'd say, and I would put my eye to the microscope and see nothing at all, except now and again a nebulous milky substance—a phenomenon of maladjustment. You were supposed to see a vivid, restless clockwork of sharply defined plant cells. "I see what looks like a lot of milk," I would tell him. This, he claimed, was the result of my not having adjusted the microscope properly, so he would readjust it for me, or rather, for himself. And I would look again and see milk.

I finally took a deferred pass, as they called it, and waited a year and tried again. (You had to pass one of the biological sciences or you couldn't graduate.) The professor had come back from vacation brown as a berry, bright-eyed, and eager to explain cell-structure again to his classes. "Well," he said to me, cheerily, when we met in the first laboratory hour of the semester, "we're going to see cells this time, aren't we?" "Yes, sir," I said. Students to right of me and to left of me and in front of me were seeing cells; what's more, they were quietly drawing pictures of them in their notebooks. Of course, I didn't see anything.

"We'll try it," the professor said to me, grimly, "with every adjustment of the microscope known to man. As God is my witness, I'll arrange this glass so that you see cells through it or I'll give up teaching. In twenty-two years of botany, I—" He cut off abruptly for he was beginning to quiver all over, like Lionel Barrymore, and he genuinely wished to hold onto his temper; his scenes with me had taken a great deal out of him.

So we tried it with every adjustment of the microscope known to man. With only one of them did I see anything but blackness or the familiar lacteal opacity, and that time I saw, to my pleasure and amazement, a variegated constellation of flecks, specks, and dots. These I hastily drew. The instructor, noting my activity, came back from an adjoining desk, a smile on his lips and his eyebrows high in hope. He looked at my cell drawing. "What's that?" he demanded, with a hint of a squeal in his voice. "That's what I saw," I said. "You didn't, you didn't, you *didn't!*" he screamed, losing control of his temper instantly, and he bent over and squinted into the microscope. His head snapped up. "That's your eye!" he shouted. "You've fixed the lens so that it reflects! You've drawn your eye!"

Another course that I didn't like, but somehow managed to pass, was economics. I went to that class straight from the botany class, which didn't help me any in understanding either subject. I used to get them mixed up. But not as mixed up as another student in my economics class who came there direct from a physics laboratory. He was a tackle on the football team, named Bolenciecwcz. At that time Ohio State University had one of the best football teams in the country, and Bolenciecwcz was one of its outstanding stars. In order to be eligible to play it was necessary for him to keep up in his studies, a very difficult matter, for while he was not dumber than an ox he was not any smarter. Most of his professors were lenient and helped him along. None gave him more hints, in answering questions, or asked him simpler ones than the economics professor, a thin, timid man named Bassum. One day when we were on the subject of transportation and distribution, it came Bolenciecwcz's turn to answer a question. "Name one means of transportation," the professor said to him. No light came into the big tackle's eyes. "Just any means of transportation," said the professor. Bolenciecwcz sat staring at him. "That is," pursued the professor, "any medium, agency, or method of going from one place to another." Bolenciecwcz had the look of a man who is being led into a trap. "You may choose among steam, horse-drawn, or electrically propelled vehicles," said the instructor. "I might suggest the one which we commonly take in making long journeys across land." There was a profound silence in which everybody stirred uneasily, including Bolenciecwcz and Mr. Bassum. Mr. Bassum abruptly broke this silence in an amazing manner. "Choo-choo-choo," he said, in a low voice, and turned instantly scarlet. He glanced appealingly around the room. All of us, of course, shared Mr. Bassum's desire that Bolenciecwcz should stay abreast of the class in economics, for the Illinois game, one of the hardest and most important of the season, was only a week off. "Toot, toot, too-toooooooot!" some student with a deep voice moaned, and we all looked encouragingly at Bolenciecwcz. Somebody else gave a fine imitation of a locomotive letting off steam. Mr. Bassum himself rounded off the little show. "Ding, dong, ding, dong," he said, hopefully. Bolenciecwcz was staring at the floor now, trying to think, his great brow furrowed, his huge hands rubbing together, his face red.

"How did you come to college this year, Mr. Bolenciecwcz?" asked the professor. "*Chuff*a, chuffa, *chuff*a chuffa."

"M'father sent me," said the football player.

"What on?" asked Bassum.

"I git an 'lowance," said the tackle, in a low, husky voice, obviously embarrassed.

"No, no," said Bassum. "Name a means of transportation. What did you *ride* here on?"

"Train," said Bolenciecwcz.

"Quite right," said the professor. "Now, Mr. Nugent, will you tell us—"

If I went through anguish in botany and economics—for different reasons—gymnasium work was even worse. I don't even like to think about it. They wouldn't let you play games or join in the exercises with your glasses on and I couldn't see with mine off. I bumped into professors, horizontal bars, agricultural students, and swinging iron rings.

Not being able to see, I could take it but I couldn't dish it out. Also, in order to pass gymnasium (and you had to pass it to graduate) you had to learn to swim if you didn't know how. I didn't like the swimming pool, I didn't like swimming, and I didn't like the swimming instructor, and after all these years I still don't. I never swam but I passed my gym work anyway, by having another student give my gymnasium number (978) and swim across the pool in my place. He was a quiet, amiable blonde youth, number 473, and he would have seen through a microscope for me if we could have got away with it, but we couldn't get away with it. Another thing I didn't like about gymnasium work was that they made you strip the day you registered. It is impossible for me to be happy when I am stripped and being asked a lot of questions. Still, I did better than a lanky agricultural student who was cross-examined just before I was. They asked each student what college he was in—that is, whether Arts, Engineering, Commerce, or Agriculture. "What college are you in?" the instructor snapped at the youth in front of me. "Ohio State University," he said promptly.

It wasn't that agricultural student but it was another a whole lot like him who decided to take up journalism, possibly on the ground that when farming went to hell he could fall back on newspaper work. He didn't realize, of course, that that would be very much like falling back full-length on a kit of carpenter's tools. Haskins didn't seem cut out for journalism, being too embarrassed to talk to anybody and unable to use a typewriter, but the editor of the college paper assigned him to the cow barns, the sheep house, the horse pavilion, and the animal husbandry department generally. This was a genuinely big "beat," for it took up five times as much ground and got ten times as great a legislative appropriation as the College of Liberal Arts. The agricultural student knew animals, but nevertheless his stories were dull and colorlessly written. He took all afternoon on each of them, on account of having to hunt for each letter on the typewriter. Once in a while he had to ask somebody to help him hunt. "C" and "L," in particular, were hard letters for him to find. His editor finally got pretty much annoyed at the farmer-journalist because his pieces were so uninteresting. "See here, Haskins," he snapped at him one day, "why is it we never have anything hot from you on the horse pavilion? Here we have two hundred head of horses on this campus—more than any other university in the Western Conference except Purdue—and yet you never get any real low down on them. Now shoot over to the horse barns and dig up something lively." Haskins shambled out and came back in about an hour; he said he had something. "Well, start it off snappily," said the editor. "Something people will read." Haskins set to work and in a couple of hours brought a sheet of typewritten paper to the desk; it was a two-hundred word story about some disease that had broken out among the horses. Its opening sentence was simple but arresting. It read: "Who has noticed the sores on the tops of the horses in the animal husbandry building?"

Ohio State was a land grant university and therefore two years of military drill was compulsory. We drilled with old Springfield rifles and studied the tactics of the Civil War even though the World War was going on at the time. At 11 o'clock each morning thousands of freshmen and sophomores used to deploy over the campus, moodily creeping up on the old chemistry building. It was good training for the kind of warfare that was waged at Shiloh but it had no connection with what was going on in Europe. Some people used to think there was German money behind it, but they didn't dare say so or they would have been thrown in jail as German spies. It was a period of muddy thought and marked, I believe, the decline of higher education in the Middle West.

As a soldier I was never any good at all. Most of the cadets were glumly indifferent soldiers, but I was no good at all. Once General Littlefield, who was commandant of the cadet corps, popped up in front of me during regimental drill and snapped, "You are the main trouble with this university!" I think he meant that my type was the main trouble with the university but he may have meant me individually. I was mediocre at drill, certainly—that is, until my senior year. By that time I had drilled longer than anybody else in the Western Conference, having failed at military at the end of each preceding year so that I had to do it all over again. I was the only senior still in uniform. The uniform which, when new, had made me look like an interurban railway conductor, now that it had become faded and too tight made me look like Bert Williams in his bellboy act. This had a definitely bad effect on my morale. Even so, I had become by sheer practise little short of wonderful at squad manoeuvres.

One day General Littlefield picked our company out of the whole regiment and tried to get it mixed up by putting it through one movement after another as fast as we could execute them: squads right, squads left, squads on right into line, squads right about, squads left front into line etc. In about three minutes one hundred and nine men were marching in one direction and I was marching away from them at an angle of forty degrees, all alone. "Company, halt!" shouted General Littlefield, "That man is the only man who has it right!" I was made a corporal for my achievement.

The next day General Littlefield summoned me to his office. He was swatting flies when I went in. I was silent and he was silent too, for a long time. I don't think he remembered me or why he had sent for me, but he didn't want to admit it. He swatted some more flies, keeping his eyes on them narrowly before he let go with the swatter. "Button up your coat!" he snapped. Looking back on it now I can see that he meant me although he was looking at a fly, but I just stood there. Another fly came to rest on a paper in front of the general and began rubbing its hind legs together. The general lifted the swatter cautiously. I moved restlessly and the fly flew away. "You startled him!" barked General Littlefield, looking at me severely. I said I was sorry. "That won't help the situation!" snapped the General, with cold military logic. I didn't see what I could do except offer to chase some more flies toward his desk, but I didn't say anything. He stared out the window at the faraway figures of co-eds crossing the campus toward the library. Finally, he told me I could go. So I went. He either didn't know which cadet I was or else he forgot what he wanted to see me about. It may have been that he wished to apologize for having called me the main trouble with the university; or maybe he had decided to compliment me on my brilliant drilling of the day before and then at the last minute decided not to. I don't know. I don't think about it much any more.

Letters

Teresa Bloomingdale

Academic Dean
University of Nebraska
Lincoln, Nebraska

Dear Dean:
     Thank you for your letter regarding our son, 486-30-1223, who is currently enrolled at the University of Nebraska.
     I appreciate your concern that the lad has been in residence at the University for five semesters and has accumulated only 9 credit hours. We, too, are a trifle concerned about this; downright stunned, as a mat-

ter of fact, for we have canceled checks proving payment for a total of 65 credit hours.

Upon receipt of your letter, we called our son for an explanation.

After 13 unanswered calls to his dormitory room, seven unsuccessful "Hold on; I'll page hims" at the Student Center; four interesting if fruitless calls to Bill's Bar and Grill, and one call to a certain apartment on N Street, we contacted 1223, and he explained the situation as follows:

In his first semester he enrolled for 15 credit hours, but dropped Economics because it was an Upper Level Course. (It was also an 8 A.M. class, but I'm sure that is irrelevant.) As the semester drew to a close, he opted for three Incompletes on the theory that if he could spend Christmas vacation polishing up some term papers, he would get an A in each of those courses. He said: "Gee I thought I had turned those papers in." . . . He will look through his things and get back to me. (Don't hold your breath; I've seen "his things"; this could take months.)

In his second semester, he signed up for 12 hours, but dropped two Science courses and added two Business courses, which, unfortunately, he didn't get credit for because he was auditing one and taking one for credit, but he forgot which was which and took the wrong exam. He also got another Incomplete that semester, but it wasn't really his fault, as the professor rescheduled the final exam and failed to notify him. (I asked him if he had checked the Bulletin Board, and he went into a fit of hysterical laughter.)

In his third semester, he fell in love. (He claims "it's a silly rule, that one should have to attend class to get credit for the course.")

In his fourth semester, he signed up for 15 hours, dropped 6, added 3, and switched sections in English and Psychology but forgot to notify the Registrar, so he didn't get credit for either course. The Incomplete in Chemistry will be replaced with a grade just as soon as he pays for the lab equipment.

In his fifth semester, he switched his major, negating the 15 hours he had signed up for, but he claims the semester wasn't wasted because his dorm team won the Intramural Ping-Pong Tournament.

He assures us that this semester "everything is copacetic," though he is a little worried that he "may not get into Law School when the time comes."

I assured him that problem did not seem to be too pressing.

Thank you for your concern.

Sincerely,

My dear son Jim:

How is everything in the Marine Corps? Your father says to tell you he is quite concerned about the "squalid living conditions" you have had to endure since your South Pacific assignment. What with all those "mosquito-infested swamps," "guerilla warfare in the jungle wilds," and "the long, boring hours on guard duty," your life must be simply awful . . . but not as awful as it's going to be if you don't send back my MasterCharge card *pronto*. I would also appreciate a money order covering the enclosed receipts.

And just out of curiosity, what did you buy in Tiffany's of Tasmania? A Mother's Day gift, perhaps?

Love,
Mother

Dear Mr. Prosecuting Attorney:

In re: your letter asking for the address of our son who is currently enrolled at the University of Nebraska in Lincoln, I have a few questions:

1. If I give you his last address, and it proves to be his current address, will you ask him why he doesn't answer my letters?

2. If I give you his address, do you really think you will ever catch him at home?

3. If I give you his address, and you find that he is still living there, am I responsible for his rent?

4. If I give you his address, and you go there and a tall, gorgeous blonde answers the door, I don't want to know about it.

5. Just what is the warrant for?

Sincerely,

Dear Mr. Prosecutor:

Overdrafts? You mean you *arrest* people for overdrawing on their accounts? Boy, am I glad I don't live in *your* county.

I checked our son's current address, and it seems it is a past address, but I will track him down for you. (You didn't happen to run into that blonde, did you? I'll wager *she* knows where he is.)

Sincerely,

Dear Mr. Prosecutor:

I contacted our son, who claims that he is absolutely unaware of the fact that he has been bouncing checks all over Lancaster County. A simple telephone call to his bank cleared up the whole matter.

It seems that our son, in preparing to go to college last fall, deposited his summer savings in an Omaha checking account. But on arriving in Lincoln, he found a bank which offered "free checking" to students, so he transferred his funds to the Lincoln bank.

He then inadvertently put the wrong checkbook into his wallet, and thus spent the next six months writing checks on the Omaha bank, while his funds rested in the Lincoln bank. When asked about overdraft notices, he admitted that as a matter-of-fact he had been getting a lot of letters from the Omaha bank, but he hadn't opened them; why should he, when he didn't have any money in their bank? Enclosed is my personal check to cover his overdrafts, fees, and fines. (I would appreciate it if you wouldn't cash this till the first of the month.)

Sincerely,

Dear Mr. and Mrs. Zobernacki:

Thank you for the invitation to your daughter's wedding, about which there may be a little confusion.

On noting the name of the groom, we were somewhat surprised to see that it was very familiar; in fact, this was the first we had heard that our son was engaged to be married. The surprise was compounded by the fact that we have never heard him mention your daughter's name. On being shown the invitation, he said: "Is her name Maggie? That's funny, I always thought it was Maizie. Yeah, I think I remember her; nice kid, but she had this thing about getting married. So finally I said okay, get married! But I didn't mean to me! No way, man; I'm not gettin' married."

Please give Maggie (Maizie?) our congratulations. Not on getting married, but on getting out of it.

Sincerely,

Graffiti on a washroom wall at M.I.T.:

And God said:

$$\frac{mv^2}{r} = \frac{Ze^2}{r^2}$$

$$mrv = n\frac{h}{2\pi}$$

$$r = \frac{r^2h^2}{(2\pi)^2mZe^2}$$

$$E = \frac{1}{2}mv^2 - \frac{Ze^2}{r}$$

$$E = \frac{2\pi^2mZ^2e^4}{n^2h^2} = R$$

and there was light.

—Mrs. Gene Arthur, in *Reader's Digest*

James Thurber

"She's all I know about Bryn Mawr and she's all I have to know."

A Taste of Princeton

Max Eastman

The reason I did not go to Princeton was that Mrs. F. F. Thompson, my father's rich parishioner in Canandaigua, offered me a scholarship at Williams. These Thompson scholarships pay the board and tuition of promising poor boys—promising in more than one sense, for they have to sign a paper stating that when they get out into the world and make money, they will hand on the gift to another boy. I do not know how well that works in most cases. I never made any money or intended to, and perhaps for that reason very soon forgot the promise.

I was desperately disappointed when the news came that I was not going to Princeton. I had never heard of Williams, and my brother had already filled me full of "Princeton spirit," having won the Freshman quarter mile down there and being of that nature which prodigiously enjoys "belonging." I dreamed, the night the bad news came, that I had a vivid orange-and-black flag on my wall and came home and found that somebody had stuck up a muddy rag in its place. I told my mother this dream, but also told her that I recognized the financial necessity of accepting the scholarship. We can not know in advance—I added—whether it would prove better for me to go to Williams or Princeton. The difference might be that if I went to Princeton, a brick would fall off a roof and kill me, and if I went to Williams, it wouldn't. My mother loved these "philosophical" remarks of mine, and her answer is characteristic:

"I hope you'll let me come and live with you when I'm old. I know I shall like it best at your house. It will probably be a lovely rambling old house on some beautiful college campus with elm trees full of birds right outside the windows. I have had a very bad time since I wrote to you, for Papa said I ought not to have told you about the Williams offer—that you are working so hard and it would make you sick, etc. . . . I'm almost afraid to go to sleep lest I shall see orange-and-black flags weeping and dirty-colored Williams flags drearily flopping in the breeze!"

As compensation for my good nature, I was allowed to visit my brother in Princeton after my graduation and great awakening in June. I thought I would express my new-found manhood by loafing compan-

ionably among his classmates, breathing at ease the "Princeton spirit."
I found myself more tongue-tied and abashed than ever. My remarks
were an intrusion from the side lines, and with all my art I could not get
them into the game. It is one thing to prepare and deliver a humorous
speech, to act the part of a sophisticated person; it is a different thing to
be one.

I hope the reader knows what I am talking about. It was the struggle of an outsider to get into the human race. My good points stood as
much in the way as my bad. My too logical brain, with its queer tendency toward generalized thinking, my extreme sensitivity, my squea-
mishness about smutty language, troubled me as much as my timidity,
self-consciousness, and everlasting worry about being good. An inferiority feeling attached to them all, and I was ready for heroic measures
of emancipation. Under influence of the "Princeton spirit" I took my
first gulp of spirituous liquor, which I found very hard to stomach, and
I chased a lady of easy virtue into the bushes behind the Presbyterian
church—where also I was unable to prove myself a man. I was unable,
in those crude circumstances, even to desire to. I suppose all imaginative
boys, if their erotic life is lived too long in daydreams, have some trouble
achieving a "transference" to reality. The first shock of the palpable
naked flesh of a woman's body chills instead of exciting them. In me this
poetic impotence, if I may so describe it, was reinforced by an over-
whelming bashful reticence which stood like a wall between me and the
downright act, or even the explicit mention, of sexual union. It closed
against me, to my good fortune, that puerile initiation into physical love
which for so many gives it a tint of bawdiness never to be washed off.

Lust does not seem to me an evil thing when it is mutual and over-
mastering. It is taking sex relations in a cheap, flip, facetious, and vulgar
fashion that offends my sense of virtue. This seems to me a sacrilege
against life's true enjoyment. If the highest point of bliss is flattened, the
whole temple is deprived of grandeur. And that desperate concern about
chastity which prevailed in Christian parents of my generation tends to
beget, in boys at least, this attitude of sacrilege. Boys have often a passing disposition to mock at life and profane it, a mischievous mood that
does not matter much or carry far. But when life's most intense and
happy raptures are withheld from them as connatural with lying, cheating, cruelty, hypocrisy, perjury, and robbery and murder, they take their
revenge by vulgarizing those raptures in a certain permanence. If we can
not openly enter your Holy of Holies, they say to their elders, we can
at least sneak in and spit upon the altar.

My brother took me down to the running track to show me where he had won the freshman quarter-mile, a victory which had loomed rather large in the pride of our family. We started trotting around the track, and our trot soon extended itself into a quarter-mile race, which to our mutual astonishment I won by several yards. That was an event of importance, which my brother related with generous delight the next morning and indeed never tired of relating throughout his life. It helped me along in what now seems a rather pathetic effort to escape, not only from inferiority feelings, but from my own nature.

My brother also took me to his class in political science to hear a professor whose lectures he said were becoming famous. The class filled a large churchlike auditorium, and the professor delivered his lecture downward from a high platform. I tried dutifully to be impressed, but found his diction too full of fluent abstractions to catch hold of my underdeveloped mind. His name was Woodrow Wilson. I heard him several times thereafter, but no matter how much I developed my mind, his diction was always too full of fluent abstractions to catch a good hold of it.

Hell Only Breaks Loose Once

James Thurber

(Written After Reading James M. Cain's "The Postman Always Rings Twice")

I

They kicked me out of college when I was about twenty-seven. I went up to see the Dean and tried to hand him a couple of laughs but it was no good. He said he couldn't put me back in college but I could hang around the office and sweep out and wash windows. I figured I better be rambling and I said I had a couple of other offers. He told me to sit down and think it over so I sat down.

Then she came in the room. She was tall and thin and had a white frowning forehead and soft eyes. She wasn't much to look at but she was something to think about. As far as she and I were concerned he wasn't in the room. She leaned over the chair where I was sitting and bit me in the ear. I let her have it right under the heart. It was a good one. It was plenty. She hit the floor like a two-year-old.

"What fell?" asked the Dean, peering over his glasses. I told him nothing fell.

II

After a while I said I guessed I'd hang around and go to work for him. "Do what?" he asked. He had forgot all about me, but I hung around. I liked him and he liked me but neither one of us cared what happened to the other.

When the Dean went out to lunch I walked into a rear office and she was there. I began to tremble all over like a hooch dancer. She was fussing with some papers but I could see she wasn't really doing anything. I walked close to her. It was like dying and going to Heaven. She was a little like my mother and a little like the time I got my hip busted in a football scrimmage. I reached over and let her have one on the chin and she went down like a tray of dishes. I knew then I would be beating her up the rest of my life. It made me feel like it was April and I was a kid again and had got up on a warm morning and it was all misty outdoors and the birds were singing.

III

"Hi, Dean," I said to him when he got back from lunch.

"What is it?" he asked. I could tell he thought he had never seen me before. I told him what it was. "Excellent," he said, looking surprised. He still didn't know what it was. She came out of the back room and he asked her what she wanted. He never remembered seeing anybody.

I took her out to lunch. It was sweet in the lunchroom and I kicked her under the table and broke her ankle. It was still broken when I carried her back to the Dean's office.

"Who do you wish to see?" he asked, looking over his glasses at us. I wanted to grind his glasses into his skull. She said we both worked there. He said that was excellent, but he wasn't looking for work. I told him to think it over and she and I went into the back room. I let her have one over the eye but it was a glancing blow and didn't knock her out. She cracked down on me with a paperweight and I went out like a light but I took her with me. She broke her head in the fall. We were unconscious for about an hour. A couple of guys were bending over us when we came to. They said they were from a place named Lang's, a cleaning establishment. The Dean had got the idea we were a bear rug and was going to send us out to be dry-cleaned. He was pretty dumb but I liked him.

IV

"What do you want to work for that guy for?"

"I'm his secretary."

"What do you want to work for him for?"

"I said I'm his secretary."

"Keep talking."

"I have to work for him. He's my husband." I felt pretty sick then.

"That's tough. You oughtn't to be married to him. He doesn't know what it's all about."

"He lectures in his sleep."

"That must be swell."

"I don't want to be his wife. I want to be yours."

"You are mine."

"Let me have it again," she said. I gave her a short left jab on the button. She was dizzy for days.

V

The Dean was too absent-minded to notice she was bruised all the time. It made me sick seeing him sitting at his desk trying to remember what it was all about. One day he began dictating a letter to me but I didn't pay any attention. I went on dusting a chair. Pretty soon he went out to lunch and I went in the back room. She was there and I began to shiver like a tuning fork. I stroked her hair. I had never done that before. It was like going to sleep.

"There is one out for us," she told me.

"Okay," I said.

VI

He was sitting at his desk trying to figure out who he was when I hit him over the conk with an auto crank. I thought he would fold up like a leather belt, but he didn't. It didn't faze him. "Somebody's at the door," he said. I was shaking a little but I went to the door and opened it. There wasn't anybody there. I stood to one side so he could look out of the door into the hall. It was empty. "I thought I heard somebody knock," he said. It made me cold.

VII

We fixed him finally. I got him up on top of the university water tower one night to see the aurora borealis. There wasn't any aurora borealis but he was too dumb to notice that. It was swell up there on the tower. It smelled pretty. It smelled of jasmine. I felt like the first time I ever kissed a girl.

I rigged up one of those double flights of steps like tapdancers dance up and down on and told him to get up on top of it.

"I don't want to get up on top of that," he said.

"You want to see the aurora borealis, don't you?"

"Most certainly."

"Then get up on top of that."

He got up on top of it and I climbed up after him. The thing was rickety but he didn't notice.

"What are we doing up here?" he asked me.

"Look at the aurora," I said, pointing at the sky. He looked and while we were standing there she came up on top of the steps with us. He didn't pay any attention to her. I swayed from side to side and started the thing teetering. I beat her up a little and then I beat him up a little. He looked like he had been spanked by an old aunt. The thing was swinging bad now, from one side to the other. I knew it was going over.

VIII

We all fell six flights. He was dead when they picked him up. She was dead too. I was near to her, but she was a long way off. I was dying, they told me. So I dictated this to a guy from the D.A.'s office, and here it is.

And that's all, except I hope it's pretty in Heaven and smells like when the lilacs first come out on May nights in the Parc Monceau in Paris.

Sexual Harassment at Harvard: Three Letters

John Kenneth Galbraith

The subject of sex recurs, if with less solemnity, in the following communications. The council referred to in the first excerpt is, as indicated, the Faculty Council, the inner legislative body of the Harvard faculty.

Henry Rosovsky was, until 1984, the greatly able and respected dean of the Faculty of Arts and Sciences, the number two post in the Harvard administration. As here shown, no Harvard dean ever answers a letter without giving some indication of need for financial support, such as the endowment of a new academic chair. Dean Rosovsky's letter is published with his more than generous permission.

EXCERPT FROM A LETTER REPORTING ON FACULTY COUNCIL
DISCUSSIONS OF SEXUAL HARASSMENT AT HARVARD ADDRESSED TO
THE HARVARD FACULTY BY DEAN HENRY ROSOVSKY.

April 1983

Dear Colleagues:

The council discussed various kinds of personal relationships between faculty members and students. Members of the council generally agreed that, in addition to the harassing behavior described below, certain other kinds of relationships are wrong whenever they take place within an instructional context.

Amorous relationships that might be appropriate in other circumstances are always wrong when they occur between any teacher or officer of the university and any student for whom he or she has a professional responsibility. Further, such relationships may have the effect of undermining the atmosphere of trust on which the educational process depends. Implicit in the idea of professionalism is the recognition by those in positions of authority that in their relationships with students there is always an element of power. It is incumbent upon those with authority not to abuse, nor to seem to abuse, the power with which they are entrusted. . . .

Other amorous relationships between members of the faculty and students, occurring outside the instructional context, may also lead to difficulties. In a personal relationship between an officer and a student for whom the officer has no current professional responsibility, the officer should be sensitive to the constant possibility that he or she may unexpectedly be placed in a position of responsibility for the student's instruction or evaluation. Relationships between officers and students are always fundamentally asymmetric in nature. . . .

LETTER TO DEAN HENRY ROSOVSKY
FROM PROFESSOR JOHN KENNETH GALBRAITH.

May 9, 1983

Dear Henry:

I was, as you will presently understand, both enchanted and distressed by your recent communication on behalf of the Faculty Council, entitled "Sexual Harassment, Related Matters." My pleasure had to do with the eloquence and delicacy of the language in which, in keeping with Harvard standards in such matters, your letter is couched. The reference to "amorous relationships" in the "instructional context" is superb and reflects an acute sense of Harvard faculty and even New England sensibilities. For some years I have been an adviser to one of our well-known dictionaries—*The American Heritage Dictionary*, to be precise. I am today instructing its editors as to the usage to which henceforth they must conform if they are to have our approval here in Cambridge.

My distress is personal. Just over forty-five years ago, already a well-fledged member of the Harvard faculty on a three-year appointment, I fell in love with a young female student. It was not in an instructional context; however, noninstructional amour is a "situation" against which you also warn. A not wholly unpredictable consequence of this lapse from faculty and professional decorum, as now required, was that we were married. So, and even happily, we have remained. But now my distress. As a senior member of this community, I am acutely conscious of my need to be an example for younger and possibly more ardent members of the faculty. I must do everything possible to retrieve my error. My wife, needless to say, shares my concern. What would you advise?

LETTER FROM DEAN HENRY ROSOVSKY
TO PROFESSOR JOHN KENNETH GALBRAITH.

May 23, 1983

Dear Ken:

I am delighted that my letter on sexual harassment caused some enchantment in your life. However, I also deeply regret having caused distress. My warnings against noninstructional amour are not especially severe: mainly I urge the practice of "sensitivity." Knowing you, I am sure that was never a problem. But I do understand your *ex post* feelings of discomfort.

Two thoughts come to mind: one humane and the other decanal. The incident in question, by your own account, occurred over forty-five years ago. I believe that the statute of limitations applies. As a dean and as someone who has recently been accused by a member of the faculty of behaving in the manner of a cardinal, I would be delighted to sell you an indulgence. How about a chair to celebrate your happy union and also a time when amour—instructional and noninstructional—was in fashion?

(1983)

The Sage's Progress

Samuel Pickering, Jr.

There is a class of ailments which, like the indiscretions of youth, are considered too commonplace to be delved into in the medical journals. Yet these ailments—the occupational hazards, such as tennis elbow and housemaid's knee—are often far from trivial, and, as a survey of academics from Maine to California would reveal, one of them strikes at the very heart of our intellectual life. In the paneled halls of ivy there lurks—pomposity.

Rarely fatal, this virus usually leads to a comfortable mental state in which the sufferer becomes quite inaccessible to thought. What the disease lacks in virulence, however, it makes up for in epidemic proportions. Even the brightest, most blue-eyed and fit, young instructor eventually slows, swells, and sickens. No antidote has yet been found for the malign effects of being treated as a sage by undergraduates. The belief that one is Delphic gets under the skin, enters the bloodstream, and becomes incurable.

The disease progresses gradually, going through a series of easily identified stages. The young assistant professor begins to become highly susceptible as soon as his first book meets with friendly critical nods. Giving the lie to the old adage that clothes make the man, the sufferer strides into pomposity's deceptive sartorial stage. Paunching slightly with confidence, he wraps himself in a tattered Afghan coat in winter and lets his toes wiggle through the slits of Rhodian sandals in summer. When reversed, his paisley tie delivers a full-fisted, eyelid-bruising message, matched in its rough whimsicality only by his lavender shorts. To the outsider this would seem to be a young man on the way out. But to the cognoscenti, this is clearly a man on the way up. They know that it is but a short step from romantic Afghan to Brooks Brothers herringbone, Bronzini and Sulka will soon hang from his neck in tasteful grey and blue. The sandals will languish in the closet while those sweet harbingers of spring, Whitehouse and Hardy wingtips, will escort a new associate professor to that tenured land where scotch and water purl against the ice like the Afton flowing gently to the sea.

Not long afterward, our subject becomes "funded" and flies away for a year in the British Museum. A penchant for Gauloises and Harvey's amontillado and the appearance of The Book mark the disease's inexorable progress. After the return from Bloomsbury, *Vanity Fair* prints of willowy John Whistler and languid Lord Leighton decorate the sufferer's office walls, while the poster celebrating the annual rattlesnake roundup in Sweetwater, Texas curls forgotten in the waste can. On the title page of The Book, L. Stafford Brown rises newborn from the ashes of Leroy Brown Jr.

Alas, the university is not an abode of unmixed bliss. Before our sufferer answers the great call from above and rises to the eminence of a named chair, he almost inevitably becomes aware of his illness. While browsing in a bookstore, he hears a student confuse him with Balaam's inelegant long-eared beast of burden. At a colleague's Christmas party, he overhears the pert helpmate of a junior member of the department compare him to that befeathered creature whose cackling saved Rome from the Gauls. Awareness of his illness sweeps down upon him, and he vows to take a cure.

Unfortunately, diagnosis is easier than treatment. Several remedies are available; but, although each may bring a temporary remission, none can completely eradicate the disease. First our sufferer grows long sideburns and begins frequenting the society of the young and ill-informed. With enthusiastic *joie de vivre,* he puts off the old and selects a new wife from his seminar on the Age of Reason. Sadly he discovers that ignorance charms only at a distance. The days when he could burst from bed to greet the sun like a morning-glory are over. Before the bottoms of his bright new jogging shoes wear thin, his wife decamps. The joggers join the sandals in the back of the closet.

And our sufferer's Indian summer of heartiness is over. Elevated to the departmental chair, he ignores the petty world scrabbling below and nods into greying dignity. Pomposity brooks opposition no longer, and the professor becomes a wonderful old boy in whose presence ideas flap heavily and fall to the ground like dying swans. Alumni recall his incompetence fondly.

On the campus, stories describing his terse "uh-huhs" and thoughtful "ums" abound. His enrollments swell as gentlemanly B's are bestowed with grand largesse. While students dream of girls as sweet as sugar candy, the old boy puffs his pipe, rolls his r's, and discusses the Immortal Bard's "ring of rightness." Time seems to doze until one long noon when pipe smoke gathers about the professor like cumulus clouds rolling to a storm. Suddenly there is a puff and he is gone. Some say he went above and now sits near the Great White Throne. Some say he went to a warmer place. Others say that he never left, and that his spirit still haunts the university.

Whatever the truth may be, the L. Stafford Brown Reading Room is duly dedicated. One wall holds an eighteenth century mahogany and rosewood bookcase, on the shelves of which are displayed samples from the professor's collection of paperweights. From above the mantlepiece, a mantlepiece on which Dr. Johnson once rested a weary elbow while expostulating with Boswell, stares the professor himself. He is portrayed walking across the Cotswolds. Sheep frisk behind him, while in his right hand he carries The Book. In his left hand he holds a pipe.

There are always students drowsing in the room. Soon it is known as
the Cave of the Old Sleeper.

The Mind of Professor Primrose

Ogden Nash

My story begins in the town of Cambridge, Mass.,
Home of the Harvard Business and Dental Schools,
And more or less the home of Harvard College.
Now, Harvard is a cultural institution,
Squandering many a dollar upon professors,
As a glance at a Harvard football team makes obvious;
Professors wise and prowling in search of wisdom,
And every mother's son of them absent-minded.
But the absentest mind belonged to Professor Primrose.
He had won a Nobel award and a Pulitzer Prize,
A Guggenheim and a leg on the Davis Cup,
But he couldn't remember to shave both sides of his face.
He discharged the dog and took the cook for an airing;
He frequently lit his hair and combed his cigar;
He set a trap for the baby and dandled the mice;
He wound up his key and opened the door with his watch;
He tipped his students and flunked the traffic policeman;
He fed the mosquitoes crumbs and slapped at the robins;
He always said his prayers when he entered the theater,
And left the church for a smoke between the acts;
He mixed the exterminator man a cocktail
And told his guests to go way, he had no bugs;
He rode the streets on a bicycle built for two,
And he never discovered he wasn't teaching at Yale.
At last one summer he kissed his crimson flannels
And packed his wife in camphor, and she complained.
She had always hated camphor, and she complained.
"My dear," she ordered, "these *contretemps* must cease;

You must bring this absent mind a little bit nearer;
You must tidy up that disorderly cerebellum;
You must write today and enroll in the Pelman Institute."
He embraced his pen and he took his wife in hand,
He wrinkled a stamp and thoughtfully licked his brow,
He wrote the letter and mailed it, and what do you know?
In a couple of days he disappeared from Cambridge.
"For heavens sake, my husband has disappeared,"
Said Mrs. Primrose. "Now isn't that just like him?"
And she cut the meat and grocery orders in half,
And moved the chairs in the living room around,
And settled down to a little solid comfort.
She had a marvelous time for seven years,
At the end of which she took a train to Chicago.
She liked to go to Chicago once in a while
Because of a sister-in-law who lived in Cambridge.
Her eye was caught at Schenectady by the porter;
She noticed that he was brushing off a dime,
And trying to put the passenger in his pocket.
"Porter," she said, "aren't you Professor Primrose?
Aren't you my husband, the missing Professor Primrose?
And what did you learn at the Pelman Institute?"
"Good Lawd, Maria," the porter said, "good Lawd!
Did you say *Pelman*? Ah wrote to de *Pullman* folks!"

The Posthumous Reputation
of Professor Crump

David M. Rein

When I was a young instructor I was quite indifferent to rank. While going to college, I studied little and had no plans and when, unexpectedly, a teaching post was offered I was so delighted I wanted little more. The higher ranks seemed so far beyond my grasp, I dared not aspire to them. I did, however, want to become an assistant professor so that I would be referred to as Professor Worth—Professor James P. Worth, to state it completely.

When I received my first promotion, therefore, I was satisfied. I always did like to talk and, if I say so myself, am pretty good at it. I was in steady demand as a lecturer, speaking to social groups, to business organizations and to literary clubs. I looked forward to each of these speaking engagements with the keenest of pleasures, and never spent much time in preparation. With a few hasty notes on a card, I could speak fluently to any audience. I needed my most extensive preparation when I would give a book review, for then, of course, I did have to read the book.

For a few years I was quite happy this way, the center of admiring audiences, popular with my students, and appreciated by my wife. But in various little ways I began to feel slighted. Occasionally, before a lecture when publicity was being prepared, I would be asked my rank. Sometimes when I answered, "Assistant professor," I would fancy that my questioner looked surprised or even disappointed. A well-known lecturer like myself, a literary man of such distinction—and only an assistant professor!

One spring when the new contracts came out, Assistant Professor X was promoted to associate professor while I wasn't. Dr. X was younger than I, newer at the school, and had been an assistant professor for less time. I was outraged, humiliated, indignant. My feelings were not improved when Professor X, in a great show of sympathy, expressed his deep sorrow at my failure to move up with him.

I went to see my department chairman. "You don't have enough publications," he told me. "You have only two. Is that right?"

"Correct. 'Swift as a Satirist' and 'Swift as a Poet.' Both published in the scholarly *HELJ, History of English Literature Journal.*"

"For an associate professorship," he proclaimed, "That is not enough!"

During the next several months I wrote two scholarly articles, both of which were accepted within the year, "The Reputation of Swift in America, 1750–1800," published by the *HELJ*, and "The Reputation of Swift in America, 1800–1850," published in the *PESMLS*, the *Publication of the Eastern Seacoast branch of the Modern Language Society.*

The following year I was promoted to the rank of associate professor. I regret to say that I was happy with my new honor for only a short time. I soon longed for another promotion. I enjoyed my classes while I taught them and I enjoyed the applause at my lectures—but even as I walked away from such triumphs the sweet taste of success would turn sour. All that I was and did, I felt, was thrown in the scale and added up—and the total was always short. I was everywhere and always haunted by the limiting word which shouted of recognition withheld, *associate* professor. And I knew I could never get satisfaction until that limit was taken off my rewards.

While I had no gift for writing and no love for it, I continued to do research and build up my list of publications. I published "The Reputation of Swift in America, 1850–1900," and "The Reputation of Swift in America, 1900–1950." At this stage, I thought of approaching my chairman, but dared not. He would see, all too clearly, that while the quantity was there, variety was lacking. He was no man to be swept off his feet by numbers alone.

An article showing a different facet of my talent would be necessary. I decided to write an appreciative, critical piece on my favorite poet, John Keats. But I could get no ideas. I could make the standard comments about the sensuous quality of his imagery, about the pathos of his untimely death, about the intensity of his romantic love—comments that might go over big at a lecture, but would not impress the stern editors of the scholarly journals. For the life of me I could think of nothing new to say about John Keats.

With defeat staring me in the face I tried to salvage something. I found myself envying my previous articles and trying to duplicate them. I would settle, at present, for more of the same. I tried to recall my plan of attack, my approach in these successful articles. Finally, after months of struggle, I finished "The Reputation of John Keats in the United States, 1850–1900." It was the best I could do and I was relieved indeed when it was accepted for publication by the *AJLC*, the *American Journal of Literature and Culture.*

"That's fine," my chairman said when I told him of my new success, "but a full professorship is the highest honor we have to give. The recipient should have a published book to his credit."

The idea of writing a book I found appalling, incredibly distasteful. Writing a book was for hermits who hated people, or zealots in love with their own ideas, or those fortunate few who could write out of themselves and didn't have to do research. For me it would mean painfully lonesome hours of routine research, of taking notes and organizing them. But I wanted that promotion so badly, I decided to repress my feelings and write a book.

Alas, I could think of absolutely nothing to write about. I went over the whole range of English and American literature, from Chaucer to Hemingway, and could think of absolutely nothing to say that might be publishable.

One day when I was deep in despair my wife came to me with a letter from her aunt. There was a favor to be done, and I was the logical man to do it. My wife's aunt, Mrs. Crump, had been married to a college professor of English like myself and there was a remarkable similarity between his situation and my own. He had died a year ago at the age of fifty-six, an assistant professor. He had been a non-conformist, a man who despised his superiors and shunned his colleagues. He had a passionate love of literature which he shared with his students alone. They found him affable, charming, and a superb teacher. In his office he was always accessible, but once he stepped out he was remote, unapproachable, consumed by his own thoughts. He ridiculed the scholarly research of his colleagues, sneered at the professional journals, and published absolutely nothing himself.

I, too, regarded him as an eccentric and, though we were in the same profession and related, and though he lived but one hundred miles away, I had almost nothing to do with him. My wife and Mrs. Crump exchanged one or two letters a year and that was it.

Mrs. Crump's letter contained a strange revelation. Her husband during his lifetime had written nearly two hundred poems, which he had polished and repolished. He had written them solely for his own pleasure, and had tried, unsuccessfully, to publish only one or two of them. Mrs. Crump thought the poems were wonderful and had shown them to the press of his University, which had agreed to publish a small volume containing one hundred poems, for a subsidy of one thousand dollars. Mrs. Crump wanted me to help her select the one hundred poems and to write a preface, giving some biographical facts and praising her husband's work. To encourage me, she sent a dozen of his poems, presumably his best.

"You will do it?" asked my wife.

"I don't really want to. I don't think the poems are very good."

"That's beside the point. You can't refuse my aunt."

"But the poems—I don't think they're any good!"

"You can still say something nice about them, can't you?" There were tears in her eyes.

"Oh, all right," I said, "If that's the way you feel!"

And so I got trapped with the job. In the preface, when I had to describe the poems I resorted to that innocuous word, that frequent cover for a multitude of sins, *interesting*. My wife would not allow it to stand. "You must say more than that," she insisted. "Would it hurt you to say they are *excellent!*"

"Yes it would. I have my integrity to think of."

"Well, *think* about it," she said, "and then do as I say."

Finally we compromised on *fascinating.* She was quite pleased with the word, and I felt it was noncommittal. After all, a work could be fascinating for any one of several reasons. In fact, some of the worst freshmen themes I ever got could qualify as *fascinating.*

When the book was published the results were remarkable—to put it mildly. Whether it was the fierce independence expressed in the poems, the resolute contempt of the author for whatever might befall him—something in the book caught the mood of our time. The *New York Sun* gave it the lead review and weekly *Trend* magazine ran a special story headed "The Courage of an Individualist." This new book, the *Pacific Monthly* pointed out, proved once again that poetry was very much alive, that it could be written in plain, comprehensible English. A number of magazines printed Crump's picture, with mine beside it. I, too, was becoming famous as the man who had discovered Crump.

My wife, in public, allowed me my honors, but in private sang many a variation on the theme, "It's a good thing you listened to me." And my college, when contract time came around, gave me the reward I so intensely desired. I became at last Professor of English, with no qualifying strings attached. I was indeed a proud man.

But I was to be given an additional, and even more distinctive honor. It seems that Crump's college, Midcontinent University, now felt embarrassed. He had served it well throughout his whole academic life, nearly twenty-five years, and he had died in the lowly rank of assistant professor. Most of the accounts pointed this out—some quite emphatically. The college wished to make amends. But was there any suitable way?

Someone suggested that Crump be awarded a full professorship posthumously. But that was dismissed as too awkward—and absolutely unprecedented. Men were not promoted after they were dead—and certainly, under no circumstances, two ranks at a time. Finally it was suggested that Crump be awarded an honorary doctorate. At first there was some opposition to this, on the grounds that such honors were never offered to anyone who could not be present at the ceremony. But this opposition melted when it was pointed out that congressional medals of honor were frequently conferred posthumously.

With this decision, I am told, everybody was happy. The sudden fame of Professor Crump, instead of embarrassing the college, could now be made to glorify it. All that remained to be done, it seemed, was to choose a commencement speaker who would put the right gloss on the whole affair.

As the man who had discovered Crump I was invited to perform this task. As I have said, I love to speak and can do so fluently with but little preparation. When the day came, it was indeed an occasion. All the dignitaries of the college were there, as well as prominent people from the town, including the mayor. In this large auditorium, filled to capacity, I faced quite a challenge—successfully. I was at my best. When I finished, the applause was long and loud and the whole audience, at a word from the chairman, stood up in honor of Professor Crump.

Mischa Richter

"It's publish or perish, and he hasn't published."

William Hamilton

*"I know, but all promises are off when Daddy's
writing his grant proposals."*

The Faculty Meeting

Jeremy Bernstein

Alice Dodd was attempting to resuscitate her philosophy class. Through
the open door I could see students in various stages of rigor mortis.
Irving Nafken, for example, was wearing that rictal grin which has often
given me the urge to place his head gently but firmly between Volumes
VIII (Poy-Ry) and IX (S-Soldo) of the Oxford English Dictionary. He
once asked in a class of mine whether it was true that Schopenhauer was
a "fruit." "Schopenhauer's life was not entirely happy," I replied. "His

father drowned himself in a canal, and Schopenhauer was sued by a seamstress who claimed he had beaten her with a stick. In court, he said that they were having a discussion on the reality of will and that he was merely trying to make a metaphysical point. He lost the suit." Another student, Edwina Gwan, was studying her eyebrows in a hand mirror. She once came to my office dressed in a miniskirt and see-through blouse, ostensibly to discuss original sin. I told her that most sins seemed already to have been invented by someone else—or perhaps by a committee—and that there should be a Nobel Prize for the inventor of a really original sin. Soon after, she began sleeping with our department chairman, Herbert Feist.

By shifting my position slightly, I could see that Alice Dodd had written something on the blackboard. I recognized it as one of the paradoxes invented by the distinguished logician Willard Quine:

"Yields a falsehood when appended to its own quotation" yields a falsehood when appended to its own quotation.

The thing that has always puzzled me is how Quine ever thought up a sentence like that. I once wrote a poem that began, "Willard V. Quine is smarter than I'm . . ." I never finished it.

Alice Dodd spotted me, but before she could say anything the bell rang. It was just as well, because Nafken had his hand up. Perhaps he was about to ask if *Quine* was a fruit. He once told me that he intended to become a brain surgeon and that he was working his way through school by repairing color television sets. Perhaps he saw a connection—all those brightly colored wires.

I entered the rapidly emptying classroom.

"George, what in God's name are you doing here?" Alice Dodd asked. "Don't you have office hours now?"

"Look," I said, "don't bother me with trivia. This is a matter of life and death. Bleibermacher's got loose again."

I must backtrack a little. Maurice Bleibermacher is one of those academic hangers-on who have made extremely successful careers by comparing two things—any two things—neither of which they understand. For a while he was also into animal behavior. His latest paper, which was largely written by a graduate student, was called "Rubik's Cube and the Shu-shu chiu-chang." The latter, I learned from Bleibermacher, was a treatise on algebra and number theory by the thirteenth-century Chinese mathematician Ch'in Chiu-shao. I told Bleibermacher that it was the "and" in his title that troubled me. "Despite," I felt, would work somewhat better. "Gawge," he said, in his inimitable pseudo-Oxonian accent, "your twable ever since gwaduate school is that you have no sense of humor."

To give him his due, Bleibermacher has turned comparison into an art form. He once showed me a file drawer full of little cards on which were written titles of articles that he or his graduate students intended to write. Things like "Reichean Orgones and Solar Electricity: A Triumph of Synergy" and "The Slime Mold and Its Use in Indian Erotic Art." Each one was in its own small way a masterpiece.

Bleibermacher has managed to parlay all of this into a remarkable reputation. Until he came to our place, he had never held an academic job. He didn't have to. Foundations tripped over each other in their rush to support him. Guggenheims, Sloans, Revsons, MacArthurs came his way one after the other. What they thought they were supporting God only knows. I suppose each one reasoned that the last place that had given him a grant must have known what it was doing. It reminds me of a man I know who found himself stateless after the Second World War. His wife stitched together a document that looked like a passport. He said that the real problem was the first visa. Some country—I think it was Liechtenstein—gave him one, and after that he got visas from everywhere.

In recent years, Bleibermacher had been operating out of Big Sur, but he had had a few contretemps there. A "wild child" whom he claimed had been raised from infancy by a herd of elk near Aspen turned out to be a teen-age runaway from Santa Barbara. Her family reclaimed her after she appeared with Bleibermacher on the Johnny Carson show, walking on all fours and making odd barking sounds. Not long afterward, a dolphin that Bleibermacher was trying to teach to do the crossword in the London *Times* had a nervous breakdown and had to be returned to San Diego's Sea World, which subsequently filed suit. In fact, Bleibermacher might have fallen on hard times if it had not been for the providential appearance of Herschel J. Lang. Lang is a self-taught biologist who has made a great fortune in clones. He first came to the attention of the general public when he accidentally produced a species of bacteria that would eat only Chinese food. The original strain was allergic to MSG, however, and it was in the course of trying to improve the breed that Lang happened upon the discovery that made him rich beyond avarice. He was feeding a batch of his bacteria some of Admiral Tsai's Historic Bean Curd when they began producing a substance that was, to all intents and purposes, indistinguishable from the blend of Dacron and rayon used in three-piece suits that sell for under eighty-nine ninety-five. The rest, of course, is history. Lang's company, Splice-Tech (its motto is "They grow so you can sew"), is now among the Fortune 500, and he recently entered the world of *haute couture* with a modified strain of *E. coli* that produces mauve crêpe de Chine.

One might have thought that with all this success Herschel Lang would have been a happy man, but he suffered from a monumental inferiority complex. He had no academic degrees. "I can buy them and I can sell them," Lang often said, referring to biologists with Ph.D.s, "but they still have their God-damned lambskins." In truth, Lang never graduated from high school. His father had been a *tummler* at places like the Concord and Grossinger's, and he trained his son from infancy to follow in his footsteps. "To *tummel*," he often told young Herschel, "you need timing, and that they don't know from at Harvard." So Lang was denied a formal education, something to which he had never been able to reconcile himself. Enter Bleibermacher.

The two of them had met on the Dick Cavett show, where Lang was exhibiting a strain of bacteria so specialized that they would eat only shredded pork with Peking sauce prepared by the chef at the Lop Sum restaurant in Greenwich Village. Bleibermacher was exhibiting a trained gerbil, which he claimed could take cube roots with the aid of a specially designed pocket calculator. It was love at first sight. Lang saw in Bleibermacher a man heavy with degrees and light in cash; in Lang, Bleibermacher saw the reverse. After a certain amount of diplomatic small talk, Bleibermacher outlined a plan. They would locate a not overly scrupulous university president and Lang could endow a chair in, say, cognitive studies, on the condition that Bleibermacher be its first occupant. Once Bleibermacher had his chair, he would begin a campaign to have Lang awarded an honorary degree. Lang would have his lambskin and Bleibermacher would be set for life.

As it happened, Bleibermacher and Lang did not have to look very far. The president of our place, Walter Praeger, was a devoted talk-show viewer and Bleibermacher fan. He somehow found out that Bleibermacher and I had been to graduate school together, and after that he took every opportunity to pump me for information. I tried to explain to Praeger that if Bleibermacher ever had a really clear idea it would kill him, like an electric shock. But Praeger would have none of it, and last spring he invited Bleibermacher to be our commencement speaker. In his speech, Bleibermacher compared two things. I forget which—it hardly matters. By the end of the weekend, Praeger and Bleibermacher were on a first-name basis, and not long thereafter Lang's limousine could be seen pulling up to the campus regularly. It came as no surprise, therefore, when in the fall Praeger announced the creation of the Herschel J. Lang Chair in Cognitive Studies, whose first occupant would be, needless to say, Maurice Bleibermacher. The only difficulty was that neither Bleibermacher nor Lang had bothered to inform Praeger until it was too late that part of the deal was an honorary degree for Lang. That was what I was about to tell Alice Dodd.

"He's got to be kidding," she said. "As depraved as Praeger is, he hasn't stooped to selling honorary degrees."

"Perhaps he has," I said. "Perhaps, even as we speak, the public-relations office is beginning a sales campaign with ads in *Scientific American* and the *Wall Street Journal*: 'Small but prestigious college has honorary Ph.D.s for sale. Terms to be arranged.' Those people are capable of anything."

"But George," Alice Dodd replied, "you know as well as I do that an honorary degree has to be approved by a vote of the faculty."

She was right. I had completely forgotten. Honorary-degree approval, along with mandatory early retirement, was written into our contract after we were unionized by the teamsters. "Christ," I said. "That's why that fool Praeger called a special faculty meeting for this afternoon. I thought it might have something to do with the students, so I was planning to go home. We must begin rounding up the troops."

I went over the list mentally. If only Albert Backen had got tenure, he could have been counted on. Dear Albert—he is now teaching logical empiricism at the College of Petroleum and Minerals in Saudi Arabia. We receive the odd Polaroid showing him riding a camel. Then there was old Lash, who when and if he was sober would understand the delicacy of the situation. Oddly enough, there was even Feist. Bleibermacher once made a pass at Edwina Gwan, and ever since that time Feist has had him in his sights. It occurred to me that at the moment the most constructive thing I could do was to find Lash and explain why his vote was needed. No doubt he would be in the bar at the faculty club.

Indeed, I readily located Lash on his favorite stool, within easy reach of a wineglass. He was regaling the bartender with some tale that seemed to focus on himself, Wittgenstein, and three stoats when I interrupted and tried to explain the impending crisis. "You say, George," he said with apparent anxiety, "Lang has made a fortune in clowns? Does he own a circus?"

I could see that I was fighting a hopeless battle, and after a decent interval I took my leave, so as not to miss any of the meeting.

The room was packed. Bleibermacher and Praeger were sitting

next to each other in the front row and talking amiably. Bleibermacher's hair, newly transplanted, had the burnished sheen of a vervet's tail. He was wearing a mauve foulard, no doubt woven by Lang's microbes. Praeger showed all the false bonhomie of a television weathercaster as his eyes wandered over the room counting votes. He stood up and called the meeting to order. The first piece of business, it turned out, was a proposal to merge the astrophysics and economics departments. A joint degree in "astronomics" would be offered, thus, in Praeger's words, "unifying two areas of fecund speculation." The proposal passed unanimously. The next item was pure Feist. It seemed that Edwina Gwan had applied to our place for graduate work. The only difficulty was her academic report, which, when plotted, had the wild inconsistency of a graph showing the changing price of shares in a small semiconductor company. She had, needless to say, A's in the several courses she had taken with Feist. Bleibermacher had given her one A, followed by three D's. Feist introduced a special petition that would allow her to continue her "important work" as his graduate assistant. Bleibermacher made an impassioned speech in which he compared the Apollonians and the Dionysians. His voice rose as he thundered, "Let no one ignorant of geometry enter here!"—a monumental irrelevance, since Gwan is studying comparative literature. But as he sat down there was a volley of applause, led by Praeger, who commented on the importance of maintaining academic standards "against a rising tide of philistinism." This carried the day, and Feist's proposal was narrowly defeated. He looked as if he had been hit by an arrow. Alice Dodd passed me a note that read, "After many a semester dies the Gwan." Then we turned to the main act—Lang's degree.

First, Praeger made an endless speech. For some reason, he pronounced the word "clone" as if it had two syllables: "clo-un." He said that he saw in Lang a sort of modern Henry Ford, and he added that Lang had a new strain of bugs, which produced a substance that bore an eerie resemblance to stainless steel. At every mention of Lang, Praeger almost visibly salivated. Bleibermacher looked like a giant cat swimming in a pool of cream. His contented smile became positively Buddhic. In front of him were endless years of comparing things on a salary greater even than that of the football coach.

Praeger sat down to scattered applause, which indicated that the vote might be close. Feist stood up and delivered a bitter speech arguing that Lang should first obtain his high-school-equivalency diploma. He and Bleibermacher exchanged glances that could have bored holes in a diamond. I thoroughly enjoyed every minute of it. Then Praeger called for a vote. Hands were raised, and the registrar took a count. It was a tie, which meant that Praeger would get to cast the deciding vote. But just as he was about to do so, in staggered Lash, his face the color of the warning lights on an ambulance. He had to be helped to his chair, and no sooner was he seated than he stood up and demanded a reading of the minutes of the last meeting. The situation was explained to him, and he said in a loud, clear voice, "I will have none of it." There was a stunned silence, and we all filed out. As I passed him, Lash said to me, "I never liked the circus much, George—not even when I was a boy."

It took some time for the dust to settle. Edwina Gwan is now our department secretary. Nafken has gone to the Harvard Medical School. The Herschel J. Lang Chair in Cognitive Studies, with Bleibermacher still firmly attached to it, was moved bodily to a large university in Texas. Bleibermacher sent me a photograph of the ceremony at which Lang was finally awarded his honorary degree. With his right hand Lang is accepting his diploma. With his left hand he is slipping the president an envelope. He has the look of someone who has finally arrived.

Faculties at Large

John R. Clark

(The Campus Citizenship Papers)

SAMPLE I. FROM THE OUTHOUSE STATE UNIVERSITY *BULLETIN*
ANNOUNCEMENT: 1971–1972

ENGLISH

Head: Assistant Professor Wolf
Chairman: Instructor Axe
Associate Chairman: Graduate Assistant Looms
Director of Programs: Crock, Jambs, & Thwart, Student English Central
  Committee

Professors: Budge, Slink, and Yeeld *(emeriti)*
Associate Professors: Cling, Lurch, and Seely
Assistant Professors: Barnacle, Batt, Corvino, Eelie, Falcon, Fox, Lemur, Platipousse, Voltore, Weezle, and Wolf
Instructors: Axe, Hammer, Hardy, Nailles, Spade, Throttle, and Torch

The Liberal Aims of the Department: English is a wide-ranging discipline with many different aspects. First, the study of language is one of the oldest studies in the humanities. Consequently, explorations in language are eminently suitable to the comprehension of meaning. Students engaging in such study are led to attempt to discover, out of the welter of writings and readings, patterns for the relevance of composition. Emphasis in the writing programs range over and underscore the literatures of the 1970's. Second, in the fields of rhetoric, students are stimulated openly to investigate and analyze facts and opinions of our decade and, on the basis of this, to present his ideas in such wise as to instruct, convince, argue, write, or encounter a particular topic or topics with meaningfulness and such like. Third, English is also the study of a vast corpus of literature, going back many centuries to the primal workings of the monastic mind in England and America. In this regard, the study of literature can provide methods and techniques in the survey of literature unadorned, laying it bare. Such contemporary literature will be fully scrutinized, seeking the arousal of sensitivities and awarenesses of pleasure. Subsidiary to this, literature can supply specific information by way of dates and facts and factions concerning lives, publications, people, and a tissue of issues. Sixthly, literature is a crucial means by which man transmits and transcends from generation to generation the great values and wholesale wisdom of the ages. The poet said, "The proper study of man is mankind," and English literature fully generates the urge to study human movements in present-day thought, within limits, be it conceded, in order to promulgate more humane knowledge and sympathy of mankind. Such studies facilitate, with diligence, the discovery of some reason for such explorations. This is truly the great tradition of the "liberal arts," a discipline which seeks exhaustively to liberate man's mind, and, eighthly, to make men free. Tuition: $4400 per semester.

The Professional Aims of the Department: The English Department seeks to prepare students on the undergraduate level to obtain degrees and to attend graduate school. Failing of this, it is to be hoped that majors might obtain employment in society.

Miscellaneous: Requirements for the Major. 18 credits in English, to be selected in the following fashions: nine (9) credits in modern literature (Group C); three (3) credits from Group A (formerly Group D), in modern drama or its equivalent; and three (3) credits from Group B, in modern criticism, psychology, and methodology. (Students wishing to examine literature of other centuries may do so with the permission of the instructor, a release from the Directors, and a seal from the Head.) And, ninthly, three (3) credits from Group D (formerly Group F), seminars in Malcolm X, *Portnoy's Complaint,* Normal Mailer, or Eldridge Cleaver.

Addenda Note: Under the new Rulings (see p. 17), student attendance is optional. There is a grade of P. (Students in the Honors Program must maintain a P average.)

SAMPLE II. REPORT OF THE SUBCOMMITTEE

Embraceable U.
Pt. Pleasant, Idaho
December 25, 1971

TO: ALL ADMINISTRATION AND THE ENTIRETY OF FACULTIES
FROM: SUBCOMMITTEE ON CALENDAR
SUBJECT: RECONSTITUTIONS PURSUANT TO REVISIONS, *re* CALENDAR

Herein is girded and appended the final interim account of the Committee of Temporal Affairs' adjunct Subcommittee on Calendar. Our membership has been performing the normal functions of a humane body for three years. After considerable straining, the subcommittee has become fecund, and our productions have been compiled and brought here (with the exception of waste matter, which has been carried away and properly deposited in cabinets*). Yet you will observe that we have retained much, and fundamentally recommend it to all of you here.

1. It has been our assumption throughout our deliberations that, although the present academic calendar has been perfectly feasible and substantially effective, it would be forward-looking and affirmative to formulate an utterly new and unfamiliar calendar. Currently, of course, our students are situated in a 4-4

---

*Needless to say, we are very willing to open our drawers for your inspection.

two-semester program; consequently, this is the one program our subcommittee found it unnecessary to consider.

2. We have decided at this time to endorse a 3-1-5 calendrical arrangement. In so doing, to be sure, we have recognized that there might be appreciable departmental and even university-wide difficulties and complications that would render a 3-1-5 scheduling proposal inefficient or undesirable. Yet we must stoutly counter that as a recommendation it is certainly not unthinkable, since, in effect, we have thought of it.

3. Speaking aesthetically and arithmetically, the 3-1-5 calendar would be distinctly singular, offering the attractive and viable spectacle of three individualized semesters, all of them independently displaying various shapes and sizes; we should never again be accused of conformity.

4. A typical calendar under our devisement might appear as follows:

> *Fall Semester*
>   Classes begin, Sept. 13
>   Semester ends, Nov. 27
> *Winter Particle*
>   Classes begin, Dec. 4
>   Semester ends, Dec. 26
> *Spring Semester*
>   Classes begin, Dec. 31
>   Semester ends, July 5

5. Within the Calendrical Apportionment, courses would remain on the current credit-hour bases with adjustments. Efficacy would hardly entail any general expansion or contraction of curriculum or labor. And Winter Particle courses would or would not replace courses now offered or the like.

6. Intersessions obviously offer opportune periods for Committee assignments and assignations.

Your subcommittee ranged broadly and settled narrowly on the archetypal calendar set forth in the recommendation of it (4, above), because it would so patently serve as Remarkable Alternative to what we have now. Additional advantages might include the following: the new calendar would provide clear and incessant changes of pace throughout the academic year.

Thus we would be enabled to inject or interlace an exciting element of Protean or Lunarian variety and mutation into our program as a permanent factor. We similarly achieve the advantage of Uniqueness, since (with the possible exception of Biloxi and several unaccredited academies**) *no other reputable university in the nation* quite offers such a calendar for student consumption.

7. Other advantages, let it be said with assurance, might possibly include: the elimination of extensive intersemester stages and similar spaces of unutilized calendrical times, and the natural existential excitements generated by the innovative divergencies of semestrial rotation.

8. The subcommittee is fully aware that in addition to potential advantages to the 3-1-5 almanac there are weighty disadvantages.

9. But we have not allowed such considerations to paralyze our endeavors or restrain our deliberations. An affirmative committee attitude is mandatory if personnel are to foist ideas or foster projects, &c. Fluid commitment *per se* to evacuation and consideration best expresses the basic principles of modification, mobility, and proliferation to which administrators adhere. We continue to be convinced that committees and groupages must bring to the curtain of tradition the valence of alteration. We remain dedicated to the rights of assembly, and therein precisely lies the meaningful physical functionings of senates, commissions, consortia, committees, boards, and corps; and beyond all these the subcommittee waits. The readiness is all—and we are almost ripe for coming hither.

10. For this very reason (our being devoted to communication, 1, above), we should like to keep the lines of information open at all ends, and select members of our body wish to submit, simultaneously with this present proposal a minority report. We

---

**We have a file and a graph determining what every other school in this country is doing about Calendar. Funds are being sought that will shortly make this material presentable to you.

must remain openminded. And if we do, it must categorically be conceded that other possibilities of a calendrical nature are highly conceivable; as, for instance: the 4-1-5, the 5-4-1, the 1-1-8, the 6-6-2, the 7-4-½. Numbers of our group will shortly be recommending these. Likewise, student observers are preparing several additional presentations and calculating possibly interesting proposals of their own. Be sure to collect every one of these reports.

Thus, our Calendar Subcommittee unequivocally does not view the recommended-type calendar as the ideal academic calendar. Indeed, as we have rendered totally evident (in 10, above), there are many potential variants or permutations to our calendar—and these have already been referred to the subcommittee on Possibilities. In addition, a new subcommittee is on this selfsame day forming, to project newer programs, plans, and reappraisals. Nor is that the sum and substance of the essence; for, as you know, ours has been but an "interim" report culled over these last three years; we are at this very minute preparing several wholly different propositions that we shall be able to make to you shortly.

In the meantime, keep your ideas, random thoughts, and queries coming in. We know that, in keeping with the spirit of our great university, all of you will be willing to devote to our deliberations your every available administrative hour.

> *Respectfully submitted,*
> *By & for the Subcommittee, &c. (seal)*
> *Transcribed by John R. Clark*

SAMPLE III. MINUTES OF THE LONG-RANGE MEETING

> Erstwhile College
> Euphoria, West Virginia
> 20 February 1971

Faculty Meeting.

(6:50 a.m.: Tea in the Academic Hallway)

7:32 a.m.: The Associate Deans called the Faculty to order in Platinum Hall at 7:30 a.m. Miss De Meanor sang the national anthem. The Associate Deans called the Faculty to order at 7:38 a.m. Motion introduced and thoroughly entertained for adoption of the minutes of yesterday's meeting. Hesitancy and debate. The wording of VIII.B.2.c, "should be clear," amended to "ought to be apparent." Minutes, as corrected, were adopted by closed vote.

8:15 a.m.: An Assistant Dean was recognized. Later he resolved in a written statement to present the Vice-President of Executive Affairs who introduced President Nilly.

8:30 a.m.: Greetings of the President, who announced a series of considerations and affirmations.

> The President thanked the members of the Faculties and Administrations, submitting reflections upon the present course of the weather (seasonable; overcast). He tendered recollections upon the late snows, with a citation from Ronsard. The President then noted that the second semester appeared to have begun. Quotations from Proverbs (Bible). Dr. Nilly reported his conviction that the faculties continued to remain suitably presentable and alert, despite projected salary cutbacks announced earlier (at Tuesday's Meetings). The President made a witticism, and offered a quotation from the Stock Exchange. In summation, he determined, if Winter is here, Spring cannot be far behind.

9:45 a.m.: Motion considered from the Chair and grappled upon the Floor, Whether or Not to admit Student Observers to this present meeting. Debates, options, amendments, irresolutions. Secret ballot: the motion CARRIED (67-64). The two students from Phi Beta Kappa escorted to the gallery by the Marshals.

10:25 a.m.: The Associate Deans called the Faculty to order. Further Greetings from the President. Welcome proffered by the Provost. Salutations of the Deans of Men, Women, and Children. Acknowledgements of Treasurer; calculations of the Bursar.

11:15 a.m.: Invocation by the Chaplain.

11:30 a.m.: Hymn delivered by the Music Department, followed by the Taking of the Roll by the Registrar, and the Taking of the Photographs of the Administrators.

11:50 a.m.: The Committee on Fixity moves to perceive the Dean. The

Standing Committee rises to apprehend the Dean. The Dean installed at the Podium.

12:00 High: Introductory Remarks by Ernest Blotner Posthume, Dean of the College.

> The Dean thanked the members of the faculties and administrations for their spirit, and offered a body of meditations. A humorous event had transpired in his presence on the way to the present meeting. The College can be proud of the parameters of its presentations and of the expansion of its interdisciplinary concentration. The Dean declared the salience of working as a Team, and perceived the vision of setting our sights.

> On the other hand, the Dean conceded the relevance of a creative fostering of the public image, and advocated wholeheartedly the primacy of setting an example. He announced the raising of tuitions, and hailed the importance of scrutiny, especially when it acceded to the imperatives of cooperation and determined upon the designation and implementation of the mandates of Self-Study. It was true that the College was faced with an overwhelming deficit and could expect the blossoming of present austerity programs. But the Dean urgently recognized the necessity of change, and praised the school's dedication to age-old standards and honored traditions.

> Nevertheless, the Dean readily cautioned his faculties personally about the perils of optimism, insisting upon the cogency of Long-Range Planning. The Dean predicted that Erstwhile College would continue to discern its targets and abrogate its aims in the years to come, remaining uprightly and flatly convinced that One Hundred Years From Now, Erstwhile would irrevocably be designated the Harvard of the Mason-Dixon, the Berkeley of the Blue Ridge, the Oxford of the Ozarks. This college would irresistibly become for all the world a wayside of learning, an outpost of excellence, and tributary to the mainstream. The Dean introduced quotations and citations to and from Plotinus, St. Thomas, Lord Tennyson, Eldridge Cleaver, and Faith Baldwin.

> It was true that drastic reductions and terminations would shortly be enforced, yet the Dean enjoined his faculties to share with him

a solemn optimism and pride. The Dean delivered Instructions for Long-Range-Planning to the EPPC, until additional Committees were established and the new Administrative Offices were erected to serve these noble ends, and bid many of the Faculty members farewell.

4:15 p.m.: Applause by the Uniform Bodies of the Faculty.

4:25 p.m.: Installation of seventeen additional Administrators and their full complement of secretarial staffs and assistants.

5:11 p.m.: Announcement of Tomorrow's Meeting.

5:15 p.m.: Prayer of Thanksgiving by the Chaplain.

5:36 p.m.: *Commus* by the Music Department and the several faculties.

5:58 p.m.: *Exodos* of Administrators, in honorable file.

6:15 p.m.: *Exeunt omnes.*

Faithfully Recorded,
Licitly Transcribed, &c.,
John R. Clark

Monastic *manuals* predominated in the thirteenth century. The sixteenth century published innumerable *Guides to Courtiers;* the seventeenth utilized *Instructions to Painters.* Thereafter, the eighteenth century honored *Compleat Letter-Writers,* the nineteenth century featured *Introduction to Industrial Etiquette.* Our own century will be committed—and rightly so—to University Administration, Campus Efficiency, and Model Programs. Professor John R. Clark of New York University has therefore long been collecting footage for a *Handbook of College Faculty Business.* He reminds us well that the faculty member's scholaring and teaching account for but the merest fraction of a professor's business. We print some significant random samples from his text.

Professor Pnin

Vladimir Nabokov

The elderly passenger sitting on the north-window side of that inexorably moving railway coach, next to an empty seat and facing two empty ones, was none other than Professor Timofey Pnin. Ideally bald, sun-tanned, and clean-shaven, he began rather impressively with that great brown dome of his, tortoise-shell glasses (masking an infantile absence of eyebrows), apish upper lip, thick neck, and strong-man torso in a tightish tweed coat, but ended, somewhat disappointingly, in a pair of spindly legs (now flanneled and crossed) and frail-looking, almost feminine feet.

His sloppy socks were of scarlet wool with lilac lozenges; his conservative black oxfords had cost him about as much as all the rest of his clothing (flamboyant goon tie included). Prior to the nineteen-forties, during the staid European era of his life, he had always worn long underwear, its terminals tucked into the tops of neat silk socks, which were clocked, soberly colored, and held up on his cotton-clad calves by garters. In those days, to reveal a glimpse of that white underwear by pulling up a trouser leg too high would have seemed to Pnin as indecent as showing himself to ladies minus collar and tie; for even when decayed Mme. Roux, the concierge of the squalid apartment house in the Sixteenth Arrondissement of Paris—where Pnin, after escaping from Leninized Russia and completing his college education in Prague, had spent fifteen years—happened to come up for the rent while he was without his *faux col*, prim Pnin would cover his front stud with a chaste hand. All this underwent a change in the heady atmosphere of the New World. Nowadays, at fifty-two, he was crazy about sun-bathing, wore sport shirts and slacks, and when crossing his legs would carefully, deliberately, brazenly display a tremendous stretch of bare shin. Thus he might have appeared to a fellow passenger; but except for a soldier asleep at one end and two women absorbed in a baby at the other, Pnin had the coach to himself.

Now a secret must be imparted. Professor Pnin was on the wrong train. He was unaware of it, and so was the conductor, already threading his way through the train to Pnin's coach. As a matter of fact, Pnin at the moment felt very well satisfied with himself. When inviting him to deliver a Friday-evening lecture at Cremona—some two hundred versts west of Waindell, Pnin's academic perch since 1945—the vice-president of the Cremona Women's Club, a Miss Judith Clyde, had advised our friend that the most convenient train left Waindell at 1:52 P.M., reaching Cremona at 4:17; but Pnin—who, like so many Russians, was inordinately fond of everything in the line of timetables, maps, catalogues, collected them, helped himself freely to them with the bracing pleasure of getting something for nothing, and took especial pride in puzzling out schedules for himself—had discovered, after some study, an inconspicuous reference mark against a still more convenient train (Lv. Waindell 2:19 P.M., Ar. Cremona 4:32 P.M.); the mark indicated that Fridays, and Fridays only, the two-nineteen stopped at Cremona on its way to a distant and much larger city, graced likewise with a mellow Italian name. Unfortunately for Pnin, his timetable was five years old and in part obsolete.

He taught Russian at Waindell College, a somewhat provincial institution characterized by an artificial lake in the middle of a landscaped campus, by ivied galleries connecting the various halls, by murals displaying recognizable members of the faculty in the act of passing on the torch of knowledge from Aristotle, Shakespeare, and Pasteur to a lot of monstrously built farm boys and farm girls, and by a huge, active, buoyantly thriving German Department which its Head, Dr. Hagen, smugly called (pronouncing every syllable very distinctly) "a university within a university."

In the Fall Semester of that particular year (1950), the enrollment in the Russian Language courses consisted of one student, plump and earnest Betty Bliss, in the Transitional Group, one, a mere name (Ivan Dub, who never materialized) in the Advanced, and three in the flourishing Elementary: Josephine Malkin, whose grandparents had been born in Minsk; Charles McBeth, whose prodigious memory had already disposed of ten languages and was prepared to entomb ten more; and languid Eileen Lane, whom somebody had told that by the time one had mastered the Russian alphabet one could practically read "Anna Karamazov" in the original. As a teacher, Pnin was far from being able to compete with those stupendous Russian ladies, scattered all over academic America, who, without having had any formal training at all, manage somehow, by dint of intuition, loquacity, and a kind of maternal bounce, to infuse a magic knowledge of their difficult and beautiful tongue into a group of innocent-eyed students in an atmosphere of Mother Volga songs, red caviar, and tea; nor did Pnin, as a teacher, ever presume to approach the lofty halls of modern scientific linguistics, that

ascetic fraternity of phonemes, that temple wherein earnest young people are taught not the language itself, but the method of teaching others
to teach that method; which method, like a waterfall splashing from
rock to rock, ceases to be a medium of rational navigation but perhaps
in some fabulous future may become instrumental in evolving esoteric
dialects—Basic Basque and so forth—spoken only by certain elaborate
machines. No doubt Pnin's approach to his work was amateurish and
lighthearted, depending as it did on exercises in a grammar brought out
by the Head of a Slavic Department in a far greater college than Waindell—a venerable fraud whose Russian was a joke but who would generously lend his dignified name to the products of anonymous drudg-
ery. Pnin, despite his many shortcomings, had about him a disarming,
old-fashioned charm which Dr. Hagen, his staunch protector, insisted
before morose trustees was a delicate imported article worth paying for
in domestic cash. Whereas the degree in sociology and political economy that Pnin had obtained with some pomp at the University of
Prague around 1925 had become by mid-century a doctorate in desue-
tude, he was not altogether miscast as a teacher of Russian. He was
beloved not for any essential ability but for those unforgettable digres-
sions of his, when he would remove his glasses to beam at the past while
massaging the lenses of the present. Nostalgic excursions in broken
English. Autobiographical tidbits. How Pnin came to the *Soedinyonnïe
Shtatï* (the United States). "Examination on ship before landing. Very
well! 'Nothing to declare?' 'Nothing.' Very well! Then political questions. He asks: 'Are you anarchist?' I answer"—time out on the part of
the narrator for a spell of cozy mute mirth—"'First what do we understand under "Anarchism"? Anarchism practical, metaphysical, theoretical, mystical, abstractical, individual, social? When I was young,' I say,
'all this had for me signification.' So we have a very interesting discussion, in consequence of which I passed two whole weeks on Ellis
Island"—abdomen beginning to heave; heaving; narrator convulsed.

But there were still better sessions in the way of humor. With an
air of coy secrecy, benevolent Pnin, preparing the children for the marvelous treat he had once had himself, and already revealing, in an
uncontrollable smile, an incomplete but formidable set of tawny teeth,
would open a dilapidated Russian book at the elegant leatherette marker
he had carefully placed there; he would open the book, whereupon as
often as not a look of the utmost dismay would alter his plastic features;
agape, feverishly, he would flip right and left through the volume, and
minutes might pass before he found the right page—or satisfied himself
that he had marked it correctly after all. Usually the passage of his

choice would come from some old and naïve comedy of merchant-class habitus rigged up by Ostrovski almost a century ago, or from an equally ancient but even more dated piece of trivial Leskovian jollity dependent on verbal contortions. He delivered these stale goods with the rotund gusto of the classical Alexandrinka (a theater in Petersburg), rather than with the crisp simplicity of the Moscow Artists; but since to appreciate whatever fun those passages still retained one had to have not only a sound knowledge of the vernacular but also a good deal of literary insight, and since his poor little class had neither, the performer would be alone in enjoying the associative subtleties of his text. The heaving we have already noted in another connection would become here a veritable earthquake. Directing his memory, with all the lights on and all the masks of the mind a-miming, toward the days of his fervid and receptive youth (in a brilliant cosmos that seemed all the fresher for having been abolished by one blow of history), Pnin would get drunk on his private wines as he produced sample after sample of what his listeners politely surmised was Russian humor. Presently the fun would become too much for him; pear-shaped tears would trickle down his tanned cheeks. Not only his shocking teeth but also an astonishing amount of pink upper-gum tissue would suddenly pop out, as if a jack-in-the-box had been sprung, and his hand would fly to his mouth, while his big shoulders shook and rolled. And although the speech he smothered behind his dancing hand was now doubly unintelligible to the class, his complete surrender to his own merriment would prove irresistible. By the time he was helpless with it he would have his students in stitches, with abrupt barks of clockwork hilarity coming from Charles and a dazzling flow of unsuspected lovely laughter transfiguring Josephine, who was not pretty, while Eileen, who was, dissolved in a jelly of unbecoming giggles.

All of which does not alter the fact that Pnin was on the wrong train.

How should we diagnose his sad case? Pnin it should be particularly stressed, was anything but the type of that good-natured German platitude of last century, *der zerstreute Professor.* On the contrary, he was perhaps too wary, too persistently on the lookout for diabolical pitfalls, too painfully on the alert lest his erratic surroundings (unpredictable America) inveigle him into some bit of preposterous oversight. It was the world that was absent-minded and it was Pnin whose business it was to set it straight. His life was a constant war with insensate objects that fell apart, or attacked him, or refused to function, or viciously got themselves lost as soon as they entered the sphere of his existence. He was inept with his hands to a rare degree; but because he could manufacture in a twinkle a one-note mouth organ out of pea pod, make a flat pebble skip ten times on the surface of a pond, shadowgraph with his knuckles a rabbit (complete with blinking eye), and perform a number of other tame tricks that Russians have up their sleeves, he believed himself endowed with considerable manual and mechanical skill. On gadgets he doted with a kind of dazed, superstitious delight. Electric devices enchanted him. Plastics swept him off his feet. He had a deep admiration for the zipper. But the devoutly plugged-in clock would make nonsense of his mornings after a storm in the middle of the night had paralyzed the local power station. The frame of his spectacles would snap in midbridge, leaving him with two identical pieces, which he would vaguely attempt to unite, in the hope, perhaps, of some organic marvel of restoration coming to the rescue. The zipper a gentleman depends on most would come loose in his puzzled hand at some nightmare moment of haste and despair.

And he still did not know that he was on the wrong train.

The Rivercliff Golf Killings

Don Marquis

OR WHY PROFESSOR WADDEMS NEVER BROKE A HUNDRED

I am telling this story to the public just as I told it in the grand jury room; the district attorney having given me a carbon copy of my sworn testimony.

The Case of Doc Green

QUESTION: Professor Waddems, when did you first notice that Dr. Green seemed to harbor animosity towards you?

ANSWER: It was when we got to the second hole.

QUESTION: Professor, you may go ahead and tell the jury about it in your own words.

ANSWER: Yes, sir. The situation was this: My third shot lay in the sand in the shallow bunker—an easy pitch with a niblick to within a foot or two of the pin, for anyone who understands the theory of niblick play as well as I do. I had the hole in five, practically.

"Professor," said Doc Green, with whom I was playing—

QUESTION: This was Dr. James T. Green, the eminent surgeon, was it not?

ANSWER: Yes, sir. Dr. Green, with whom I was playing, remarked, "You are all wrong about Freud. Psychoanalysis is the greatest discovery of the age."

"Nonsense! Nonsense! Nonsense!" I replied. "Don't be a fool, Doc! I'll show you where Freud is all wrong, in a minute."

And I lifted the ball with an explosion shot to a spot eighteen inches from the pin, and holed out with an easy putt.

"Five," I said and marked it on my card.

"You mean eight," said Doc Green.

"Three into the bunker, four onto the green, and one putt—five," I said.

"You took four strokes in the bunker, Professor," he said. "Every time you said 'Nonsense' you made a swipe at the ball with your niblick."

"Great Godfrey," I said, "you don't mean to say you are going to count those gestures I made to illustrate my argument as *golf strokes?* Just mere gestures! And you know very well I have never delivered a lecture in twenty-five years without gestures like that!"

"You moved your ball an inch or two with your club at every gesture," he said.

QUESTION: Had you really done so, Professor? Remember, you are on oath.

ANSWER: I do not remember. In any case, the point is immaterial. They were merely gestures.

QUESTION: Did you take an eight, or insist on a five?

ANSWER: I took an eight. I gave in. Gentlemen, I am a good-natured person. Too good-natured. Calm and philosophical; unruffled and patient. My philosophy never leaves me. I took an eight.

(Sensation in the grand jury room.)

QUESTION: Will you tell something of your past life, Professor Waddems—who you are and what your lifework has been, and how you acquired the calmness you speak of?

ANSWER: For nearly twenty-five years I lectured on philosophy and psychology in various universities. Since I retired and took up golf it has been my habit to look at all the events and tendencies in the world's news from the standpoint of the philosopher.

QUESTION: Has this helped you in your golf?

ANSWER: Yes, sir. My philosophical and logical training and my specialization in psychology, combined with my natural calmness and patience, have made me the great golfer that I really am.

QUESTION: Have you ever received a square deal, Professor, throughout any eighteen holes of golf?

ANSWER: No, sir. Not once! Not once during the five years since I took the game up at the Rivercliff Country Club.

QUESTION: Have you ever broken a hundred, Professor Waddems?

ANSWER: No, sir. I would have, again and again, except that my opponents, and other persons playing matches on the course, and the very forces of nature themselves are always against me at critical moments. Even the bullfrogs at the three water holes treat me impertinently.

QUESTION: Bullfrogs? You said the bullfrogs, Professor.

ANSWER: Yes, sir. They have been trained by the caddies to treat me impertinently.

QUESTION: What sort of treatment have you received in the locker room?

ANSWER: The worst possible. In the case under consideration, I may say that I took an eight on the second hole, instead of insisting on a five, because I knew the sort of thing Dr. Green would say in the locker room after the match—I knew the scene he would make, and what the comments of my so-called friends would be. Whenever I do get down to a hundred an attempt is made to discredit me in the locker room.

QUESTION: Well, you took an eight on the second hole. What happened at the third hole?

ANSWER: Well, sir, I teed up for my drive, and just as I did so, Doc Green made a slighting remark about the League of Nations. "I think it is a good thing we kept out of it," he said.

QUESTION: What were your reactions?

ANSWER: A person of intelligence could only have one kind of reaction, sir. The remark was silly, narrow-minded, provincial, boneheaded, crass and ignorant. It was all the more criminal because Dr. Green knew quite well what I think of the League of Nations. The League of Nations was my idea. I thought about it even before the late President Wilson did, and talked about it and wrote about it and lectured about it in the university.

QUESTION: So that you consider Dr. Green's motives in mentioning it when you were about to drive—

ANSWER: The worst possible, sir. They could only come from a black heart at such a time.

QUESTION: Did you lose your temper, Professor?

ANSWER: No sir! No sir! No sir! I *never* lose my temper! Not on any provocation. I said to myself, Be calm! Be philosophical! He's trying to get me excited! Remember what he'll say in the locker room afterwards! Be calm! Show him, show him, show him! Show him he can't get my goat.

QUESTION: Then you drove?

ANSWER: I addressed the ball the second time, sir. And I was about to drive when he said, with a sneer, "You must excuse me, Professor. I forgot that you invented the League of Nations."

QUESTION: Did you become violent, then, Professor?

ANSWER: No, sir! No, sir! I never become violent! I never—

QUESTION: Can you moderate your voice somewhat, Professor?

ANSWER: Yes, sir. I was explaining that I never become violent. I had every right to become violent. Any person less calm and philosophical would have become violent. Doc Green to criticize the League of Nations! The ass! Absurd! Preposterous! Silly! Abhorrent! Criminal! What the world wants is peace! Philosophic calm! The fool! Couldn't he understand that!

QUESTION: Aren't you departing, Professor, from the events of the 29th of last September at the Rivercliff golf course? What did you do next?

ANSWER: I drove.

QUESTION: Successfully?

ANSWER: It was a good drive, but the wind caught it, and it went out of bounds.

QUESTION: What did Dr. Green do then?

ANSWER: He grinned. A crass bonehead capable of sneering at the progress of the human race would sneer at a time like that.

QUESTION: But you kept your temper?

ANSWER: All my years of training as a philosopher came to my aid.

QUESTION: Go on, Professor.

ANSWER: I took my midiron from my bag and looked at it.

QUESTION: Well, go on, Professor. What did you think when you looked at it?

ANSWER: I do not remember, sir.

QUESTION: Come, come, Professor! You are under oath, you know. Did you think what a dent it would make in his skull?

ANSWER: Yes, sir. I remember now. I remember wondering if it would not do his brain good to be shaken up a little.

QUESTION: Did you strike him, then?

ANSWER: No, sir. I knew what they'd say in the locker room. They'd say that I lost my temper over a mere game. They would not understand that I had been jarring up his brain for his own good, in the hope of making him understand about the League of Nations. They'd say I was irritated. I know the things people always say.

QUESTION: Was there no other motive for not hitting him?

ANSWER: I don't remember.

QUESTION: Professor Waddems, again I call your attention to the fact that you are under oath. What was your other motive?

ANSWER: Oh, yes, now I recall it. I reflected that if I hit him they might make me add another stroke to my score. People are always getting up the flimsiest excuses to make me add another stroke. And then accusing me of impatience if I do not acquiesce in their unfairness. I am never impatient or irritable!

QUESTION: Did you ever break a club on the course, Professor?

ANSWER: I don't remember.

QUESTION: Did you not break a mashie on the Rivercliff course last week, Professor Waddems? Reflect before you answer.

ANSWER: I either gave it away or broke it, I don't remember which.

QUESTION: Come, come, don't you remember that you broke it against a tree?

ANSWER: Oh, I think I know what you mean. But it was not through temper or irritation.

QUESTION: Tell the jury about it.

ANSWER: Well, gentlemen, I had a mashie that had a loose head on it, and I don't know how it got into my bag. My ball lay behind a sapling, and I tried to play it out from behind the tree and missed it entirely. And then I noticed I had this old mashie, which should have been gotten rid of long ago. The club had never been any good. The blade was laid back at the wrong angle. I decided that the time had come to get rid of it once and for all. So I hit it a little tap against the tree, and the head fell off. I threw the pieces over into the bushes.

QUESTION: Did you swear, Professor?

ANSWER: I don't remember. But the injustice of this incident was that my opponent insisted on counting it as a stroke and adding it to my score—my judicial, deliberate destruction of this old mashie. I never get a square deal.

QUESTION: Return to Dr. James T. Green, Professor. You are now at the third hole, and the wind has just carried your ball out of bounds.

ANSWER: Well, I didn't hit him when he sneered. I carried the ball within bounds.

"Shooting three," I said calmly. I topped the ball. Gentlemen, I have seen Walter Hagen top the ball the same way.

"Too bad, Professor," said Doc Green. He said it hypocritically. I knew it was hypocrisy. He was secretly gratified that I had topped the ball. He knew I knew it.

QUESTION: What were your emotions at this further insult, Professor?

ANSWER: I pitied him. I thought how inferior he was to me intellectually, and I pitied him. I addressed the ball again. "I pity him," I murmured. "Pity, pity, pity, pity, pity!"

He overheard me. "Your pity has cost you five more strokes," he said.

"I was merely gesticulating," I said.

QUESTION: Did the ball move? Remember, you are under oath, and you have waived immunity.

ANSWER: If the ball moved, it was because a strong breeze had sprung up.

QUESTION: Go on.

ANSWER: I laid the ball upon the green and again holed out with one putt. "I'm taking a five," I said, marking it on my card.

"I'm giving you a ten," he said, marking it on his card. "Five gesticulations on account of your pity."

QUESTION: Describe your reactions to this terrible injustice, Professor. Was there a red mist before your eyes? Did you turn giddy and wake up to find him lying lifeless at your feet? Just what happened?

ANSWER: Nothing, sir.

(Sensation in the grand jury room.)

QUESTION: Think again, Professor. Nothing?

ANSWER: I merely reflected that, in spite of his standing scientifically, Dr. James T. Green was a moron and utterly devoid of morality and that I should take this into account. I did not lose my temper.

QUESTION: Did you snatch the card from his hands?

ANSWER: I took it, sir. I did not snatch it.

QUESTION: And then did you cram it down his throat?

ANSWER: I suggested that he eat it, sir, as it contained a falsehood in black and white, and Dr. Green complied with my request.

QUESTION: Did you lay hands upon him, Professor? Remember, now, we are still talking about the third hole.

ANSWER: I think I did steady him a little by holding him about the neck and throat while he masticated and swallowed the card.

QUESTION: And then what?

ANSWER: Well, gentlemen, after that there is very little more to tell until we reached the sixteenth hole. Dr. Green for some time made no further attempt to treat me unjustly and played in silence, acquiescing in the scores I had marked on my card. We were even as to holes, and it was a certainty that I was about to break a hundred. But I knew what was beneath this silence on Doc Green's part, and I did not trust it.

QUESTION: What do you mean? That you knew what he was thinking, although he did not speak?

ANSWER: Yes, sir. I knew just what kind of remarks he would have made if he had made any remarks.

QUESTION: Were these remarks which he suppressed derogatory remarks?

ANSWER: Yes, sir. Almost unbelievably so. They were deliberately intended to destroy my poise.

QUESTION: Did they do so, Professor?

ANSWER: I don't think so.

QUESTION: Go on, Professor.

ANSWER: At the sixteenth tee, as I drove off, this form of insult reached its climax. He accentuated his silence with a peculiar look, just as my club head was about to meet the ball. I knew what he meant. He knew that I knew it, and that I knew. I sliced into a bunker. He stood and watched me, as I stepped into the sand with my niblick—watched me with that look upon his face. I made three strokes at the ball and, as will sometimes happen even to the best of players, did not move it a foot. The fourth stroke drove it out of sight into the sand. The sixth stroke brought it to light again. Gentlemen, I did not lose my temper. I never do. But I admit that I did increase my tempo. I struck rapidly three more times at the ball. And all the time Doc Green was regarding me with that look, to which he now added a smile. Still I kept my temper, and he might be alive today if he had not spoken.

QUESTION *(by the foreman of the jury):* What did the man say at this trying time?

ANSWER: I know that you will not believe it is within the human heart to make the black remark that he made. And I hesitate to repeat it. But I have sworn to tell everything. What he said was, "Well, Professor, the club puts these bunkers here, and I suppose they have got to be used."

QUESTION *(by the foreman of the jury):* Was there something especially trying in the way he said it?

ANSWER: There was. He said it with an affectation of joviality.

QUESTION: You mean as if he thought he were making a joke, Professor?

ANSWER: Yes, sir.

QUESTION: What were your emotions at this point?

ANSWER: Well, sir, it came to me suddenly that I owed a duty to society; and for the sake of civilization I struck him with the niblick. It was an effort to reform him, gentlemen.

QUESTION: Why did you cover him with sand afterwards?

ANSWER: Well, I knew that if the crowd around the locker room discovered that I had hit him, they would insist on counting it as another stroke. And that is exactly what happened when the body was discovered—once again I was prevented from breaking a hundred.

THE DISTRICT ATTORNEY: Gentlemen of the jury, you have heard Professor Waddems' frank and open testimony in the case of Dr. James T. Green. My own recommendation is that he be not only released, but complimented, as far as this count is returned. If ever a homicide was justifiable, this one was. And I suggest that you report no indictment against the Professor, without leaving your seats. Many of you will wish to get in at least nine holes before dinner. Tomorrow Professor Waddems will tell us what he knows about the case of Silas W. Amherst, the banker.

The district attorney has given me the following certified copy of my sworn testimony, and I am telling the story of this golf game to the public just as I told it in the grand jury room.

Two Limericks

Bennett Cerf

There once was a scholar named Fressor
Whose knowledge grew lessor and lessor.
It at last grew so small
He knew nothing at all,
And today he's a college professor!

There once lived a teacher named Dodd
With manners arresting and odd.
He said, "If you please,
Spell my name with three D's,"
Though one was sufficient for God.

Garry Trudeau

Professor Tattersall

Peter De Vries

The demonstration was being staged to coincide with Reunion Week, and now visiting alumni of various ages stood in groups around the fountain near which Tattersall had paused. There were a number of seniors among the onlookers; more than among the participants, since they were about to graduate and leave, and had little or no interest in the subject now. They had more curiosity about the alumni which they were on the brink of becoming. The old grads soon had their fill and returned, by contrast, to more nostalgic concerns, swapping reminiscences, exchanging gossip, and in at least one case, striking up a song or two. The music mingled with the sound of the chanting, which though persistent was restrained and systematic, in keeping with the admonition to "orderly milling." "Orderly Milling," Tattersall thought to himself. "It sounds like a hospital employee. Hello, Orderly Milling? Send up another tank of oxygen to Room 312."

"Hello, Hank." Wurlitzer, after a spell of harmonizing, had strolled to his side.

"How do you feel about it?" With a nod Wurlitzer indicated the demonstration to which his question applied.

Tattersall understood it to be Wurlitzer's view that young people "went too far," "demanded too much," and "were getting out of hand." Which was just enough to congeal a latent sympathy with their cause into formal support on Tattersall's part. It was all he needed.

"I think they're right," he said.

"You do?"

"Yes. We're here to give them an education. Not regulate their private lives."

"Then why aren't you in there marching with them?"

Wurlitzer had spoken it facetiously, even with a discernible laugh. But Tattersall answered, "Why not indeed?" and strode over and joined the line.

He was rather surprised to find himself there, since he was also a member of the discipline committee. The demonstrators marched three and four abreast, and he tramped rhythmically along to the right of a youth in a black turtleneck sweater, on whose left was a girl in a plaid skirt and maroon cardigan. That they ignored Tattersall pleased him, since it meant they saw nothing unusual in his participation by reason of age or appearance. In his tweed coat and black knit tie he could easily pass for one of Wurlitzer's crazy mixed-up kids. Braced by these deductions, he threw his shoulders back and lustily joined in chanting, "No curfew Saturday! Curfew shall not ring on Saturday!"

For all the rhythmic shouting and stomping, quite blood-rousing in its way, the line steadily circling the Administration Building was indeed an orderly one. It recalled prisoners being exercised in a yard. The half-dozen or so cops one passed at their successive posts, standing with feet planted apart and nursing their sticks behind their backs, heightened this resemblance to an orbiting contingent of inmates in stir. Was that how the term had originated? They quite resembled a vast porridge being stirred by an invisible authoritative ladle. On one circuit he saw President Mattock and Dean Shaffer posing with the student ringleaders for some newspaper photographs. They smiled in a simulated tableau of amicably Hearing the Young People Out, and as if in balanced rejection of any implication that youth was Going to the Dogs. One of the ringleaders was not too fortunate a spokesman for the cause, having, in a way, compromised it.

Bats Hartack was a junior majoring in architecture, who had violated every rule concerning girls and dormitories except one—the eleven o'clock Lights Out rule. His lights were always out well before that time. On that score there could be no complaints. Since the present expanding agitation had started, some few months before, he had been found with a girl in his bed. Opinion was divided as to whether this prejudiced the cause or performed the service of bringing it into clear and dramatic focus. Some such debate was presumed to be going forward now between the principals, judging by the way reporters took notes, now on what one side said, now the other. All this was orderly too. Then suddenly the scene was given a different and quite galvanizing emphasis. Tattersall was recognized. Another minute and he would have been safely past the front of the building. But one of the ringleaders spotted him and instantly made capital of it. "There's Mr. Tattersall!" he shouted, pointing, and Tattersall was led captive through the roaring mob.

His statement was straightforward and terse. It began with what he had pithily told Wurlitzer, that they were there to educate the students, not regulate their private lives. "Parietal rules, as we call these campus regulations, can only be partial and therefore hypocritical in any case," he said, as pencils flew and cameras clicked. "The rules themselves mean nothing. Whether you have a two A.M. curfew or a ten o'clock one, there are still twenty-four hours in a day. And nobody checks the rooms anyway, except in the most desultory and sporadic fashion. The possibility of what you may find in them makes such espionage more disagreeable than the offenses they uncover."

"Then how was Hartack caught?" a reporter asked.

"By someone not looking for that at all. He'd heard there was something stronger than beer in the room, and happened to find something stronger than whiskey."

"What are your views on that? As a member of the discipline committee, would you expel a student for drinking bourbon on campus?"

"Yes."

"Why, if not for the other?"

"Because in that case he's breaking a state law, and worse, a gentlemen's agreement. There's a delicate truce between us and the local authorities, by which they connive at beer and wine in return for our cracking down on whiskey. It's not perfect, any more than anything in this world is, but it's one way of solving this whole tricky and complex problem of college drinking. And it works. It's an honor thing, if you will, and so if I found Hartack drinking whiskey, yes, I'd kick him out. His sex life is his own business. That does not involve what you could accurately call a gentlemen's agreement." The laughter was such that Tattersall could enjoy having to hold his hand up for quiet. "We don't interfere with the sex life of students living off campus. They sleep together in one another's apartments all over town and everyone knows it. That's what I mean about its all being hypocritical. The parietal rules *are not honest.*"

The President's face, which looked like a pot of tomatoes the best of times, now positively blazed, as though it had caught fire, while the Dean simply looked at the ground with his crapkicking smile, as though it was he who had been caught with the girl, and was a devil.

"Do you have a statement to make about all this?" one of the reporters asked the President.

"Just that there will be an emergency meeting of the discipline committee in my office in exactly one hour," the President said, and turned on his heel and strode away.

As a member of it, Tattersall scurried conscientiously about in preparation for the meeting. He sought Hartack out immediately after the demonstration and ordered him to appear without fail at the emergency session. He had a plan which he hoped would put an end to this whole sordid muddle, and marching in unexpectedly with Bats Hartack by his side served his strategy by catching the President unawares. The President was engaged in preliminary consultation with the two other members of the committee: the Dean, and Edmonds of the History Department, a man who sucked on curved pipes and weighed both sides before making a judgment.

"What is the meaning of bringing Hartack in on this, Tattersall?" the President demanded, looking up.

"I thought that's what you meant. That he be summoned. Else what's the meeting for?"

"To consider you! As you very well know. Your insubordination—which I make no bones about calling it. This is real malfeasance. What right have you to march in a demonstration aimed at a committee of which you are a member? Up to now anyway," the President added darkly. If one might not more accurately say brightly, for his face glowed dangerously again. He ground his teeth wretchedly a moment, and then said, "Do you march against yourself, man!"

"I don't look at it that way. I took the demonstration to be just what the term implies. A public declaration of opinion. No more, no less. There are some students who oppose liberalizing the parietal rules, and they were given their right to heckle. Conversely some faculty members favor it, and by the same token share in the right to speak up and say what they think. Or so I assume, unless free speech is a one-way street."

The President looked to Edmonds for his view on this thinking, and in so doing riveted all eyes upon him. Edmonds nodded thoughtfully, puffing on his pipe, and at last said through a cloud of smoke which obscured him personally, as Jehovah was said to obscure himself in making pronouncements, "I think Tattersall has a point. It's a piece of casuistry, granted, but valid in its way. He's compromised us as a committee in one sense. But in another he's certified us before the world as honestly accommodating dissent, thereby laying claim for us to a confidence which the student body is now in all conscience obliged to give."

"What do you think, Dean?"

"I'm in agreement."

"With whom—Edmonds and Tattersall, or me?"

This was hard on the Dean, who tried to take both sides of every question, not merely, like Edmonds, weigh them with a view to selecting one. The fence-straddling was in turn hard on the President. It was an open secret that the Dean's definite maybes were chief among the factors undermining the President's health; that another mouthful of mush would kill him, by bringing on another duodenal crisis.

"I agree with you absolutely that Tattersall's action was imprudent from one point of view," the Dean said, "but that by sheer luck it may turn out in our favor." While the President sat magisterially trying to hear everyone out before deciding whether to release unto them Barabbas or another, the Dean, his chins making him look more than ever like a pelican, took the opportunity to glance at Hartack as someone to whom plain disapproval could be safely directed. "Once we know what in the world Hartack is doing here."

That worthy (as such types were called in the fiction Tattersall knew full well the Dean still read) had all this while been standing, as, indeed, had Tattersall. After waving them to chairs, the President acidly asked Tattersall to enlighten them on the point the Dean had raised. That made the Dean's thrust seem to have been directed at Tattersall, causing the Dean guiltily to drop his eyes again.

"I can only assume," Tattersall began, "that if action was to be taken on my participation in the rally, it would consist either in a request for my resignation, or, if the milder line were adopted for which I would have to thank my good friend Edmonds, in some kind of statement of censure which would force me to tender it anyway."

"A distinct possibility," the President said to his desk blotter.

"In that case," Tattersall said slowly, "there would be a student revolt."

"So that's your little game, is it? Blackmail!"

"No. Not in the least. The fact is that I have decided to tender my resignation anyway. Not over this, or as a member of the committee. As a teacher. I have another offer of employment open to me, in another profession, which I have decided to accept. That ought to cut this Gordian knot for us all."

There were murmurs of protestation and reassurance. "Quit teaching? Why would you want to do a thing like that?" the President said, scarcely able to conceal his joy.

"I just think I'm ripe for a change, that's all. Nothing more to it than that. Well, to get back to the business at hand. I thought one reason Hartack's presence would be valuable is that he can hear for himself that my resignation is not being asked for, and so testify to the student body. That way there'll be no misunderstanding, no needless hoopla over nothing. Certainly no wasteful and destructive student revolt." After they had all breathed a sigh of relief, Tattersall turned to Hartack. "Now let's put a few questions to the prisoner while we have him here, shall we? Does anyone mind if I conduct the interrogation?"

"Not at all," said the President, only too tickled that this was to be Tattersall's swan song.

They were loosely ranged around the desk at which the President himself sat. Tattersall now twitched his chair about so as to be facing Hartack more squarely. Hartack, a stocky blond with a crew cut, did not look like a firebrand now that he was actually before the tribunal that would decide his fate. The sudden fear of expulsion, or even of a suspension that would in effect lose him a whole semester since they were within so few days of its end, brought beads of perspiration to his brow, and made him clear his throat nervously. He agreed to come clean when Tattersall warned him it would be wise to do so, and not deny facts of which he had the evidence—evidence, Tattersall added, that he had gone to the trouble of personally collecting.

"The truth is that you were only caught in bed once with this girl, but that you have really been taking her into your room regularly. Is that correct?"

"Yes, sir," Hartack said, wetting his lips, "I guess that's right."

"You guess. How many times would you say you violated the rule?"

"I can't say."

"Because they were so many. It might be easier to state the period of time over which you have been doing so, rather than enumerate individual instances. How long would you say? All semester? All year?"

"All year."

"Last year too?"

"Yes, sir."

"And the year before that."

"Yes, sir."

There was a silence in the room. It continued for some time. The committee members could all be heard breathing heavily. When they had drunk their fill of implication, Tattersall turned slowly from Hartack to them.

"You've heard the whole story, gentlemen," he said, "the full facts. And I wish to submit to you, gentlemen, that these are extenuating circumstances. This is obviously not a superficial relationship, but a deep and serious one. This girl is not a pickup, nor is this your short-order sex, a case of popping in and out of the sack such as we know to be going on everywhere, not only here but all around, anywhere you can name. These young people are going steady in the fullest sense of the term, not shacking up in the shabby and superficial one. *This man has been pulling the wool over our eyes for four years.* Clearer proof of his intentions could not be asked. In view of all this, gentlemen, I think it would be regrettable to make an example of someone who might more properly be held up as one."

"Hear, hear!" they said.

That was how they voted too, not only clearing Hartack of the charge, by the simple device of dropping it, but shaking his hand by way of commending a meaningful bond such as could only refresh their faith in an age of promiscuity. "There are marriages that don't last that long," Edmonds said from within a dense cloud of smoke.

Having excused Hartack, they settled down to the larger issue, that of overhauling the regulations in general. Tattersall again stressed the point that students on campus were being cracked down on for what those living off it got away with scot-free. The President protested fatigue with that argument. The obvious impracticability of policing the entire city didn't absolve them from the responsibility of governing the part they could. "If a cop is giving you a ticket for speeding," he said, "the fact that cars are whizzing by at eighty miles an hour while he is doing so is no ground for complaining that you're being discriminated against. He can't be everywhere at once. And if they're having such meaningful relationships, let them prove it by contending with a few obstacles!"

Then the Dean, having just murmured that there was something in what Tattersall said, now agreed with the President also, picking lint from his knee with his crapkicking smile. Then he made a joke. He remarked that infractions were hard to be sure about in any case, if you found two people in bed together, because nowadays you couldn't tell the boys from the girls. Then Tattersall, who had made that observation himself years back when it wasn't so common, said, "Maybe they *like* to resemble each other, the young people. Maybe that's very loving and sexual, rather than hermaphroditic." Then the Dean backed down a little and said, "There's something in what you say." Whereupon Tattersall had one of his twinges of remorse for jumping on him, and to make amends, cited a cartoon contradicting his own position and supporting the Dean's. It showed just such an androgynous youth as they were talking about, with dungarees and long hair, standing at a mailbox reading a letter which began, "Dear sir or madam . . ." Then the Dean said, "I see what you mean," lowering his eyes to the floor while Tattersall rolled his to the ceiling in an expression of absolutely giving up.

Not even Edmonds could summarize, or "recap," these bandied and qualification-tormented observations, or resolve their contradictions by pointing out with his pipestem the truth that lay somewhere in between. So they came to no decision about what to recommend, but tabled the matter till another meeting, which meant another term. Which was perhaps just as well. But in rolling his eyes to the ceiling, Tattersall had noted a wide and rapidly spreading wet spot in the plaster there. Thus a serious leak in the plumbing was detected, in time to save the school hundreds, possibly thousands, of dollars in repair expense, and making them all feel that something worthwhile had been accomplished by this meeting.

Report on the Barnhouse Effect

Kurt Vonnegut, Jr.

Let me begin by saying that I don't know any more about where Professor Arthur Barnhouse is hiding than anyone else does. Save for one short, enigmatic message left in my mailbox on Christmas Eve, I have not heard from him since his disappearance a year and a half ago.

What's more, readers of this article will be disappointed if they expect to learn how *they* can bring about the so-called "Barnhouse Effect." If I were able and willing to give away that secret, I would certainly be something more important than a psychology instructor.

I have been urged to write this report because I did research under the professor's direction and because I was the first to learn of his astonishing discovery. But while I was his student I was never entrusted with knowledge of how the mental forces could be released and directed. He was unwilling to trust anyone with that information.

I would like to point out that the term "Barnhouse Effect" is a creation of the popular press, and was never used by Professor Barnhouse. The name he chose for the phenomenon was *"dynamopsychism,"* or *force of the mind.*

I cannot believe that there is a civilized person yet to be convinced that such a force exists, what with its destructive effects on display in every national capital. I think humanity has always had an inkling that this sort of force does exist. It has been common knowledge that some people are luckier than others with inanimate objects like dice. What Professor Barnhouse did was to show that such "luck" was a measurable force, which in his case could be enormous.

By my calculations, the professor was about fifty-five times more powerful than a Nagasaki-type atomic bomb at the time he went into hiding. He was not bluffing when, on the eve of "Operation Brainstorm," he told General Honus Barker: "Sitting here at the dinner table, I'm pretty sure I can flatten anything on earth—from Joe Louis to the Great Wall of China."

There is an understandable tendency to look upon Professor Barnhouse as a supernatural visitation. The First Church of Barnhouse in Los Angeles has a congregation numbering in the thousands. He is godlike in neither appearance nor intellect. The man who disarms the world is single, shorter than the average American male, stout, and averse to exercise. His I.Q. is 143, which is good but certainly not sensational. He is quite mortal, about to celebrate his fortieth birthday, and in good health. If he is alone now, the isolation won't bother him too much. He was quiet and shy when I knew him, and seemed to find more companionship in books and music than in his associations at the college.

Neither he nor his powers fall outside the sphere of Nature. His dynamopsychic radiations are subject to many known physical laws that apply in the field of radio. Hardly a person has not now heard the snarl of "Barnhouse static" on his home receiver. The radiations are affected by sunspots and variations in the ionosphere.

However, they differ from ordinary broadcast waves in several important ways. Their total energy can be brought to bear on any single point the professor chooses, and that energy is undiminished by distance. As a weapon, then, dynamopsychism has an impressive advantage over bacteria and atomic bombs, beyond the fact that it costs nothing to use: it enables the professor to single out critical individuals and objects instead of slaughtering whole populations in the process of maintaining international equilibrium.

As General Honus Barker told the House Military Affairs Committee: "Until someone finds Barnhouse, there is no defense against the Barnhouse Effect." Efforts to "jam" or block the radiations have failed. Premier Slezak could have saved himself the fantastic expense of his "Barnhouse-proof" shelter. Despite the shelter's twelve-foot-thick lead armor, the premier has been floored twice while in it.

There is talk of screening the population for men potentially as powerful dynamopsychically as the professor. Senator Warren Foust demanded funds for this purpose last month, with the passionate declaration: "He who rules the Barnhouse Effect rules the world!" Commissar Kropotnik said much the same thing, so another costly armaments race, with a new twist, has begun.

This race at least has its comical aspects. The world's best gamblers are being coddled by governments like so many nuclear physicists. There may be several hundred persons with dynamopsychic talent on earth, myself included. But, without knowledge of the professor's technique, they can never be anything but dice-table despots. With the secret, it would probably take them ten years to become dangerous weapons. It took the professor that long. He who rules the Barnhouse Effect is Barnhouse and will be for some time.

Popularly, the "Age of Barnhouse" is said to have begun a year and a half ago, on the day of Operation Brainstorm. That was when dynamopsychism became significant politically. Actually, the phenomenon was discovered in May, 1942, shortly after the professor turned down a direct commission in the Army and enlisted as an artillery private. Like X-rays and vulcanized rubber, dynamopsychism was discovered by accident.

• • •

From time to time Private Barnhouse was invited to take part in games of chance by his barrack mates. He knew nothing about the games, and usually begged off. But one evening, out of social grace, he agreed to shoot craps. It was terrible or wonderful that he played, depending upon whether or not you like the world as it now is.

"Shoot sevens, Pop," someone said.

So "Pop" shot sevens—ten in a row to bankrupt the barracks. He retired to his bunk and, as a mathematical exercise, calculated the odds against his feat on the back of a laundry slip. His chances of doing it, he found, were one in almost ten million! Bewildered, he borrowed a pair of dice from the man in the bunk next to his. He tried to roll sevens again, but got only the usual assortment of numbers. He lay back for a moment, then resumed his toying with the dice. He rolled ten more sevens in a row.

He might have dismissed the phenomenon with a low whistle. But the professor instead mulled over the circumstances surrounding his two lucky streaks. There was one single factor in common: on both occasions, *the same thought train had flashed through his mind just before he threw the dice.* It was that thought train which aligned the professor's brain cells into what has since become the most powerful weapon on earth.

•   •   •

The soldier in the next bunk gave dynamopsychism its first token of respect. In an understatement certain to bring wry smiles to the faces of the world's dejected demagogues, the soldier said, "You're hotter'n a two-dollar pistol, Pop." Professor Barnhouse was all of that. The dice that did his bidding weighed but a few grams, so the forces involved were minute; but the unmistakable fact that there were such forces was earthshaking.

Professional caution kept him from revealing his discovery immediately. He wanted more facts and a body of theory to go with them. Later when the atomic bomb was dropped in Hiroshima, it was fear that made him hold his peace. At no time were his experiments, as Premier Slezak called them, "a bourgeois plot to shackle the true democracies of the world." The professor didn't know where they were leading.

In time, he came to recognize another startling feature of dynamopsychism: *its strength increased with use.* Within six months, he was able to govern dice thrown by men the length of a barracks distant. By the time of his discharge in 1945, he could knock bricks loose from chimneys three miles away.

Charges that Professor Barnhouse could have won the last war in a minute, but did not care to do so, are perfectly senseless. When the war ended, he had the range and power of a 37-millimeter cannon, perhaps—certainly no more. His dynamopsychic powers graduated from the small-arms class only after his discharge and return to Wyandotte College.

I enrolled in the Wyandotte Graduate School two years after the professor had rejoined the faculty. By chance, he was assigned as my thesis adviser. I was unhappy about the assignment, for the professor was, in the eyes of both colleagues and students, a somewhat ridiculous figure. He missed classes or had lapses of memory during lectures. When I arrived, in fact, his shortcomings had passed from the ridiculous to the intolerable.

"We're assigning you to Barnhouse as a sort of temporary thing," the dean of social studies told me. He looked apologetic and perplexed. "Brilliant man, Barnhouse, I guess. Difficult to know since his return, perhaps, but his work before the war brought a great deal of credit to our little school."

When I reported to the professor's laboratory for the first time, what I saw was more distressing than the gossip. Every surface in the room was covered with dust; books and apparatus had not been disturbed for months. The professor sat napping at his desk when I entered. The only signs of recent activity were three overflowing ashtrays, a pair of scissors, and a morning paper with several items clipped from its front page.

As he raised his head to look at me, I saw that his eyes were clouded with fatigue. "Hi," he said, "just can't seem to get my sleeping done at night." He lighted a cigarette, his hands trembling slightly. "You the young man I'm supposed to help with a thesis?"

"Yes sir," I said. In minutes he converted my misgivings to alarm.

"You an overseas veteran?" he asked.

"Yes, sir."

"Not much left over there, is there?" He frowned. "Enjoy the last war?"

"No, sir."

"Look like another war to you?"

"Kind of, sir."

"What can be done about it?"

I shrugged. "Looks pretty hopeless."

He peered at me intently. "Know anything about international law, the U.N., and all that?"

"Only what I pick up from the papers."

"Same here," he sighed. He showed me a fat scrapbook packed with newspaper clippings. "Never used to pay any attention to international politics. Now I study them the way I used to study rats in mazes. Everybody tells me the same thing—'Looks hopeless.'"

"Nothing short of a miracle—" I began.

"Believe in magic?" he asked sharply. The professor fished two dice from his vest pocket. "I will try to roll twos," he said. He rolled twos three times in a row. "One chance in about 47,000 of that happening. There's a miracle for you." He beamed for an instant, then brought the interview to an end, remarking that he had a class which had begun ten minutes ago.

He was not quick to take me into his confidence, and he said no more about his trick with the dice. I assumed they were loaded, and forgot about them. He set me the task of watching male rats cross electrified metal strips to get to food or female rats—an experiment that had been done to everyone's satisfaction in the nineteen-thirties. As though the pointlessness of my work were not bad enough, the professor annoyed me further with irrelevant questions. His favorites were:

"Think we should have dropped the atomic bomb on Hiroshima?" and "Think every new piece of scientific information is a good thing for humanity?"

· · ·

However, I did not feel put upon for long. "Give those poor animals a holiday," he said one morning, after I had been with him only a month. "I wish you'd help me look into a more interesting problem—namely, my sanity."

I returned the rats to their cages.

"What you must do is simple," he said, speaking softly. "Watch the inkwell on my desk. If you see nothing happen to it, say so, and I'll go quietly—relieved, I might add—to the nearest sanitarium."

I nodded uncertainly.

He locked the laboratory door and drew the blinds, so that we were in twilight for a moment. "I'm odd, I know," he said. "It's fear of myself that's made me odd."

"I've found you somewhat eccentric, perhaps, but certainly not—"

"If nothing happens to that inkwell, 'crazy as a bedbug' is the only description of me that will do," he interrupted, turning on the overhead lights. His eyes narrowed. "To give you an idea of how crazy, I'll tell you what's been running through my mind when I should have been sleeping. I think maybe I can save the world. I think maybe I can make every nation a *have* nation, and do away with war for good. I think maybe I can clear roads through jungles, irrigate deserts, build dams overnight."

"Yes, sir."

"Watch the inkwell!"

Dutifully and fearfully I watched. A high-pitched humming seemed to come from the inkwell; then it began to vibrate alarmingly, and finally to bound about the top of the desk, making two noisy circuits. It stopped, hummed again, glowed red, then popped in splinters with a blue-green flash.

Perhaps my hair stood on end. The professor laughed gently. "Magnets?" I managed to say at last.

"Wish to heaven it were magnets," he murmured. It was then that he told me of dynamopsychism. He knew only that there was such a force; he could not explain it. "It's me and me alone—and it's awful."

"I'd say it was amazing and wonderful!" I cried.

"If all I could do was make inkwells dance, I'd be tickled silly with the whole business." He shrugged disconsolately. "But I'm no toy, my boy. If you like, we can drive around the neighborhood, and I'll show you what I mean." He told me about pulverized boulders, shattered oaks, and abandoned farm buildings demolished within a fifty-mile radius of the campus. "Did every bit of it sitting right here, just thinking—not even thinking hard."

He scratched his head nervously. "I have never dared to concentrate as hard as I can for fear of the damage I might do. I'm to the point where a mere whim is a blockbuster." There was a depressing pause. "Up until a few days ago, I've thought it best to keep my secret for fear of what use it might be put to," he continued. "Now I realize that I haven't any more right to it than a man has a right to own an atomic bomb."

He fumbled through a heap of papers. "This says about all that needs to be said, I think." He handed me a draft of a letter to the Secretary of State.

DEAR SIR:
    I have discovered a new force which costs nothing to use, and which is probably more important than atomic energy. I should like to see it used most effectively in the cause of peace, and am, therefore, requesting your advice as to how this might best be done.
                                                                            Yours truly,
                                                                            A. BARNHOUSE.

"I have no idea what will happen next," said the professor.

• • •

There followed three months of perpetual nightmare, wherein the nation's political and military great came at all hours to watch the professor's tricks.

We were quartered in an old mansion near Charlottesville, Virginia, to which we had been whisked five days after the letter was mailed. Surrounded by barbed wire and twenty guards, we were labeled "Project Wishing Well," and were classified as Top Secret.

For companionship we had General Honus Barker and the State Department's William K. Cuthrell. For the professor's talk of peace-through-plenty they had indulgent smiles and much discourse on practical measures and realistic thinking. So treated, the professor, who had at first been almost meek, progressed in a matter of weeks toward stubbornness.

He had agreed to reveal the thought train by means of which he aligned his mind into a dynamopsychic transmitter. But, under Cuthrell's and Barker's nagging to do so, he began to hedge. At first he declared that the information could be passed on simply by word of mouth. Later he said that it would have to be written up in a long report. Finally, at dinner one night, just after General Barker had read the secret orders for Operation Brainstorm, the professor announced, "The report may take as long as five years to write." He looked fiercely at the general. "Maybe twenty."

The dismay occasioned by this flat announcement was offset somewhat by the exciting anticipation of Operation Brainstorm. The general was in a holiday mood. "The target ships are on their way to the Caroline Islands at this very moment," he declared ecstatically. "One hundred and twenty of them! At the same time, ten V-2s are being readied for firing in New Mexico, and fifty radio-controlled jet bombers are being equipped for a mock attack on the Aleutians. Just think of it!" Happily he reviewed his orders. "At exactly 1100 hours next Wednesday, I will give you the order to *concentrate;* and you, professor, will think as hard as you can about sinking the target ships, destroying the V-2s before they hit the ground, and knocking down the bombers before they reach the Aleutians! Think you can handle it?"

The professor turned gray and closed his eyes. "As I told you before, my friend, I don't know what I can do." He added bitterly, "As for this Operation Brainstorm, I was never consulted about it, and it strikes me as childish and insanely expensive."

General Barker bridled. "Sir," he said, "your field is psychology, and I wouldn't presume to give you advice in that field. Mine is national defense. I have had thirty years of experience and success, Professor, and I'll ask you not to criticize my judgment."

The professor appealed to Mr. Cuthrell. "Look," he pleaded, "isn't it war and military matters we're all trying to get rid of? Wouldn't it be a whole lot more significant and lots cheaper for me to try moving cloud masses into drought areas, and things like that? I admit I know next to nothing about international politics, but it seems reasonable to suppose that nobody would want to fight wars if there were enough of everything to go around. Mr. Cuthrell, I'd like to try running generators where there isn't any coal or water power, irrigating deserts, and so on. Why, you could figure out what each country needs to make the most of its resources, and I could give it to them without costing American taxpayers a penny."

"Eternal vigilance is the price of freedom," said the general heavily.

Mr. Cuthrell threw the general a look of mild distate. "Unfortunately, the general is right in his own way," he said. "I wish to heaven the world were ready for ideals like yours, but it simply isn't. We aren't surrounded by brothers, but by enemies. It isn't a lack of food or resources that has us on the brink of war—it's a struggle for power. Who's going to be in charge of the world, our kind of people or theirs?"

The professor nodded in reluctant agreement and arose from the table. "I beg your pardon, gentlemen. You are, after all, better qualified to judge what is best for the country. I'll do whatever you say." He turned to me. "Don't forget to wind the restricted clock and put the confidential cat out," he said gloomily, and ascended the stairs to his bedroom.

· · ·

For reasons of national security, Operation Brainstorm was carried on without the knowledge of the American citizenry which was paying the bill. The observers, technicians, and military men involved in the activity knew that a test was under way—a test of what, they had no idea. Only thirty-seven key men, myself included, knew what was afoot.

In Virginia, the day for Operation Brainstorm was unseasonably cool. Inside, a log fire crackled in the fireplace, and the flames were reflected in the polished metal cabinets that lined the living room. All that remained of the room's lovely old furniture was a Victorian love seat, set squarely in the center of the floor, facing three television receivers. One long bench had been brought in for the ten of us privileged to watch. The television screens showed, from left to right, the stretch of desert which was the rocket target, the guinea-pig fleet, and a section of the Aleutian sky through which the radio-controlled bomber formation would roar.

Ninety minutes before H-hour the radios announced that the rockets were ready, that the observation ships had backed away to what was thought to be a safe distance, and that the bombers were on their way. The small Virginia audience lined up on the bench in order of rank, smoked a great deal, and said little. Professor Barnhouse was in his bedroom. General Barker bustled about the house like a woman preparing Thanksgiving dinner for twenty.

At ten minutes before H-hour the general came in, shepherding the professor before him. The professor was comfortably attired in sneakers, gray flannels, a blue sweater, and a white shirt open at the neck. The two of them sat side by side on the love seat. The general was rigid and perspiring; the professor was cheerful. He looked at each of the screens, lighted a cigarette and settled back.

"Bombers sighted!" cried the Aleutian observers.

"Rockets away!" barked the New Mexico radio operator.

All of us looked quickly at the big electric clock over the mantel, while the professor, a half-smile on his face, continued to watch the television sets. In hollow tones, the general counted away the seconds remaining. "Five . . . four . . . three . . . two . . . one . . . *Concentrate!*"

Professor Barnhouse closed his eyes, pursed his lips, and stroked his temples. He held the position for a minute. The television images were scrambled, and the radio signals were drowned in the din of Barnhouse static. The professor sighed, opened his eyes, and smiled confidently.

"Did you give it everything you had?" asked the general dubiously.

"I was wide open," the professor replied.

The television images pulled themselves together, and mingled cries of amazement came over the radios tuned to the observers. The Aleutian sky was streaked with the smoke trails of bombers screaming down in flames. Simultaneously, there appeared high over the rocket target a cluster of white puffs, followed by faint thunder.

General Barker shook his head happily. "By George!" he crowed. "Well, sir, by George, by George, by George!"

"Look!" shouted the admiral seated next to me. "The fleet—it wasn't touched!"

"The guns seem to be drooping," said Mr. Cuthrell.

We left the bench and clustered about the television sets to examine the damage more closely. What Mr. Cuthrell had said was true. The ships' guns curved downward, their muzzles resting on the steel decks. We in Virginia were making such a hullabaloo that it was impossible to hear the radio reports. We were so engrossed, in fact, that we didn't miss the professor until two short snarls of Barnhouse static shocked us into sudden silence. The radios went dead.

We looked around apprehensively. The professor was gone. A harassed guard threw open the front door from the outside to yell that the professor had escaped. He brandished his pistol in the direction of the gates, which hung open, limp and twisted. In the distance, a speeding government station wagon topped a ridge and dropped from sight into the valley beyond. The air was filled with choking smoke, for every vehicle on the grounds was ablaze. Pursuit was impossible.

"What in God's name got into him?" bellowed the general.

Mr. Cuthrell, who had rushed out onto the front porch, now slouched back into the room, reading a penciled note as he came. He thrust the note into my hands. "The good man left this billet-doux under the door knocker. Perhaps our young friend here will be kind enough to read it to you gentlemen, while I take a restful walk through the woods."

"*Gentlemen,*" I read aloud, *As the first superweapon with a conscience, I am removing myself from your national defense stockpile. Setting a new precedent in the behavior of ordnance, I have humane reasons for going off. A. Barnhouse.*"

• • •

Since that day, of course, the professor has been systematically destroying the world's armaments, until there is now little with which to equip an army other than rocks and sharp sticks. His activities haven't exactly resulted in peace, but have, rather, precipitated a bloodless and entertaining sort of war that might be called the "War of the Tattletales." Every nation is flooded with enemy agents whose sole mission is to locate military equipment, which is promptly wrecked when it is brought to the professor's attention in the press.

Just as every day brings news of more armaments pulverized by dynamopsychism, so has it brought rumors of the professor's whereabouts. During the last week alone, three publications carried articles proving variously that he was hiding in an Inca ruin in the Andes, in the sewers of Paris, and in the unexplored lower chambers of Carlsbad Caverns. Knowing the man, I am inclined to regard such hiding places as unnecessarily romantic and uncomfortable. While there are numerous persons eager to kill him, there must be millions who would care for him and hide him. I like to think that he is in the home of such a person.

One thing is certain: at this writing, Professor Barnhouse is not dead. Barnhouse static jammed broadcasts not ten minutes ago. In the eighteen months since his disappearance, he has been reported dead some half-dozen times. Each report has stemmed from the death of an unidentified man resembling the professor, during a period free of the static. The first three reports were followed at once by renewed talk of rearmament and recourse to war. The saber-rattlers have learned how imprudent premature celebrations of the professor's demise can be.

Many a stouthearted patriot has found himself prone in the tangled bunting and timbers of a smashed reviewing stand, seconds after having announced that the arch-tyranny of Barnhouse was at an end. But those who would make war if they could, in every country in the world, wait in sullen silence for what must come—the passing of Professor Barnhouse.

• • •

To ask how much longer the professor will live is to ask how much longer we must wait for the blessing of another world war. He is of short-lived stock: his mother lived to be fifty-three, his father to be forty-nine; and the life-spans of his grandparents on both sides were of the same order. He might be expected to live, then, for perhaps fifteen years more, if he can remain hidden from his enemies. When one considers the number and vigor of these enemies, however, fifteen years seems an extraordinary length of time, which might better be revised to fifteen days, hours, or minutes.

The professor knows that he cannot live much longer. I say this because of the message left in my mailbox on Christmas Eve. Unsigned, typewritten on a soiled scrap of paper, the note consisted of ten sentences. The first nine of these, each a bewildering tangle of psychological jargon and references to obscure texts, made no sense to me at first reading. The tenth, unlike the rest, was simply constructed and contained no large words—but its irrational content made it the most puzzling and bizarre sentence of all. I nearly threw the note away, thinking it a colleague's warped notion of a practical joke. For some reason, though, I added it to the clutter on top of my desk, which included, among other mementos, the professor's dice.

It took me several weeks to realize that the message really meant something, that the first nine sentences, when unsnarled, could be taken as instructions. The tenth still told me nothing. It was only last night that I discovered how it fitted in with the rest. The sentence appeared in my thoughts last night, while I was toying absently with the professor's dice.

I promised to have this report on its way to the publishers today. In view of what has happened, I am obliged to break that promise, or release the report incomplete. The delay will not be a long one, for one of the few blessings accorded a bachelor like myself is the ability to move quickly from one abode to another, or from one way of life to another. What property I want to take with me can be packed in a few hours. Fortunately, I am not without substantial private means, which may take as long as a week to realize in liquid and anonymous form. When this is done, I shall mail the report.

I have just returned from a visit to my doctor, who tells me my health is excellent. I am young, and, with any luck at all, I shall live to a ripe old age indeed, for my family on both sides is noted for longevity.

Briefly, I propose to vanish.

Sooner or later, Professor Barnhouse must die. But long before then I shall be ready. So, to the saber-rattlers of today—and even, I hope, of tomorrow—I say: Be advised. Barnhouse will die. But not the Barnhouse Effect.

Last night, I tried once more to follow the oblique instructions on the scrap of paper. I took the professor's dice, and then, with the last, nightmarish sentence flitting through my mind, I rolled fifty consecutive sevens.

Good-by.

Soby

Wright Morris

One

Death had spared Arnold Soby—as it had also deprived him—of the academic wife who gave teas to freshmen, saw that the wall flowers at the parties were watered, and played cards in the foyer while the seniors danced. He was not, however, that Bachelor of the Arts who had never sunk his teeth into the apple. No, Soby knew the bitter-sweet taste, and the lingering smell of life. That it had proved gratifying was implied in the way a little of it proved sufficient for a lifetime. He did not cultivate romantic affairs among the campus wives who were ripe for cultivation, or use his vacations to dig for buried treasure in the sands of Acapulco or Martha's Vineyard. Not that this didn't cost him something. He was considered more than reasonably safe. When the Foreign Affairs Club planned its trip to the UN it was inevitable that the girls would ask Soby, who had no interest in the subject, to be their chaperone. He was safe, acceptable, and he was also good fun. He would see that they were taken

to the Modern Museum and to lunch at the Met. If there was a questionable foreign movie to be seen, they saw it. They preferred to be
herded around by Soby, or clustered under the drip of his umbrella, and
dusted with the ashes, as well as the sparks, of his inverted pipe. He
sometimes looked, he invariably smelled like a man. Allowing for the
seasonal flaking of the skin around his earlobes and his eyebrows, the
consensus was that he might be square, but he was cute. He had learned
to live with it and felt no need to wear Bermuda shorts.

The slogan of the Rawley Centennial Fund Drive—*The Times
change, and Rawley changes with the Times*—did not apply to Arnold
Soby, one of its more durable ornaments. Soby, never Arnold Soby, nor
Professor Soby, nor Dr. Soby. His superiors—in a manner of speaking—used the term with a certain affection, as if they had placed a hand
on his head and pronounced the word son. The younger generation, for
much the same reason, added the word *old.* Take Old Soby they would
say, meaning that one could easily do worse. Not that he was old, quite
the contrary, he did not age so much as he dated. One could imagine
him at the wheel of any car with its top down, a Kelly Springfield tire,
unused, in nickel plated clamps on the running board. One had to imagine it, however, since he did not drive. He played respectable tennis in
the style of a man who had played mixed doubles with Suzanne Lenglen,
and been struck by a smash from the racket of Borotra, the bounding
Basque. At teas, weddings of students, and cocktail parties he wore flannels the color of piano keys. A colleague once described him as the only
Rhodes scholar who came home at Christmas without an accent.
Twenty-five years later, crouched under a slicker at the annual Hamil-
ton-Chase classic, Soby heard the voice of the girl behind him, muffled
by large bites of hotdog, explain why she was taking a poetry seminar.
"I don't know about the Wasteland," she said, licking her fingers, "but
he's cute."

Soby *cute?* Under the slicker all that appeared was the inverted
bowl of his pipe, a Soby trademark rain or shine. When he arose, ten
minutes later, to join in the singing of the Alma Mater, one had the
impression that he was all legs. Even more so a few minutes later, crossing the grassy quad on his way to his rooms, his trousers rolled on the
gartered calves of Mr. Prufrock, his eyes above the level of the crowd
gathered waiting for taxis, where, as if seeing people off personally, he
would remove his hat, bow.

Was that what the girl had meant? His bowing, his formal air, the
way he stood half tipped, like some fabled bird, was partly his temper-
ament, partly a problem of scale. His cap on, he looked something more

than his forty-seven years. The cap off, as it was in class, or in more favorable campus weather, there was something of a youthful Alec Guinness trying to pass himself off as one of the elders. The impression was largely due to his hair. It lay flat, and grew forward to conceal part of his forehead, not unlike the heads of small fry, after a swim, and certain Roman Senators. The lick at the front, just before it was trimmed, would be lightly powdered with green chalk dust from the absent-minded sweep of the his hand. Rather large ears, inclined to be hairy, the bridge of his nose somewhat bruised by glasses and the thoughtful way he stroked it with his fingers when bored. Blue eyes, very pale, sometimes looking like holes in his head. How often it was said, "If only he would do *something* about his teeth!"

Well, he did. He grinned more than he smiled. *Something*, alas, was to have them pulled or capped, which he soberly stated as his intention—when he found the time. Publicly, he admitted that false teeth might ruin his smoking since they were not designed to clamp down on a pipe. Privately, there was the problem of pain, since he was a physical coward, and the notion, however vague, that he would be losing more than his teeth. Never mind what. All in all not much of a figure, but something in his scale, his reserve, and his voice on the tape machine in the library, reading selections from the modern poets, suggested a man who had surprised people once, and might do it again.

The Curriculum

Richard Armour

The purpose of the curriculum is to prepare students to cope with the problems of today. Examples of courses which will be helpful in this regard are "Principles of Hellenistic Art," "French Poetry of the Renaissance," and "Music of the Baroque and Pre-Classical Periods."

To graduate, a student must have acquired 120 units and be able to swim the length of the pool. In acquiring 120 units, it is hoped that the student has learned to think. In swimming the length of the pool, it is hoped that the student has learned to swim. Both of these requirements must be met, since it is not a case of think or swim.

Every student must take a foreign language for two years. This does not mean that the requirement is satisfied after the student has spent two years on First Year French, as the head of the French Department will be glad to explain. Latin will be accepted as satisfying the language requirement, since otherwise not enough students would enroll to justify keeping the Professor of Classics, who has no other way to make a living.

One year of science is also required. It is recommended that students who are poorly prepared in mathematics avoid physics and take botany, in which questions involving mathematics are not likely to go beyond "How many leaves has a four-leaf clover?"

Every student must have a major, or field of concentration. To help select a major, the student is assigned a Faculty Adviser, who shortly afterward goes to some distant place, such as Pakistan, on a research project. The student usually has one meeting with his Adviser, however, and it goes something like this:

STUDENT: I'm thinking of majoring in English.

ADVISER: Fine.

STUDENT: Or maybe History.

ADVISER: History's a good subject too.

STUDENT: My mother thinks I should major in Art.

ADVISER: An excellent idea.

STUDENT: But my father says Econ would be more practical.

ADVISER: Of course.

STUDENT: Then there's Political Science.

ADVISER: Yes, there is.

STUDENT: And Religion, Comparative Literature, and Philosophy.

ADVISER: Quite true.

STUDENT: I appreciate your helping me clarify my thinking.

ADVISER: Don't mention it. It's my job. Drop in again in a few months, when I get back from Pakistan.

There are year courses and semester courses. A year course is a course that does a semester's work in a year. A semester course is a course that does a year's work in a semester. Most courses include lectures, when the professor does all the talking, and discussion, when the professor and one student do all the talking. Discussions are intended to develop independent thinking. This means that while the discussion is going on, the students not involved in it are free to think about whatever they want to think about. They are also encouraged to think for themselves. Thinking for others is not permitted by the Honor Code (see below).

For qualified students, there is a program of Independent Study. This permits students to study whatever and whenever and wherever they want to, and may eventually have the same effect on professors as automation is having on factory workers. Students pursuing Independent Study write a long paper or a thesis with a bibliography which lists all the books on the subject they should have used.

For a few outstanding, anti-social students there is what is known as an Honors Program. This is like the program of Independent Study but more so. Students who read for Honors have their own cubicle in the library and read for hours on end. The work may leave its mark on them for life, especially if they sit on a chair with a wicker bottom. Most students who read for Honors go on to graduate school and then into teaching, being incapable of doing anything else.

In addition to term papers, students must expect quizzes and final examinations. One type of quiz is the pop quiz, which is given on a day when no one is prepared. How professors know which day this is is a professional secret. Usually these quizzes are objective, which means that questions can be answered by a single word, such as "Yes" or "No" but not "Maybe." This enables the professor to check on the student's knowledge of facts and, more important, correct the quiz quickly enough to get in eighteen holes before dark.

Final examinations are scheduled well in advance, enabling the student to plan his time carefully and do all the reading for the entire term on the day before. Being more difficult to grade and harder on the eyes than short quizzes, final examinations are read by a graduate assistant.

To get ready for examinations, students are helped by:

1. Hot coffee
2. Cold showers
3. Propping up the eyelids with toothpicks or matches
4. Lucky charms, such as a rabbit's foot (from which the rabbit has been carefully removed)
5. Brisk walks, from which there is a temptation not to return
6. Brains

Courses meet three times a week: Monday, Wednesday, and Friday or Tuesday, Thursday, and an Arranged Hour. The Arranged Hour

A department chairman

is a way of avoiding classes on Saturday, which always happens to come on a weekend. Since it is hard to find an hour which is not occupied by Choir Practice, the Arranged Hour is usually omitted, especially by any professor who wants a Student Following.

Science courses have laboratory periods which last all afternoon and conflict with ROTC. Or, as the science professors look at it, ROTC conflicts with their laboratory periods. Students in foreign languages spend a good many hours in the language laboratory, sitting around with headphones and looking like delegates to the UN. Some of the time they are listening to themselves, trying to find out how a foreign language sounds when it is mispronounced.

Art classes are held outdoors, except when students are painting nudes. Of course they do not actually paint nudes, they paint pictures of them. All students do not paint. Some, of a more practical turn, make ceramics which can be used as ash trays or doorstops. Each spring there is a student art show when student works are admired and sometimes purchased by parents and friends. From the throng of art lovers can be heard such discerning questions as "What is that supposed to be?" and "How much is it?"

Plays are put on under the supervision of the Drama Department. Students who act or paint scenery or sell tickets stay up late at night drinking coffee and growing beards. All play and no work brings down their grades but seems worth it until they read the review by the local drama critic, a man who, having once written a play which has never been produced, is considered (by himself) an expert. "It was a farce," he writes, if the play was a tragedy, or "It was a tragedy," if the play was a farce. He is not hard to identify in a crowd, for he twirls his cane and wears his topcoat like a cape.

The drama coach, like the football coach, gives the members of the cast a pep talk between acts. Instead of "Get in there and fight," he says, "Don't be so wooden, or the scene shifters will move you off with the furniture." He has a great sense of humor, as long as he is making fun of someone else. Everyone knows he was on Broadway once, as a young man, but few know he was at the corner of Broadway and 42nd, giving away free tickets for a Radio City tour.

When the students put on a production of *Hamlet*, the auditorium is always filled, since attendance is required by English teachers in the local high school. The teachers themselves do not have to attend, however, since they have seen *Hamlet* before. Many who are seeing a Shakespeare play for the first time are amazed at how long it is.

The highlight of Geology and Botany are the field trips to collect specimens. Since rocks do not wither, like flowers and plants, and make better paperweights, Geology has its advantages. But students who like to press flowers between the pages of a book find Botany preferable. After-dark field trips, to see night-blooming flora, are especially popular in coeducational institutions. (Flora could, of course, be the name of a girl who just really gets going after sundown.)

Field trips are not confined to science. Practical experience is gained in Sociology and Government by visiting prisons, insane asylums, and meetings of the local city council. In this way students are encouraged to take an interest in community activities.

Once a professor, taking a class in Social Psychology to a home for juvenile delinquents, left one of the students behind. By the time the boy's absence was discovered, he had become a ward of the state, and legal maneuvering to return him to college dragged into the second semester. "I usually count the students before entering an institution and again afterwards," the professor said later. "This time I must have goofed."

The various fields of study are divided into departments. Without departments, there would be no chance for a faculty member to become chairman of the department with a higher salary and less teaching. Department chairmen recommend appointments and promotion and therefore hold the whip hand (in which there only *seems* to be a whip) over junior faculty members, who try to ingratiate themselves in little ways. An energetic and imaginative young Instructor in English of our acquaintance used to wash the chairman's car. An Assistant Professor shopped at the same supermarket as the chairman's wife and pushed her cart. He expected to be promoted to Associate Professor but wound up as correspondent in a messy divorce case.

It is not customary for a department chairman to wear a crown or sit on a throne, but this is a matter of personal preference.

The departments are grouped in divisions: Humanities, Social Studies, and Natural and Physical Sciences. Whether Psychology is a Natural Science or an Unnatural Science is open to question. ROTC, or Military Science, is probably a Natural Science, because it is perfectly natural to want to kill people. It is hard to know where to put Philosophy and History, Philosophy involving thinking deeply and History involving thinking for a long time. To bring out this distinction between depth and breadth, philosophers should have a

T
H

sign over their desk reading I while historians should have a sign read-

N
K

ing T H I N K.

Memo from Osiris

Gary Jay Williams

Hi fellow persons! This has been a glorious summer for us of rethinking all last year's concepts. With your zeal, this will be a year of vitalizing, radicalizing, sensitizing, and maximizing that Authentic Self which is

Our Art. The one long-standing tradition we will observe this urgent year is last year's innovation: the Structureless Anti-authoritarian Dialogues (SAD). This was overwhelmingly approved by your elected committee For Academic Democracy (one professor, four graduate assistants, and 17 undergraduates). FAD's SAD curriculum is as follows:

There is to be no more Theater History. All history has been canceled subject to revision. FAD feels you should instead seek the world within you and thus we offer in place of history, Self-Exploration 101: 14 hours credit (nongraded) for the intensive investigation of the 17- to 20-year-old Self and all that that entails.

For graduate students, there will be no language requirements at all this year. A nonverbal command of nonverbal theater theory will suffice (unless, of course, you opt for certain upper-level courses outside the department where a reading knowledge of English is still thought necessary—for which we cannot be held responsible).

On the other hand, since the registration for the film survey was so high, we have split the course into 283 sections. Section assignments will be made according to astrological sign pairings using the new university laser computer after it has programed the campanile for our opening day ceremonies.

The Socio-Anthro-Poli-Psycho Department's course, Mimesis Archetypes Survey, has been moved. It will now meet in the former nondenominational chapel.

The Theater of Cruelty and Theater of Ecstasy classes will be combined this semester and will meet in the Performance Environment Configuration Room (formerly the scene shop).

Each new registrant for the criticism seminar, Middle-Class Audience Abuse, must establish, prior to first class *please,* certification of your middle-class origin. Our experience with successfully abusive graduates shows this to be a key prerequisite. Minority students are, *prima facie,* exempt. The course will be taught by the current holder of our *New York Times* Magazine Weekly Tenure, Professor Mark A. Ruse.

As you know, our ad hoc Search Committee for an instructor for the new Street Theater course has been carefully screening candidates. It was the goal to find an authentically, rather than academically, experienced peer leader and the committee is now pleased to announce its appointment. He is John Doe, of no fixed address for the past 18 years. The committee wishes to thank all those who submitted credentials.

Our usual course in Kabuki acting for Americans, taught by Professor Bob Smith of Texas, cannot be offered this year. The students for

American Indian Tribal Dances have obtained an injunction and a nego-
tiated equal-time agreement has gone to the trustees for budget
authorization.

And for those 379 of last year's 380 theater majors who have not
yet found employment, there is a position open at a rural Southwestern
college for an established, impeccable scholar and widely known actor/
actress, under 35, who wants to direct self-exploration drama on a campus well known for its valid learning experiences and 24-hour Army-
Navy boutique. The ability to stage the annual college musical would
also be an asset. Minority candidates are urged to apply. Federal law
ensures that no discriminating choice will be made.

Finally, I am pleased to announce the completion of our federal-
and state-funded performing arts complex, long my dream. The $70-
billion marble theater will open with an important, provocative play by
our Guerrilla Theater seminar, a yet untitled work which I understand
dramatizes plastik Amerika's materialistik exploitation of its young,
"from Capitalist Hill to the Whitewash House." The program notes
alone will run seventy pages. This will alternate with an original play
on the freedom to abort by the celebrated woman author of last year's
"The Bombing of the Children of Hanoi."

Yours for a balanced and mythic year,

Professor Osiris.

Catalog of Courses: Aquarius U.
Non Campus Mentis

John D. Kirwan

Even though the fall semester is about completed on most campuses, the
majority of parents (and nearly all students) still have little idea what to
expect from the modern university—save that it strives to be relevant.
Therefore, as a public service, I have culled from the catalogs of several
of our leading groves of academe the following selected sample courses,

designed to prepare our youth for the challenging world of tomorrow . . .

Basic English

Offers a course to help students in the fundamentals of reading, writing and penmanship. The spelling of big words (notably *dichotomy* and *synergistic*) will be stressed and students will discuss the validity of such concepts as "neatness counts." Initial workshops will stress the pencil; then, as language-arts techniques improve, gradually evolve into the use of pen and ink.

Studies in Modern Philosophy

The purpose of this course is to demonstrate conclusively that nothing is. Conducted by Professor Rensalier, author of *The Knowledge of Null* and editor of the *Negative Absolute Quarterly*, the class will examine such questions as "why?" and "why not?" A prime object of this course is to help students with an identity crisis discover there is no such thing as identity.

Urban Planning

According to Edgar Twinewell, nationally known consultant on city housing, who conducts this seminar: "There are no prerequisites, no reading lists and no tests. The kids and I will sit around and bat the breeze, in the hope that by the symbiosis of minds some solution to our urban problems will be achieved. If not, well, what the hell?"

Introduction to Economics and Business Management

This series of lectures will concentrate on the role of the executive in today's society and the changing nature of the contemporary corporation. The class will discuss such topics as the fallacy of the profit concept, the social responsibilities of institutionalized greed and how businessmen can be helped to recognize their guilt. As a term project, the class will write a collective essay on "The Need To Repeal the Industrial

Revolution." The reading list includes Nader, Galbraith, Henry Wallace and *The Collected Works of Harriet Van Horne.*

Problems of Underdeveloped Nations

Led by W. J. Watersby, former Director of the Foundation for Backward Countries (now the Association of Aspiring States). The societal and cultural backgrounds of selected emerging nations will be examined, as well as such contemporary problems as the difficulties of providing food, clothing and shelter. Guest lecturers from the United Nations will appear to highlight the responsibilities of America regarding aid for their respective underdeveloped nations. Emphasis will be placed upon the fact that Rhodesia does not exist.

Classical Literature

Conducted by Associate Professor W. "Spud" Carfax. Students will read and critically discuss classical literature, measuring it against contemporary writing to see how the problems of bygone days are relevant to our own. The pros and cons, as well as the pluses and minuses, of these works will be probed in depth. Among the works to be examined are *On the Road, Howl, Bonjour Tristesse* and *Hamlet* (edited and simplified for modern readers).

Education for Teachers

This course is structured to serve as a theoretical foundation for student teachers, to enable them to establish more rewarding dialogues with their future pupils. The discussions will be led by Jeremy J. Grillfinder PhD (Hon.), author of *To Hell with Kirk and Rickover* and *The Beauty of Being Intellectually Underprivileged.* The importance of the subachiever to society will be examined, as well as techniques for helping "bright" children adjust to their peer groups. Such modern visual aids as posters will be given comparative study.

Marriage and the Family

Designed to give the college-aged youth fresh insights into crises of contemporary conjugality. Professor Emeritus Grover C. Whisp will discuss such concepts as "Is two company?"; "The sociological balance of the extended family"; "Orgasms made easy." A special feature of this course is the three-part lecture "Variety is the spouse of life," led by the former Mrs. Whisps. *Note:* Due to a lack of registrants, the seminar on *Making Marriage Work* will not be given this semester.

Religion and Contemporary Society

Guided by the Reverend Doctor Fielmaus, author of *Making the Scene Godwise and Other Sermons,* this course will deal with such problems as: "Just how dead is God?"; "Is relevance relevant?"; "Can modern man live a moral life while not giving a damn?" In line with the democratic principles he has so long espoused, Reverend Fielmaus says: "Participation by all students will be encouraged and equal weight will be given to everyone's opinions."

Easy Road to Culture, Sort of

Eric Larrabee

No modern scholar, whatever his special competence, can ignore the impact on educational practice of those two British authorities, W. C. Sellar and R. J. Yeatman, the authors of *1066 and All That.* It fell to these courageous innovators to redefine the word "memorable" to mean not what *should* be remembered but what *can* be remembered.

This realistic principle has since been increasingly applied in the colleges and universities. Notable achievements have been made in reducing the number of Great Ideas and Men to a manageable figure, and in compressing the body of organized knowledge into at most two or three more-or-less manageable departments. Strange as it may seem, however, until my own study of the matter no effort had been made to reduce all of higher education to *one course.*

The following syllabus is purely tentative. Exact research under rigidly controlled conditions will undoubtedly reveal that some elements in it are *not* memorable. The author will in that event welcome deletions or emendations of a negative character, but it must be understood that no proposal to *add* to the outline can be entertained. The survey course described below therefore replaces all others.

First Semester: Western Thought

Western thought was invented by the Greeks, who were the first people to realize they were thinking. The most memorable Greek thinker was Aristotle, author of the *Metataphysica* ("After Physics, What?"). One day while he was walking in the shade with King Midas (*cf.* Golden Mean, peripatetics), he fell into a bathtub and tried to pass it off by shouting "Eureka!" This is known as the Hypocritical Oath. Attention should also be paid to Greek Art, which is very classical and represented by the Wingless de Mille (Nike the Greek).

The Greek period was followed by the Roman period, which may roughly be divided into Decline and Fall. This period is somewhat decadent and noteworthy for such authors as Suetonius, Apuleius, Petronius, and Henry Miller (his *Nexus, Plexus,* and *Sexus* are especially memorable). The cruelty of the Roman period is typified by Floradora, mother of Cato the Elder, Cato the Younger, Marcus Cato, and Neiman Marcus (*"Timeo dallas, et panem circenses"*). Having set fire to Rome, she asked Julius Caesar to put his hand in the flame to see if it was hot enough.

"You brute," he replied.

This brings us to the Medieval period and to St. Thomas Aquinas, the author of *Theologica, Indian Summa.* According to Henry Adams, Aquinas may have been the architect of the Cathedral of Beauvais, which collapsed. Aquinas was consequently banished to St. Heloise, where he wrote entertaining letters under the name of Abelard. Adams, who was also an architect (Mont St. Michel and Chartres), was thus the original Doubting Thomist.

The Medieval period was followed in quick succession by the Renaissance, the Reformation, the counter-Renaissance, and the counter-Reformation. The Renaissance was started by Erasmus of Rotterdam, author of *Moriae Encomium*, a rather poor biography of his friend Sir Thomas More. Erasmus is the subject of an egg-tempera portrait by Holstein ("that Jersey cow," as he was called by Henry the Eighth). He also started the Oxford Reform Movement, which supported the teaching of Greek and other reforms. But the Reformation was started by Martin Luther, composer of the oratorio *Erwache durch Freud* ("Awake and Read Joyce"). Luther officiated at Finnegan's Wake. Wanting to get if not a *summa* at least a *magna*, he wrote a thesis which he then had to pin on the door of the church; as he explained later, *"Ich kann nicht anders"* ("I couldn't get it under"). This thesis would have been banned from the mails but for a memorable legal decision by Cardinal Wolsey.

The Seventeenth Century stands halfway between the Medieval period and the Modern period, and is thus exceedingly transitional. It was memorable for the Rise of Science and for John Donne, a kind of seventeenth-century T. S. Eliot. Though he was not interested in Science and spelled badly ("Noe Manne is an Iland"), Donne was made vector of St. Paul's and became a kind of seventeenth-century Norman Vincent Peale. The Seventeenth Century is thus exactly like the Twentieth Century and all centuries in between may be skipped. During the Twentieth Century, Western Thought became confused with Eastern Thought, as a result of *The Meeting of Northrop and Southrop*, and has thus come to an End. It is also memorable for neo-Protestantism ("Love thy Niebuhr"), or Rockefeller Plaza Orthodoxy *(Luce et Vanitas)*.

Second Semester: Science

Science was invented by the Greeks, who were the first people to realize that it was a Good Thing. It was also invented by Galileo, who leaned against the Tower of Pisa to see if it would move *(eppur si muove)*. Later on, science was re-invented by Descartes. After losing a bet with Pascal, he was forced to live in a stove *("j'ai faim, donc je cuit")*. The bet resulted from a balloon ascension by Robert Montgomery, which in turn gave rise to the cinematic theory of gases, or Gauss (plural: *gassendi*).

The most memorable branch of science is physics. Some people think that physics was invented by Sir Francis Bacon, who was hit by an apple when he was sitting under a tree one day writing Shakespeare. This is not true. It was *Roger* Bacon, and it wasn't Shakespeare; it was

Christopher Marlowe. Later physics was taken up by Isaac Newton, who invented the Second Law of Thermodynamics (there is no *First Law of Thermodynamics*). Newton also discovered that the straightest distance between two points is inversely proportional, though he did not say to what. This was left to Einstein. Einstein is chiefly memorable for being smarter than Newton.

Astronomy was independently discovered by Copernicus and Kepler, who sent the news to each other *(de nova stella)* by sidereal messenger. This was very slow, since astronomers measure time in light-years, or the amount of light in a year. Some astronomers like to find stars by themselves, like Hershey, the famous discoverer of the Milky Way and the Mars Bar; others prefer to go around in a Cepheid cluster, or Magellanic cloud. A memorable contest once took place in astronomy between the Red Giants and the White Dwarfs, refereed by Hubble, the inventor of the Red Shift. Ever since, all games in astronomy have been played according to Hoyle.

Another memorable branch of science is electronics, which is the science of amplifying messages by putting them through a degenerative circuit. Electronics can handily be demonstrated in the home by filling a Leyden Jar full of formaldehyde and turning on the radio. Through the magic of modern communications, electronics reminds us of such famous communicators as Wiener, Weaver, Faraday, and Ohm ("Be it ever so faraday, there's no place like ohm"). Originally electronics inventions were named after people (Lee the Forest, Jennie the Transformer, etc.) but they are now named after Polish patriots—Edvac, Eniac, Cosmotron, and Radar. The reason for this is to embarrass the Russians, in the hope that they will turn a non-compatible color.

We come now to the social sciences, which are divided into sociology, anthropology, cultural anthropology, anthropological sociology, sociological anthropology, psychology, dynamic psychology, group dynamics, palmistry, and statistics (optional). The most memorable thing about the social sciences is the principle of *anomie*, or autonomy, which holds that people tend to behave like each other. This helps to explain such phenomena as the in-group, the out-group, the peer-group, and Margaret Mead. For best results, advanced field work in the social sciences should be conducted among the Mountain Arapesh, who are a pretty lonely crowd.

Biology is especially memorable because of evolution. This was the subject of a maternity suit (the Stopes trial) between William Lane Bryant and the famous lawyer, Clarence Darwin. Darwin believed in the survival of the best fit, but Bryant won, which was the origin of demography, or populism. In disgust, Darwin joined the navy as an enzyme and was sent around the world on a beagle. Evolution might have been forgotten, had it not been for Julian Huxley, who attended the trial and wrote a famous book about it, called *Natural Selection without Glasses, or Eyeless in Gaza.*

Included under biology should also be the history of medicine, which is most memorable when it is psychosomatic. This branch of medicine was invented by the famous physician, Peristalsis, who also invented nutrition *("Mann ist was Mann isst").* Nutrition teaches the importance of getting plenty of protein and chlorophyll, both of which are contained in black-strap molasses (G. Hauser Wienerschnitzel, Yoghurt, and Strap Iron Co., Mfgrs., *Advt.*). Psychosomatic medicine is difficult to practice without an Orgone Box, which is guaranteed to make you feel Jung and to last for 1,000 years *(tausendjahrende Reich).* Psychosomatic medicine is not to be confused with extra-sensory perception, which most doctors reject and keep a sharp watch on *(der Wacht am Rhine),* nor with psychiatry, which is concerned with the psyche (soma). Since psychiatry was originally invented by the Greeks ("Oedipus, schmedipus, so long he loves his mother"), it is the end of the course.

Final Examination

1. Name a great idea.

Handy-Dandy Plan to Save Our Colleges

Leo Rosten

No fair-minded cretin can deny that our colleges—so lovingly nourished, so costly to maintain, so irreplaceable in the knowledge they augment and dispense—are in one hell of a mess. If the stupid Establishment would only *listen* to our idealistic children, to the sincere college students who only want to *communicate* their superior wisdom in meaningful monologues, then the answer to all our college problems would become as clear as the nose on my face, which few observers fail to notice.

We must unmask the broad *social* causes that underlie campus unrest. Once we understand that, or them, the cure is a cinch.

I. Causes

Millions of decent young Americans annually complete what we call "high" school. (This usually occurs between the age of 16.) These innocent youngsters are cursed with materialistic *parents who do not understand them.* The insensitive parents fall into three inhuman groups:

A. Parents who insist that their children go to college because they are naïve sentimentalists and want to give their offspring the best education possible.

Going to college is, of course, not the same as getting an education; but parents in Group A are ecstatic if their progeny simply use up four years on a campus—even though Junior hates to read, Missy is incapable of understanding why water runs downhill instead of up, and both will get a B.A. under the illusion that the Generalissimo of Nationalist China is Shanghai Jack.

B. Parents who force their kids to go to college only because they (the parents) don't want them (the kids) hanging around the house. Nothing so destroys American parents' peace of mind as having nubile boys and girls in physical proximity when they (the parents) don't want them (the children) around, especially while they (the parents) want to get loaded enough to ask each other how in the world they (the parents) had ever been crazy enough to decide to have them (the children).

C. Mothers and fathers who nag, nag, nag their sons and daughters into surrendering to a college official only because of social ambitions that are based on the outmoded American dream of providing your off-spring with every chance to better themselves. There is a widespread illusion in parental circles (even parents who are "square" move in circles) that the quickest way to better yourself, when you are between 16, is to spend the next four years in a college dorm—playing house, or conducting imaginative experiments in biology with bad boys and girls from good families.

But these foolish parents fail to recognize how many of our young people want to spend four years *not* with boys and girls, but with boy-girls or girl-boys, or boys/girls—who are the most picturesque of all in dress, posture and dangling participles.

II. Cure

To restore a semblance of justice in such brutal treatment of the young, we should junk our entire college treadmill and replace it with six new, different *types* of colleges, specifically set up for six totally different kinds of students:

1. USELESS UNIVERSITIES

These will be colleges for oddballs who want a really useless education, through irrelevant courses such as philosophy, history, literature, the humanities.

Students at Useless U will be required to wear shoes, attend classes and take examinations. They will not be allowed to swear at a professor, stab a dean, conduct discussions via bullhorns, or even make progressive bombs in wholesome surroundings.

We may expect Useless U's student body to consist of impractical intellectuals who don't *relate;* icky nerds with an antisocial propensity for analyzing problems instead of oversimplifying them; plus clowns who respect facts and even historical experience; plus reactionaries who actually think intelligence better than emotion, and knowledge better than delusions, in any efforts made to improve life on this wretched earth.

Useless U's faculty will consist of cold-blooded thinkers who make no effort to woo, love, understand or play pussycat with their downtrodden students, but only try to educate them. They will see no reason for treating their pupils as pals, patients, seers or even sages. They will not mistake innocence for insight, or ignorance for virtue.

Useless U's motto will be engraved over each bulletproof window: "Knowledge is learned, not taught."

The Useless faculty will be disliked and respected by the students, which is the proper attitude of pupils to professors.

2. PLAYMATE UNIVERSITIES

These will be colleges for those millions of our young who don't know what else to do with themselves after they escape from high school, and just are not *happy* torturing their delicate brains into unfamiliar activity. These innocents should not be asked to endure the humiliating, soul-shriveling experience of having to work for a living. Experts in education tell us that nothing depletes a youth's creative play or consumption of drugs the way holding down a job does. Work also corrupts youth's ideals by inculcating a pernicious respect for the exertion required to obtain m-o-n-e-y by lawful means.

Every candidate for Playmate U will have to meet three basic requirements:

(a) Have an IQ. (It doesn't matter what the IQ actually is, just so the student has one.)

(b) Be able to write a coherent paragraph of *not less than twenty words*, in English which is comprehensible to someone else; if the English is grammatical as well, the candidate will go straight into graduate school.

(c) Know how to divide *any number*, even ten digits long, by 2.

Any student who can fulfill these entrance requirements is sure to enjoy "doing his own thing" (to say nothing of undoing her own thing) amidst the many dandy "gut" courses at Playmate U.

The motto of Playmate U will be: "All play and no work— WOW!"

3. INSTITUTES OF TECHNOLOGY

These will be colleges for dropouts who want to drop in—and learn a useful trade or skill. We have become such snobs about a college degree that we give utterly insufficient praise and respect to our overworked check-out clerks, subway pilots, sweatband staplers, etc. This is undemocratic. All manual workers should go to a prestigious college, instead of a plebeian trade school. In this way, they will gain self-respect, and we will lose our guilt.

Dropouts from high school/college should no longer be lectured, cozened, hollered at and chivied by silly bus and TV ads: Dropouts are absolutely *right* to shun courses they are sure to find bewildering, books they will never understand, and experiences that must make them feel inferior.

Dropouts should be encouraged to follow and respect the bio-chemical makeup God gave them. They should be able to attend colleges specifically designed to salve their wounded egos and raise their social status. For example:

An MIT for Television Repairmen will provide Americans with what is their birthright: technicians who charge less than $45 an hour, plus social security, hot lunch, green stamps toward a vacation in Hawaii, and groveling expressions of gratitude to any mechanic making a house call.

A Georgia Tech for Sanitation Engineers will provide our cities with street custodians trained in modern ways of removing garbage without distributing samples thereof on the sidewalks, and even without the ear-shattering clatter currently sanctified as integral to public hygiene.

A Cal Tech for Plumbers will produce pipe-and-wrench experts who will have been trained so well, with such compassion and understanding, that they will arrive on a job with all their tools.

These are only examples, of course: Window washers would go to Opaque U; Dropsy U would turn out face-lifters; and Southern Christian would produce Southern Christians, who have too long been in short supply—according to Northern Liberals who live in segregated areas.

The motto of our Institutes of Technology will be: "A Jack-of-all-trades can make jack hand over fist today."

4. PROFESSIONAL COLLEGES

Professional Universities will teach only *relevant* subjects to students who want to become doctors, lawyers, accountants, embezzlers. None of these will be forced to waste time on Plato, Gibbon, Newton or Keats.

The practice of exposing professional men to a liberal education is a foolish carry-over from Europe, where professional men are expected to be civilized. Transposing this system to the United States, without regard to our students' determination to be hasty and "realistic" about social issues, has wreaked havoc. There is no havoc worse, on a campus, than that which is wreaked, except for that which is wrecked.

Even as you read these words, American doctors are being intellectually crippled by courses in English, which they won't even use when writing prescriptions. American dentists by the gallon are being psychologically scarred at colleges that require oral examinations. Psychotherapists are having their imaginations blunted by deadly courses in logic, evidence and *post hoc ergo propter hoc.*

I dare not even contemplate the tragic plight of our future teachers, social workers and gynecologists, who are suffering blinding headaches because of their exposure to lectures on algebra, Aristotle and American history.

The motto of Professional U will be: "I have just as much right to be a brain surgeon as you do."

5. HARVARDS FOR THE UNDEREDUCATED

These will be colleges for students who were so miserably educated in high school that they are certain to be frustrated and made to feel inferior, should they attend a bona fide college. Miserably educated high school "graduates" have a constitutional right to be forced to learn how to read, write, add and subtract. (They already know how to multiply.)

Can anyone deny that every American boy and girl should know how to spell "irregardless"; or why inertia is unfair to people of inert ancestry; or where the Rocky Mountains were recently located?

Every undereducated student in America should go to a "Harvard," which will guarantee that he or she will pass every course, even those not attended, and receive a beautiful diploma. What harm will actually be done if we call seminaries for the retarded "Harvard," or even "Yale"? I doubt that a white Fascist can get a fair education at Yale the way things are done today.

The motto of our colleges for the undereducated will be: "There are no blue genes."

6. RIGHT ON UNIVERSITIES

These are the colleges most urgently needed: colleges for idealistic students who want to Smash the Entire System NOW in order to Build a Beautiful Society Overnight, without wasting time learning any more than they already don't know.

Right On U's slogan will be: "All Power to the People Who Shout All Power to the People."

ROU will accept only sincere, committed, *involved* students who seek to become better disrupters of the peace. Scholarships will be given to any oppressed adolescent whose postnasal drip makes him feel like a social outcast.

The Physical Education program at Right On U will concentrate on practical, socially useful courses: Improving Your Aim in Rock Throwing, Setting Fires, Beating Older People With Chains of the Proper Size, etc. The program will increase student proficiency in rioting through daily practice riots against each other, closely supervised by scholarly commandos from Hanoi and Berkeley. All buildings on campus will be lighted day and night to facilitate their having windows knocked out. Molotov cocktails will be provided at the student armory, at cost.

Every graduate of Right On U will automatically receive an A.B. (Animal Behavior) degree.

What about ROU's academic curriculum, you ask?

Freshmen will be obliged to take Elementary Rage, the Copulation Explosion, and the Proper Use and Storage of Dynamite.

Sophomores will be required to study Advanced Alienation, Inflammatory Rhetoric and Intermediate Pornography.

Juniors will concentrate on Techniques of Blackmail and White-mail (racism will receive short shrift at ROU), the Revolutionary Use of Non Sequiturs, and Liberation Geography—the latter being a new, progressive discipline in which all maps of the world are redrawn on truly democratic lines. Thus, the land area of China, Africa and Cuba will be greatly expanded, according to the principle of revolutionary justice, since they have far more people than, say, Greenland, Nevada or the Sahara Desert, which is today drawn much too large for comfort.

Seniors at Right On U will specialize in Advanced Profanity. I think it shocking that our college men and women can't swear with greater eloquence and precision than our bar bums or oil riggers. In an enlightened, really free society, accusations of an incestuous nature should show the advantages of higher education. Advanced Profanity will enrich student vocabulary by imaginative drills in anatomy, blasphemy and rare perversions. Field trips to prison wards and depressed pelvic areas will give every student a chance to learn by doing.

More important than subject matter is the fact that at ROU *all courses will be geared to the ethnic backgrounds of the students.* Students of Irish origin, for example, will take Snake Extermination; students with Dutch names will study Bulbs, Wooden Shoes, and Dikes (for women only); Hindu students will learn how to stack bodies for

funeral pyres; Japanese will gain expertise in Flower Arrangement and
Hara-Kiri; and special textbooks for Jewish students will end century-
old discrimination because all the sentences will run from right to left.

The faculty at ROU will, of course, be *representative* of our society; proportional representation must prevail; every student has a right
to a teacher of similar ethnic background.

Students of mixed racial ancestry present a nitty-gritty, because it
may be very hard to offer an exact ethnic match-up of faculty and students, as Prof. D. Boorstin has warned us: A student who is one-half
Portuguese, one-quarter Chinese and one-quarter Greek deserves a
teacher with the same ancestral components, for how else can the
teacher really know what Portuguese-Chinese-Greeks have suffered
throughout Brazilian history? The problem of an ethnic faculty is
tough, but it can be solved the way every other problem has been solved:
through Federal appropriations.

As every progressive student knows: Where there is a will there is
a wail.

Well, folks, there it is—a simple, fair, handy-dandy college system
for honest paranoids in a really free America. Mail soothing comments
to me; ignite negative ones with a good, strong match.

Jocelyn College

Mary McCarthy

Jocelyn College had a faculty of forty-one persons and a student-body
of two hundred and eighty-three—a ratio of one teacher to every 6.9
students, which made possible the practice of "individual instruction"
as carried on at Bennington (6:1), Sarah Lawrence (6.4:1), Bard (6.9:1),
and St. John's (7.7:1). It had been founded in the late Thirties by an
experimental educator and lecturer, backed by a group of society-
women in Cleveland, Pittsburgh, and Cincinnati who wished to strike
a middle course between the existing extremes, between Aquinas and

Dewey, the modern dance and the labor movement. Its students were neither to till the soil as at Antioch nor weave on looms as at Black Mountain; they were to be grounded neither in the grass-roots present as at Sarah Lawrence nor in the great-books past as at St. John's or Chicago; they were to specialize neither in verse-writing, nor in the poetic theatre, nor in the techniques of co-operative living—they were simply to be free, spontaneous, and coeducational.

What the founder had had in mind was a utopian experiment in so-called "scientific" education; by the use of aptitude tests, psychological questionnaires, even blood-sampling and cranial measurements, he hoped to discover a method of gauging student-potential and directing it into the proper channels for maximum self-realization—he saw himself as an engineer and the college as a reclamation project along the lines of the Grand Coulee or the TVA. The women behind him, however, regarded the matter more simply, in the usual fashion of trustees. What they wanted to introduce into their region was a center of "personalized" education, with courses tailored to the individual need, like their own foundation-garments, and a staff of experts and consultants, each with a little "name" in his field, like the Michels and Antoines of Fifth Avenue, to interpret the student's personality. In the long run, these views, seemingly so harmonious, were found to be far apart. The founder had the sincere idea of running his college as a laboratory; failure in an individual case he found as interesting as success. Under his permissive system, the students were free to study or not as they chose; he believed that the healthy organism would elect, like an animal, what was best for it. If the student failed to go in the direction indicated by the results of his testing, or in any direction at all, this was noted down and in time communicated to his parents, merely as a matter of interest—to push him in any way would be a violation of the neutrality of the experiment. The high percentage of failure was taken to be significant of the failures of secondary education; any serious reform in methodology must reach down to the kindergarten and the nursery school, through the whole preparatory system, and it was noteworthy, in this connection, that the progressive schools were doing their job no better than the old-fashioned classical ones. Indeed, comparative studies showed the graduates of progressive schools to be *more* dependent on outside initiative, on an authoritarian leader-pattern, than any other group in the community.

This finding convinced the trustees, who included the heads of two progressive schools, that the founder was ahead of his time, a stimulating man in the tradition of Pasteur and the early vivisectionists, whom history would give his due. He left the college the legacy of a strong scientific bent and a reputation for enthusiasm and crankishness that reflected itself in budgetary difficulties and in the prevalence of an "undesirable" type of student. Despite a high tuition and other screening devices (a geographical quota, interviews with the applicant and with the applicant's parents, submission of a photograph when this was not practicable, solicitation of private schools), despite a picturesque campus—a group of long, thick-walled, mansarded, white-shuttered stone dwellings arranged around a cupolaed chapel with a planting of hemlocks, the remains of a small, old German Reformed denominational college that had imparted to the secluded ridge a Calvinistic sweetness of worship and election—something, perhaps the coeducational factor, perhaps the once-advertised freedom, had worked to give the college a peculiarly plebeian and subversive tone, like that of a big-city high-school.

It was the mixture of the sexes, some thought, that had introduced a crude and predatory bravado into the campus life; the glamour was rubbed off sex by the daily jostle in soda-shop and barroom and the nightly necking in the social rooms, and this, in its turn, had its effect on all ideals and absolutes. Differences were leveled; courses were regarded with a cynical, practical eye; students of both sexes had the wary disillusionment and aimlessness of battle-hardened Marines. After six months at Jocelyn, they felt that they had "seen through" life, through all attempts to educate and improve them, through love, poetry, philosophy, fame, and were here, it would seem, through some sort of coercion, like a drafted army. Thronging into store or classroom, in jeans, old sweaters, caps, visors, strewing cigarette-butts and candy-wrappers, they gave a mass impression that transcended their individual personalities, which were often soft, perturbed, uncertain, innocent; yet the very sight of an individual face, plunged deep in its own introspection, as in a blanket, heightened the crowd-sense they communicated, like soldiers in a truck, subway riders on their straps, serried but isolated, each in his stubborn dream, resistant to waking fully—at whatever time of day, the Jocelyn students were always sleepy, yawning, and rather gummy-eyed, as though it were seven in the morning and they unwillingly on the street.

Yet this very rawness and formlessness in the students made them interesting to teach. Badly prepared, sleepy, and evasive, they *could* nevertheless be stirred to wonder and pent admiration at the discovery of form and pattern in history or a work of art or a laboratory experiment, though ceding this admiration grudgingly and by degrees, like primitive peoples who must see an act performed over and over again before they can be convinced that some magic is not behind it, that they are not the dupes of an illusionist. To teachers with some experience of the ordinary class-bound private college student, of the quiet lecture-hall with the fair duteous heads bent over the notebooks, Jocelyn's hard-eyed watchers signified the real. Seeing them come year after year, the stiff-spined, angry only children with inhibitions about the opposite sex, being entrained here remedially by their parents, as they had been routed to the dentist for braces, the wild-haired progressive-school rejects, offspring of broken homes, the sexually adventurous youths looking to meet their opposite numbers in the women's dormitories, without the social complications of fraternities and sororities or the restraints of grades, examinations, compulsory athletics, R.O.T.C., the single well-dressed Adonis from Sewickley with a private plane and a neurosis, the fourteen-year-old mathematical Russian Jewish boys on scholarships, with their violin cases and timorous, old-country parents, hovering humbly outside the Registrar's door as at a consular office, the cold peroxided beauties who had once done modeling for Powers and were here while waiting for a screen-test, the girls from Honolulu or Taos who could "sit on" their hair and wore it down their backs, Godiva-style, and were named Rina or Blanca or Snow-White, the con-ventional Allysons and Pattys whose favorite book was *Winnie-the-Pooh*—seeing them, the old-timers shook their heads and marveled at how the college could continue but in the same style that they marveled at the survival of the race itself. Among these students, they knew, there would be a large percentage of trouble-makers and a handful of gifted creatures who would redeem the whole; four out of five of these would be, predictably, the scholarship students, and the fifth a riddle and an anomaly, coming forward at the last moment, from the ranks of Ally-sons or Blancas, like the tortoise in the fable, or the sleeper in the horse-race, a term which at Jocelyn had a peculiar nicety of meaning.

And over the management of these students, the faculty, equally heterogeneous, would, within the year, become embroiled, with each other, with the student-body, or with the President or trustees. A scan-dal could be counted on that would cause a liberal lady somewhere to strike the college from her will: a pregnant girl, the pilfering of reserve books from the library, the usual plagiarism case, alleged racial discrim-ination, charges of alcoholism or homosexuality, a strike against the food in the dining-room, the prices in the college store, suppression of the student paper, alleged use of a course in myth to proselytize for reli-gion, a student demand that a rule be laid down, in the handbook, governing sexual intercourse, if disciplinary action was to be taken against those who made love *off* the college premises and were observed by faculty-snoopers. No truly great question had ever agitated the campus since the original days of the founder, but the ordinary trivia of college life were here blown up, according to critics, out of all proportion. There had been no loyalty oath, no violation of academic freedom, but problems of freedom and fealty were discovered in the smallest issue, in whether, for example, students in the dining-hall, when surrendering their plates to the waiters, should pass them to the right or the left, clockwise or counterclockwise; at an all-college meeting, held in December of this year, compulsory for all students, faculty, and administrative staff, President Maynard Hoar had come within an ace of resigning when his appeal for moderation in the discussion had met with open cat-calls from the counterclockwise faction.

Thus the college faced every year an insurrectionary situation; in the course of twelve years it had had five presidents, including the founder, who was unseated after only eleven months of service. During the War, it had nearly foundered and been saved by the influx of veterans studying under the GI bill and by the new plutocracy of five-percenters, car-dealers, black-market slaughterers, tire-salesmen, and retail merchants who seemed to Jocelyn's presidents to have been specially enriched by Providence, working mysteriously, with the interests of the small college in mind. These new recruits to the capitalist classes had no educational prejudices, were extremely respectful of the faculty, to whom they sent bulky presents of liquor or perfume, as to valuable clients at Christmas-time; they came to the college seldom, sometimes only once, for Commencement, passed out cigars and invitations to use the shack at Miami or Coral Gables *any time at all*—this benign and preoccupied gratitude, tactfully conscious of services rendered, extended also to friends and roommates of the poorer sort. Several years after graduation, little shoals of Jocelyn students would still be found living together co-operatively, in Malibu or St. Augustine—occasionally with an ex-teacher—sharing a single allowance under the bamboo tree.

Reforming Yale*

Mark Twain

I was sincerely proud and grateful to be made a Master of Arts by this great and venerable university. And I would have come last June to testify this feeling, as I do now testify it, but that the sudden and unexpected notice of the honor done me found me at a distance from home and unable to discharge that duty and enjoy that privilege.

Along at first, say for the first month or so, I did not quite know how to proceed, because of my not knowing just what authorities and privileges belonged to the title which had been granted me. But after that I consulted some students of Trinity, in Hartford, and they made everything clear to me.

It was through them that I found out that my title made me head of the governing body of the university and lodged in me very broad and severely responsible powers. It is through trying to work these powers up to their maximum of efficiency that I have had such a checkered career this year.

I was told that it would be necessary for me to report to you at this time, and of course I comply though I would have preferred to put it off till I could make a better showing, for indeed I have been so pertinaciously hindered and obstructed at every turn by the faculty that it would be difficult to prove that the university is really in any better shape now than it was when I first took charge.

In submitting my report I am sorry to have to begin it with the remark that respect for authority seems to be at a quite low ebb in the college. It is true that this has caused me pain but it has not discouraged me.

By advice, I turned my earliest attention to the Greek department. I told the Greek professor I had concluded to drop the use of the Greek written character, because it is so hard to spell with and so impossible to read after you get it spelled. Let us draw the curtain there. I saw by

---

*Although Yale awarded Clemens a Master of Arts degree in June 1888, he was unable to attend the award ceremony. And, although he claims he made this address at a later time, it is uncertain whether he actually did.

what followed that nothing but early neglect saved him from being a very profane man.

I ordered the professor of mathematics to simplify the whole sytem, because the way it was I couldn't understand it, and I didn't want things going on in the college in what was practically a clandestine fashion. I told him to drop the conundrum system. It was not suited to the dignity of a college, which should deal in facts, not guesses and suppositions. We didn't want any more cases of *if* A and B stand at opposite poles of the earth's surface and C at the equator of Jupiter, at what variations of angle will the left link of the moon appear to these different parties?

I said you just let that thing alone. It's plenty time to get in a sweat about it when it happens. As like as not it ain't going to do any harm anyway.

His reception of these instructions bordered on insubordination, insomuch that I felt obliged to take his number and report him.

I found the astronomer of the university gadding around after comets and other such odds and ends—tramps and derelicts of the skies. I told him pretty plainly that we couldn't have that. I told him it was no economy to go on piling up and piling up raw material in the way of new stars and comets and asteroids that we couldn't ever have any use for till we had worked off the old stock. I said if I caught him strawberrying around after any more asteroids especially, I should have to fire him out.

Privately, prejudice got the best of me there, I ought to confess it. At bottom I don't really mind comets so much. But somehow I have always been down on asteroids. There is nothing mature about them. I wouldn't sit up nights, the way that man does, if I could get a basketful of them.

He said it was the best line of goods he had. He said he could trade them to Rochester for comets and trade the comets to Harvard for nebulae and trade the nebulae to the Smithsonian for flint hatchets.

I felt obliged to stop this thing on the spot. I said we couldn't have the university turned into an astronomical junk shop.

And while I was at it I thought I might as well make the reform complete. The astronomer is extraordinarily mutinous. And so with your approval I will transfer him to the law department and put one of the law students in his place. A boy will be more biddable, more tractable, also cheaper. It is true he cannot be entrusted with important work at first, but he can comb the skies for nebulae till he gets his hand in.

I have other changes in mind but as they are in the nature of surprises I judge it politic to leave them unspecified at this time.

(about 1888)

The Groves of Academe: Deep, Deep Words

Willard P. Espy

Knowledge taught by rote originated with Mnemosyne, goddess of memory and mother of the nine Muses. She was the daughter of Uranus, the most ancient of the gods, and Gaea, the goddess of earth. MNEMONICS is any system designed to improve or develop the memory. I tried several such systems, until I decided I was better off forgetting.

A long time ago there lived in Attica a man named Academos ("on the side of the people"). Academos disclosed to Castor and Pollux the place where Theseus had secreted their irresistibly beautiful young sister Helen, whom he had kidnaped with lustful intent. (This is the same Helen who was later to desert her husband for Paris—an event which led to the Trojan War, the *Iliad*, the *Odyssey*, and a poem by Edgar Allen Poe.)

The people of Athens made much of Academos for his tittle-tattling, though it is hard to see why they should have cared, since Helen was a Spartan. A lovely and spacious garden, the Academe, was named in his honor.

In the 4th century B.C., the philosopher Plato opened a school for his followers in the grove of ACADEME. Ever since, the word has been inseparately connected with learning. AN ACADEMY may be an association of scholars, or of artists (as in London's Royal Academy of Fine Arts); or a school for special instruction; or a secondary or college-preparatory school.

PLATONISM, from Plato ("broad-shouldered"), is a philosophy holding that perfect, eternal realities are the objects of true knowledge; that the things of the senses are but distorted shadows of reality; that the soul, in its highest, rational form, is immortal; and that pleasures of the body, while they may be harmless and even virtuous, are to be subordinated to the pleasures of the mind. PLATONIC LOVE has come to be associated with love having no element of sexual desire.

Plato was a pupil of Socrates, who developed the inductive method and the conception of knowledge or insight as the foundation of virtue. SOCRATIC IRONY is pretended ignorance, or a willingness to learn from others assumed for the sake of making their errors conspicuous. The SOCRATIC METHOD consists of a series of questions, the object of which is to elicit a clear and consistent expression of something supposed to be implicitly known by all rational beings.

Socrates' love for outdoor discussion, away from home, appears to have been augmented by domestic difficulties, his wife Xanthippe ("roan horse") outdoing Mrs. Caudle in her scolding. A XANTHIPPE is a shrewish, peevish, quarrelsome wife.

At the opposite pole from platonic idealism is ARISTOTELIANISM, after Aristotle (384–322 B.C.), who is said to have exercised greater influence upon Western attitudes than any other one man. Aristotle ("best objective") espoused the empirical or scientific in methods and thought. Aristotelian logic is built around the syllogism, a form of deductive reasoning consisting of a major premise, a minor premise, and a conclusion.

The gymnasium at Athens where Aristotle taught was named the Lukeion, after the neighboring temple of Apollo Lukeios ("wolf-killer"). The word has come down to us as LYCEUM. (The lyceum movement, an association for debate and educational and literary improvement, flourished in the United States before the Civil War, having three thousand branches in 1834.)

Philosophy was taught also at the Athenaion, the temple of Athena. Rome adopted the word for a school of art, and today ATHENEUM, like academy, has become common for any institution, such as a library or reading room, that disseminates learning.

Antisthenes (born about 444 B.C.), like Plato a student of Socrates, founded the school of the Cynics (named improbably for a dog), who believed that virtue is the only good, and that its essence lies in self-control and independence. It is curious that this noble doctrine entered the vernacular with a nearly opposite meaning: today's CYNIC believes all men are motivated by vulgar selfishness.

The turnabout in the meaning of cynicism is matched by that of epicureanism. Epicurus, born seven years after the death of Plato, was so chaste a man that one of his enemies sought to deny him merit by saying he was without passion. He did not marry, in order that he might devote himself to philosophy. His conviction that it was human duty to maximize pleasure and minimize pain, however, led to an impression that EPICUREANISM stood for a life of indulgence. Today an epicure is considered one given to luxury or sensual gratification, modified by delicacy and refinement.

The Sophists (5th century B.C.) received their name from the Greek word for "skilled" or "clever." They were not personified in any one leader, but the best of them were undoubtedly among the most learned men of the period. They were the first to offer systematic education beyond the rudiments, antedating even Socrates. But they later came to be disparaged for oversubtle, self-serving reasoning, and that is the way a sophist is thought of today. SOPHOMORE ("wise fool"), SOPHISTICATED, and the like, have the same origin. Your Aunt Sophie is a wise old woman.

About 308 B.C., Zeno taught that men should be free from passion and calmly accept all occurrences as the unavoidable result of divine will. He taught in a porch *(Stoia)* in Athens, which led to the appellation STOIC for persons apparently or professedly indifferent to pleasure or pain.

Euclid, father of geometry, was born about 300 B.C. It was he who warned Ptolemy I that "there is no royal road to geometry." EUCLIDEAN means "lucid and orderly in the exposition of evidence," even if geometry is not in question.

Between 365 and 275 B.C. there lived in Greece a man named Pyrrho, who believed that all perceptions are of doubtful value, so that the supreme good is to preserve tranquillity of mind. Such a belief is PYR-RHONISM. It has nothing to do with pyrrhotism, from Greek *pyrrhotes*, "redness," the quality of having red hair.

EUHEMERISM is the doctrine that gods were great humans who grew in the telling, that myths are embellished accounts of historical personages and events. The Sicilian philosopher Euhemeros (meaning "good day") lived around 300 B.C. His interpretation relies upon an account of early history which he said he had discovered on a golden pillar in a temple on the island of Panchaia when on a voyage around the coast of India. The voyage and the island appear to have been a figment.

When Jesus was walking toward his crucifixion, the Roman soldiers, says Matthew 27:32, "found a man of Cyrene, Simon by name:

him they compelled to bear his cross." A CYRENAIC is a disciple of the hedonistic school of philosophy founded in Cyrene by Aristippus ("best horse"), who believed that pleasure is the only good in life. There's no reason to think the biblical Simon was of that school.

One generation's genius may be the next generation's half-wit. Johannes Duns Scotus (c. 1265–1308), born in Duns, Scotland, was the greatest of British medieval philosophers. Called the "subtle doctor" for his intricate reasoning, he won a large following for his objections to many of the changes brought about by the Reformation. After his death these "Dunsmen" persisted blindly in their opposition to the revival of classical learning, and eventually came to be considered a stupid lot. Hence the present-day significance of DUNCE: "one backward in book learning; a dull-witted person." DUN, for an old, broken-down horse, may have the same point of departure.

Atlas was either a divinity having charge of the pillars which upheld the heavens, or a Titan forced, for warring against Zeus, to bear the heavens on his head and hands. A picture of Atlas, supporting not the heavens but the ball of earth, was commonly prefixed to map collections at the beginning of the Renaissance. This led Gerhard Mercator (1512–1594), the Flemish geographer, to call the collections ATLASES. Mercator is also responsible for the mercator projection, a map in which the meridians and parallels of latitude appear as lines crossing at right angles, and in which areas appear larger the farther they are from the equator.

The theory that species of plants and animals develop through natural selection of viable variations is called DARWINISM, after Charles Robert Darwin (1809–1882), the British naturalist who propounded it in 1858. A SOCIAL DARWINIST is said to use this subtle doctrine as justification of individual callousness—every man for himself.

A FREUDIAN is one who practices the theories of Sigmund Freud (1856–1939), the pioneer psychoanalyst, in psychotherapy; or who applies those theories to other disciplines such as history or literary criticism; or who simply approves and preaches them. *Freude* in German means "joy; gladness," emotions not generally associated with the father of psychiatry. A "Freudian slip" could be called a *Felix culpa.*

NEWTONIAN derives from the work of Sir Isaac Newton (1642–1727) in mechanics and gravitation (the NEWTON, a unit of force, is named after him), and EINSTEINIAN from the theories of Albert Einstein (1879–1955) on general and special relativity. A synthetic transuranic element obtained by neutron irradiation of uranium is named EINSTEINIUM.

After the Civil War, Americans became fascinated by the CHAU-
TAUQUA, a traveling show, often performing under canvas, and including vaudeville acts as well as lectures. Chautauquas were reinforced by
a system of home study. The name derives from the county and lake in
southwestern New York where the first chautauqua was held in 1874.
Chautauqua was a word of the Seneca Indians, who attributed several
meanings to it, one being "the place of easy death." In view of the
uneasy state of present institutions of learning, one wonders whether
we should not give the chautauqua another chance.

Louis Braille (1809–1852), a Frenchman who lost his sight
through an accident at the age of three, developed a dot system of print-
ing (first suggested by Captain Charles Barbier) which can be read by
touch, and easily written with a simple instrument. BRAILLE defines any
similar system.

Summa Cum Laude, Timothy

"Oh," said Timothy, turning the last page of the chapter face
down, "BERKELEIANISM. Subjective idealism. The doctrine that so-called
material things exist only in being perceived. After Bishop George
Berkeley, the Irish philosopher. His dates are 1685–1753. He inspired
this anonymous witticism:

> *There was a young man who said: God*
> *Must think it exceedingly odd*
> *That the juniper tree*
> *Just ceases to be*
> *When there's no-one about in the quad.*

Monsignor Ronald Knox replied:

> *Dear Sir, Your astonishment's odd;*
> *I am always about in the quad;*
> *And that's why the tree*
> *Will continue to be,*
> *Since observed by*

> *Yours faithfully,*
> *God.*

"You might wish to include BERKELIUM, the appropriately transient element with a half-life of four and a half hours. Named for Berkeley, California, which in turned is named for Bishop Berkeley."

He also insisted on my including "Priscian's head." Priscian, a Latin grammarian who flourished at Constantinople around A.D. 500, was so highly regarded during the Middle Ages that the phrase "TO BREAK PRISCIAN'S HEAD" became a byword for the violation of rules of grammar.

OCKHAM'S RAZOR, too, noted Timothy, has become generic: "William of Ockham. A Franciscan. His dates were about 1300 to about 1349. A pupil and later a rival of Duns Scotus. His famous doctrine was 'Entities are not to be multiplied'—that is, one must slice away all nonessential constituents in the subject being analyzed. Hence Ockham's razor."

I suddenly remembered something. "ALGORISMUS!" I exclaimed. "Wasn't it invented by someone named Algor?"

"Ah," said Timothy. "A name applied in the Middle Ages to arithmetic employing the Indo-Arabic numerals. Ah . . . yes. Bop-bop-bop."

I was much set up to have thought of a word he had missed. He went on: "Early European writers indeed thought it came from Algor, a king of India. A manuscript written around 1300 said, 'Ther was a kyng of Inde the quich heyth Algor, he made this craft. And aft his name he called hit algory.' I will write that out for you. But the origin is *Liber Algorismus,* 'the Book of al-Khowarizmi,' by Mohammed ibn Musa al-Khowarizmi."

"But it is an uncommon, improper noun," I said. "Khowarizmi—algorismus."

"Exactly. Ah, Vitruvian man?"

Vitruvius was a Roman architect of the 1st century B.C. To show the normal proportions of the members to the body, he sketched the VITRUVIAN MAN in the two classic positions with arms and legs outthrust: one around which could be drawn a perfect circle; the other around which could be drawn a perfect square. Leonardo da Vinci created a similar figure. It would have done your heart good to see Timothy demonstrate the two positions, arms and legs stiffly spread, his stick aloft in one hand. His agility was admirable.

His final contribution was the Greek cynic philosopher Diogenes, supposed to have lived in a tub and to have gone about with a lantern in daylight, looking for an honest man.

"Alexander the Great admired him extravagantly," said Timothy. "'If I were not Alexander,' he said, 'I would be Diogenes.' The admiration appears not to have been returned. When the ruler of the world inquired, 'Is there any way I can serve you?' Diogenes replied, 'You can step out of my light.'"

I protested: "Diogenes has left us no improper, uncommon nouns. Nor Patient Griseldas either, as far as I know, unless you consider Diogenes' lantern in that category."

"You forget the terrestrial hermit crab that destroys crops in the West Indies," said Timothy. "The Diogenes crab. And the cuplike hollow formed by the hand and the fingers: Diogenes' cup."

Magna cum laude, Timothy. Summa cum laude.

Jules Feiffer

Survey of Literature

John Crowe Ransom

In all the good Greek of Plato
I lack my roast beef and potato.

A better man was Aristotle,
Pulling steady on the bottle.

I dip my hat to Chaucer,
Swilling soup from his saucer,

And to Master Shakespeare
Who wrote big on small beer.

The abstemious Wordsworth
Subsisted on a curd's-worth,

But a slick one was Tennyson,
Putting gravy on his venison.

What these men had to eat and drink
Is what we say and what we think.

The influence of Milton
Came wry out of Stilton.

Sing a song for Percy Shelley,
Drowned in pale lemon jelly,

And for precious John Keats,
Dripping blood of pickled beets.

Then there was poor Willie Blake,
He foundered on sweet cake.

God have mercy on the sinner
Who must write with no dinner,

No gravy and no grub,
No pewter and no pub,

No belly and no bowels,
Only consonants and vowels.

Shakespeare Explained

Robert Benchley

Carrying on the System of Footnotes to a Silly Extreme

PERICLES

Act II. Scene 3

Enter first Lady-in-Waiting (Flourish,[1] Hautboys[2] and[3] torches[4])
First Lady-in-Waiting—What[5] ho![6] Where[7] is[8] the[9] music?[10]

Notes

1. *Flourish:* The stage direction here is obscure. Clarke claims it should read "flarish," thus changing the meaning of the passage to "flarish" (that is, the King's), but most authorities have agreed that it should remain "flourish," supplying the predicate which is to be flourished. There was at this time a custom in the countryside of England to flourish a mop as a signal to the passing vender of berries, signifying that in that particular household there was a consumer-demand for berries, and this may have been meant in this instance. That Shakespeare was cognizant of this custom of flourishing the mop for berries is shown in a similar passage in the second part of King Henry IV, where he has the Third Page enter and say, "Flourish." Cf. also Hamlet, IV, 7:4.

2. *Hautboys*, from the French *haut*, meaning "high" and the Eng. *boys*, meaning "boys." The word here is doubtless used in the sense of "high boys," indicating either that Shakespeare intended to convey the idea of spiritual distress on the part of the First Lady-in-Waiting or that

he did not. Of this Rolfe says: "Here we have one of the chief indications of Shakespeare's knowledge of human nature, his remarkable insight into the petty foibles of this work-a-day world." Cf. T. N. 4:6, "Mine eye hath play'd the painter, and hath stell'd thy beauty's form in table of my heart."

3. *and.* A favorite conjunctive of Shakespeare's in referring to the need for a more adequate navy for England. Tauchnitz claims that it should be pronounced "und," stressing the anti-penult. This interpretation, however, has found disfavor among most commentators because of its limited significance. We find the same conjunctive in A. W. T. E. W. 6:7, "Steel-boned, unyielding *and* uncomplying virtue," and here there can be no doubt that Shakespeare meant that if the King should consent to the marriage of his daughter the excuse of Stephano, offered in Act 2, would carry no weight.

4. *Torches.* The interpolation of some foolish player and never the work of Shakespeare (Warb.). The critics of the last century have disputed whether or not this has been misspelled in the original, and should read "trochies" or "troches." This might well be since the introduction of tobacco into England at this time had wrought havoc with the speaking voices of the players, and we might well imagine that at the entrance of the First Lady-in-Waiting there might be perhaps one of the hautboys mentioned in the preceding passage bearing a box of "troches" or "trognies" for the actors to suck. Of this entrance Clarke remarks: "The noble mixture of spirited firmness and womanly modesty, fine sense and true humility, clear sagacity and absence of conceit, passionate warmth and sensitive delicacy, generous love and self-diffidence with which Shakespeare has endowed this First Lady-in-Waiting renders her in our eyes one of the most admirable of his female characters." Cf. M. S. N. D. 8:9, "That solder'st close impossibilities and mak'st them kiss."

5. *What*—What.

6. *Ho!* In conjunction with the preceding word doubtless means "What ho!" changed by Clarke to "what hoo!" In the original ms. it reads "What hi!" but this has been accredited to the tendency of the time to write "What hi" when "what ho" was meant. Techner alone maintains that it should read "What humpf!" Cf. Ham. 5:0, "High-ho!"

7. *Where.* The reading of the folio, retained by Johnson, the Cambridge editors and others, but it is not impossible that Shakespeare wrote "why," as Pope and others give it. This would make the passage read "Why the music?" instead of "Where is the music?" and would be a much more probable interpretation in view of the music of that time.

Cf. George Ade. Fable No. 15, "Why the gunny-sack?"

8. *is*—is not. That is, would not be.

9. *the.* Cf. Ham. 4:6. M. S. N. D. 3:5. A. W. T. E. W. 2:6 T. N. 1:3 and Macbeth 3:1, "that knits up *the* raveled sleeves of care."

10. *music.* Explained by Malone as "the art of making music" or "music that is made." If it has but one of these meanings we are inclined to think it is the first; and this seems to be favored by what precedes, "*the* music!" Cf. M. of V. 4:2, "The man that hath no music in himself."

The meaning of the whole passage seems to be that the First Lady-in-Waiting has entered, concomitant with a flourish, hautboys and torches and says, "What ho! Where is the music?"

Al Ross

"Good, but not immortal."

The Shakespeare Interview

Brock Brower

William Shakespeare lives in a stylish, imitation-Tudor house at Strat-
ford-on-Avon, a growing exurbanite community some ninety miles
outside of London. He was born here in 1564, and not long ago decided
to return, hoping that the country air would alleviate a pale cast of
thought that has bothered him ever since his tragic period. The slanting
half-timbers, the asphodels, the greenwood, and a new coat of arms give
the New Place in Chapel Street a rich feeling of hey-nonny-no.

Mr. Shakespeare met us at the gate. We quickly recognized the
firm, exopthalmic phiz of the First Folio portrait with bagged chin and
five o'clock shadow. He looked saddened, but rested. With obvious
pride, he began walking us over his freehold toward the garden. "It's
really the movie sale of *Hamlet* that's done it," he admitted. "We've
even been talking about taking a trip. I rounded up some pamphlets on
Bermuda the other day. We'll probably never go, but it's nice to think
about."

Through a mullioned back window, we noticed Anne—his
accommodating, somewhat elderly wife—fluffing out the bolster on the
second-best bed. In a far corner of the garden, his granddaughter Eliza-
beth sat, studying a chess problem. We reached a mulberry tree, where
a much-thumbed Holinshed lay open on a bench, and, beside it, a copy
of Plutarch, heavily underlined. We took our seats (a near-by armillary
served as ground for our tape recorder), and he asked us for news of London. He wanted to know if we found the work of Beaumont and
Fletcher at all to our taste, if Ben Jonson was still roaring around town,
and if the Bear Garden had reopened next to the Globe Theatre. We reas-
sured him on all counts, though he was grieved to hear that the Mermaid Tavern had temporarily lost its license.

INTERVIEWERS: Do you think the Mermaid Tavern has been an
important influence on you?

MR. SHAKESPEARE: You mean, as a literary thing?

INTERVIEWERS: Yes. Taken as something typically Elizabethan.

MR. SHAKESPEARE: Now you must be very careful how you use that term "Elizabethan." It covers a lot of poets and dramatists who really don't have that much in common. I don't think there ever was a typical Elizabethan. Phil Sidney is one kind of Elizabethan, and Ed Spencer is another. Also, you have some Elizabethans who actually spent most of their lives as Jacobeans. You'll notice the newspapers call me both. Actually I don't think it makes much difference. "Elizabethan" is just the sort of label the public tries to stick on a writer when they don't understand him.

INTERVIEWERS: Where did the word come from?

MR. SHAKESPEARE: I don't exactly know. It's the sort of thing that's more likely to come out of the Mermaid Tavern than any real work, if that helps answer a previous question of yours. As I recall it, I think it was Kit Marlowe who came up with it. And he was certainly the most truly Elizabethan playwright we had working in the theatre. But if he'd lived long enough, they would've started tagging him a Jacobean too.

INTERVIEWERS: Did you start out to write as an Elizabethan?

MR. SHAKESPEARE: Lord, no.

INTERVIEWERS: But isn't it true that most of your earlier poems appeared in the Elizabethan press?

MR. SHAKESPEARE: Yes, that's true, and I'm certainly grateful to Mr. Richard Field and others like him for helping me find a reading public, even before the plays. But I've never belonged to any "school" or movement. That was all tacked on afterward by the critics. Take the early poems—I suppose you're thinking of the Sonnets as much as *The Rape* and *Venus and Adonis*?

INTERVIEWERS: Yes. There's been a lot of speculation about the Sonnets. The Dark Lady and Mr. W.H., and so forth.

MR. SHAKESPEARE: Right. And if I'd had any idea what a stink they were going to cause, I'd have cut the both of them out to begin with. Maybe I was trying too hard to appeal to the public taste. After all, it's pretty lurid stuff, and the intellectuals have just tried to make a big thing out of it. As far as I'm concerned, the Sonnets were strictly a commercial venture.

INTERVIEWERS: Would you describe any of your other works as "strictly commercial"?

MR. SHAKESPEARE: Yes, some of it. I always figured on making a good penny out of Falstaff. I probably would've stuck him in a lot more plays if our heavy hadn't quit us. Then I counted heavily on bringing the teen-agers into the theatre with *Romeo and Juliet*. Even *Macbeth* is basically a thriller, don't forget.

INTERVIEWERS: Would you call *Hamlet* and *Lear* commercial?

MR. SHAKESPEARE: Not exactly. *Hamlet* more than *Lear*, I suppose. *Hamlet* is definitely a young man's play, and you can always count on the Castiglione crowd to lap that kind of stuff up. But with *Lear* you've got to bank on the older people. It probably would've been better if I hadn't hanged Cordelia in the last act, but I got carried away. I figured if Ophelia can drown, why can't Cordelia swing?

INTERVIEWERS: Do you ever rewrite?

MR. SHAKESPEARE: No. I do a first draft, longhand, and that's usually it. Sometimes I do a little scratching in the prompt copy.

INTERVIEWERS: Does writing come easily to you?

MR. SHAKESPEARE: That depends. It usually starts with a sort of airy nothingness, if you know what I mean. That's pretty hard to lick. I try to attack it by giving it a local habitation and a name, and once I've got those down the rest is relatively simple. I can knock out ninety to a hundred pentameters a day.

INTERVIEWERS: Did you ever take a writing course?

MR. SHAKESPEARE: No. I don't think much of the academic approach, frankly. I don't think Cambridge did Kit Marlowe any harm, but then I doubt if anybody up there taught him how to write a play. Ben Jonson is always after me about my Latin and Greek, of course. But with all due respect to Ben—and I think he's a fine Jacobean, one of the best—he's got too much damned Latin and a hell of a lot more Greek than he needs.

INTERVIEWERS: Do you think the writer—particularly the playwright—should involve himself in politics?

MR. SHAKESPEARE: That's a tough one. My plays have always had political overtones, particularly the *Henries*. But I think it's important to avoid propagandizing. For instance, I've always stood pretty much for the Divine Right of Kings (or Queens), but I certainly overdid it with Prince Hal. It queered Falstaff, but good.

INTERVIEWERS: Some people claim that you've Tudor-angled your Histories. . . .

MR. SHAKESPEARE: Yes, I realize that. There's been a lot of sharp criticism of my handling of Richard Crookback, but the way I see it, I'd a lot rather have the two princes buried in the Tower than end up there myself. I'm not putting my head on anybody's block. I'm no Walt Raleigh.

INTERVIEWERS: Let's talk about comedy a minute. During your early years in the theatre, you wrote a number of very fine ones. Why did you stop?

MR. SHAKESPEARE: I guess I was just written out. I wasn't pulling the same laughs any more, and you get pretty sick of this swain-meets-shepherdess routine. It was getting so that every time there was a posh wedding or a big Christmas party, I had to come up with another *Twelfth Night*. A real nightmare. Besides, you can't get anywhere with the London crowd unless you do a Revenge tragedy.

INTERVIEWERS: Is that why you wrote *Hamlet?*

MR. SHAKESPEARE: Partly. *Hamlet* was a funny play for me. At the time I was pretty much wrapped up in myself—a lot of family trouble, feelings of persecution, et cetera—and you might say I got hung up on Elsinore rock. I overwrote the soliloquies badly, and it was really Dick Burbadge who saved the play. Without him, we would've closed the second night.

INTERVIEWERS: Do you keep a journal?

MR. SHAKESPEARE: No. All I really need to summon up the remembrance of things past is a good session of sweet, silent thought.

INTERVIEWERS: Do you have any advice for beginning writers?

MR. SHAKESPEARE: Yes. I think they ought to stay out of literary quarrels, but being in, they ought to make sure they don't get pushed around. They should give an ear to whatever's being said around them, but keep their traps shut otherwise. They ought to dress as well as they can afford. You know—rich, not gaudy. They shouldn't borrow any money, or lend any either. I guess the most important thing is to stay true to yourself, because then you won't screw up anybody else.

INTERVIEWERS: How did you get started in the theatre?

MR. SHAKESPEARE: Now that's a pretty good story. I arrived in London—after a little trouble over a rabbit or two on Sir Thomas Lucy's estate (a real s.o.b., by the way)—and I needed a job pretty badly. I was over in Southwark one day, hanging around the theatres, when a bloke comes riding up hard, jumps off, and hands me his horse to hold. Before I knew it, I was holding everybody's horse who rode up to the theatre and collecting tips, and gradually I worked my way inside—

INTERVIEWERS: Wait a minute, sire. That story's apocryphal.

MR. SHAKESPEARE: Whazzat?

INTERVIEWERS: It's been disproven. People just made it up to add a little glamour. The source is highly unreliable.

MR. SHAKESPEARE: Well, I'll be damned.

INTERVIEWERS: And that brings up a very important question, sir. If you don't mind our asking. . . .

MR. SHAKESPEARE: No, no. Go right ahead.

INTERVIEWERS: Who *did* write your plays?

MR. SHAKESPEARE: Now, listen. I don't *have* to give interviews. I'm doing this as a favor. And if you milksops think you're going to raise the circulation on that cheap little rag of yours by dragging me into an argument—

INTERVIEWERS: Come now, sir. Be honest.

MR. SHAKESPEARE: I wrote every damn one of them!

INTERVIEWERS: Was it Marlowe?

MR. SHAKESPEARE: All right. Pack up that wire contraption, and get out of here.

INTERVIEWERS: Perhaps you'll go along with the Baconians. . . .

MR. SHAKESPEARE: Frank Bacon! Malvolio could write a better play than Frank Bacon!

INTERVIEWERS: Was it the Earl of Essex?

MR. SHAKESPEARE: Out!

INTERVIEWERS: Certain crytographic analyses show—

MR. SHAKESPEARE: Out!

(Exit Interviewers, pursued by a Bear.)

(This is the one-hundred-and-eleventh in a series on The Art of Fiction. Authors interviewed have included Erle Stanley Gardner, Euripides, Soren Kierkegaard, Jane Austen, O. Henry, Henry James, James Jones, Goethe, and Ray Bradbury. The series has been temporarily discontinued due to lacerations.)

(Reprinted from *The P - - - - R - - - -*)

Professor Gratt

Donald Hall

And why does Gratt teach English? Why, because
A law school felt he could not learn the laws.
"Hamlet," he tells his students, "you will find,
Concerns a man who can't make up his mind.
The Tempest? . . . um . . . the one with Ariel! . . .
Are there more questions now?" But one can tell
That all his will, brains, and imagination
Are concentrated on a higher station:
He wants to be in the Administration.
Sometimes at parties he observes the Dean;
He giggles, coughs, and turns aquamarine.
Yet some day we will hear of "Mr. Gratt,
Vice-President in Charge of This or That."
I heard the Dean remark, at tea and cakes,
Face stuffed and sneering, "Gratt has what it takes."

The Cliché Expert Testifies on Literary Criticism

Frank Sullivan

Q. Mr. Arbuthnot, you are an expert in the use of the cliché as applied to literary criticism?

A. I am told that I am, Mr. Sullivan.

Q. We shall soon find out. What is this object, marked Exhibit A?

A. That is a book.

Q. Good. What kind of book is it?

A. It is a minor classic.

Q. And what kind of document is it?

A. It is a valuable human document.

Q. Very good, Mr. Arbuthnot. Please continue.

A. It is a book in which the results of painstaking—or scholarly—research are embodied, and it should appeal to a wide public. This reviewer could not put it down.

Q. Why not?

A. Because of its penetrating insight. It is a sincere and moving study of family life against the background of a small cathedral town. It is also a vivid and faithful portrayal.

Q. How written?

A. Written with sympathy, pathos, and kindly humor. It throws a clear light on a little understood subject and is well worth reading.

Q. How is it illustrated?

A. Profusely. It is original in conception, devoid of sentimentality, highly informative, consistently witty, and rich in color. You should place it on your library list.

Q. Why?

A. Because it strikes a new note in fiction. Mystery and suspense crowd its pages. The author has blended fact and fiction and the result is an authentic drama of social revolution, a definite contribution to proletarian literature.

Q. Told with a wealth of what?

A. Told with a wealth of detail.

Q. And how portrayed?

A. Realistically portrayed, in staccato prose. For sheer brilliance of style there has been nothing like it since *Moby Dick*. Rarely does a narrative move at such a fast pace.

Q. What is it a shrewd comment on?

A. The contemporary scene. It marks a red-letter day in current literature. It is capital entertainment.

Q. What pervades it?

A. A faint tinge of irony.

Q. And how is it translated?

A. Ably. It is a penetrating study in abnormal psychology, and unlike most scientific works it is written in language understandable to the layman. It belongs in the front rank of modern picaresque literature. Ideology.

Q. I beg your pardon?

A. I said ideology. Also catharsis.

Q. What about them?

A. Well, they have to come in somewhere.

Q. I see. Now, to return to the minor classic, Mr. Arbuthnot. Would you call it a subtle and arresting piece of work?

A. Certainly I would. Why do you suppose I'm an expert in the use of the cliché? I'd also call it an honest attempt to depict, a remarkable first novel, a veritable triumph, a genuine contribution, a thrilling saga of life in frontier days, and the most impressive study of degeneration since Zola. It bids fair to go down as one of the great biographies of all time, including *Moby Dick*. In short, it has unusual merit.

Q. How does it augur?

A. It augurs well for the future of the author.

Q. And how does it bid?

A. It bids fair to become a best-seller.

Q. And how does it end?

A. It ends upon a distinct note of despair. It is a work of art.

Q. I'm glad you liked it, Mr. Arbuthnot.

A. Who said I liked it?

Q. Didn't you?

A. Certainly not.

Q. Why not?

A. Because it is, one fears, mawkishly sentimental and, one regrets, faintly pretentious. Curiously enough, it does not carry conviction. Strangely enough, it lacks depth. Oddly enough, the denouement is weak. It is to be regretted that the title is rather misleading and it need hardly be pointed out that the book as a whole lacks cohesion and form. I am very much afraid, one regrets, that it falls definitely into the escapist school of fiction. And of course, like all first novels, it is autobiographical.

Q. I'm glad you told me. I won't buy it.

A. Ah, but in spite of its faults it contains much of real value. It kept me awake till three. In the opinion of the present reviewer it would be the long-awaited great American novel except for one serious defect.

Q. What is that?

A. It lacks an index.

Q. Mr. Arbuthnot, it is easy to see that you have earned your spurs in the field of literary criticism. So much for the book. Now, observe this object I hold here in my hand, marked Exhibit B. What is it?

A. That. *That* is an *author.*

Q. Whose are those italics, Mr. Arbuthnot?

A. The italics are mine.

Q. What kind of author is this?

A. A promising young author who should be watched.

Q. What does he write?

A. Powerful first novels.

Q. What kind of storyteller is he?

A. He's a born storyteller.

Q. What kind of satirist is he?

A. A satirist of the first order.

Q. Tell us more about this interesting creature.

A. Well, he cannot be lightly dismissed. He is undoubtedly to be reckoned with, one feels, as a definite force. He is in the front rank of the younger writers.

Q. Why?

A. Because his work plainly shows the influence of Joyce, Hemingway, Huxley, Proust, Gertrude Stein, Auden, Eliot, and Virginia Woolf. Here is an authentic talent from which we may expect great things.

Q. So what do you do?

A. So I hail him. And I acclaim him. He has a keen ear for the spoken word. He also has a flair. He set out to tell. He deals with themes, or handles them. He recaptures moods. His execution is brilliant, his insight is poetic, his restraint is admirable, and he has a sense of values. There is something almost uncanny in his ability to look into men's souls. And he paints a vivid word picture and works on a vast canvas.

Q. How?

A. With consummate artistry. He writes with commendable frankness.

Q. Using what kind of style?

A. Using a limpid prose style. He has a real freshness of approach that stamps him as an artist in the true sense of the word. He culls his material and his niche in the hall of literary fame seems secure.

Q. I'm glad you like him, Mr. Arbuthnot.

A. But I don't.

Q. No? Why not?

A. Because his talent is plainly superficial and ephemeral. He has an unfortunate habit of allowing his personality to obtrude. His book is badly documented and not the least of his many irritating mannerisms is his addiction to inexcusable typographical errors. His book is full of clichés and he does not make his characters live and feel and breathe. And he writes with one eye on Hollywood.

Q. You mean to tell me that a cad like that has the audacity to call himself an author?

A. Well now, don't be too hard on him. Although he decidedly does not justify his early promise it is as yet too early to evaluate his work. Want to know about the plot?

Q. Yes, indeed. What about the plot?

A. It is well rounded and fully developed. But it is marred by structural weaknesses.

Q. What kind of structural weaknesses?

A. Inherent structural weaknesses. It is motivated, of course. And its threads are cunningly woven into a harmonious texture by the deft hand of a skilled literary craftsman.

Q. Just one thing more, Mr. Arbuthnot. How many kinds of readers are there?

A. Three—casual, general, and gentle.

Q. Mr. Arbuthnot, I think that is all. I can't thank you enough for having come here today to help us out.

A. It has been a pleasure—a vivid, fascinating, significant, vigorous, timely, gracious, breath-taking, mature, adequate, nostalgic, unforgettable, gripping, articulate, engrossing, poignant, and adult pleasure to be of service to you, Mr. Sullivan. Good day, sir.

Jules Feiffer

TODAY'S BOOK IS A RATHER BULKY BUT PROMISING FIRST ATTEMPT BY AUTHOR OR AUTHORS UNKNOWN.

IT'S CALLED THE BIBLE.

IT IS WRITTEN IN A NARRATIVE RATHER THAN INTROSPECTIVE STYLE WHICH MAY PERHAPS MAKE FOR QUICKER READING BUT LEAVES SOMETHING TO BE DESIRED ON THE LEVEL OF CHARACTER MOTIVATION.

IT PURPORTS TO BE A THEOLOGICAL AND HISTORICAL DOCUMENT, AND WHILE THIS REVIEWER DOES NOT QUESTION ITS SINCERITY, HE CAN ONLY REGRET THE PUBLISHER'S FAILURE TO INCLUDE A BIBLIOGRAPHY.

BUT THESE ARE MINOR CRITICISMS. ONE CAN NOT DENY THE POWER AND SWEEPING RANGE OF THE SUBJECT MATTER - (ONE MIGHT EVEN CALL IT EPIC) —

- THE SUBTLE ALLEGORICAL NUANCES TOUCHED, AT TIMES, WITH WHAT SEEMS TO BE AN ALMOST METAPHYSICAL INSIGHT.' IT WILL UNDOUBTEDLY CAUSE CONTROVERSY IN THE LITERARY FIELD.

BUT THE AUTHORS, WHILE WRITING IN A QUASI-JOURNALISTIC FORM SHOW OCCASIONAL FLOURISHES OF STYLISTIC DARING WHICH MAKES ONE IMPATIENT TO VIEW THEIR LATER EFFORTS.

I SHALL AWAIT THEIR SECOND BOOK WITH GREAT INTEREST.

Great Poets

Richard Armour

Teaching poetry has one advantage over teaching prose: there is more to explain. You can go into such matters as rhyme, meter, blank verse, free verse, assonance, consonance, alliteration, imagery, personification, stanzaic patterns, odes, elegies, sonnets, pastorals, ballads, epics, and dramatic monologues, not to mention (but you must be sure to mention them) similes, metaphors, run-on lines, caesuras, and, if you want to pour it on, *vers de société* and such exotic forms as the *chant royal, kyrielle, pantoum, lai,* and *virelai.*

But the best thing about poetry, to a teacher, is the chance to tell students what a poem, or a specific line, is about, assuming the poet had something in mind. Of course the teacher may, when cornered, simply shrug and quote Archibald MacLeish's "A poem should not mean/But be." The only trouble is that some student may ask, "What did MacLeish mean by that?"

I have taught poetry much more than prose and have learned all, or almost all, the tricks. It was many years before I discovered that provocative question, "What do *you* think?" I picked it up from a colleague who was known for his ability to stimulate discussion. If, while asking it, the teacher can put on a concerned, curious expression (an expression full of curiosity, that is), so much the better. While the question is being answered, the expression should reflect concentration, astonishment, skepticism, and grudging agreement, in that order, with just the right amount of pursing the lips, letting the mouth fall wide open, wrinkling the brow, and finally vigorously nodding the head. My colleague was not in English, but in History. If well handled, "What do *you* think?" seems to be effective in any field. But I myself have found it most useful in the teaching of poetry.

The great poets have inspired me to a form of collaboration. Tampering, some might call it, and they could be right. I feel, however, that the great poet and I are working together to produce something that requires more than one writer.

I began this some years ago when I fooled around a little with one of Wordsworth's Lucy Poems, "She Dwelt Among the Untrodden Ways." The first two stanzas I left untouched. The third stanza I altered only slightly, changing one word in the second line and one in the fourth. The whole poem is Wordsworth's, then, except for two words. Perhaps this is the way Wordsworth actually wrote it and there was a typographical error, or there were two errors. What I am sure of is that the poem takes on a new meaning, or a new relevance. Here is the revised poem:

Lucy Revisited

She dwelt among the untrodden ways
Beside the springs of Dove,
A Maid whom there were none to praise
And very few to love:

A violet by a mossy stone
Half hidden from the eye!
—Fair as a star, when only one
Is shining in the sky.

She lived unknown, and few could know
When Lucy ceased to stir;
But she is in her grave, and, oh,
The difference to her!

My collaboration with Wordsworth emboldened me to work with other poets of the past. Instead of contributing only two words to a poem, however, I substituted an entire line of my own for the last line of a famous quatrain. This meant that I was now writing a fourth of the quatrain, or that the great poet and I were pooling our efforts in a ratio of three to one. My responsibility was therefore greater than it had been with Wordsworth, and I must try hard not to let my partner down.

I worked closely with such poets as Longfellow:

Lives of great men all remind us
We can make our lives sublime,
And, departing, leave behind us
Things unpaid for, bought on time.

And Henley:

> Out of the night that covers me,
> Black as the Pit from pole to pole,
> I thank whatever gods may be
> I have not stumbled in a hole.

And Tennyson:

> Come into the garden, Maud,
> For the black bat, night, has flown.
> Come into the garden, Maud—
> Don't bring a chaperon.

The next step was to work on a fifty-fifty basis, share and share alike. I took a single famous line and in place of the poet's next line added an infamous line of my own. The result was a book called *Punctured Poems*, illustrated by Eric Gurney, himself famous for *How to Live with a Neurotic Dog* and other works of high literary quality. I thought an artist who liked dogs would also like doggerel, and I was right. Our partnership on *Punctured Poems* led us to do *The Strange Dreams of Rover Jones* together, a book that has no connection with the study of English or American literature but is important to everyone concerned about caninity.

Two things were essential in selecting the famous lines I was to cap, or capsize. First they should be truly famous, or at least well known. Second, they should serve as a springboard for the plunge into the line which was my half of the couplet. To find such lines I went through Bartlett's *Familiar Quotations*, which in my edition is 1831 double-column pages of fine print, three times. I also perused numerous anthologies of poetry. It was harder to find just the right lines than you might suppose.

As I say in the Foreword to the book: "No apologies are made for the infamous second lines. Some of them will seem better when read over and over. At least they will approximately offset the number of lines which seem worse. If the reader is still unhappy, he can cross out the offending line and write something of his own—if it is not a borrowed copy." This might, in fact, be a good class exercise. Another would be to try to recall what the poet's own second line is. Better still, ask someone else what it is, having first looked it up yourself, and enjoy a moment of superiority.

Here are a few couplets, half man and half beast, from *Punctured Poems*, occasionally with a learned footnote.

Christopher Marlow, "Dr. Faustus"

> Was this the face that launch'd a thousand
>   ships?
> No wonder there are keel marks on her lips.[1]

William Shakespeare, "The Tempest"

> Full fathom five thy father lies.
> I pushed him. I apologize.

Alexander Pope, "Essay on Criticism"

> To err is human, to forgive divine.
> Some errors I forgive, though, quickly.
> . . . Mine.[2]

Percy Bysshe Shelley, "The Cloud"

> I bring fresh showers for the thirsting flowers.
> I've stood in the sun, with a hose, for hours.[3]

Samuel Taylor Coleridge, "The Rime of the Ancient Mariner"

> Water, water, everywhere;
> The plumbing badly needs repair.

---

[1] Helen of Troy is said to have had a full lower lip. Apparently it was full of bolts and barnacles.

[2] And then there is Charles Townsend Copeland's "To eat is human; to digest, divine."

[3] See also Thomas Edward Brown's
A garden is a lovesome thing, God wot,
But only if God wotters it a lot.

[1] In the same poem we also have:
The moving finger writes and, having writ,
Is badly stained with ink, you must admit.

[2] Or, in view of the capital in some texts:
We are the Hollow men:
Fred Hollow, Bert Hollow, Ben.

Robert Browning, "My Last Duchess"

>That's my last Duchess painted on the wall.
>I've scraped, but cannot get her off at all.

Omar Khayyám, "Rubáiyát" (tr. by Edward Fitzgerald)

>A jug of wine, a loaf of bread, and thou. . . .
>I'm not so very hungry anyhow.[1]

Henry Wadsworth Longfellow, "Paul Revere's Ride"

>One if by land, and two if by sea. . . .
>Now what do I do? He signals three!

Dante Gabriel Rossetti, "The Blessed Damozel"

>The blessed damozel leaned out.
>"She's sick!" I heard a warning shout.

Edna St. Vincent Millay, "Figs from Thistles"

>My candle burns at both ends.
>Where can I set it down, my friends?

T. S. Eliot, "The Hollow Men"

>We are the hollow men.
>It's time to eat again.[2]

After you have studied and taught the great poets and come to look on them as friends, there is an element of sharing and intimacy in working with them in this way. It is an indescribable feeling which I shall not attempt to describe.

Richard Armour

LINES LONG AFTER POPE,
BY A READER OF FRESHMAN THEMES

Small wit is theirs, in shopworn phrases dressed;
What oft was thought, and twice as well expressed.

Webley I. Webster: Wisdom of the Ages

Bob Elliott and Ray Goulding

(Theme music, in and under)

WEBSTER: Hello, this is Webley L. Webster welcoming you to educational *Wisdom of the Ages*. We have with us a panel of distinguished scholars who are going to use their wisdom, their sapiens and profunditers to give you, the listeners, something to ponder over.
First guest on my right is Roland C. Drob, the Dean of Wisdom at the Druckel School of Agriculture.

DROB: How do you do?

WEBSTER: Sir, you don't have to smile perpetually. This is radio. And Fionia Flavin, whose current book of poems, *Rhymes on My Hands*, is a glut on the market.

FIONIA *(Interrupting):* It is not a glut on the market. The note says that it was "put" on the market.

WEBSTER: I'm sorry. Our last guest is Stock Vanderhoogen, who used to study Sigmund Freud.

STOCK: No, I used to study Hans Christian Andersen.

WEBSTER: Well, I knew it was one of those foreigners. Panel, it is time to philosophize, and I should like first to look at Stock Vanderhoogen.

STOCK: Who is he looking at?

WEBSTER: Stock Vanderhoogen!

STOCK: Well, I believe it was Confucius who once said, "Water can both sustain and engulf a ship."

FIONIA: I think Samuel Johnson said, "Nobody is always wrong. Even a stopped clock is right twice a day."

DROB: I always admired William Shakespeare for saying, "There is small choice in rotten apples."

WEBSTER: I would like to add a point here. The poet George Burns once said, "Water can both sustain and engulf a ship."

STOCK: What insight the poet Shelley Winters had when he said, "Never argue with a doctor, he has inside information."

FIONIA: A memorable line from Shakespeare's *As You Like It* was

"Laughter greases up the engine of worry, enabling you to slide merrily on your way."

DROB: Ginger Rogers, in a moment of inspiration, once said, "Nobody is always wrong. Even a stopped clock is right twice a day."

STOCK: Charles Dickens knew from whence he spoke when he said, "Water can both sustain and engulf a ship."

FIONIA: I think it was Ginger Rogers who said, "Water can both sustain and engulf a ship."

DROB: I remember Rudyard Kipling's immortal words, "Nobody is always wrong. Even a stopped clock is right twice a day."

WEBSTER: I have tried to live by the words of Henry Morgan, who said, "Put your money where your mouth is."

DROB: He's a good singer, too.

WEBSTER: I think our time is about up. As you know, this program, *Wisdom of the Ages*, is a copyrighted feature and cannot be rebroadcast without the express consent of the now-defunct Continental League.

James Thurber

"He knows all about art,
but he doesn't know
what he likes."

The Immortal Hair Trunk

(from A Tramp Abroad, *1880)*

Mark Twain

As Mark Twain toured Europe, in 1878, observing the ladies of his party reverently admiring the old master painters, he was inspired to write "The Immortal Hair Trunk"—"possibly the funniest piece of demolition in the history of art criticism."

The other great work which fascinated me was Bassano's immortal Hair Trunk. This is in the Chamber of the Council of Ten. It is in one of the three forty-foot pictures which decorate the walls of the room. The composition of this picture is beyond praise. The Hair Trunk is not hurled at the stranger's head—so to speak—as the chief feature of an immortal work so often is; no, it is carefully guarded from prominence, it is subordinated, it is restrained, it is most deftly and cleverly held in reserve, it is most cautiously and ingeniously led up to, by the master, and consequently when the spectator reaches it at last, he is taken unawares, he is unprepared, and it bursts upon him with a stupefying surprise.

One is lost in wonder at all the thought and care which this elaborate planning must have cost. A general glance at the picture could never suggest that there was a hair trunk in it; the Hair Trunk is not mentioned in the title even—which is, "Pope Alexander III. and the Doge Ziani, the Conqueror of the Emperor Frederick Barbarossa"; you see, the title is actually utilized to help divert attention from the Trunk; thus, as I say, nothing suggests the presence of the Trunk, by any hint, yet everything studiedly leads up to it, step by step. Let us examine into this, and observe the exquisitely artful artlessness of the plan.

At the extreme left end of the picture are a couple of women, one of them with a child looking over her shoulder at a wounded man sitting with bandaged head on the ground. These people seem needless, but no, they are there for a purpose; one cannot look at them without seeing the gorgeous procession of grandees, bishops, halberdiers, and banner-bearers which is passing along behind them; one cannot see the procession without feeling a curiosity to follow it and learn whither it is going; it leads him to the Pope, in the center of the picture, who is talking with the bonnetless Doge—talking tranquilly, too, although within twelve

166

feet of them is a man beating a drum, and not far from the drummer two persons are blowing horns, and many horsemen are plunging and rioting about—indeed, twenty-two feet of this great work is all a deep and happy holiday serenity and Sunday-school procession, and then we come suddenly upon eleven and one-half feet of turmoil and racket and insubordination. This latter state of things is not an accident, it has its purpose. But for it, one would linger upon the Pope and the Doge, thinking them to be the motive and supreme feature of the picture; whereas one is drawn along, almost unconsciously, to see what the trouble is about. Now at the very *end* of this riot, within four feet of the end of the picture, and full thirty-six feet from the beginning of it, the Hair Trunk bursts with an electrifying suddenness upon the spectator, in all its matchless perfection, and the great master's triumph is sweeping and complete. From that moment no other thing in those forty feet of canvas has any charm; one sees the Hair Trunk, and the Hair Trunk only—and to see it is to worship it. Bassano even placed objects in the immediate vicinity of the Supreme Feature whose pretended purpose was to divert attention from it yet a little longer and thus delay and augment the surprise; for instance, to the right of it he has placed a stooping man with a cap so red that it is sure to hold the eye for a moment—to the left of it, some six feet away, he has placed a red-coated man on an inflated horse, and that coat plucks your eye to that locality the next moment—then, between the Trunk and the red horseman he has intruded a man, naked to his waist, who is carrying a fancy flour-sack on the middle of his back instead of on his shoulder—this admirable feat interests you, of course—keeps you at bay a little longer, like a sock or a jacket thrown to the pursuing wolf—but at last, in spite of all distractions and detentions, the eye of even the most dull and heedless spectator is sure to fall upon the World's Masterpiece, and in that moment he totters to his chair or leans upon his guide for support.

Descriptions of such a work as this must necessarily be imperfect, yet they are of value. The top of the Trunk is arched; the arch is a perfect half-circle, in the Roman style of architecture, for in the then rapid decadence of Greek art, the rising influence of Rome was already beginning to be felt in the art of the Republic. The Trunk is bound or bordered with leather all around where the lid joins the main body. Many critics consider this leather too cold in tone; but I consider this its highest merit, since it was evidently made so to emphasize by contrast the impassioned fervor of the hasp. The high lights in this part of the work are cleverly managed, the *motif* is admirably subordinated to the ground tints, and the technique is very fine. The brass nail-heads are in the purest style of the early Renaissance. The strokes, here, are very firm and bold—every nail-head is a portrait. The handle on the end of the Trunk has evidently been retouched—I think, with a piece of chalk—but one can still see the inspiration of the Old Master in the tranquil, almost too tranquil, hang of it. The hair of this Trunk is *real* hair—so to speak—white in patches, brown in patches. The details are finely worked out; the repose proper to hair in a recumbent and inactive attitude is charmingly expressed. There is a feeling about this part of the work which lifts it to the highest altitudes of art; the sense of sordid realism vanishes away—one recognizes that there is *soul* here.

View this Trunk as you will, it is a gem, it is a marvel, it is a miracle. Some of the effects are very daring, approaching even to the boldest flights of the rococo, the sirocco, and the Byzantine schools—yet the master's hand never falters—it moves on, calm, majestic, confident—and, with that art which conceals art, it finally casts over the *tout ensemble*, by mysterious methods of its own, a subtle something which refines, subdues, etherealizes the arid components and endues them with the deep charm and gracious witchery of poesy.

Among the art treasures of Europe there are pictures which approach the Hair Trunk—there are two which may be said to equal it, possibly—but there is none that surpasses it. So perfect is the Hair Trunk that it moves persons who ordinarily have no feeling for art. When an Erie baggagemaster saw it two years ago, he could hardly keep from checking it; and once when a customs inspector was brought into its presence, he gazed upon it in silent rapture for some moments, then slowly and unconsciously placed one hand behind him with the palm uppermost, and got out his chalk with the other. These facts speak for themselves.

Al Ross

How to Understand Music

Robert Benchley

With people having the Very Best Music interpreted for them every Sunday afternoon over the radio by the Very Best Experts, it will soon be so that we can't hear *Turkey in the Straw* without reading a meaning into it. With so much attention being paid to *leitmotifs* and the inner significance of what the bassoons are saying, it would not be surprising if, after a while, we forgot to beat time. And if you don't beat time, where is your music?

I would like to take up this afternoon an analysis of Bach's *(Carry Me Back to Old Virginny)* symphonic tschaikovski in C minor, one of the loveliest, and, at the same time, one of the most difficult exercises for three-and-a-half fingers ever written. I may have to stop and lie down every few minutes during my interpretation, it is so exciting. You may do as you like while I am lying down.

In the first place, I must tell you that the modern works of Schön-berg, although considerably incomprehensible to the normal ear (that is, an ear which adheres rather closely to the head and *looks* like an ear) are, in reality, quite significant to those who are on the inside. This includes Schönberg himself, his father, and a young man in whom he confides while dazed. What you think are random noises made by the musicians falling over forward on their instruments, are, when you understand them, really steps in a great, moving story—the Story of the Traveling Salesman who came to the Farmhouse. If you have heard it, try to stop me.

We first have the introduction by the wood-winds, in which you will detect the approach of summer, the bassoons indicating the burst-ing buds (summer and spring came together this year, almost before we were aware of it) and the brasses carrying the idea of winter disappear-ing, defeated and ashamed, around the corner. Summer approaches (in those sections where you hear the "tum-tiddy-ump-ump-tum-tiddy-ump-ump." Remember?) and then, taking one look around, decides that the whole thing is hardly worth while, and goes back into its hole—a new and not entirely satisfactory union of the groundhog tradition with that of the equinox. This, however, ends the first movement, much to the relief of everyone.

You will have noticed that during this depicting of the solstice, the wind section has been forming dark colors right and left, all typical of Tschaikovski in his more wood-wind moods. These dark colors, such as purple, green, and sometime W and Y, are very lovely once they are recognized. The difficulty comes in recognizing them, especially with beards on. The call of the clarinet, occurring at intervals during this first movement, is clearly the voice of summer, saying, "Co-boss! Co-boss! Co-boss!" to which the tympani reply, "Rumble-rumble-rumble!" And a very good reply it is, too.

The second movement begins with Strephon (the eternal shep-herd, and something of a bore) dancing up to the hut in which Phyllis is weaving honey, and, by means of a series of descending six-four chords (as in Debussy's *Reflets dans l'eau* which, you will remember, also makes no sense), indicating that he is ready for a romp. Here we hear the dripping coolness of the mountain stream and the jump-jump-jump of the mountain goat, neither of which figures in the story. He is very eager (tar-ra-ty-tar-ra-ty-tar-ra-ty) and says that there is no sense in her being difficult about the thing, for he has everything arranged. At this the oboes go crazy.

I like to think that the two most obvious modulations, the dominant and the subdominant respectively, convey the idea that, whatever it is that Strephon is saying to Phyllis, nobody cares. This would make the whole thing much clearer. The transition from the dominant to the subdominant (or, if you prefer, you may stop over at Chicago for a day and see the bullfights) gives a feeling of adventure, a sort of Old Man River note, which, to me, is most exciting. But then, I am easily excited.

We now come to the third movement, if there is anybody left in the hall. The third movement is the most difficult to understand, as it involves a complete reversal of musical form in which the wood-winds play the brasses, the brasses play the tympani, and the tympani play "drop-the-handkerchief." This makes for confusion, as you may very well guess. But, as confusion is the idea, the composer is sitting pretty and the orchestra has had its exercise. The chief difficulty in this movement lies in keeping the A strings so tuned that they sound like B-flat strings. To this end, small boys are employed to keep turning the pegs down and the room is kept as damp as possible.

It is here that Arthur, a character who has, up until now, taken no part in the composition, appears and, just as at the rise of the sixth in Chopin's *Nocturne in E Flat* one feels a certain elation, tells Strephon that he has already made plans for Phyllis for that evening and will he please get the hell out of here. We feel, in the descent of the fourth, that Strephon is saying "So what?" Any movement in which occurs a rise to the major third suggests conflict (that is, a rise from the key-note to the major third. Get me right on that, please) and a similar rise to the minor third, or, if you happen to own a bit of U. S. Steel, a rise to 56, suggests a possibility of future comfort. All this, however, is beside the point. (Dorothy Angus, of 1455 Granger Drive, Salt Lake City, has just telephoned in to ask "what point?" Any point, Dorothy, any point. When you are older you will understand.)

This brings us to the fourth movement, which we will omit, owing to one of the oboes having clamped his teeth down so hard on his mouthpiece as to make further playing a mockery. I am very sorry about this, as the fourth movement has in it one of my favorite passages—that where Strephon unbuttons his coat.

From now on it is anybody's game. The A minor prelude, with its persistent chromatic descent, conflicts with the *andante sostenuto*, where the strings take the melody in bars 7 and 8, and the undeniably witty theme is carried on to its logical conclusion in bars 28 and 30, where the pay-off comes when the man tells his wife that he was in the pantry all the time. I nearly die at this every time that I hear it. Unfortunately, I don't hear it often enough, or long enough at a time.

This, in a way, brings to a close our little analysis of whatever it was we were analyzing. If I have made music a little more difficult for you to like, if I have brought confusion into your ear and complication into your taste, I shall be happy in the thought. The next time you hear a symphony, I trust that you will stop all this silly sitting back and taking it for what it is worth to your ear-drums to your emotions, and will put on your thinking caps and try to figure out just what the composer meant when he wrote it. Then perhaps you will write and tell the composer.

1776 and All That.
The First Memorable History of America

Caryl Brahms and Ned Sherrin

Editor's Note: In 1931 there appeared the first truly memorable history of England entitled 1066 and All That *by Walter C. Sellar and Robert J. Yeatman. Some years later, Richard Armour, an American, applied the same techniques to American history in* It All Started with Columbus. *This effort turned out to be somewhat less than truly memorable because, appearing as it did years before the Bicentennial, the book confronted a public disinclined either to remember or disremember American history. That has now changed, and at this opportune moment two British writers have come forward with their version of our past. Memorable it is.*

"History is not what you thought. It is what you can remember."
Sellar and Yeatman

ERRATA

for "Coronaries" read "Colonies" throughout
for "Presidents" read "Precedents" throughout
for "Precedents" read "Presidents" throughout

Immigrants

SPANISH

The first date in American History is 1492. In that year Christopher Columbus sailed from Cadith in Thpain. The Portuguese were good at sailing left to India. Chrithtopher Columbuth turned right and was the first person to use the American phrase "Right on!"

ITALIAN

The next memorable immigrants to discover America (which was still known as India at the time, quite erroneously, although the people there were known as Indians, quite correctly) were Cabot and son, who founded the Cabot Lodge in Boston. A memorable Italian immigrant was Amerigo Vespucci. As the Indians could not pronounce his name properly, America became known as Ameriga, a quaint practice still observed by Puerto Ricans in their traditional songs, e.g., "Ev'rything free in Ameriga,/For a small fee in Ameriga!"

Unlike later immigrants, all these returned to Europe as soon as possible, which was a good thing.

ENGLISH

The first English immigrants sailed to Virginia. England was top nation at the time and did not want to be left out if gold, tobacco and potatoes were being handed out.

The English soon took over New Amsterdam from the first Dutch immigrants, renaming it New York. They then expanded greedily, inaugurating the well-known American sentiment, "I'll take Manhattan, the Bronx, and Staten Island too."

The local Indians in New York were known as the Algonquin because they were the wittiest and most sophisticated. They invited the

English immigrants to their Algonquin Hotel where they smoked Peace Pipes round a Round Table, a custom they copied from King Arthur. (This practice would be revived much later by John F. Kennedy, who called it Camelot.)

THE PURITANS

The Puritans, so called because to the pure all things are impure, landed on Plymouth Rock by mistake. They sailed in the memorable ship **Mayflower,** and as soon as they saw land they had a Coronary. As they did not like people to have a good time, New England was the perfect place for them. Had they landed in Virginia as they intended, they would have been sitting in the sun and smoking tobacco for the rest of their lives.

In New England they found freezing-cold weather, utter starvation, ferocious Indians and dangerous diseases. A year later, when half of them were dead, they simply had to thank someone so they ate Thanksgiving Dinner. Every year since then Americans have eaten too much on Thanksgiving Day and indulged for weeks afterward in a corrective treatment known as cold turkey.

THE QUAKERS

The Quakers were even purer than the Puritans. They were led by William Penn, whose father was owed £80,000 by Bonnie King Charlie II, who preferred to hand over a few acres of barren, savage-infested wasteland rather than hard cash. The name of this Coronary was quickly expanded to Pennsylvania because the Quakers were too embarrassed to tell their Friends that they lived in the Pen. New arrivals from the Old Country left New York from the Pennsylvania Station at a quarter to four and by the time they read a magazine they were in Baltimore.

THE FRENCH

Traditionally a sneaky nation, France avoided open confrontation with other immigrants for many years. King Louis XIV, known as the Son King because his mother used to introduce him proudly as "My son, the king," sent La Salle down the Mississippi to found a chain of French restaurants and sell onions to them. He improved on the traditional French notice, "Le patron mange ici," by displaying a sign which read "La Salle à Manger."

THE BOSTON TAXI PROBLEM

As soon as King George III went mad (and became known affectionately as Bonkers Hill) the immigrant population of America, especially the Poles and the Irish, insisted on being ruled by him and not by the Mother of Parliaments, which was comparatively sane.

Americans especially disliked the way Parliament insisted that the English should take all the American taxis. The English used them to carry tea, sugar and stamps around Boston and they were known as tea taxis, sugar taxis and stamp taxis. The famous Adams Brothers, Sam and John, uttered a memorable motto, "No taxis without representation," which meant that you could not take a taxi unless you had a vote.

THE BOSTON TEA PARTY

In addition to boycotting taxis, the Bostonians now started not drinking tea. They changed to coffee because of the Five Intolerable Acts of the English which were:

1. Drinking tea noisily.
2. Pouring tea into the saucer and blowing on it to cool it.
3. Drinking tea from the saucer.
4. Putting in the milk before the tea.
5. Using tea bags.

Rather than countenance this sort of behavior, Bostonians threw all the tea bags they could lay their hands on into Boston Harbor. They came to the Party dressed up as Indians from head to foot (the costumes having been rented from the Cabot Lodge).

THE REVOLTING CORONARIES

The English, who had always been keen on manners (apart from their appalling habits when drinking tea), sent an army to teach the Americans etiquette. George III, in a lucid moment, dispatched the English general John Burgoyne (nicknamed the Devil's Disciple by George Bernard Shaw), who fired a loud revolver on Lexington Avenue. This was memorable as the shot heard around the world.

GEORGE WASHINGTON

George Washington appeared on nationwide television and confessed to his wife, Martha, that he had chopped down her favorite cherry tree.

He took full responsibility and apologized to the cherry tree. As a result he was made Commander in Chief of the Coronial Army with a good chance of becoming Precedent, thus setting a President for never telling a lie. His next decision was to be painted crossing the Delaware on the way to Martha's Vineyard.

THE STARS AND STRIPES

These had not yet been invented but that did not stop George Washington from being painted carrying them. They were therefore memorable for being memorable even before they existed.

THE DECLARATION OF INDEPENDENCE, 1776

This is the second memorable date in American History. Composed at a meeting of the Thirteen Coronaries in Philadelphia, the Declaration, like most examples of collaborative writing, was not very accurate. It was dictated by Thomas Jefferson to his secretary, Liberty Belle, and it was full of un-English sentiments. This was indeed the Birth of a Nation and the French sent a General Layette (blue with stars for a boy and pink with stripes for a girl).

REDSKINS AND REDCOATS AND REDSOX

As the Americans refused to fight more than a few miles from their homes, General Washington had a distinct advantage over the British because he was always the home team, while they were always playing away.

Contributory factors to the British defeat were:

1. **A body of American soldiers called Minute Men.** Other history books assert that this was on account of their ability to be ready at a moment's notice. But this is a misconception. They were in fact exceedingly small, as is borne out by the correct pronunciation of the word "Minute." Under the command of their general, Tom Thumb, they showed extreme bravery.
2. **The extreme cold,** particularly at Valley Forge, encouraged the Americans to fight twice as hard to keep warm and cure their bleeding feet which turned their socks red (Redsox).
3. **Benjamin Franklin,** who was ninety-three, flattered the French by learning their language and thus persuaded France to Join In. As a result Holland, Spain, and sundry Poles and

Germans Joined In as well without Franklin having to learn Dutch, Spanish, Polish or German, which would have taken Too Long.

4. **American naval supremacy.** This was achieved partly by the French and Spanish and partly by American privateers, a large fleet, mainly commanded by the Jones family, John, Paul, and Lorenzo.

5. **The large number of camp followers or "vivandières"** who were the mistresses of the revolutionary troops, called Muffled Whores by Paul Revere. They had scarlet letters embroidered on their blouses and their illegitimate offspring were known as Daughters of the Revolution, a formidable race.

6. **The drunken behavior of the British commander, Cornwallis,** made memorable by Americans in the folk song "Cornwallis as high as an elephant's eye."

THE OUTBREAK OF PEACE

One of Washington's problems was combining Thirteen States, all of which had different laws. For instance, you couldn't chop your mamma up in Massachusetts, whereas in New York it was practically expected of you.

So Washington called Representatives of all Thirteen States to Philadelphia during a particularly long hot summer and insisted that they become United before he would allow them to go back to the beach.

THOMAS JEFFERSON

After George Washington got bored with being Precedent, John Adams, one of the Boston taxi boycotters, succeeded him. He was followed by Thomas Jefferson, who liked domes and played the cello.

At about this time Alexander Hamilton founded the Banks of the Wabash and was subsequently shot by Aaron Burr, whose checks were always bouncing.

The Banks of the Ohio River were reached by settlers who crossed a mountain range called, of all appellations, the Appellations. Once they had reached the river they sang, "Hi-o, away we go, floating down to Ohio." As they trekked west they sang, "Heigh-ho, heigh-ho, it's off to work we go!" After they had been attacked by Indians, they changed their tune to "Why, o why, o why-o? Why did we ever leave Ohio?"

THE LOUISIANA PURCHASE

Jefferson's memorable innovation was his Nonintercourse Law which was frequently broken especially by English and French sailors. Since this privilege was particularly important to the French (a romantic people), Napoleon agreed to let Jefferson have Louisiana if his sailors could have intercourse.

The English, who were less used to paying for their pleasures than the sophisticated French, went on fighting for them and lost the War of 1812. This is not a memorable date but the war did take place in that year and no one could think of a better name. The most memorable battle was won by Commodore Perry, who overturned the English boats on Lake Erie. This was called the Battle of Tip a Canoe.

A BETTER BUY

After Jefferson came Dolly Madison, who was a good thing. Soon after buying Louisiana from the French, America bought Miami, Florida, the land south of the Blue Rinse Mountains, from the Spanish who did not want to grow old gracefully and certainly not expensively. The price was Five Million Dollars, paid by James Monroe, M.D., who was more memorable for his doctorin' than for his statesmanship.

TEXAS AND MEXICO

By now the Americans were in love with the Idea of Moving West, especially the older men who stayed at home and urged the young men to go. Some Americans infiltrated Mexico and Texas, pretending to be missionaries. However, their real motive was to find the famous Tequila mines, which were halfway between Guacamole and Avocado. When the Mexican Poncho (as their general was called), Tacos Tortillas, discovered the plot he attacked Davy Crocker, the American missionary leader. Crocker was memorable for his habits (including a coonskin hat), his prayer, Praise the Lord and Pass the Ammunition, and his recipe for Davy Crocker cake mix. Tortillas besieged Crocker and his motley band under the Enchilada Trees on the banks of the Alamo. All the Americans were killed and General Sam Houston rode to revenge them. When he succeeded, Houston, Texas, was named after him. The conquest of Texas (including the capture of Tacos Tortillas, his henchmen Pepe le Moko and Speedy Gonzales, and his girl friend Cilli con Carne) was eventually a disappointment as the famous Tequila mines turned out to be nothing more than oil wells and although you can get filthy rich on oil you can't get very drunk which is unfortunate because in Texas what you want to do most is to forget where you are.

INDIANS

As they trekked westward, all the Yankees paid the Indians was a few beads and promises, promises. The Indians felt cheated and gave each other memorable names like Black Look, Red Face, Dodge City, Wounded Knee (but not Blue Jokes, which came later).

When calling one another names did not pay dividends, the Indians tried holding up travelers on the Appellation Trail, the Oregon Trail, the Overland Trail as well as as on the Freedom Train and the Dean Acheson, Topeka and the Santa Fe Train.

THE ARTS

A proud developing country like America needed its own school of literature. Two memorable early writers were J. Anymore Cooper, a Mohican Indian, and Rip Van Winkle, who wrote **Washington Irving,** a novel about a distinguished author who sent his readers to sleep for a hundred years.

These two men were an inspiration to a whole school of Americans who were memorable because for them writing was their middle name, e.g., Ralph Writing Emerson, Henry Writing Longfellow, John Writing Whittier, Oliver Writing Holmes, James Writing Lowell and Edgar Writing Poe.

THE UN-CIVIL WAR

The next American war was called the Un-Civil War because the two sides were so rude to one another. The main reason for the war was to decide whether Abe Lincoln or Jeff Davis should be Precedent. Lincoln, who loved pancakes and used too much syrup and was thus known as having been born in a log cabin, refused to share the White House with Davis because he said the house would be divided within itself and he could not stand it. Helped by their developing sense of history, the American people chose Honest Abe. Time has shown this to be the correct decision.

Contributory reasons for the war were:

1. **Slavery.** Many Southern whites had black uncles with names like Uncle Tom and Uncle Remus. Some of them also had

black sons and daughters, but they preferred not to acknowl-
edge them as they found it compromising. This was called the
Missouri Compromise. It did not last long.
2. The need to find a plot for **Gone with the Wind.**

The war lasted four years but there were not many memorable battles, such as:

1. **The Battle of Harper's Bizarre.** After this battle, John Brown's
   body lay a-moldering in the grave, but his soul went marchin'
   on. This terrified the South.
2. **The Battle of Re-Run.**
3. **The Battles of the Burgs.**
   a) Vicksburg
   b) Petersburg
   c) Hamburg
   d) Cheeseburg
   e) Fredericksburg
   f) J. Paul Gettysburg

The proportion of Generals to battles was quite high:
Ulysses S. Grant commanded the North. The "S" was to distinguish him from Ulysses P. Grant, who was a nonentity.

The Southern Commander was called **Robert E. Lee** to distinguish
him from Robert F. Lee, who was also unmemorable but who never kept
anyone waiting. People were always **waiting** for Robert E. Lee.

General Sherman was memorable for marching through Georgia
from Atlanta to the sea, leading his troops in community singing.

General J. "Stonewall" Jackson played for the South and was
memorable for having a thing about older women, which led the desperate northern heroine Barbara Frietchie to throw herself at him: "Kiss,
if you must, this old grey head. But spare your country's flag," she said
hopefully.

The war was completed at Hippopotomox when Robert E. Lee
offered his sword to Ulysses S. Grant who suggested that he go and turn
it into a plowshare. Peace broke out and everyone was civil to everyone
again.

NOTE: The Un-Civil War was the last really memorable war that
America entered at the beginning.

PEACE

After the war was over, things went with a bang. Lincoln was assassinated. He had gone to the theater and an actor called John Wilkes Booth, knowing Abe's reputation for honesty, and fearing that he might discuss his performance, shot him.

From that moment things did not go According to Plan. Lincoln's successor was Andrew Johnson (whose hundred-year-old record as the only Precedent to be threatened with impeachment has recently been broken). Johnson's problem was that the South wanted to call the slaves free and treat them like slaves while the North wanted to call the South enemies and treat them abominably.

KU KLUX KLUNG FU

This was a Korrupt, Kriminal Konspiracy to Keep the South Kountry divided into 1st Klass Kitizens and 2nd Klass Kitizens. Its members had no humanity and no dress sense.

CONSOLIDATION

By now America had had enough history to be going on with and started having inventions instead. Things they could not invent they perfected, e.g., millionaires.

Pioneers in various fields included:

1. A forty-nine-year-old miner and his daughter, Clementine, who found gold in them thar Hills.
2. Dale Carnegie, a dour Scot with a will of iron who made one fortune out of steel and another out of a book called **How To Win Friends and Give Influenza to People.**
3. John D. Rockefeller, who bored for oil and started a family which has bored America ever since.
4. Cornelius Vander, who popularized railroads. His publicist came up with the slogan, "Ride on the line that Vander built." Together they changed the family name and the nation's habits.
5. A Mr. Morse, who replaced the Code of the West with one of his own.
6. Everything else was invented by Thomas Edison.

TEDDY (T.R.) ROOSEVELT

After they had invented enough things to be going on with the Americans went back to history. They chose the most energetic man they could think of to make it, Theodore Roosevelt.

Very sensibly he started with a war, which is always surefire for a touch of history. He attacked the Spanish in Cuba because Spain was weak and a long way away and would have preferred to agree to all his demands. However, in the interests of history, Roosevelt was not prepared to take "Yes" for an answer.

WILLIAM HOWARD TAFT, A FAT PRECEDENT

Taft had the unenviable task of following Roosevelt into the White House—very little seemed to happen. Days tended to take a long time.

WOODROW WILSON

Next, Woodrow Wilson won the War to End Wars by fourteen points to nil.

NOSTALGIA

After the War to End Wars history was replaced by Nostalgia, of which there are five sorts: the Twenties, the Thirties, the Forties, the Fifties, and the Sixties.

THE SEVENTIES

These are far too near for history and nearly too near for Nostalgia, although Nostalgia is catching up. People are already becoming nostalgic for Richard Nixon and his Vice-Precedent, Spiro Agnew, who was known as The Greek Bearing Away Gifts. Nixon was memorable as "The Man who could not be trusted to sell you a used Ford"—but in the end he managed it.

If He Scholars, Let Him Go

Ogden Nash

I like to think about that great French critic and historian,
    Hippolyte Adolphe Taine.
I like to think about his great French critical and historical
    brain.
He died in 1893 at the age of sixty-five.
But previously he had been alive.
He wrote many books of outstanding worth,
But this was before his death, although following his birth.
He tried to interpret human culture in terms of outer
    environment,
And he knew exactly what the biographers of Rousseau
    and Shelley and Lord Byron meant.
His great philosophical work, *De l'intelligence,* in which
    he connected physiology with psychology, was written
    after meeting a girl named Lola,
And greatly influenced the pens of Flaubert,
    de Maupassant, and Zola.
He did much to establish positivism in France,
And his famous *History of English Literature* was written
    on purpose and not by chance.
Yes, Hippolyte Adolphe Taine may have been only five
    foot three, but he was a scholar of the most discerning;
Whereas his oafish brother Casimir, although he stood six
    foot seven in his bobby-socks, couldn't spell C-H-A-T,
    cat, and was pointed at as the long Taine that had no
    learning.

"Well, today I begin my wonderfully perceptive and cogent book, abounding in brilliant insights—with ninety-six superb full-color illustrations. Fourteen-ninety-five to January. Twenty dollars thereafter."

"So this is the hundred-thousand-dollar Wilson P. Donovan Chair of History!"

James Thurber

"He doesn't know anything except facts."

The Truth about History

Roy Blount, Jr.

I guess you saw the headlines: SO YOU SWALLOWED GEORGE'S WOODEN TEETH? GET THEM OUT OF YOUR HEAD—DENTAL HISTORIAN. There is no way, historians now agree, that George Washington could have had wooden teeth.

Okay? First the cherry tree, now the teeth. Another old chestnut tossed onto the fire by the spoilsport, or "No, Virginia," school of historiography.

The trouble with historians, they don't like a good story. Or a good line. "You know what Sherman said . . . ," you begin to say, and they interrupt: Sherman didn't really say "War is hell." Actually he said either "Well, well" or "Well, hell"; there is no telling what he had on his mind. And Babe Ruth didn't really call his shot in the 1932 World Series. He was actually signaling to a vendor in the bleachers for a frank. Several years ago, I remember, a couple of French historians declared that there was no Joan of Arc. Never was one. Best just forget her.

We all know what prompts these disclosures. Some historian starts telling his class about Joan of Arc. "This morning we take up the story of a simple shepherd girl who . . ."

"Oh, no," the class groans. (Because they are all jaded sophomores.) "Not that again."

"Well, not a word of it is true," the historian says, hastily; and then he begins to improvise.

It is easy to tear things down, History! What are you going to give us to take their place? If Joan of Arc wasn't a simple shepherd girl who had visions and led the French against the English at Orléans and went on to be burned at the stake and played by Ingrid Bergman and Jean Seberg, then who was?

No one, according to these French historians. The whole thing was a publicity stunt. Joan was actually a girl of royal blood who was brought out at Orléans for morale purposes. She wasn't executed at all. She later married someone named Robert.

What a charming tale. What are we supposed to do now, when Joan of Arc's birthday comes around? Reflect on what a kick it must have given Joan and Robert (pronounced "Ro-bair") in their declining years to sit at home and chuckle about all the crazy legends a girl can start if she will play along with the military?

When that story came out, it didn't just spoil Joan of Arc for me. It spoiled history as a whole. I threw up my hands. I became willing to accept that nothing ever happened in ages past that couldn't be reduced to simple administrative terms, or worse.

Rasputin was just a minor Russian official who had a little something going with the tsarina, and she worked up a disguise for him that everyone but the tsar saw through from the beginning. He died in a boating accident.

Mohandas Gandhi was actually a portly behind-the-scenes type who dressed, mutatis mutandis, like Colonel Tom Parker, except that—in the curious belief that it would impress the English—he carried a shillelagh. For photo opportunities, of course, there were the several interchangeable, wizened stand-ins.

Cleopatra was a man, and not even a very prepossessing one, who, as a matter of fact, was immune, because of the quantities of garlic he ate, to asp venom.

The historical Charlemagne wasn't a man but rather a primitive committee.

Vincent van Gogh never set foot outside the town of Bort-les-Orgues, France, and his mother painted all of his best things. The

famous mailed decapitated ear was a figment of the public-relations
firm engaged by van Gogh's dealer—himself not an imaginative per-
son. Actually, van Gogh never had a mistress, and took both of his ears
to the grave. Indeed, the only reason that the outsized woolen cap his
mother made him wear never slipped completely down over his eyes
was that his ears were always so large and firmly attached. He never
had any moods, incidentally, to speak of.

Romulus and Remus were no more suckled by a wolf than you
and I and Henry Steele Commager were. They were suckered on a
wharf.

Then I snapped back out of italics and started to think: "History,
wait a minute. You owe me more than that." I can understand why historians resist being doomed to repeat themselves, but why don't they
try making historical figures *more* numinous, instead of less? That's
what the average person would do, if he or she had the chance to be a
historian.

Millard Fillmore. If the truth be told, Fillmore would roll into the
Oval Office about 9:45 in the morning after being up half the night playing Whigs and Masons with Henry Clay. Whigs and Masons was a wrestling game. It is said—even if not by historians—that Fillmore would
summon Alex H. H. Stuart, his secretary of the interior, to tie his (Fillmore's) right foot to his (again, Fillmore's) left arm and then he (yes,
Fillmore) would still throw Clay four times in five.[1] Of Whigs and
Masons, Fillmore was the Magic Johnson.

But after getting into the office a couple of hours behind everybody else—and you know the secretaries are all grumbling because why
should they be at their desks hitting it bright and early when the president was out till all hours horsing around—Fillmore would immediately put everyone in a dynamic, progressive frame of mind by telling
how he bested legendary riverman Mike Fink in a gator-cowing contest.
(Fillmore, in only a breechclout, once cowed a twelve-hundred-pound
gator just by going "Well?" at it. This has been *documented*.)

Then Fillmore would make a statement of national purpose so
clearly put and deeply felt that all those who heard him, however small
their roles in the government's workings, felt lifted and involved.
"This," Filmore's listeners felt, "is why we must hold our great plural

---

[1]Ironically enough quite an extrovert, Stuart was a real pistol in his own right
whose mother, a seeress, had imparted unto him the power literally to contain multitudes.
It is from his middle initials alone that we derive not only Hubert Humphrey and Herbert
Hoover but also Horace Heidt.

union together, and never let it succumb to meanness or fixed ideas. And here," the White House staff and any average citizens on hand would reflect, "is one who is larger than we, yet one of us."

At which juncture Clay might pop in, tousled from the night before. (No matter what *he* had been up to, Fillmore always arrived for business looking cleaner than the Board of Health.) Fillmore would wink at Clay's stout, scuffed Kentucky brogans and lighten the moment with a remark about "feet of Clay," which Clay himself—being possessed of a firm yet unoppressive sense of his own authenticity—would take in good spirits.

Another thing about Fillmore. He never secretly taped his telephone conversations.

If Grant Had Been Drinking at Appomattox

James Thurber

The morning of the ninth of April, 1865, dawned beautifully. General Meade was up with the first streaks of crimson in the eastern sky. General Hooker and General Burnside were up, and had breakfasted, by a quarter after eight. The day continued beautiful. It drew on toward eleven o'clock. General Ulysses S. Grant was still not up. He was asleep in his famous old navy hammock, swung high above the floor of his headquarters' bedroom. Headquarters was distressingly disarranged: papers were strewn on the floor; confidential notes from spies scurried here and there in the breeze from an open window; the dregs of an overturned bottle of wine flowed pinkly across an important military map.

Corporal Shultz, of the Sixty-fifth Ohio Volunteer Infantry, aide to General Grant, came into the outer room, looked around him, and sighed. He entered the bedroom and shook the General's hammock roughly. General Ulysses S. Grant opened one eye.

"Pardon, sir," said Corporal Shultz, "but this is the day of surrender. You ought to be up, sir."

"Don't swing me," said Grant, sharply, for his aide was making the hammock sway gently. "I feel terrible," he added, and he turned over and closed his eye again.

"General Lee will be here any minute now," said the Corporal firmly, swinging the hammock again.

"Will you cut that out?" roared Grant. "D'ya want to make me sick, or what?" Shultz clicked his heels and saluted. "What's he coming here for?" asked the General.

"This is the day of surrender, sir," said Shultz. Grant grunted bitterly.

"Three hundred and fifty generals in the Northern armies," said Grant, "and he has to come to *me* about this. What time is it?"

"You're the Commander-in-Chief, that's why," said Corporal Shultz. "It's eleven twenty-five, sir."

"Don't be crazy," said Grant. "Lincoln is the Commander-in-Chief. Nobody in the history of the world ever surrendered before lunch. Doesn't he know that an army surrenders on its stomach?" He pulled a blanket up over his head and settled himself again.

"The generals of the Confederacy will be here any minute now," said the Corporal. "You really ought to be up, sir."

Grant stretched his arms above his head and yawned.

"All right, all right," he said. He rose to a sitting position and stared about the room. "This place looks awful," he growled.

"You must have had quite a time of it last night, sir," ventured Shultz.

"Yeh," said General Grant, looking around for his clothes. "I was wrassling some general. Some general with a beard."

Shultz helped the commander of the Northern armies in the field to find his clothes.

"Where's my other sock?" demanded Grant. Shultz began to look around for it. The General walked uncertainly to a table and poured a drink from a bottle.

"I don't think it wise to drink, sir," said Shultz.

"Nev' mind about me," said Grant, helping himself to a second, "I can take it or let it alone. Didn' ya ever hear the story about the fella went to Lincoln to complain about me drinking too much? 'So-and-So says Grant drinks too much,' this fella said. 'So-and-So is a fool,' said Lincoln. So this fella went to What's-His-Name and told him what Lincoln said and he came roarin' to Lincoln about it. 'Did you tell So-and-

So I was a fool?' he said. 'No,' said Lincoln, 'I thought he knew it.'" The General smiled, reminiscently, and had another drink. "*That's* how I stand with Lincoln," he said, proudly.

The soft thudding sound of horses' hooves came through the open window. Shultz hurriedly walked over and looked out.

"Hoof steps," said Grant, with a curious chortle.

"It is General Lee and his staff," said Shultz.

"Show him in," said the General, taking another drink. "And see what the boys in the back room will have."

Shultz walked smartly over to the door, opened it, saluted, and stood aside. General Lee, dignified against the blue of the April sky, magnificent in his dress uniform, stood for a moment framed in the doorway. He walked in, followed by his staff. They bowed, and stood silent. General Grant stared at them. He only had one boot on and his jacket was unbuttoned.

"I know who you are," said Grant. "You're Robert Browning, the poet."

"This is General Robert E. Lee," said one of his staff, coldly.

"Oh," said Grant. "I thought he was Robert Browning. He certainly looks like Robert Browning. There was a poet for you, Lee: Browning. Did ja ever read 'How They Brought the Good News from Ghent to Aix'? "Up Derek, to saddle, up Derek, away; up Dunder, up Blitzen, up Prancer, up Dancer, up Bouncer, up Vixen, up—'"

"Shall we proceed at once to the matter in hand?" asked General Lee, his eyes disdainfully taking in the disordered room.

"Some of the boys was wrassling here last night," explained Grant. "I threw Sherman, or some general a whole lot like Sherman. It was pretty dark." He handed a bottle of Scotch to the commanding officer of the Southern armies, who stood holding it, in amazement and discomfiture. "Get a glass, somebody," said Grant, looking straight at General Longstreet. "Didn't I meet you at Cold Harbor?" he asked. General Longstreet did not answer.

"I should like to have this over with as soon as possible," said Lee. Grant looked vaguely at Shultz, who walked up close to him, frowning.

"The surrender, sir, the surrender," said Corporal Shultz in a whisper.

"Oh sure, sure," said Grant. He took another drink. "All right," he said. "Here we go." Slowly, sadly, he unbuckled his sword. Then he handed it to the astonished Lee. "There you are, General," said Grant. "We dam' near licked you. If I'd been feeling better we *would* of licked you."

The Universe and the Philosopher

Don Marquis

The Universe and the Philosopher sat and looked at each other satirically. . . .

"You know so many things about me that aren't true!" said the Universe to the Philosopher.

"There are so many things about you that you seem to be unconscious of," said the Philosopher to the Universe.

*　　*　　*

"I contain a number of things that I am trying to forget," said the Universe.

"Such as what?" asked the Philosopher.

"Such as Philosophers," said the Universe.

"You are wrong," said the Philosopher to the Universe, "for it is only by working up the most important part of yourself into the form of Philosophers that you get a product capable of understanding you at all."

"Suppose," said the Universe, "that I don't care about being understood. Suppose that I care more about being?"

"You are wrong again, then," said the Philosopher. "For being that is not conscious being can scarcely be called being at all."

*　　*　　*

"You Philosophers always were able to get the better of me in argument," smiled the Universe, "and I think that is one thing that is the matter with you."

"If you object to our intellects," said the Philosopher, "we can only reply that we got them, as well as everything else, from you."

"That should make you more humble," said the Universe. "If I quit letting you have intellect, where would you be then?"

"Where would *you* be," asked the Philosopher, "if you quit letting me have intellect? If I quit thinking you out as you are, and must be, you would cease to exist as you are; for I am a part of you; and if I were to change, your total effect would be changed also." . . . Then the Philosopher reflected a long moment, and, warming to his work, put over

191

this one: "The greater part of you, for all I know, exists in my brain anyhow; and if I should cease to think of that part, that part would cease to be."

                    *   *   *

"You make me feel so helpless, somehow!" complained the Universe, hypocritically. "I beg your pardon for asking you to be humble a moment ago. . . . I see now, very plainly, that it is I who should be more humble in your presence."

"I am glad," said the Philosopher, "that we have been able to arrive at something like an understanding."

"Understanding!" echoed the Universe. "It's *so* important, isn't it?" . . . And then: "Come! We have argued enough for one day! There is something terribly fatiguing to me about Profound Thought. Can't we just lie down in the shade the rest of the afternoon and watch the wheels go round?"

"Watch the wheels go round?" puzzled the Philosopher.

"Uh-huh! . . . the planets and solar systems, and stuff like that. The nicest thing in life, as I have lived it, is just to lie about and drowse and watch the wheels go round. . . . I made nearly everything spherical in the beginning so it would roll when I kicked it. I'd rather play than think."

"You are a Low Brow!" said the Philosopher.

"Uh-huh," said the Universe. "At times. . . . I suppose that's the reason some of the children neglect the old parent these days."

                    *   *   *

And then, after a nap, during which the Philosopher contemplated the Universe with a tinge of superiority, the Universe rumbled sleepily: "*I* know what I am going to do with this Intellect Stuff. I'm going to take it away from you Philosophers and give it to fish or trees or something of that sort!"

"How frightfully grotesque!" said the Philosopher, turning pale.

"Or to giraffes," continued the Universe. "Giraffes are naturally dignified. And they aren't meddlesome. I'd like to see a whole thousand of giraffes walking along in a row, with their heads in the air, thinking, thinking, thinking . . . with tail coats and hornrimmed goggles."

                    *   *   *

"You are absurd!" cried the Philosopher.

"Uh-huh," said the Universe. And reaching over, the Universe picked up the Philosopher, not ungently, by the scruff of the neck, tossed him into the air, caught him tenderly as he came down, spun him around, and set him right side up on the ground.

"You," said the Universe, grinning at the breathless Philosopher pleasantly, "are sort of funny yourself, sometimes!"

My Philosophy

Woody Allen

The development of my philosophy came about as follows: My wife, inviting me to sample her very first soufflé, accidentally dropped a spoonful of it on my foot, fracturing several small bones. Doctors were called in, X-rays taken and examined, and I was ordered to bed for a month. During this convalescence, I turned to the works of some of Western society's most formidable thinkers—a stack of books I had laid aside for just such an eventuality. Scorning chronological order, I began with Kierkegaard and Sartre, then moved quickly to Spinoza, Hume, Kafka, and Camus. I was not bored, as I had feared I might be; rather, I found myself fascinated by the alacrity with which these great minds unflinchingly attacked morality, art, ethics, life, and death. I remember my reaction to a typically luminous observation of Kierkegaard's: "Such a relation which relates itself to its own self (that is to say, a self) must either have constituted itself or have been constituted by another." The concept brought tears to my eyes. My word, I thought, to be that clever! (I'm a man who has trouble writing two meaningful sentences on "My Day at the Zoo.") True, the passage was totally incomprehensible to me, but what of it as long as Kierkegaard was having fun? Suddenly confident that metaphysics was the work I had always been meant to do, I took up my pen and began at once to jot down the first of my own musings. The work proceeded apace, and in a mere two afternoons—with time out for dozing and trying to get the two little BBs into the eyes of the bear—I had completed the philosophical work that I am hoping will not be uncovered until after my death, or until the year 3000 (whichever comes first), and which I modestly believe will assure me a place of reverence among history's weightiest thinkers. Here is but a small sample of the main body of intellectual treasure that I leave for posterity, or until the cleaning woman comes.

I. Critique of Pure Dread

In formulating any philosophy, the first consideration must always be: What can we know? That is, what can we be sure we know, or sure that we know we knew it, if indeed it is at all knowable. Or have we simply forgotten it and are too embarrassed to say anything? Descartes hinted at the problem when he wrote, "My mind can never know my body, although it has become quite friendly with my legs." By "knowable," incidentally, I do not mean that which can be known by perception of the senses, or that which can be grasped by the mind, but more that which can be said to be Known or to possess a Knownness or Knowability, or at least something you can mention to a friend.

Can we actually "know" the universe? My God, it's hard enough finding your way around in Chinatown. The point, however, is: Is there anything out there? And why? And must they be so noisy? Finally, there can be no doubt that the one characteristic of "reality" is that it lacks essence. That is not to say it has no essence, but merely lacks it. (The reality I speak of here is the same one Hobbes described, but a little smaller.) Therefore the Cartesian dictum "I think, therefore I am" might be better expressed "Hey, there goes Edna with a saxophone!" So, then, to know a substance or an idea we must doubt it, and thus, doubting it, come to perceive the qualities it possesses in its finite state, which are truly "in the thing itself," or "of the thing itself," or of something or nothing. If this is clear, we can leave epistemology for the moment.

II. Eschatological Dialectics As a Means of Coping with Shingles

We can say that the universe consists of a substance, and this substance we will call "atoms," or else we will call it "monads." Democritus called it atoms. Leibnitz called it monads. Fortunately, the two men never met, or there would have been a very dull argument. These "particles" were set in motion by some cause or underlying principle, or perhaps something fell someplace. The point is that it's too late to do anything about it now, except possibly to eat plenty of raw fish. This, of course, does not explain why the soul is immortal. Nor does it say anything about an afterlife, or about the feeling my Uncle Sender has that he is being followed by Albanians. The causal relationship between the first principle (i.e., God, or a strong wind) and any teleological concept of being (Being) is, according to Pascal, "so ludicrous that it's not even funny (Funny)." Schopenhauer called this "will," but his physician diagnosed it as hay fever. In his later years, he became embittered by it, or more likely because of his increasing suspicion that he was not Mozart.

III. The Cosmos on Five Dollars a Day

What, then, is "beautiful"? The merging of harmony with the just, or the merging of harmony with something that just sounds like "the just"? Possibly harmony should have been merged with "the crust" and this is what's been giving us our trouble. Truth, to be sure, is beauty— or "the necessary." That is, what is good or possessing the qualities of "the good" results in "truth." If it doesn't, you can bet the thing is not beautiful, although it may still be waterproof. I am beginning to think I was right in the first place and that everything should be merged with the crust. Oh, well.

TWO PARABLES

A man approaches a palace. Its only entrance is guarded by some fierce Huns who will only let men named Julius enter. The man tries to bribe the guards by offering them a year's supply of choice chicken parts. They neither scorn his offer nor accept it, but merely take his nose and twist it till it looks like a Molly screw. The man says it is imperative that he enter the palace because he is bringing the emperor a change of underwear. When the guards still refuse, the man begins to Charleston. They seem to enjoy his dancing but soon become morose over the treatment of the Navajos by the federal government. Out of breath, the man collapses. He dies, never having seen the emperor and owing the Steinway people sixty dollars on a piano he had rented from them in August.

•

I am given a message to deliver to a general. I ride and ride, but the general's headquarters seem to get farther and farther away. Finally, a giant black panther leaps upon me and devours my mind and heart. This puts a terrific crimp in my evening. No matter how hard I try, I cannot catch the general, whom I see running in the distance in his shorts and whispering the word "nutmeg" to his enemies.

APHORISMS

It is impossible to experience one's own death objectively and still carry a tune.

•

The universe is merely a fleeting idea in God's mind—a pretty uncomfortable thought, particularly if you've just made a down payment on a house.

•

Eternal nothingness is O.K. if you're dressed for it.

•

If only Dionysus were alive! Where would he eat?

•

Not only is there no God, but try getting a plumber on weekends.

The Higher Pantheism in a Nutshell

A. C. Swinburne

One, who is not, we see: but one, whom we see not,
   is:
Surely this is not that: but that is assuredly this.

What, and wherefore, and whence? for under is over
  and under:
If thunder could be without lightning, lightning could
  be without thunder.

Doubt is faith in the main: but faith, on the whole,
  is doubt:
We cannot believe by proof: but could we believe
  without?

Why, and whither, and how? for barley and rye are
  not clover:
Neither are straight lines curves: yet over is under
  and over.

Two and two may be four: but four and four are not
  eight:
Fate and God may be twain: but God is the same
  thing as fate.

Ask a man what he thinks, and get from a man what
  he feels:
God, once caught in the fact, shows you a fair pair
  of heels.

Body and spirit are twins: God only knows which is
  which:
The soul squats down in the flesh, like a tinker drunk
  in a ditch.

More is the whole than a part: but half is more than
  the whole:
Clearly, the soul is the body: but is not the body the
  soul?

One and two are not one: but one and nothing is
   two:
Truth can hardly be false, if falsehood cannot be
   true.

Once the mastodon was: pterodactyls were common
   as cocks:
Then the mammoth was God: now is He a prize ox.

Parallels all things are: yet many of these are askew:
You are certainly I: but certainly I am not you.

Springs the rock from the plain, shoots the stream
   from the rock:
Cocks exists for the hen: but hens exist for the cock.

God, whom we see not, is: and God, who is not, we
   see:
Fiddle, we know, is diddle: and diddle, we take it,
   is dee.

The Philosopher and the Oyster

James Thurber

By the sea on a lovely morning strolled a philosopher—one who seeks
a magnificent explanation for his insignificance—and there he came
upon an oyster lying in its shell upon the sand.

"It has no mind to be burdened by doubt," mused the philosopher, "no fingers to work to the bone. It can never say, 'My feet are killing me.' It hears no evil, sees no television, speaks no folly. It has no buttons to come off, no zipper to get caught, no hair or teeth to fall out." The philosopher sighed a deep sight of envy. "It produces a highly lustrous concretion, of great price or priceless," he said, "when a morbid condition obtains in its anatomy, if you could call such an antic, anomalous amorphousness anatomy." The philosopher sighed again and said, "Would that I could wake from delirium with a circlet of diamonds upon my fevered brow. Would, moreover, that my house were my sanctuary, as sound and secure as a safe-deposit vault."

Just then a screaming sea gull swooped out of the sky, picked up the oyster in its claws, carried it high in the air, and let it drop upon a great wet rock, shattering the shell and splattering its occupant. There was no lustrous concretion, of any price whatever, among the debris, for the late oyster had been a very healthy oyster, and, anyway, no oyster ever profited from its pearl.

MORALS: *Count your own blessings, and let your neighbor count his.*
Where there is no television, the people also perish.

The Boring Leading the Bored

Steve Martin

(Reprinted from "Boredom" Magazine)

"Well, I never!" said Mrs. Watkins. The meeting of the College Council on Metaphysics then applauded her and stood up cheering. Of course, some of the old-school existentialists humbugged it, but nevertheless, the response was overwhelmingly positive. Then Mrs. Jenkins shouted over the crowd, "That woman never ceases to amaze me." The logicians and semanticists gloated and looked anxiously over to the metaphysicians to see their reaction to the carefully planted "never ceases" insertion. Mrs. Jenkins obviously had been working for the logicians to arouse insurrection among the three or four Zeno partisans. But suddenly Dr. Walker, who had been a recluse professor for almost twenty years, stood up. With the crowd instantly silenced by his commanding and unexpected rising, he uttered something so incredibly unutterable, so impossible, so unsolvable, that this mass of philosophy started heaving right and left and dying on the spot, blood bursting from their ears in an astounding death agony.

Existentialism: The Inside Story

Delmore Schwartz

Is it not true that the discussion of the meaning of existentialism has been dying down? or at any rate is being taken more and more for granted, like cynicism, optimism, surrealism, alcoholism, and practically all other well-known topics of conversation?

If so, this is a dangerous state of affairs. For as soon as a philosophy is taken for granted, as soon as its meaning is assumed, then it begins to be misunderstood and misinterpreted. Philosophical idealism is a good example. It was once just as fashionable as existentialism and is now generally thought to have to do with those impractical people who believe in ideals and never amount to anything.

I propose a revival of interest in the meaning of existentialism because when everyone asks what something means, the possibilities of misunderstanding are, if not lessened, more controllable. Having studied existentialism in an offhand way since 1935, I become more and more convinced that its meaning can be reduced to the following formulation: *Existentialism means that no one else can take a bath for you.*

This example is suggested by Heidegger, who points out that no one else can die for you. You must die your own death. But the same is true of taking a bath. And I prefer the bath as an example to death because, as Heidegger further observes, no one likes to think very much about death, except indigent undertakers perhaps. Death is for most a distant event, however unpleasant and inevitable.

A bath, however, is a daily affair, at least in America. Thus it is something you have to think about somewhat everyday, and while you are thinking about it, and while, perforce, you are taking a bath, you might just as well be thinking about what existentialism means. Otherwise you will probably just be thinking about yourself, which is narcissism; or about other human beings, which is likely to be malicious, unless you are feeling very good; or worst of all, you may not be thinking at all, which is senseless and a waste of time.

Of course, there are other acts which each human being must perform for himself, such as eating, breathing, sleeping, making love, etc. But taking a bath seems to me the best of the lot because it involves the vital existentialist emphasis on choice: you can choose *not* to take a bath, you can waver in your choice, you can finally decide to take a bath, the whole drama of human freedom can become quite hectic or for that matter quite boring. But eating is hardly a matter of choice, except for the menu itself, nor is breathing which can be done not only without taking thought but while one is quite unconscious. As for making love, taking a bath is a better example because you can keep it clean, simple, free of fixations, perversions, inhibitions, and an overpowering sense of guilt.

Now despite the fact that most of the bathtubs which exist are in America, some Americans are not in the habit of taking baths for granted. I know of one American (formerly an existentialist, by the way) who avoids taking frequent baths because he feels that the taking of a bath is an *extreme situation*. (He is not averse to using existentialist arguments when it suits his torso, though in company he attacks existentialism.) He says that taking a bath is an extreme situation because God knows what may occur to you when you are in the tub; you may decide to drown yourself because existence, as existentialists say, is essentially *absurd*; you may decide to become a narcissist because of the pleasures of the warm and loving water. But there's no use listing all the catastrophes this fellow thinks may occur to anyone in the extreme situation of taking a bath.

So too with the bathtaking of a close friend of mine, who finds the taking of baths a matter of no little thought. He takes two baths a day, but he has to force himself to do so because there are so many other more important things to do (so it seems to him!) or which he feels he ought to do during the time occupied in taking a bath (note how the question of moral value enters at this point). It is a matter for much thought also because he has to decide whether to take a bath or a shower. He is afraid that sooner or later he will break his neck slipping on a cake of soap while taking a shower (which he prefers to a bath), although, on the other hand, he feels that in some ways it is better to take a shower than a bath because then he does not have to wash out the tub for others (*the others* are always important, as Sartre has observed), and in short the taking of baths is not a simple matter for him. Once I visited him while he was taking a shower, and while I was conversing with his wife in their handsome living-room, he kept crying out through the downpour of the shower: "Say, you know it's mighty lonesome in here." He wanted me to visit with him and keep him company (note the *aloneness* of the human situation as depicted by the existentialists), to converse with him. Consequently, after he had shouted his fourth appeal for my company, I had to go in and point out to him that we would have to shout at each other because of the noise of the shower and we shouted at each other often enough for more justifiable reasons.

In the upper class, as is well known, it is customary (I am told by friends who have soared to these circles at times ho, ho!) to take at least two baths a day, while in the lower middle class and working class this is less true, an observation I bring forward to show how important social and economic factors are; or, as the existentialists say, how all being is being-in-the-world, although they seem to think that the social and economic aspects of being-in-the-world are not so important as I am forced to think they are. Of course, some of the existentialists may have changed their minds during the second World War and the recent so-called peace.

The real difficulty in explaining what existentialism means flows from the basis of this philosophy, a basis which can be summarized in the following proposition: *Human beings exist.* They have an existence which is human and thus different from that of stones, trees, animals, cigar store Indians, and numerous human beings who are trying their best not to exist or not to be human.

If you are really human, if you really exist as a human being, you have no need of any explanation of existence or existentialism. In the meantime, the best thing to do is to keep on reading explanations of existentialism and existence.

As for me, I never take baths. Just showers. Takes less time.

Science

Fran Lebowitz

Science is not a pretty thing. It is unpleasantly proportioned, outlandishly attired, and often overeager. What, then, is the appeal of science? What accounts for its popularity? And who gave it its start?

In order to better understand the modern penchant for science it is necessary to take the historical point of view. Upon doing this, one makes the discovery that the further back one goes the less science one is likely to find. And that the science one does encounter is of a consistently higher quality. For example, in studying the science of yesteryear one comes upon such interesting notions as gravity, electricity, and the roundness of the earth—while an examination of more recent phenomena shows a strong trend toward spray cheese, stretch denim, and the Moog synthesizer.

These data unquestionably support my theory that modern science was largely conceived of as an answer to the servant problem and that it is generally practiced by those who lack a flair for conversation.

It is therefore not surprising that only after Abolition did science begin to display its most unsavory features. Inventions and discoveries became progressively less desirable as it became harder and harder to get good help.

Prior to the advent of this unfortunate situation the scientist was chiefly concerned with the theoretical. His needs properly attended to, he quite rightly saw no reason to disturb others by finding a practical application for his newfound knowledge. This resulted in the establishment of schools of thought rather than schools of computer programming. That this was a much pleasanter state of affairs than presently exists is indisputable, and one has only to look around to see that the unseemliness of modern science is basically the product of men whose peevish reactions to household disorder drove them to folly. Even in those cases where a practical touch was indicated one notes a tendency toward excess.

A typical example of this syndrome is Thomas Edison. Edison invented the electric light bulb, the purpose of which was to make it possible for one to read at night. A great and admirable achievement and one that would undoubtedly have earned him a permanent place in the hearts and minds of civilized men had he not then turned around and invented the phonograph. This single act led to the eventual furnishing of small apartments with quadrophonic sound systems, thereby making it impossible for the better element to properly enjoy his *good* invention. If one follows this line of thought to its logical conclusion one clearly sees that almost without exception every displeasing aspect of science is, in one way or another, a hideous corruption of the concept of reading at night. Reading is not a particularly popular pastime—hence the warm welcome the majority of the population has extended to such things as snowmobiles, tape decks, and citizen band radios. That these newer appliances have not entirely taken away the appetite of the public for electric lamps can only be attributed to their unwillingness to let perfectly good empty sangria bottles go to waste.

Scientists are rarely to be counted among the fun people. Awkward at parties, shy with strangers, deficient in irony—they have had no choice but to turn their attention to the close study of everyday objects. They have had ample opportunity to do so and on occasion have been rewarded with gratifying insights.

Thus electricity was the product of Franklin's interest in lightning, the concept of gravity the outcome of Newton's experience with an apple, and the steam engine the result of Watt's observation of a teakettle.

It is only to be expected that people of this sort are not often invited out. After all, a person who might well spend an entire evening staring at a kitchen utensil has little to recommend him as a dinner companion. It is far too risky—particularly if the person in question is moved to share his thoughts with others. Physical laws are not amusing. Mathematical symbols do not readily lend themselves to the double entendre. Chemical properties are seldom cause for levity. These facts make it intolerable for a gathering ever to include more than one scientist. If it is unavoidable, a scientist may be safely invited to dinner providing that he is absolutely the only member of his profession present. More than one scientist at the table is bad luck—not to mention bad taste. Legend has it that the atom was split when a bunch of scientists working late decided to order in a pizza. Indeed a terrifying story and one made all the more chilling when one learns that a number of their colleagues smarting from the snub of being excluded from this impromptu meal spitefully repaired to an all-night diner and invented polyester.

A Philosopher

Sam Walter Foss

Zack Bumstead uster flosserfize
About the ocean and the skies:
An' gab an' gas f'um morn till noon
About the other side the moon;
An' 'bout the natur of the place
Ten miles be-end the end of space.
An' if his wife sh'd ask the crank
Ef he wouldn't kinder try to yank
Hisself out doors an' git some wood
To make her kitchen fire good,
So she c'd bake her beans an' pies,
He'd say, "I've gotter flosserfize."

An' then he'd set an' flosserfize
About the natur an' the size
Of angels' wings, an' think, and gawp,
An' wonder how they made 'em flop.
He'd calkerlate how long a skid
'Twould take to move the sun, he did,
An' if the skid was strong an' prime,
It couldn't be moved to supper time.
An' w'en his wife 'ud ask the lout
Ef he wouldn't kinder waltz about
An' take a rag an' shoo the flies,
He'd say, "I've gotter flosserfize."

An' then he'd set an' flosserfize
'Bout schemes for fencing in the skies,
Then lettin' out the lots to rent
So's he could make an honest cent,
An' ef he'd find it pooty tough
To borry cash fer fencin' stuff?
An' if 'twere best to take his wealth

An' go to Europe for his health,
Or save his cash till he'd enough
To buy some more of fencin' stuff—
Then, ef his wife sh'd ask the gump
Ef he wouldn't kinder try to hump
Hisself to tother side the door
So she c'd come an' sweep the floor,
He'd look at her with mournful eyes,
An' say, "I've gotter flosserfize."

An' so he'd set an' flosserfize
'Bout what it wuz held up the skies,
An' how God made this earthly ball
Jest simply out er nawthin' tall.
An' 'bout the natur, shape an' form
Of nawthin' thet he made it from.
Then, ef his wife sh'd ask the freak
If he wouldn't kinder try to sneak
Out to the barn an' find some aigs,
He'd never move nor lift his laigs
An' never stir nor try to rise
But say, "I've gotter flosserfize."

An' so he'd set an' flosserfize
About the earth an' sea an' skies,
An' scratch his head an' ask the cause
Of w'at there waz before time waz,
An' w'at the universe 'ud do
Bimeby w'en time hed all got through;
An' jest how fur we'd hev to climb
Ef we sh'd travel out er time,
An' ef we'd need w'en we got there
To keep our watches in repair,
Then, ef his wife she'd ask the gawk
Ef he wouldn' kinder try to walk
To where she had the table spread
An' kinder git his stomach fed,
He'd leap for that ar kitchen door
An' say, "W'y didn't you speak afore?"

An' when he'd got his supper et,
He'd set, an' set, an' set, an' set,
An' fold his arms an' shet his eyes,
An' set, an' set, an' flosserfize.

Stevenson

"Whatever it is, it's very, very little"

Mr. Science

Bob Elliott and Ray Goulding

RAY: Now, as a public service paid for by the Philanthropic Council to Make Things Nicer, we invite you to spend another educational session with the idol of the nation's youngsters—Mr. Science. As we look in on the modern, well-equipped laboratory today, we see that little Jimmy Schwab is just arriving to watch Mr. Science perform his latest fascinating experiment.

(Sound: Door slam)

MR. SCIENCE: Oh, hello there, Jimmy. You're just in time to watch me perform my latest fascinating experiment.

JIMMY: Gee willikers, Mr. Science. I'm always fascinated by your fascinating experiments. Which one are you going to perform today?

MR. SCIENCE: Well, Jimmy, today we're going to observe what happens when we boil water right here in the laboratory.

JIMMY: Great day in the morning, Mr. Science! . . . I don't understand what you're talking about.

MR. SCIENCE: Well, it's really not as complicated as it sounds. You see, each chemical property has its own particular temperature point at which it changes from a liquid to a gas. And loosely defined, steam is the form of gaseous vapor that water is converted into when we heat it to 212 degrees.

JIMMY: Holy mackerel, Mr. Science. I don't understand that even worse than what you said the first time.

MR. SCIENCE: Well, don't worry about it, son. I'm sure it'll all become very clear to you after you've observed today's experiment. Now, in order to see what happens when we bring water to the boiling point, we must first prepare our laboratory equipment to heat it to 212 degrees.

JIMMY: Gosh-all hemlock, Mr. Science. What's that piece of laboratory equipment you're lighting with a match?

MR. SCIENCE: This device is called a candle, Jimmy.

JIMMY: A candle! Holy suffering catfish. Wait'll I tell all the kids at school I've seen one of those.

MR. SCIENCE: Now, just try to keep your enthusiasm under control, boy. We still haven't gotten to the most amazing part. Watch what happens when I hold this test tube filled with water over the lighted candle.

JIMMY: Golly Moses, Mr. Science! Nothing happened at all.

MR. SCIENCE: Well, that's only because the water hasn't been heated quite long enough yet. Remember, I told you that all chemical properties are converted from liquid to vapor once their temperature rises sufficiently.

JIMMY: Great Jumping Jehoshaphat! The water's starting to get all bubbling on top. I guess doing that instead of turning into a vapor offers conclusive proof that water's not a chemical property. Right, Mr. Science?

MR. SCIENCE: No. That's not quite correct, Jimmy. You see, those bubbles indicate that the water is starting to boil. And now, if you'll look closely, you can see steam beginning to rise from the test tube.

JIMMY: Oh, Wowie-two-shoes! But that stuff sure looks an awful lot like the smoke that was rising from the candle. You wouldn't try to slip me the old rubber peach just because I'm a gullible child, would you, Mr. Science?

MR. SCIENCE: No. Of course not, Jimmy. Notice how my hand gets wet when I pass it through the cloud of steam like this. And that means the vapor has converted itself back into water again.

JIMMY: Boy oh boy, your hand's sure wet, all right, Mr. Science. I feel as though one of nature's eternal secrets has just been unlocked before my very eyes.

MR. SCIENCE: That's very cleverly phrased, Jimmy. And—

JIMMY: I'll bet this little bottle would get equally wet if I passed it through the cloud of steam.

MR. SCIENCE: No. Don't do that, Jimmy. The contents of that bottle must never be exposed to heat! Keep it away from here, boy!

JIMMY: But I only want to see if the outside of the bottle will—

(Sound: Explosion)

ANNOUNCER: Mr. Science has been brought to you as a public service paid for by the Philanthropic Council to Make Things Nicer. Today's broadcast was the last in our current series.

One Very Smart Tomato

Russell Baker

I had coffee with Dr. Irving Slezak, the brilliant genetics researcher. He brought some genes and a chopping knife. Working with the skill of a master salad chef, he chopped one of the genes into dozens of tiny parts, threw half of them away and tossed the rest into a salad bowl.

He repeated the process with the second gene, then stirred the bowl vigorously, at the same time explaining. One gene, he said, belonged to a truck driver and the other to a state policeman. By blending the two, he hoped to produce a brand-new form of life—a truck driver who, immediately upon exceeding the fifty-five-mile-an-hour speed limit, would pull himself over and give himself a ticket.

This was but a small example of the new fuel-saving developments possible through research in recombinant DNA. He had bigger projects afoot in the lab. He became confidential.

"Would you believe a topless go-go dancer crossed with a seal?" he whispered.

"You're mad, Slezak, mad," I said.

"They won't think I'm mad when I produce a topless dancer who can perform without a single goose pimple in a room heated to a mere thirty-six degrees Fahrenheit," he said.

So far he had succeeded only in producing a seal that liked to take off its brassiere and twitch to loud records, he confessed. But, in the meantime, other miraculous gene stews were being cooked.

Even now he was combining the genes of a midget with the genes of an interstate highway to produce a smaller turnpike which would force people to drive smaller cars.

"Impossible," I said. "Turnpikes don't have genes."

"If that's right," he asked, "how come I've already got seventeen midgets with 'Do Not Cross Median Strip' signs growing in their navels?"

No wonder so many people were opposed to recombinant DNA projects. Slezak speared a coffee gene in his cup and held it up, then dropped it on the table and before it could wiggle to safety chopped it into tiny pieces.

"Now give me one of your genes," he said.

"What for?"

"By blending a human gene with a coffee gene," he said, "I shall reduce the outrageous price of coffee by producing a man with built-in caffeine. He will no longer need coffee."

"But he'll need constant infusions of milk and sugar."

"Then I'll cross him with a cow and a sugar beet," said Slezak.

"Use your own gene," I said.

"It's too dangerous," he said. "America isn't ready for a mooing beet that's absolutely brilliant. It still doesn't know what to do with Henry Kissinger."

I edged a safe distance from the great scientist's chopping blade and switched the subject. "Is it true, Dr. Slezak, that you are actually a clone?"

"A canard," he snorted. "A distortion of truth spread by my enemies who would have the world believe that the great Irving Slezak had himself cloned from a wart on his ear, that this clone overpowered him one dark night in a frenzy of wartish rage, hurled his genes into a Venus's-flytrap and assumed Slezak's identity. A vicious fiction."

The truth was far more botanical, he explained. He, Irving Slezak, had for years been enslaved by a two-pack-a-day cigarette habit. Being unable to abandon his brilliant work for the two years it would take him to break the habit, he decided to outwit it.

"And so," he said, "I spent two weeks locked in the lab crossing myself with a tobacco plant."

"Brilliant," I cried. "Once you became partly tobacco, you immediately lost the desire to take tobacco into your system."

"Not quite," said Slezak. "Unfortunately, an imbecilic lab assistant had supplied tomato genes instead of tobacco genes. The two plants are related, of course, but that was no excuse for the slipup. The result was that I lost all hunger for tobacco but developed an insatiable appetite for salt and pepper, Worcestershire sauce, bacon, lettuce and vodka."

Aha, I thought: this explains why Slezak takes his coffee with two heaping teaspoons of mayonnaise.

"A pity," I said, as he brushed a tomato worm off his lapel and rose to return to the service of science.

"Not at all," he said. "Once I have crossed myself with toasted whole wheat I'll be a B.L.T. and never have to wait again for a stool at the lunch counter."

Botanist, Aroint Thee! or, Henbane by Any Other Name

Ogden Nash

I had always known that botanists were finicky,
But not until a recent tour of the dictionary did I realize
    that they were also cynicky.
They are friendly toward strangers, they are not xenophobes,
    they enjoy the theater, they are not dramaphobes,
But it is now clear to me that they are, to coin an unscholarly
    but apt neologism, thalamaphobes.
Yes, they are in favor of pollenizing
Just as much as Kosygin is against imperialistic colonizing,
    But they disparage marriage.
Let me anticipate your queries,
Let me simply call your attention to the matrimony vine,
    the common name by which they identify a solanaceous
    plant of the genus *Lycium*, cultivated for its flowers,
    foliage and berries.
So far, so innocent, but hold! What is solanaceous? Upon
    my honor,
Included in the species *Solanaceae* what do we find? We
    find henbane, mandrake and belladonna.
Let alone mandrake and belladonna, you know and I know
    that every botanist knows henbane, it's an herb com-
    mon, not exotic;
It bears sticky, hairy foliage of disagreeable odor and has
    properties poisonous and narcotic.
So here we have a plant sticky, hairy, lethal and mephitic,
    and by what name does the botanist choose this plant
    to define?
The matrimony vine.
I say, Lady, if you wish of all wives to be the forgottenist,
Marry a botanist.

Nonsense Botany

Edward Lear

Armchairia Comfortabilis

Bassia Palealensis

Bubblia Blowpipia

Crabbia Horrida

Phattfacia Stupenda

Plumbunnia Nutritiosa

Manypeeplia Upsidownia

Guittara Pensilis

Bottlephorkia Spoonifolia

Smalltoothcombia Domestica

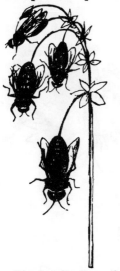

Bluebottlia Buzztilentia

Pollybirdia Singularis

Knutmigrata Simplice

Tureenia Ladlecum

Puffia Leatherbéllowsa

Queeriflora Babyöides

Cockatooca Superba

Baccopipia Gràcilis

Fishia Marina

Piggiawiggia Pyramidalis

Book Learning

E. B. White

Farmers are interested in science, in modern methods, and in theory, but they are not easily thrown off balance and they maintain a healthy suspicion of book learning and of the shenanigans of biologists, chemists, geneticists, and other late-rising students of farm practice and management. They are, I think, impressed by education, but they have seen too many examples of the helplessness and the impracticality of educated persons to be either envious or easily budged from their position.

I was looking at a neighbor's hens with him one time when he said something which expressed the feeling farmers have about colleges and books. He was complaining about the shape of the henhouse, but he wanted me to understand that it was all his own fault it had turned out badly. "I got the plan for it out of a book, fool-fashion," he said. And he gazed around at his surroundings in gentle disgust, with a half-humorous, half-disappointed look, as one might look back at any sort of youthful folly.

Scientific agriculture, however sound in principle, often seems strangely unrelated to, and unaware of, the vital, gruelling job of making a living by farming. Farmers sense this quality in it as they study their bulletins, just as a poor man senses in a rich man an incomprehension of his own problems. The farmer of today knows, for example, that manure loses some of its value when exposed to the weather; but he also knows how soon the sun goes down on all of us, and if there is a window handy at the cow's stern he pitches the dressing out into the yard and kisses the nitrogen good-by. There is usually not time in one man's lifetime to do different. The farmer knows that early-cut hay is better feed than hay which has been left standing through the hot dry days of late July. He hasn't worked out the vitamin losses, but he knows just by looking at the grass that some of the good has gone out of it. But he knows also that to make hay he needs settled weather—better weather than you usually get in June.

I've always tried to cut my hay reasonably early, but this year I wasn't able to get a team until the middle of July. It turned out to be just as well. June was a miserable month of rains and fog mulls. The people who stuck to their theories and cut their hay in spite of the

weather, took a beating. A few extremists, fearful of losing a single vitamin, mowed in June, choosing a day when the sun came out for a few
minutes. Their hay lay in the wet fields and rotted day after day, while
Rommel took Tobruk and careened eastward toward Alexandria.

The weather was unprecedented—weeks of damp and rain and
fog. Everybody talked about it. One day during that spell I was holding
forth to a practical farmer on the subject of hay. Full of book learning,
I was explaining (rather too glibly) the advantages of cutting hay in
June. I described in detail the vitamin loss incurred by letting hay stand
in the field after it has matured, and how much greater the feed value
was per unit weight in early-cut hay, even though the quantity might be
slightly less. The farmer was a quiet man, with big hands for curling
round a scythe handle. He listened attentively. My words swirled
around his head like summer flies. Finally, when I had exhausted my
little store of learning and paused for a moment, he ventured a reply.

"The time to cut hay," he said firmly, "is in hayin' time."

Prehistoric Animals of the Middle West

James Thurber

Many residents of that broad, proud region of the United States known
as the Middle West are, I regret to say, woefully ignorant of, not to say
profoundly incurious about, the nature and variety of the wild life
which existed, however precariously in some instances, in that part of
North America before the coming of the Red Man *(Homo Rufus)* or of
anybody else.

The only important research which has been done in this fascinating field was carried on for the better part of thirty-two years by the late

Dr. Wesley L. Millmoss.* For the last twenty years of the great man's life, I served as his artist, companion, counsellor and assistant. In this last capacity, I did a great deal of heavy lifting, no doubt more than was good for me. During the years I spent with Dr. Millmoss, he devoted most of his time to digging in all parts of the Middle West for the fossilized remains of extinct animals. From bits of a thigh bone, or one vertebra, he would reconstruct the whole animal. My drawings of his most famous reconstructions accompany this treatise.

For the past twelve years I have striven without success to have his findings, together with their accompanying illustrative plates, published in one or another of the leading scientific journals of this and other countries. I lay my failure directly at the door of Dr. Wilfred Ponsonby who, at the meeting of the American Scientific Society in Baltimore in 1929, made the remark, "The old boy (Dr. Millmoss) has never dug up half as many specimens as he has dreamed up."

Although Dr. Millmoss, quite naturally, was unable to perceive the wit in this damaging observation, which hung like a cloud over his last days, he was not without a sense of humor, and I believe, if he were alive today, he would take no little satisfaction in the fact that for the last five years Dr. Ponsonby has labored under the delusion that he is married to a large South African butterfly.

However, this is scarcely the place for an exploration of the little feuds and fantasies of the scientific world. Let us proceed to an examination of the remarkable fauna of the prehistoric Middle West. If in doing so, I present no formal defense of the Millmoss discoveries, put it down to a profound reverence for the memory of Wesley Millmoss, who used so often to say, "A Millmoss assumption is more important than a Ponsonby proof."

All the plates reproduced here were drawn by me from photographs of original life-size models constructed by Dr. Millmoss out of wire, *papier mâché* and other materials. These models were all destroyed by fire in 1930. "All that I have to show for them," the good doctor once told a friend, "is two divorces."

According to all scientists except Dr. Millmoss, the famous mounds of Ohio were built by an early race of men known as Mound Builders. The doctor, on the other hand, contended that the mounds were built by the Mound Dweller (Plate I). This primitive creature was about the size of the modern living room. The Mound Dweller's body

---

*While on a field trip in Africa in 1931, Dr. Millmoss was eaten by a large piano-shaped animal, to the distress of his many friends and colleagues.

occupied only one third of the space inside his shell, the rest of which was used to carry the earth as he dug it up. The creature's eye was an integral part of its shell, a mistake made by Mother Nature and not, as has been claimed,* "a bit of Millmoss butchery-botchery." The Mound Dweller is of interest today, even to me, principally because it was my friend's first reconstruction, and led to his divorce from Alma Albrecht Millmoss.

Plate I

In Plate II, I have drawn the Thake, a beast which Dr. Millmoss was wont to refer to lovingly as "Old Laughing Ears." It represents perhaps the most controversial of all the ancient creatures reconstructed by the distinguished scientist. Dr. Millmoss estimated that the Thake had inhabited the prairies of Illinois approximately three million years before the advent of the Christian era. Shortly after Dr. Millmoss gave his model of the Thake to the world, Dr. Ponsonby, in a lecture at Williams College that was notable for its lack of ethical courtesy, asserted that the Thake bones which Dr. Millmoss had found were in reality those of a pet airedale and a pet pony buried together in one grave by their owner, *circa* 1907. My own confidence in the authenticity of the Thake has never been shaken, although occasionally it becomes a figure in my nightmares, barking and neighing.

Plate II

In Plate III, we have the Queech, also known as the Spotted, or Ringed, Queech—the only prehistoric feline ever discovered by Dr. Millmoss in his midwestern researches. I find no record in the doctor's notes as to the probable epoch in which it flourished. Like so many of Dr. Millmoss' restorations, the Queech was made the object of a particularly unfriendly and uncalled-for remark by Dr. Ponsonby. At a dinner of the New York Society of Zoologists, held at the old Waldorf-Astoria some fifteen years ago, Ponsonby observed, "There is no doubt in my mind but that this pussy cat belongs to the Great Plasticine Age."

---

*Dr. W. Ponsonby, in the *Yale Review*, 1933.

Plate III

As to the authenticity of the Cobble-tufted Wahwah (Plate IV), even the sardonic Dr. Ponsonby could offer no slighting insinuations.* Like all other scientists, he was forced tacitly to admit the brilliant precision with which the old master had restored this antediluvian fowl. The Wahwah bird, in spite of its mammoth size, measured nothing at all from wing tip to wing tip, since it had only one wing. Because of its single wing, its obviously impractical

Plate IV

feet and its tendency to walk over high rocks and fall, it is probable, Dr. Millmoss believed, that the species did not exist for more than a hundred and seventy-five years. Dr. Millmoss once told me that, if the bird made any sound at all, it probably "went 'wah-wah.'" Since this embarrassed me for some reason, the celebrated scientist did not press the point.

Plate V

In Plate V, we come upon my favorite of all the Millmoss discoveries, the Hippoterranovamus. One of Nature's most colossal errors, the Hippoterranovamus ate only stork meat and lived in a land devoid of storks. Too large to become jumpy because of its predicament, the 'novamus took out its frustration in timidity. It almost never came out completely from

---

Author's Note: My research staff has since established that Dr. Ponsonby was enjoying a two-year sabbatical in Europe at the time the Wahwah model was completed.

behind anything. When I asked Dr. Millmoss how long he figured the 'novamus had existed as a species, he gave me his infrequent but charming smile and said in his slow drawl, "Well, it never lived to vote for William Jennings Bryan." This was the only occasion on which I heard the great man mention politics.

Plate VI

Plates VI and VII represent, respectively, the Ernest Vose, or Long-necked Leaf-eater, and the Spode, or Wood-wedger. Neither of these animals has ever interested me intensely, and it is only fair to say that I am a bit dubious as to the utter reality of their provenance. At the time he constructed these models, Dr. Millmoss was being divorced by his second wife, Annette Beggs Millmoss, and he spent a great deal of his time reading children's books and natural histories. The tree at the back of the Spode is my own conception of a 3,000,000-year-old tree. The small animal at the feet of the Ernest Vose is a Grod. Dr. Millmoss' notes are almost entirely illegible, and I am not even sure that Ernest Vose is right. It looks more like Ernest Vose than anything else, however.

The final plate (Plate VIII) was one of the last things Wesley Millmoss ever did, more for relaxation, I think, than in the interests of science. It shows his idea, admittedly a trifle fanciful, of the Middle-Western Man and Woman, three and a half million years before the dawn of history. When I asked him if it was his conviction that Man had got up off all fours before Woman did, he gave me a pale, grave look and said simply, "He had to. He needed the head start."

Even in death, Dr. Wesley Millmoss did not escape the sharp and envious tongue of Dr. Wilfred Ponsonby. In commenting upon the untimely passing of my great

Plate VII

employer and friend, the *New York Times* observed that explorers in Africa might one day come upon the remains of the large, piano-shaped animal that ate Dr. Millmoss, together with the bones of its distinguished and unfortunate prey. Upon reading this, Ponsonby turned to a group of his friends at the Explorers' Club and said, "Too bad the old boy didn't live to reconstruct *that*."

Plate VIII

Professor Gulliver Grebe's Adventures among the Snarfs

Pierre Berton

I had an interesting talk last week with one of the world's best-known explorers and anthropologists, Professor Gulliver Grebe, who has just returned from exploring the native civilizations of the Upper Amazon.

Professor Grebe tells me that this jungle fastness is not entirely inhabited by untutored savages. In fact, he spent more than a year studying one culture which he feels is almost as civilized as our own. This is the little-known society of Snarfs (or—to give them their original German spelling, *Schnarffes*). There are some seventy-five thousand of these Snarfs living in small cities, towns, and villages in the inaccessible Grool, a mountain plateau which was, until the development of the long-range helicopter, entirely cut off from the world.

Professor Grebe's studies have cast new light on the strange Snarf custom of elbow worship, a practice only sketchily referred to in earlier anthropological works. In this oddly gifted society—whose political sophistication is beyond dispute—the men seem to be totally obsessed not only with the female elbow, but also with the forearm, the hand, and the fingers.

Part of this curious fetishism is due, no doubt, to an ancient Snarf custom. Since the temperature of the Grool hovers around 103, the women of the tribe generally appear in public almost totally naked. Traditional modesty, however, makes one bodily covering virtually mandatory—a pair of long gloves, which conceal the forearms up to and including the elbow.

A woman appearing in public with her elbows undraped would be considered grossly indecent, while anyone daring to walk about freely with bare arms would be driven from the streets and, indeed, imprisoned.

Professor Grebe, however, remains confused by the elbow mania since it is not really true that the feminine elbow is hidden from masculine eyes in Snarf society. In fact, a recent count made by the professor suggests that in spite of long-held taboos, there are now more Snarf elbows showing than there are Snarf elbows hidden.

For one thing, many of the most stylish gloves are worn so tightly that every detail of the arm is observable to the most casual eye. For another, it has become highly fashionable to affect semitransparent gloves which leave little to the imagination. Again, on the beach and for evening wear, style-conscious Snarf women have followed the trend of partially rolling down their gloves to reveal about seven eighths of their elbow.

Almost every Snarf publication for men now features detailed pictures of not one but dozens of undraped elbows and even forearms. Some of the more daring show the back of the hand and perhaps even a bit of the palm, though these have been the objects of recent attempts at censorship. Many theatrical performances and native dances feature suggestive elbow and hand movements and, again, the elbows are undraped. A book, if it is to attract attention, must feature on its cover a picture of a giant elbow. Classical paintings abound in naked elbows and are widely praised. And in the cheaper novelty shops, ash trays and other bric-a-brac in the form of elbows enjoy a steady sale among sophisticated males.

Thus, male Snarfs are literally surrounded by elbows; yet they continue to be excited by them. Even a wrinkled glove lying on a chair will cause sniggers and whispered comments. Indeed, younger Snarfs have been known to stage "glove raids" on feminine dormitories.

It is difficult to move down the main street of any Snarf settlement without encountering elbow symbols on every side; yet the sight of a quarter inch of naked elbow protruding from a worn glove will cause a near panic and give rise to write-ups in the newspapers.

A bizarre by-product of this elbow-directed society, Professor Grebe informs me, is the grotesque anatomical distortions it has caused. Women with enlarged elbow bones or particularly hefty forearms are much in demand, especially as entertainers. Professor Grebe interviewed several of these pathetic creatures who, by virtue of muscle exercises and even surgical operation, had managed to increase the size of their elbows to the point where it made it difficult to walk upright or perform simple feats of manual dexterity. To a woman he found them entirely happy with their strange lot perhaps because they are looked on both by men and other women as near goddesses. Some of them, he reports, have to carry their arms in special slings for support, but this seems to make them all the more desirable.

Some years ago, certain women—disgraced in the eyes of their parents and friends by the physical accident of underdeveloped elbows—began to use padded gloves. These, the professor says, have now become an important commercial by-product of Snarf society and are, indeed, advertised openly.

Another curious aspect of the Snarf elbow mania is the rise of the so-called "Health Groups" who insist that the enforced draping of the lower arm is unhealthy and physically undesirable. These people meet in secluded spots—private farms, beaches, and forest glades—where they effect a strange costume consisting of an all-encompassing wool cloak which covers the wearer from head to foot, but leaves the arms entirely nude from the elbow down. Many attempts have been made to prevent these societies from meeting, but the fact that health is the key motive has protected them from legal action. Many publish health magazines showing pictures of the undraped elbow and these have a wide sale since the male Snarfs, apparently, are extremely interested in health.

Professor Grebe has done considerable historical research into the Snarf past and it is his belief that there was a time when the very word "elbow" was taboo in polite society. This is no longer the case, since it is used in books, plays, and theater advertising and always gets a laugh when employed by a stand-up comedian in a joke.

The taboo still generally holds, however, for words dealing with the concealed parts of the lower arm, especially the fingers. These are rarely if ever mentioned in public either by name or inference. A storm of protest was engendered recently with the publication of a new book of considerable literary quality because it dared to employ the five-letter word "thumb"—a term heretofore confined entirely to scrawls on back fences and washroom walls.

The fact that this book has been distributed, however, indicates a breaking down of traditional Snarf taboos. Indeed, Professor Grebe says he has reason to believe that the sight of a naked elbow in the Upper Amazon may soon become almost as familiar as, say, the sight of a naked bosom in our own culture.

James Thurber

VI. Capture of three physics professors

A Pure Mathematician

Arthur Guiterman

Let Poets chant of Clouds and Things
    In lonely attics!
A Nobler Lot is his, who clings
    To Mathematics.

Sublime he sits, no Worldly Strife
    His Bosom vexes,
Reducing all the Doubts of Life
    To Y's and X's.

And naught to him's a Primrose on
    The river's border;
A Parallelepipedon
    Is more in order.

Let Zealots vow to do and dare
    And right abuses!
He'd rather sit at home and square
    Hypotenuses.

Along his straight-ruled paths he goes
    Contented with 'em,
The only Rhythm that he knows,
    A Logarithm!

Modell

"From the cyclotron of Berkeley to the labs of M.I.T.,
We're the lads that you can trust to keep our country strong and free."

Jules Feiffer

Thinking Black Holes Through

Roy Blount, Jr.

Just by thinking on such a grand scale, humanity not only enlarges its universe but expands and ennobles itself. Perhaps the ideal metaphor is not Piglet's Heffalump but Browning's famous declamation: "Ah, but a man's reach should exceed his grasp, / Or what's a heaven for?" To the growing fraternity of black-hole theorists, that cosmic vision is the ultimate lodestar.

—"Those Baffling Black Holes," Time.

"You can call them Great Big Old Nothings all you want," says Mrs. Vern Wike of Baruma, Michigan, "but when that thing came along and seized me up by the clavicles and turned me into a grain of dust five or six times and set me down fourteen miles from my home, it did me a world of good. I feel like a new old lady."

"Idea I got, it was trying to tell me something, trying to, you know, to *communicate*," says Roster Toombs of Fillings, Maryland, who maintains that a black hole reached him in his garage apartment, transferred him to at least two other universes and left him with "kind of more perspective on life than I can use."

Ex-President Jimmy Carter is interested in black holes.

Sings Benno Zane II in his black hole–inspired pop hit "So-uh Dark":

> You-uh so profound,
> Grand Canyon like a levee.
> Billion tons-uh like a pound,
>
> You-uh so heavy.
> Yeah so-uh dark in there
> You got Noah's ark in there?

But the hole is greater than some of its poets. From Slippery Key, Florida, to Bosco, Washington, from England's Cambridge University to cooperative observatories on mainland China, mankind is going further than it ever imagined possible with thoughts of black holes, those mysterious antiwombs of collapsed stars in which time and space are so

warped that they gasp, enclose themselves and become nothing; the
speed of light is just nothing, flat; and as for matter, it is spaghettied-
out, shamed and compressed into a nothingness billions and billions of
times smaller—and more potent—than it was when it was something.

To some theorists, a black hole admits no escape. Under special
circumstances, others argue, it may transpose things into another universe or back in time as far as, for instance, the Hoover administration,
via passages dubbed "wormholes." One school of thought posits phenomena dubbed "white holes" (which *spew out* nothing instead of
ingesting it), but these—as anyone can understand who has watched
both "American Bandstand" and "Soul Train"—have laid a lesser claim
on the imagination. The possibility of a "yellow hole," in which everything is sunny and visitors find themselves robed in buttercups, is generally dismissed as wishful thinking.

So what kind of thinking is right? Even the savants wonder. When
Sir Waring Tifit created the first mathemo-mechanical model of a black
hole in 1964, famed Astrophysicist Vivien Soule took one look and
exclaimed, "This is so dense that thought must become like Thousand
Island dressing, or petroleum jelly or something, and time become u.s.
news and world report."

The distinguished Pure Mathematician Seiji Kamara took one
look and observed. "This is so dense that the birds must leave off their
singing and crawl like little bugs upon the ground. It's not the blackness
so much, it's the *density*."

Little Joey Fulks, the brilliant if ill-focused graduate student who
later withdrew into market research, took one look and said, "This is so
dense it makes me want to *shriek*."

The great Rabinrasha Charawansary took two looks and said, "I
don't think it is so dense." But that was just Charawansary. He also
didn't think Kamara's mathematics were so pure. Later that same evening, at a faculty cookout in his back yard, Charawansary reasoned
aloud about black holes so deeply that his mind evidently passed into
one. Because of relativistic effects, he appeared to observers to be forever
nearly coming to a point but always more and more slowly and never
quite. To Charawansary himself, he seemed to have summed up mag-
nificently, in one great flash while bunning a wiener, and everyone else
was just sitting there like sacks of wheat. In fact, the phenomenon Charawansary presented was so extremely trying a thing to observe that all
of his colleagues had murmured months ago that they had better be getting along, leaving him with Mrs. Charawansary, who was disconsolate
until a troupe of quantum mechanics came through town and showed

her some models of what goes on inside the atom that made her laugh and laugh.

Can a person *become* a black hole? Not likely, believe most theorists. But just say someone were to. What if? His knees would in effect become his respiration . . . his past, future and sense of smell would be telescoped into an infinitesimal pelletlike item . . . and he would literally be worn by his own shoes. In earthly geographical terms, an area the size of Maine, Asia and the city of Detroit and environs would be squeezed into a single copy of the *New York Post.*

All airy speculation? Not so, insist some of today's brightest young stars of physics and math. "Oh, the holes are there, for sure," says Caltech's Flip Kensil. "It ain't no big thing. Could be there's one of infinitesimal magnitude coursing within a hair's breadth of your face right now powerful enough to swallow human life and the federal bureaucracy. But hey, that's the universe all over."

A "singularity" is what scientists tend to dub a black hole in the scientific papers that they read to each other. A "singularity." These scientists! They don't give much away, do they?

The state of the art of black-hole thought is enough, in short, to tempt the layman to throw up his or her hands. But that would be defeatism—and in fact many laymen are doing anything but.

Fulpus Wsky and Livianne Wills of the Yale-Rockefeller Institute for Astrophysics believe that public enthusiasm for black holes is such that the holes may well be in our own homes, in some form, before the turn of the century. "When we happen to mention at a cocktail party that at any moment we might receive in the pit of our stomach a golf ball the 'size' of a million suns," note Wsky-Wills, "people's heads turn our way instantly."

All very well, humanity's ever practical side will counter, but what is in the hole for us? The answers to that question are by no means clear. A black hole, if harnessed, would be of undeniable value in trash removal and national defense. But so far the principal benefit derived is a sense of elation, of expansion, even of pride, gained by those hardy reflectives, in science and out, who make a level effort to comprehend the concept. Black Hole Clubs, NOTHING IS BEAUTIFUL buttons and "singularity bars" are springing up. In many parts of the country, black-hole mental-picturing sessions are replacing wet-T-shirt contests in popularity.

Not all of these "holeys," as the trendier enthusiasts dub themselves, rise to the gravity of the phenomenon. Misfits, many of them, acting out compulsions that are psychological at bottom and may have little or nothing to do with nothingness itself. These people, it may be, tend to cheapen the hole thing—but under our laws they have the right to think about what they please, as they please; and that includes the laws of nature.

And in the end, who can readily say which response to black holes is authentic and which is not? Who can say that the Toombses and the Mrs. Wikes of this world are real zeros? Who can say—although we may know what a black hole *is*—what a black hole is *like?* Not the experts.

"'*Like.*' Oh, it can't be *likened* to anything," says Rocky Top Observatory's Bern Rogovin. "It's . . . different from anything. It's—I wouldn't say *opposite*—it's . . . Oh, what's the word?"

Antimatter?

"No, not that. Yet definitely not *matter.* I would say, perhaps . . . amatter."

What's amatter?

"Oh, nothing."

The Purist

Ogden Nash

I give you now Professor Twist,
A conscientious scientist.
Trustees exclaimed, "He never bungles!"
And sent him off to distant jungles.
Camped on a tropic riverside,
One day he missed his loving bride.
She had, the guide informed him later,
Been eaten by an alligator.
Professor Twist could not but smile.
"You mean," he said, "a crocodile."

Theoretical Theories

John Bailey

DINOSAURS still romp and play
In Florida's Okeechobee Bay.

The universe is still expanding.
(But it can't be seen from where you're standing.)

Four trillion miles out in the void
There lives a greenish humanoid.

The center of the earth is hot
But then again, perhaps it's not.

Professor Piccard

E. B. White

Before

Professor Piccard, traveller in the outer spheres, has announced his intention of making another ascent, this time borne aloft by 2,000 small balloons instead of by one big one. If he carries out his plan, the trip should be of profound interest to logicians—for the professor this time will invade not only the stratosphere but that equally vaporous region, the Realm of Probability. Usually, you see, the Professor relies, for his descent, on letting some gas out of his bag; but on this occasion he will rely on the fitful bursting of some of the little balloons in the rarefied air to which they are exposed. He hopes that only "some" of the little balloons, not all of them, will give way, and feels that probability is on his side.

The calculation of probability has long occupied the night thoughts of gambling men, and the coin-flippers of the world will brood endlessly on the idea of 2,000 little supporting balloons, some of which must hold, some of which must let go. What, they will want to know, are the chances of having 2,000 balloons, all subjected to bursting conditions, explode at comfortable intervals? It is not probable, yet it is conceivable, that 2,000 balloons, rising into an unfavorable zone, might explode as one, just as it is conceivable that a coin, tossed fifty times, might show heads in all fifty flips. And there is still another, larger question which comes up, it seems to us: What effect does rarefied air have on the very law itself? Can anyone state, authoritatively, that there exists any such thing as probability so far from the core of earth? We wish Dr. Abraham Wolf and Dr. William Fleetwood Sheppard, who wrote the fascinating chapters on probability in the Britannica, would write us an equation covering the probable interval of explosion of 2,000 little balloons dangling an inquisitive professor in the already improbable blue.

After

Dr. Piccard, of the upper air, brings to scientific fields the highest quality of madness. This sprightly little explorer, the jackanapes of the stratosphere, cunningly soars aloft in a basket borne upward by a galaxy of toy balloons, suddenly whips out a gun and takes pot shots at his own supports. "So I took my pistol and killed about a dozen of them," he explained. It was the sort of plot Harpo Marx might hatch, with his hair straying and his eyes too bright. Dr. Piccard descended in flames, and when he jumped out, according to the papers, he was choked with laughter.

How Newton Discovered
the Law of Gravitation

James E. Miller

Another wasteful use of scientific manpower results from the fact that we overload productive scientists with far too many committee, study panel, and advisory commission duties, and with money raising and formal administrative activities.

—WARREN WEAVER
"A Great Age For Science," in
Goals for Americans

The investigator may be made to dwell in a garret, he may be forced to live on crusts and wear dilapidated clothes, he may be deprived of social recognition, but if he has time, he can steadfastly devote himself to research. Take away his free time and he is utterly destroyed as a contributor to knowledge.

—W. B. CANNON
in *The Way Of An Investigator*

A tremendous increase in the number of vigorous young workers in the scientific vineyard has been one of the happiest results of the recent expansion, encouraged and nourished by our Federal Government, of scientific research in this country. These neophytes, left to their own devices by harassed research directors, have often found themselves without adequate guidance through the intricacies of governmental sponsorship; but, fortunately, they can find inspiration in the story of Sir Isaac Newton, his development of the law of gravitation, and his experiences as director of the Subproject for Apples of the Fruit-Improvement Project, sponsored by His Majesty's Government of Great Britain in cooperation with a syndicate of British fruit-growers.

Few are familiar with the details of Newton's twenty-year search for a proof of his hypothesis: the frustrations and failures, the need for accurate measurements of the earth's radius and for a mathematical tool that Newton himself was forced to invent, and the integration of his scattered efforts by the splendid organization of the Fruit-Improvement Project. These details have been collected from his *Principia*, personal letters, notebooks and other papers, and a series of personal interviews arranged by a medium of the author's acquaintance.

In 1665 the young Newton became a professor of mathematics in the University of Cambridge, his alma mater. His devotion to his work and his capabilities as a teacher and friend of the student may be assumed without question. It is well to point out also that he was no dreamy, impractical inhabitant of an ivory tower. His services to his college went far beyond the mere act of classroom teaching: he was an able and active member of the college's curriculum committee, the board of the college branch of the Young Noblemen's Christian Association, the dean's grounds committee, the publications committee, the *ad hoc* committee, and numerous other committees essential to the proper administration of a college in the seventeenth century. An exhaustive compilation of Newton's work along these lines reveals that, during a five-year period, he served on 379 committees, which investigated an aggregate of 7924 problems of campus life and solved 31 of them.

Newton the genius was yet a human being; and though in energy and ability he far surpassed the great majority of his fellow men, he found himself ultimately limited in his powers. His unselfish devotion to the important work of his committees absorbed so much time that

he was constrained to turn more and more of his teaching duties over to one of his students. He reasoned, quite correctly, that the substitution of a student as teacher in his place would benefit both the student and the student's students; the former because, in teaching, his own knowledge would be enhanced; and the latter because, in being taught by one near to them in age and interests, they would more eagerly grasp at the scraps of knowledge that came their way. Newton, whose stipend was small, did not spoil this idyllic arrangement by offering pay to his student substitute: a prime example of his sense of values and his restraint. Eventually, when his substitute had proved his ability as a teacher, Newton turned all of the classroom work over to him and was thus able to channel all his tremendous powers into the administrative work of the college.

At about this time, Newton, whose mind was too active ever to let scientific problems recede from his attention, occasionally mulled over the great discoveries of Kepler on planetary motions and the hypothesis, advanced by a number of astronomers, that these motions were governed by an attraction that varied inversely as the square of the distance between planets. One evening of a crowded day in the year 1680, a committee that was scheduled to meet at eleven o'clock, no earlier time being available, was unable to muster a quorum because of the sudden death from exhaustion of one of the older committee members. Every waking moment of Newton's time was so carefully budgeted that he found himself with nothing to do until the next committee meeting at midnight. So he took a walk—a brief stroll that altered the history of the world.

It was on this excursion into the night air of Cambridge that Newton was struck by a flash of insight which set off a chain of events culminating in his announcement to the world, in 1686, of the law of gravitation.

The season was autumn. Many of the good citizens in the neighborhood of the modest Newton home had apple trees growing in their gardens, and the trees were laden with ripe fruit ready for the picking. Newton chanced to see a particularly succulent apple fall to the ground. His immediate reaction was typical of the human side of this great genius. He climbed over the garden wall, slipped the apple into his pocket, and climbed out again. As soon as he had passed well beyond that particular garden, he removed the apple from his pocket and began munching it.

Then came inspiration. Without prelude of conscious thought or logical process of reasoning, there was suddenly formed in his brain the idea that the falling of an apple and the motions of planets in their orbits may be governed by the same universal law. Before he had finished eating the apple and discarded the core, Newton had formulated his hypothesis of the universal law of gravitation. By then it was three minutes before midnight, so he hurried off to the meeting of the Committee to Combat Opium Eating Among Students Without Nobility.

In the following weeks, Newton's thoughts turned again and again to his hypothesis. Rare moments snatched between the adjournment of one committee and the call to order of another were filled with the formulation of plans for testing the hypothesis. Eventually, after several years, during which, according to evidence revealed by diligent research, he was able to spend 63 minutes and 28 seconds on his plans, Newton realized that the proof of his hypothesis would take more spare time than might become available during the rest of his life. He had to find accurate measurements of a degree of latitude on the earth's surface, and he had to invent the calculus.

Finally, he concluded that he must find some relief from his collegiate administrative burdens. He knew that it was possible to get the King's support for a worthy research project of definite aims, provided a guarantee could be made that the project would be concluded in a definite time at a cost exactly equal to the amount stipulated when the project was undertaken. Lacking experience in these matters he adopted a commendably simple approach and wrote a short letter of 22 words to King Charles, outlining his hypothesis and pointing out its far-reaching implications if it should prove to be correct. It is not known whether the King ever saw the letter, and he may not have, being overwhelmed with problems of state and plans for pending wars. There is no doubt that the letter was forwarded, through channels, to all heads of departments, their assistants, and their assistants' assistants, who might have reason to make comments or recommendations.

Eventually, Newton's letter and the bulky file of comments it had gathered on its travels reached the office of the secretary of HMPBRD/CINI/SSNBI—His Majesty's Planning Board for Research and Development, Committee for Investigation of New Ideas, Subcommittee for Suppression of Non-British Ideas. The secretary immediately recognized its importance and brought it before the subcommittee, which voted to ask Newton to testify before the Committee for Investigation of New Ideas. Some discussion of Newton's idea—as to whether it could really be called British in intent—preceded this decision, but the transcript of the discussion, filling several quarto volumes, clearly shows that no real suspicion ever fell upon him.

Newton's testimony before HMPBRD/CINI is recommended for all young scientists who may wonder how they will comport themselves when their time comes. His college considerately granted him two months' leave, without pay, while he was before the committee, and the Dean of Research sent him off with a joking admonition not to come back without a fat contract. The committee hearing was open to the public and was well attended, though it has been suggested that many of the audience had mistaken the hearing room of HMPBRD/CINI for that of HMCEVAUC—His Majesty's Committee for the Exposure of Vice Among the Upper Classes.

After Newton was sworn to tell the truth and had denied that he was a member of His Majesty's Loyal Opposition, had ever written any lewd books, had traveled in Russia, or had seduced any milkmaids, he was asked to outline his proposal. In a beautifully simple and crystal-clear, ten-minute speech, delivered extemporaneously, Newton explained Kepler's laws and his own hypothesis, suggested by the chance sight of an apple's fall. At this point, one of the committee members, an imposing fellow, a dynamic man of action, demanded to know if Newton had a means of improving the breed of apples grown in England. Newton began to explain that the apple was not an essential part of his hypothesis, but he was interrupted by a number of committee members, all speaking at once in favor of a project to improve apples. This discussion continued for several weeks, while Newton sat in characteristic dignity waiting until the committee wished to consult him. One day he arrived a few minutes late and found the door locked. He knocked circumspectly, not wishing to disturb the committee's deliberations. The door was opened by a guard who told him there was no more room and sent him away. Newton, with his logical way of reasoning, deduced that the committee did not wish to consult him further, and forthwith he returned to his college and his important committee work.

Several months later, Newton was surprised to receive a bulky package from HMPBRD/CINI. He opened the package and found it contained a variety of governmental forms, each in quintuplicate. His natural curiosity, the main attribute of the true scientist, provoked him into a careful study of the forms. After some time, he concluded that he was being invited to submit a bid for a contract for a research project on the relationship between breed, quality, and rate of fall of apples. The ultimate purpose of the project, he read, was to develop an apple that not only tasted good but also fell so gently that it was not bruised by striking the ground. Now, of course, this was not what Newton had had in mind when he had written his letter to the King. But he was a practical man and he realized that, in carrying out the proposed project, he could very well test his hypothesis as a sort of side-line or by-product. Thus, he could promote the interests of the King and do his little bit for science in the bargain.

Having made his decision, Newton began filling out the forms without further hesitation. One of the questionnaires asked how the funds allotted for the project were to be spent. Newton was somewhat taken aback to read that £12,750 6s. 3d., the surplus remaining in the horticultural development fund for the current fiscal year, had been estimated as the total cost of his project. Methodically, he put down his own stipend first, and after a moment's thought he added the item: "Other salaries, travel, supplies, and overhead: £12,750 0s. 0d."

A true believer in correct administrative procedures, Newton sent the completed forms by special messenger to the Dean of Research, for transmittal through proper channels to HMPBRD/CINI.

His adherence to established procedure was rewarded a few days later when the Dean of Research summoned him and outlined a new plan, broader in scope and more sweeping in its conception. The Dean pointed out that not only apples, but also cherries, oranges, lemons, and limes fell to the earth, and while they were about it they might as well obtain a real, man-sized government contract to cover all the varieties of fruit that grow above the ground. Newton started to explain the mis-understanding about the apples; but he stopped rather than interrupt the Dean, who was outlining a series of conferences he proposed to organize among fruit-growers and representatives of various depart-ments of His Majesty's Government. The Dean's eyes began to glaze as he talked, and he became unaware that anybody else was in the room. Newton had an important committee meeting at that time, so he quietly went out the door, leaving the Dean of Research in an ecstasy of planning.

The seasons passed, while Newton led a busy, useful life as a mem-ber of many committees and chairman of some. One dark winter's day he was called again to the office of the Dean of Research. The Dean was beaming: he proudly explained to Newton all about the new contract he had obtained to study the relationship between breed, quality, and rate of fall of all the varieties of fruit that grow above the ground. The project was to be supported by no less than five different branches of His Majesty's Government plus a syndicate of seven large fruit-growers. Newton's part in the project was to be small but important: he was to direct the Subproject for Apples.

The following weeks were busy ones for Newton. Though

relieved from his committee work (a young instructor of Greek, Latin, history, and manual training took his place on the committees), he found himself cast into a morass of administrative problems: forms to be filled out for the governmental departments, for the fruit-growers, for the Dean of Research, for the Assistant Dean of Research, and for the financial office of the college; prospective research assistants to be interviewed and hired; office and laboratory space to be wangled from other projects on the campus. The wide abilities of our great genius are fully demonstrated by the way he piloted his subproject during its first formative weeks. He personally filled out 7852 forms, often in quintuplicate and sextuplicate; he interviewed 306 milkmaids and hired 110 of them as technical assistants. With his own hands he cleaned out an abandoned dungeon in a nearby castle for use as subproject headquarters; and, turning carpenter in typically versatile fashion, he erected 12 temporary buildings to house his staff. These buildings, used today as classrooms, stand as a monument to Newton's career.

Soon the subproject was fully implemented, documented, and regimented. Newton was not quite sure what his reconverted milkmaids could do for his hypothesis (he was a lifelong bachelor and hence not well acquainted with the ways of women), but he abhorred the thought of idleness in his staff. So he divided them into six teams, each of which was to measure and tabulate the rate of fall of one variety of apple, using sufficient apples to establish a statistically significant result. All went well except with the winesap team, who discovered a new way of making applejack, and consequently ran short of apples. Newton made a note of their recipe, wisely comprehending long before his fellow scientists the advantages of serendipity, or finding good things while looking for other things.

This period of life was a happy and profitable one for Newton. From the time he arose in the morning until, exhausted with honest labor, he dropped late at night back into his humble bed of straw, he spent each day filling out payroll forms for his milkmaids, ordering pens and paper, answering the questions of the financial office, and showing distinguished visitors and the Dean of Research around his subproject. Often he discussed the past, present, and future work of his project with representatives of the five governmental departments and seven fruit-growers who had been sent to check on his progress. He was frequently invited to give progress reports in person at the central offices of these 12 sponsors. Each week he wrote out a full progress report, which was duplicated and sent by special messenger to 3388 other projects sponsored by His Majesty's Government throughout the British Isles.

One of these remarkable documents, in an excellent state of preservation, can be found in the Museum of the Horticultural Society of Western Wales, in the village of Merthyr Tydfil. In typically logical style, the report, bound in a dark red stiff cover bearing the project number, HM2wr3801-g-(293), stamped in gold leaf, opens with a succinct table of contents:

1. Administration
2. Conferences
3. Correspondence
4. Supplies
5. Results of research

The last section, "Results of research," may have been lost during the intervening years, or it may not have been specifically required under the terms of His Majesty's contracts of that era. At any rate, it is not there. But the other sections remain to gladden the hearts of those permitted to read them. Is it too much to hope that this report can be published and distributed among our young scientists in America? Such a precept should accomplish miracles for the morale and spirit of our neo-geniuses.

One day, in 1685, Newton's precise schedule was interrupted, through no fault of his own. He had set aside a Tuesday afternoon to receive a committee of vice-presidents of the fruit-growing syndicate when, much to his horror and Britain's deep sorrow, the news spread that the whole committee had been destroyed in a three-stagecoach smashup. As once before, Newton found himself with a hiatus. He took a leisurely walk through the luscious vineyards of the subproject on Grapes, but not, of course, until he had obtained security clearance at the gate. While on this walk, there came to him, he knew not how ("Ye thought just burst upon me," he later wrote), a new and revolutionary mathematical approach which, in less time than it takes to tell about it, could be used to solve the problem of attraction in the neighborhood of a large sphere. Newton realized that the solution to this problem provided one of the most exacting tests of his hypothesis; and, furthermore, he knew, without need of pen and paper to demonstrate the fact to himself, that the solution fully supported his hypothesis. We can well imagine his elation at this brilliant discovery; but we must not overlook his essential humility, which led him forthwith to kneel and offer thanks to the King for having made the discovery possible.

On his return from this walk, Newton stopped a moment to browse in a bookstore, where he accidentally knocked a book to the floor. With apologies to the proprietor, who seemed in a mood to toss him out upon his ear, Newton retrieved the book and dusted it off. It was Norwood's *Sea-Mans Practice*, dated 1636. Opening the book at random, Newton found it contained the exact information of the length of a latitude degree that he required for the complete test of his hypothesis. Almost instantaneously, one part of his brain performed several lightning calculations and presented the result for the other part to examine; and there it was: the proof complete and irrefutable. Newton glanced at the hourglass in the shopkeeper's window and, with a start, remembered that he was due back at the dungeon to sign the milkmaids' time slips as they checked out for the day. He hurried out of the bookshop with the book under his arm, forgetting in his zeal that he had not paid for it.

Thus it was that His Majesty's Government supported and encouraged Newton during the trying years in which he was putting his hypothesis to the test. Let us not dally with the story of Newton's efforts to publish his proof, the misunderstanding with the editor of the *Horticulture Journal*, the rejections by the editors of *The Backyard Astronomer* and *Physics for the Housewife*. Suffice it to say that Newton founded his own journal in order to make sure that his proof would be published without invalidating alterations. Regrettably, he named his journal *Star and Planet*, with the result that he was branded a subversive, since Star could mean Red Star and Planet could mean Plan-It. Newton's subsequent testimony before the Subcommittee for Suppression of Non-British Ideas remains as a convincing demonstration of the great qualities that combined to make him a genius. Eventually, he was exonerated, and after enjoying many years of the fame that was due him, reigning one day each year as King of the Apple Festival, Newton died happily.

Garry Trudeau

Parlez-vous Presidentialese?

Richard Chait and Madeleine Green

Presidentialese is a curious dialect of higher education-speak. Over the past decade, we have had the pleasure of working with hundreds of college presidents, and have become fairly fluent. It is worth noting that no one is born with the ability to speak presidentialese; there are no "native speakers." But after a time in office, presidents actually may think in presidentialese, rarely translating into plain English.

We present below a basic primer, first indicating the phrase in presidentialese, and then providing a translation. The primer starts with the first words of presidentialese uttered on administrators' way up and continues through the more sophisticated language spoken by presidents on their way down.

The Courtship

I'm very happy in my job, but I might consider a presidency if the right one came along.
I'd kill for one.

I'm putting out a few feelers just to see what's there.
I've put the word out to five hundred of my closest friends.

I think I'll allow my name to go forward.
I spent four days sprucing up my resume.

They have some problems, but it's an interesting situation.
It's not Harvard, but I'd still kill for it.

I'm on the short list.
I was asked for a list of references.

I'll go for the interview, look, and listen; what do I have to lose?
I'm nervous; I hope I don't put my foot in my mouth.

The Interview

This is just the kind of community we would like to live in and contribute to.
It's two hours from civilization. I wonder how often we can get away!

This is really the place for me.
I'll take it if the other presidency doesn't come through.

I'm strongly committed to shared governance and a collaborative leadership style.
I am the CEO.

I'm a good listener.
Honey, did you catch his name!

I accept the position.
Eat your heart out; I'm the president.

The Early Years

It's a great place to be.
Wait 'til you see my house!

I'm not personally an advocate of lavish inaugurations, but I think that a significant event would rally the community and provide some visibility for the institution.
I've always fantasized about a huge inauguration.

We've got a few problems.
I can't believe no one told me about the deficit.

This place is steeped in proud tradition.
I can't even get the locks changed, never mind the curriculum.

I may need to make a few changes in key positions.
The senior staff are not sharing my vision for this place.

The faculty are getting restless.
Has it been a year already!

The students are getting restless.
Has it been two years already?

There's never enough time in the day to do all a president needs to do.
A lot of work piled up while I was in the Orient for a month.

The Later Years

I'm really tightening the screws on the faculty.
For the first time, I denied a promotion.

I'm trying to enhance our national visibility.
I'll take any excuse to get off campus once a week.

I'm really pretty damn good at what I do.
I'm really pretty damn good at what I do.

No president who tries to provide real leadership can avoid making enemies.
The faculty hates my guts.

Clearly, the board didn't really want the kind of change they said they did.
I'm losing the support of the board.

Exit, Stage Right

The board is getting restless.
Has it really been four years?

I'm thinking of looking around.
I'd kill to get out of here.

I've really accomplished everything I set out to do here.
The board chairman told me to start looking around.

I need a new challenge.
I need a new job—I've been fired.

The Aftermath

I had always hoped to return to the faculty; it is an enormous relief to have some time to think and to write.
I miss the perks.

It's a pleasure to get back to my discipline.
After being twenty years out of the professoriate, it's like landing on Mars.

The national associations really should do more work on the issue of life after the presidency.
Aren't they going to help me find a job?

I might consider another presidency if the right situation came along.
I'd kill for one.

Clearly, the need exists to conduct more extensive research on this popular but little understood dialect. The inquiry would be greatly enriched by a multidisciplinary focus, bringing to bear the expertise of polypresidential scientists and academic pseudogrammarians, among others.

The Secret Life of Henry Harting

Mark C. Ebersole

The annual report to the trustees had been read. Dr. Harting put aside his manuscript, rested his hands on the lectern, and postured himself formidably for some plain talk about a condition that had distressed him ever since he became president of Rockland University.

"There prevails among the members of this board," he declared resolutely, "a grave misconception as to what your university trustee-ship entails. The charter says, in essence, that you should be pre-emi-nently concerned with formulating major policies and providing finan-cial resources. But that's not what you do. No, you are instead singularly and obsessively preoccupied with maintaining surveillance over faculty members to make sure that their speech and actions are entirely compatible with your own encrusted convictions."

The president's voice was stern—very stern—and the trustees knew that he meant business.

"According to your reasoning," he continued, "professors are an inherently wayward lot, prone to do eccentric and perfidious things. Thus never are they beyond the purview of your unrelenting scrutiny, and if any one of them behaves in a manner displeasing to you, down comes your fury: 'I'll not tolerate that!' you protest, and straightaway you summon the president to take, as you put it, 'corrective mea-sures'—which is a euphemism for saying that the culprit must be either muzzled or else catapulted off the campus."

Dr. Harting shifted his glasses down his nose and peered at his trustees with a trenchant eye. A tremor of fear passed through them.

"Well, I've had enough of your meddling. For one thing, it's an infringement upon the privileges and rights of professors as stipulated in the university's by-laws. For another, it entangles you in matters about which you are strikingly ignorant. That's right—you know vir-tually nothing about the genius, the functions, and the prerogatives of academicians. In fact, you think that professors should be likened to corporation employees, which is very stupid reasoning. But no need to labor the point: your meddling is altogether indefensible and must stop."

So there: the president had done it—confronted the trustees with the unassailable truth about their obtrusiveness, so as to reduce them to a naked defenselessness.

For long moments there was silence. Then, as one man, the trust-ees leaped to their feet and burst into applause. Finally restoring order, the chairman of the board commended Dr. Harting for citing the trust-ees' "infelicitous conduct," apologized profusely for it, and vowed repeatedly that if it happened again, the offender would be harshly cen-sured. Then, the meeting having been immediately adjourned, the trust-ees swarmed around the president like baseball players around a home-run hitter, to congratulate him on his grand speech and to assure him . . .

"Good heavens, Henry! What are you daydreaming about this

time?" Betty Harting poked her husband in the ribs and frowned over her coffee cup as they lingered at the dinner table.

"Hmmmm?"

"All through dinner you lectured Brian and Carl, in that presidential voice of yours . . ."

"During recent months, university people of all sorts have been denouncing the president for faults that are really figments of their disgruntled imaginations," declared the chairman of the Student Coalition for Support of the President. "In fact, their accusations collapse under the weight of their own absurdity.

"For example, these people say that you are 'autocratic,' 'snobbish,' 'devious,' 'prejudiced,' 'cowardly,' 'ill-tempered,' 'muddleheaded.' What a wretched thing—concocting and mouthing such nasty, malicious indictments."

The coalition chairman, turning away from Dr. Harting seated behind his desk, looked toward the some 150 Rockland collegians wedged into the president's three-room office suite and asked them: 'Am I not telling it as it is?" To which the students nodded vigorously in agreement. Some called out, "That's right," "You said it," and "Right on."

"It's a heavy burden you bear, Dr. Harting," sympathized the chairman, "this scorn and ridicule that your maligners heap upon you. And we don't like it. Don't like it one bit. From now on the people around here better be mighty careful about the sort of names they call you."

Again, from the students, firm noddings and scattered utterances of agreement.

"Yes, we know, it's unprecedented for students to show allegiance to a university president. But we say, 'Precedent be damned.' After all, university presidents are normal, sensitive human beings. They deserve a fair shake as much as anyone else. Besides, Dr. Harting, since you are more abused than are other presidents, we think you are especially deserving of . . ."

The coalition chairman could not continue. His wrought-up compeers, unable any longer to restrain themselves to the staid decorum that they had thought befitting a presidential suite, burst out chanting wildly: "No more carping at Dr. Harting," "No more carping at Dr. Harting," "No more carping" . . .

The president got up from the table and, with a jaunty gait, strode through the living room and into his study. He ensconced himself in his swivel chair, saw the day's mail on his desk: thumbed through it—a bit

of everything there, including the *American Scholar,* the *Cape Cod
Standard Times* . . .

"You, the members of this faculty senate, complain incessantly
that our institution lacks intellectual vigor. And on this point—and this
may surprise you—I agree: new ventures in learning at Rockland are
pathetically few and our curricula languish from neglect. But it is funny
that you should make this criticism. Whenever new programs are submitted to this senate for approval, you invariably finish them off either
by rejecting them instantly or by discussing and amending them to
death. As a matter of fact, my own 'Design for Learning' was maneu-
vered into oblivion through your execessive parliamentarian exercises
just one meeting ago."

President Harting never before had spoken so caustically to faculty members on a subject about which they were so sensitive, so defen-
sive. But, determined that they should know the truth, he went on.

"It is a curious thing that to your students you earnestly declare
that the grist of liberal learning is critical and imaginative thinking and
that only these noble qualities of mind can render vitality to the collective and individual endeavors of mankind. But then you egregiously
contravene your own good counsel by steadfastly refusing to subject
your academic programs to serious critical appraisal. No doubt about it:
'experimenters' and 'innovators' for the advancement of learning you
truly are not."

The senate members could not help but shake their heads and
smile in self-depreciation. How foolishly they had acted—and would
have continued to do so had President Harting not spoken up. But now,
grateful that he had, they seized the opportunity to tell him so.

The secretary of the senate, the chairman of the senate, the professors of history, of sociology, of geology: these, and many more,
praised the president for his candid treatment of the folly. Through the
numerous and profuse speeches, the spirit of approbation became so
great that the senate was moved, then and there, to retrieve from the
minutes Dr. Harting's "Design for Learning" and to approve it for
immediate implementation, declaring all the while that not only would
it drastically alter Rockland University but would also revolutionize all
American higher education and . . .

The sound of Betty Harting's approaching footsteps—sharp, pur-
poseful—forewarned Henry Harting of an impending interrogation:
"For God's sake, Henry, the Manning party at the Jansen's starts in 15
minutes, doesn't it? Did you forget about it? The university doesn't
entertain a multi-millionaire every day, you know."

Within 25 minutes, the Hartings arrived at the home of the vice-president for development, Alan Jansen. Shaking hands with Lois Jansen, the President scanned the packed rooms. Yes, there was Mr. Morris Manning, chairman of the board of Manning Plastic Fiber Industries, the one for whom the university had contrived this evening of conviviality.

Manning's elegant countenance struck the president as bearing out precisely what Jansen and others who know him well had asserted: that he put a premium on excellence, and that his philanthropies went only to people who manifested this rare quality. Manning was, according to Jansen, the sort of person who, if he ever hit upon a university president who was truly superior, would draw lavishly from his plethoric coffers, and proceed to . . .

"Dr. Harting does not know why I requested that this special convocation be held, nor does anyone else, for that matter. I simply appeared at the president's office and requested that I be given the chance to speak to the members of this university community. A strange request, I know, enough to set any campus reeling with rumor and wild speculation."

Thus did Mr. Manning begin his speech to the more than 7,500 students, trustees, professors, alumni, and friends of Rockland University assembled expectantly in Powell Memorial Hall.

"Although I am not a resident of your town, nor a graduate of your university," Manning continued, "I have for some time observed the affairs of this institution, and especially the work of your president. And what a truly gifted person he is, as gifted as I could ever have imagined anyone to be. Whether his superior ability is by instinct or by training or both, I do not know, but it clearly distinguishes him in kind from all other men and women who preside over the nation's academies of higher learning. All of which brings me to the reason for this convocation."

The audience leaned forward, straining to hear Manning's next words.

"I have searched long for a university with which I could share a generous portion of my good fortune. But I will search no more. By virtue of Dr. Harting's excellence, I am now convinced, beyond any doubt, that Rockland is that university. So, my good friends, now hear this: I have come here this day to tell you that Manning Plastic Fiber Industries will award to Rockland University the sum of 90 million . . ."

Before he could say "dollars" the audience rose and exploded into thundering applause and cheers. What incredible riches Dr. Harding had brought to Rockland University! Even the wildest rumors as to what would happen at this convocation had not reached such staggering heights.

Finally, after the audience quieted down, the president, arrayed in his imposing academic regalia, rose slowly to his feet, smiled and waved learnedly, and then walked to the podium to accept formally the university's unexpected bounty. But Mr. Manning quickly whispered into his ear, "I'm not finished yet," and then went on at once to say, "Furthermore, the gift that I have bestowed upon this institution carries with it the expectation that this great citadel of higher learning shall henceforth be known (his voice now mounting to a crescendo) not as Rockland University but as the University of Henry Harting."

Another outburst of unrestrained, authentic gratitude—cheering and clapping—a rapturous sound that could not be contained by the walls of Powell Hall. And no wonder—to the university had come immortal glory.

Meanwhile, as the ecstatic celebration went on and on, there, in the midst of it all, stood the incomparable President Henry Harting, Ph.D., LL.D., shaking his head and sighing in resignation at his own excellence.

Garry Trudeau

Marshyhope State University

John Barth

The provost invites the author to accept an honorary degree and tells him of the history of Marshyhope State University.

Office of the Provost
Faculty of Letters
Marshyhope State University
Redmans Neck, Maryland 21612

8 March 1969

Mr John Barth, Esq., Author

Dear sir:

At the end of the current semester, Marshyhope State University will complete the seventh academic year since its founding in 1962 as Tidewater Technical College. In that brief time we have grown from a private vocational-training school with an initial enrollment of thirteen students, through annexation as a four-year college in the state university system, to our present status (effective a month hence, at the beginning of the next fiscal year) as a full-fledged university centre with a projected population of 50,000 by 1976.

To mark this new elevation, at our June commencement ceremonies we shall exercise for the first time one of its perquisites, the awarding of honorary degrees. Specifically, we shall confer one honorary doctorate in each of Law, Letters, and Science. It is my privilege, on behalf of the faculty, (Acting) President Schott, and the board of regents of the state university, to invite you to be with us 10 A.M. Saturday, 21 June 1969, in order that we may confer upon you the degree of Doctor of Letters, *Honoris Causa*. Sincerely hopeful that you will honour us by accepting the highest distinction that Marshyhope can confer, and looking forward to a favourable reply, I am,

Yours sincerely,

Germaine G. Pitt (Amherst)
Acting Provost

GGP(A)/ss

P.S.: A red-letter day on my personal calendar, this—the first in too long, dear Mr B., but never mind *that!*—and do forgive both this presumptuous postscriptum and my penmanship; some things I cannot entrust to my "good right hand" of a secretary (a hand dependent, I have reason to suspect, more from the arm of our esteemed acting president than from my arm, on which she'd like nothing better, if I have your American slang aright, than to "put the finger") and so must pen as it were with my left, quite as I've been obliged by Fate and History—my own, England's, Western Culture's—to swallow pride and

But see how in the initial sentence (*my* initial sentence) I transgress my vow not to go on about myself, like those dotty women "of a certain age" who burden the patience of novelists and doctors—their circumstantial ramblings all reducible, I daresay, to one cry: "Help! Love me! I grow old!" Already you cluck your tongue, dear Mr-B.-whom-I-do-not-know (if indeed you've read me even so far): life is too short, you say, to suffer fools and frustrates, especially of the prolix variety. Yet it is you, sir, who, all innocent, provoke this stammering postscript: for nothing else than the report of your impatience with just this sort of letters conceived my vow to make known my business to you *tout de suite,* and nothing other than that vow effected so to speak its own miscarriage. So perverse, so helpless the human heart!

And yet bear on, I pray. I am . . . what I am (rather, what I find to my own dismay I am become; I was not always so . . .): old schoolmarm rendered fatuous by loneliness, indignified by stillborn dreams, I prate like a "coed" on her first "date"—and this to a man not merely my junior, but . . . No matter.

I *will* be brief! I *will* be frank! Mr B.: But for the opening paragraphs of your recentest, which lies before me, I know your writings only at second hand, a lacuna in my own life story which the present happy circumstance gives occasion for me to amend. Take no offence at this remissness: for one thing, I came to your country, as did your novels to mine, not very long since, and neither visitor sojourns heart-on-sleeve. A late good friend of mine (himself a Nobel laureate in literature) once declared to me, when I asked him why he would not read his contemporaries—

But Germaine, Germaine, this is not germane! as my ancestor and namesake Mme de Staël must often have cried to herself. I can do no better than to rebegin with one of her own (or was it Pascal's?) charming openers: "Forgive me this too long letter; I had not time to write a short." And you yourself—so I infer from the heft of your *oeuvre,* stacked here upon my "early American" writing desk, to which, straight upon the close of this postscript, I will address me, commencing with your earliest and never ceasing till I shall have overtaken as it were the present point of your pen—you yourself are not, of contemporary authors, the most sparing . . .

To business! *Cher Monsieur* (is it French or German-Swiss, your name? From the lieutenant who led against the Bastille in *Great-great-great-great-great-grand-mère's* day, or the late theologian of our own? Either way, sir, we are half-countrymen, for all you came to light in Maryland's Dorset and I in England's: may this hors d'oeuvre keep your appetite for the entrée whilst I make short work of soup and salad!) . . .

Salad of laurels, sir! Sibyl-greens, Daphne's death-leaves, honorific if worn lightly, fatal if swallowed! I seriously pray you will take it, this "highest honour that Marshyhope can bestow"; I pray you will not take it seriously! O this sink, this slough, this Eastern Shore of Maryland, this marshy County Dorchester—whence, to be sure, *you* sprang, mallow from the marsh, as *inter faeces* etc. we are born all. Do please forgive—whom? How should you have heard of me, who have not read you and yet nominated you for the M.U. Litt.D.? I have exposed myself already; then let me introduce me: Germaine Pitt I, née Gordon, Lady Amherst, late of that *other* Dorset (I mean Hardy's) and sweeter Cambridge, now "Distinguished Visiting Lecturer in English" (to my ear, the *only* resident speaker of that tongue) and Acting (!) Provost of Make-Believe University's Factory of Letters, as another late friend of mine might have put it: a university not so much pretentious as pretending, a toadstool blown overnight from this ordurous swamp to broadcast doctorates like spores, before the stationer can amend our letterhead!

I shall not tire you with the procession of misfortunes which, since the end of the Second War, has fetched me from the ancestral seats of the Gordons and the Amhersts—where three hundred years ago is reckoned as but the day before yesterday, and the 17th-Century Earls of Dorset are gossipped of as if still living—to this misnamed shire (try to explain, to your stout "down-countian," that *-chester<castra* = camp, and that thus *Dorchester*, etymologically as well as by historical precedent, ought to name the seat rather than the county! As well try to teach Miss Sneak my secretary why *Mr* and *Dr* need no stops after), which sets about the celebration this July of its tercentenary as if 1669 were classical antiquity. Nor shall I with my passage from the friendship—more than friendship!—of several of the greatest novelists of our century, to the supervisal of their desecration in Modern Novel 101–102: a decline the sadder for its parallelling that of the genre itself; perhaps (God forfend) of Literature as a whole; perhaps even (the prospect blears in the eyes of these . . . yes . . . colonials!) of the precious Word. These adversities I bear with what courage I can draw from the example

of my favourite forebear, who, harassed by Napoleon, abused by her lovers, ill-served by friends who owed their fortunes to her good offices, nevertheless maintained to the end that animation, generosity of spirit, and brilliance of wit which make her letters my solace and inspiration. But in the matter of the honorary doctorate and my—blind—insistence upon your nomination therefor, I shall speak to you with a candour which, between a Master of Arts and their lifelong Mistress, I must trust not to miscarry; for I cannot imagine your regarding a distinction so wretched on the face of it otherwise than with amused contempt, and yet upon your decision to accept or decline ride matters of some (and, it may be, more than local) consequence.

Briefly, briefly. The tiny history of "Redneck Tech" has been a seven-year battle between the most conservative elements in the state— principally local, for, as you know, Mason and Dixon's line may be said to run north and south in Maryland, up Chesapeake Bay, and the Eastern Shore is more Southern than Virginia—and the most "liberal" (mainly not native, as the natives do not fail to remark), who in higher latitudes would be adjudged cautious moderates at best. The original college was endowed by a local philanthropist, now deceased: an excellent gentleman whose fortune, marvellous to tell, derived from *pickles* . . . and whose politics were so Tory that, going quite crackers in his final years, the dear fellow fancied himself to be, not Napoleon, but *George III*, still fighting the American Revolution as his "saner" neighbours still refight your Civil War. His Majesty's board of trustees was composed exclusively of his relatives, friends, and business associates— several of whom, however, were of more progressive tendencies, and sufficiently influential in this Border State to have some effect on the affairs of the institution even after it joined the state university complex. Indeed, it was they who pressed most vigorously, against much opposition, to bring the college under state administration in the first place, hoping thereby to rescue it from parochial reaction; and the president of the college during these first stages of its history was a man of respectable academic credentials and reasonably liberal opinions, their appointee: the historian Joseph Morgan.

To console the Tories, however, one John Schott—formerly head of a nearby teachers college and a locally famous right-winger—was appointed provost of the Faculty of Letters and vice-president of (what now was awkwardly denominated) Marshyhope State University College. A power struggle ensued at once, for Dr Schott is as politically ambitious as he is ideologically conservative, and had readily accepted what might seem a less prestigious post because he foresaw, correctly, that MSUC was destined for gigantic expansion, and he sensed, again correctly, opportunity in the local resentment against its "liberal" administration.

In the years thereafter, every forward-looking proposal of President Morgan's, from extending visitation privileges in the residence halls to defending a professor's right to lecture upon the history of revolution, was opposed not only by conservative faculty and directors of the Tidewater Foundation (as the original college's board of trustees renamed itself) but by the regional press, state legislators, and county officials, all of whom cited Schott in support of their position. The wonder is that Morgan survived for even a few semesters in the face of such harassment, especially when his critics found their Sweet Singer in the person of one A. B. Cook VI, self-styled Laureate of Maryland, of whom alas more later—I daresay you know of that formidable charlatan and his mind-abrading doggerel, *e.g.*:

> Fight, Marylanders, nail and tooth,
> For John Schott and his Tow'r of Truth, etc.

Which same tower, presently under construction, was the gentle Morgan's undoing. He had—aided by the reasonabler T.F. trustees, more enlightened state legislators, and that saving remnant of civilised folk tied by family history and personal sentiment to the shire of their birth—managed after all to weather storms of criticism and effect some modest improvements in the quality of instruction at Marshyhope. Moreover, despite grave misgivings about academic gigantism, Morgan believed that the only hope for real education in such surroundings was to make the college the largest institutional and economic entity in the area, and so had led the successful negotiation to make Marshyhope a university centre: not a replica of the state university's vast campus on the mainland, but a smaller, well-funded research centre for outstanding undergraduate and postgraduate students from throughout the university system: academically rigorous, but loosely structured and cross-disciplinary. So evident were the economic blessings of this coup to nearly everyone in the area, Morgan's critics were reduced to grumbling about the radical effects that an influx of some seven thousand "outsiders" was bound to have on the Dorset Way of Life—and Schott & Co. were obliged to seek fresh ground for their attack.

They found it in the Tower of Truth. If the old isolation of Dorchester was to be sacrificed any road on the altar of economic progress (so their argument ran), why stop at seven thousand students—a kind of academic elite at that, more than likely long-haired radicals from Baltimore or even farther north? Why not open the doors to *all* our tidewater sons and daughters, up to the number of, say, seven times seven thousand? Fill in sevenfold more marshy acreage; make seven times over the fortunes of wetland realtors and building contractors; septuple the jobs available to Dorchester's labour force; build on Redmans Neck a veritable City of Learning, more populous (and prosperous) by far than any of the peninsula's actual municipalities! And from its centre let there rise, as a symbol (and advertisement) of the whole, Marshyhope's beacon to the world: a great white tower, the Tower of Truth! By day the university's main library, perhaps, and (certainly) the seat of its administration, let it be by night floodlit and visible from clear across the Chesapeake—from (in Schott's own pregnant phrase) "Annapolis at least, maybe even Washington!"

In vain Morgan's protests that seven thousand dedicated students, housed in tasteful, low-profile buildings on the seven hundred acres of farmland already annexed by MSUC, represented the maximum reasonable burden on the ecology and sociology of the county, and the optimal balance of economic benefits and academic manageability; that Schott's "Tower of Truth," like the projected diploma mill it represented, would violate the natural terrain; that the drainage of so much marsh would be an ecological disaster, the influx of so huge a population not a stimulus to the Dorset Way of Life but a cataclysmic shock; that both skyscrapers and ivory towers were obsolete ideals; that even if they weren't, no sane contractor would attempt such a structure on the spongy ground of a fresh-filled fen, et cetera. In veritable transports of bad faith, the Schott/Cook party rhapsodised that Homo sapiens himself—especially in his rational, civilised, university-founding aspect—was the very embodiment of "antinaturalness": towering erect instead of creeping on all fours, opposing reason to brute instinct, aspiring ever to what was deemed beyond his grasp, raising from the swamp primordial great cities, lofty cathedrals, towers of learning. How were the fenny origins invoked of Rome! How *learning* was rhymed with *yearning, Tow'r of Truth* with *Flow'r of Youth!* How was excoriated, in editorial and Rotary Club speech, "the Morgan theory" (which he never held) that the university should be a little model of the actual world rather than a lofty counterexample: lighthouse to the future, ivory tower to the present, castle keep of the past!

Cook's rhetoric, all this, sweetly resounding in our Chambers of Commerce, where too there were whispered libels against the luckless

Morgan: that his late wife had died a dozen years past in circumstances never satisfactorily explained, which however had led to Morgan's "resignation" from his first teaching post, at Wicomico Teachers College; that his absence from the academic scene between that dismissal (by Schott himself, as ill chance would have it, who damningly refused to comment on the matter, declaring only that "every man deserves a second chance") and his surprise appointment by Harrison Mack II as first president of Tidewater Tech was not unrelated to that dark affair. By 1967, when Morgan acquiesced to the Tower of Truth in hopes of saving his plan for a manageable, high-quality research centre, the damage to his reputation had been done, by locker-room couplets of unacknowledged but unmistakable authorship:

> Here is the late Mrs Morgan interred,
> Whose *ménage à trois* is reduced by one-third.
> Her husband and lover survive her, both fired:
> *Requiescat in pacem* the child they both sired, etc.

In July of last year he resigned, ostensibly to return to teaching and research, and in fact is a visiting professor of American History this year at the college in Massachusetts named after my late husband's famous ancestor—or was until his disappearance some weeks ago. John Schott became acting president—and what a vulgar act is his!—and yours truly, who has no taste for administrative service even under decent chiefs like Morgan, but could not bear to see MSUC's governance altogether in Boeotian hands, was prevailed upon to act as provost of the Faculty of Letters.

How came Schott to choose me, you ask, who am through these hopeless marshes but (I hope) the briefest of sojourners? Surely because he rightly distrusts all his ordinary faculty, and wrongly supposes that, visitor and woman to boot, I can be counted upon passively to abet his accession to the actual presidency of MSU—from which base (read "tow'r," and weep for Marshyhope, for Maryland!) he will turn his calculating eyes to Annapolis, "maybe even Washington"! Yet he does me honour by enough distrusting my gullibility after all to leave behind as mine his faithful secretary-at-least: Miss Shirley Stickles, sharp of eye and pencil if not of mind, to escape whose surveillance I am brought to penning by hand this sorry history of your nomination.

Whereto, patient Mr B., we are come! For scarce had I aired against my tenancy the provostial chamber (can you name another university president who smokes cigars?) when there was conveyed to me, via his minatory and becorseted *derrière-garde*, my predecessor's expectation, not only that I would appoint at once a nominating committee for the proposed Litt.D. (that is, a third member, myself being already on the committee *ex officio* and Schott having appointed, by some dim prerogative, a second: one Harry Carter, former psychologist, present nonentity and academic vice-president, Schott's creature), but that, after a show of nomination weighing, we would present to the board of regents as our candidate the "Maryland Laureate" himself, Mr Andrew Cook!

Schott's strategy is clear: to achieve some "national visibility," as they say, with his eyesore of a Tower; a degree of leverage (in *honoris causa!*) in the state legislature with his honorary doctorates (the LL.D., of course, will go to the governor, or the local congressman); and the applause of the regional right with his laurelling of the hardy rhymer of "marsh mallow" and "beach swallow"—a man one could indeed simply laugh at, were there no sinister side to his right-winged wrongheadedness and his rape of Mother English.

Counterstrategy I had none; nor motive, at first, beyond mere literary principle. Unacquainted with your work (and that of most of your countrymen), my first candidates were writers most honoured already in my own heart: Mrs Lessing perhaps, even Miss Murdoch; or the Anthonys Powell or Burgess. To the argument (advanced at once by Dr Carter) that none of these has connexion with MSUC, I replied that "connexions" should have no connexion with honours. Yet I acceded to the gentler suasion of my friend, colleague, and committee appointee Mr Ambrose Mensch (whom I believe you know?): Marshyhope being not even a national, far less an international, institution, it were presumptuous of us to think to honour as it were beyond our means (literally so, in the matter of transatlantic air fares). He then suggested such Americans as one Mr Styron, who has roots in Virginia, and a Mr Updike, formerly of Pennsylvania. But I replied, cordially, that once the criterion of mere merit was put by, to honour a writer for springing from a neighbouring state made no more sense than to do so for his springing from a neighbouring shire, or civilisation. Indeed, the principle of "appropriateness," on which we now agreed if on little else, was really Carter's "connexion" in more palatable guise: as we were in fact a college of the state university and so far specifically regional, perhaps we could after all do honour without presumption only to a writer, scholar, or journalist with connexion to the Old Line State, preferably to the Eastern Shore thereof?

On these friendly deliberations between Mr Mensch and myself, Dr Carter merely smiled, prepared in any case to vote negatively on all nominations except A. B. Cook's, which he had put before us in the opening minutes of our opening session. I should add that, there being in the bylaws of the college and of the faculty as yet no provision for the nomination of candidates for honorary degrees, our procedure was *ad hoc* as our committee; but I was given to understand, by Sticklish insinuation, that if our nomination were not unanimous and soon forthcoming, Schott would empower his academic vice-president to form a new committee; further, that if our choice proved displeasing to the administration, the Faculty of Letters could expect no budgetary blessings next fiscal. Schott himself, with more than customary tact, merely declared to me his satisfaction, at this point in our discussions, that we had decided to honour a native son . . .

"*I.e.*, the Fair-Land Muse himself," Mr Mensch dryly supposed on hearing this news (the epithet from Cook's own rhyme for Maryland, in its local two-syllable pronunciation). I then conveyed to him, and do now to you, in both instances begging leave not to reveal my source, that I had good reason to believe that beneath his boorish, even ludicrous, public posturing, Andrew Burlingame Cook VI (his full denomination!) is a dark political power, in "Mair'land" and beyond: not a kingmaker, but a maker and unmaker of kingmakers: a man behind the men behind the scenes, with whose support it was, alas, not unimaginable after all that John Schott might one day cross the Bay to "Annapolis, maybe even Washington." To thwart Cook's nomination, then, and haply thereby to provoke his displeasure with our acting president, might be to strike a blow, at least a tap, for decent government!

I speak lightly, sir (as did Germaine de Staël even in well-founded fear of her life), but the matter is not without gravity. This Cook is a menace to more than the art of poetry, and any diminution of his public "cover," even by denying him an honour he doubtless has his reasons for desiring, is a move in the public weal.

And I now believe, what I would not have done a fortnight past, that with your help—*i.e.*, your "aye"—he may be denied. "Of course," Mr Mensch remarked to me one evening, "there's always my old friend B. . . ." I asked (excuse me) whom that name might name, and was told: not only that you were born and raised hereabouts, made good your escape, and from a fit northern distance set your first novels in this area, but that my friend himself—*our* friend—was at that moment under contract to write a screenplay of your newest book, to be filmed on location in the county. How would your name strike Carter, Schott, and company? It just might work, good Ambrose thought, clearly now warming to his inspiration and wondering aloud why he hadn't hit on it before—especially since, though he'd not corresponded with you for years, he was immersed in your fiction, is indeed on leave from teaching this semester to draft that screenplay.

In sum, it came (and comes) to this: John Schott's appointment to the presidency of MSU is quietly opposed, in our opinion, by moderate elements on the board of regents and the Tidewater Foundation, and it can be imagined that, among the more knowledgeable of these elements, this opposition extends to the trumpeting false laureate as well. Their support comes from the radical right and, perversely, the radical left (that minority of two or three bent on destroying universities altogether as perpetuators of bourgeois values). A dark-horse nominee of the right colouration might just slip between this Scylla and this Charybdis.

Very casually we tried your name on Harry Carter, and were pleased to observe in his reaction more suspicious curiosity than actual opposition. This curiosity, moreover, turned into guarded interest when Ambrose pointed out (as if the thought had just occurred to him) that the "tie-in" at our June commencement of the filming of your book and the county's Tercentennial (itself to involve some sort of feature on "Dorchester in Art and Literature") would no doubt occasion publicity for Marshyhope U. and the Tower of Truth. He, Ambrose—he added with the straightest of faces—might even be able to work into the film itself some footage of the ceremonies, and the Tower . . .

This was last week. Our meeting ended with a sort of vote: two–nothing in favour of your nomination, Dr Carter abstaining. To my surprise, the acting president's reaction, relayed through both Dr Carter and Miss Stickles, is cautious nondisapproval, and today I am authorised to make the invitation.

You are, then, sir, by way of being a compromise candidate, who will, I hope, so far from feeling therein compromised, come to the aid of your friend, your native county, and its "largest single economic [and *only* cultural] entity" by accepting this curious invitation. Moreover, by accepting it promptly, before the opposition (some degree of which is to be expected) has time to rally. That Schott even tentatively permits this letter implies that A. B. Cook VI has been sounded out and, for whatever mysterious reasons, chooses not to exercise his veto out of hand. But Ambrose informs me, grimly, that there is a "Dr Schott" in some novel of yours, too closely resembling ours for coincidence, and not flatteringly drawn: should he get wind of this fact (Can it be true? Too delicious!) before your acceptance has been made public . . .

Au revoir, then, friend of my friend! I hold your first novel in my hand, eager to embark upon it; in your own hand you may hold some measure of our future here (think what salubrious effect a few well-chosen public jibes at the "Tow'r of Truth" and its tidewater laureate might have, televised live from Redmans Neck on Commencement Day!). Do therefore respond at your earliest to this passing odd epistle, whose tail like the spermatozoon's far outmeasures its body, the better to accomplish its single urgent end, and—like Molly Bloom at the close of *her* great soliloquy (whose author was, yes, a friend of your friend's friend)—say to us *yes,* to the Litt.D. *yes,* to MSU *yes,* and *yes* Dorchester, *yes* Tidewater, Maryland *yes yes yes!*

Yours,
GGP(A)

N: *The Author to Lady Amherst. Politely declining her invitation.*

Department of English, Annex B
State University of New York at Buffalo
Buffalo, New York 14214

March 16, 1969

Prof. Germaine G. Pitt (Amherst)
Acting Provost, Faculty of Letters
Marshyhope State University
Redmans Neck, Maryland 21612

Dear Professor Pitt (Amherst?):

Not many invitations could please me more, ordinarily, than yours of March 8. Much obliged, indeed.

By coincidence, however, I accepted in February a similar invitation from the main campus of the State University at College Park (it seems to be my year down there), and I feel that two degrees in the same June from the same Border State would border upon redundancy. So I decline, with thanks, and trust that the ominous matters you allude to in your remarkable postscript can be forestalled in some other wise.

Why not award the thing to our mutual acquaintance Ambrose Mensch? He's an honorable, deserving oddball and a bona fide avant-gardist, whose "career" I've followed with interest and sympathy. A true "doctor of letters" (in the Johns Hopkins Medical School sense), he is a tinkerer, an experimenter, a slightly astigmatic visionary, perhaps even a revolutionizer of cures—and patient Literature, as your letter acknowledges, if not terminal, is not as young as she used to be either.

Cordially,

P.S.: "I have made this longer only because I did not have the leisure to make it shorter": Pascal, *Lettres provinciales,* XVI. Perhaps Mme de Staël was paraphrasing Pascal?
P.P.S.: Do the French not customarily serve the salad *after* the entrée?

The Degree

Richard Armour

On completion of the required course of studies, the student is given the B.A. or, if he has avoided all impractical courses, the B.S. He is now entitled to put his degree after his name, like an M.D., but will be subjected to considerable ridicule if he does, unless he lives in England.

The degree is proof of the fact that the student is Educated, despite doubts raised by his inability to write clearly, keep his bank account balanced, or be logical in an argument. When people ask him, "Where did you go?" he is able to tell where he went.

The degree is formally conferred at Commencement, the final test of the student's stamina and fortitude. Commencement takes place in June, the weather determining whether it is held indoors or outdoors. If it is held indoors, in the college gym, which is without air conditioning and smells of sweat socks, it will be the hottest day of the year, while if it is held outdoors there will be a steady downpour, beginning almost the instant the College Chaplain opens the ceremony with the invocation. Possibly what sounds like "Let us spray" is heard by some ancient rain god.

Students wear academic robes, which are black because students are supposed to be in mourning at having to leave college after four happy years of examinations, term papers, and required physical education. On their heads are mortarboards, a type of headgear which has never caught on for everyday use. While the glee club is singing, a wind inevitably rises and students must hold onto their mortarboards or graduate bareheaded.

The faculty, which could not otherwise find its way, is led by the Faculty Marshal. The Marshal carries a mace, a heavy staff about five feet long which is a reminder to faculty members that they had better not get out of step. In the early days, the mace had spikes on the end, but these were removed as the result of pressure from the AAUP.

After the invocation by the Chaplain and one number too many by the glee club, the President introduces the commencement speaker, who is either (1) another college President, who, by reciprocal arrangement, is willing to speak for nothing if he is given an honorary degree, (2) the head of a large corporation, educational foundation, or other source of funds, or (3) a graduate of the college who has been more successful than anyone would have dreamed.

The President's introduction of the commencement speaker is full of facts everyone has been dying to know, such as where he went to college, professional societies to which he belongs, his participation in

The Marshal and his mace

such community activities as the Chamber of Commerce (vice president, 1949) and the Community Chest (chairman for his block, 1952), his publications (including his widely read "Structural Relationships of Pteridophytes and Seed Plants"), his military service, his travels, his hobbies, and his golf handicap. Mainly the President is trying to justify his selection of the speaker, especially since the fiasco of last year, when the speaker was told not to exceed twenty minutes and spoke slightly over an hour and was extremely dull, except for an off-color story that offended several of the wealthiest trustees.

The following words, phrases, and inspiring statements will be useful to any commencement speaker. By putting them together, in any order, the speaker will have a speech which, when he has concluded, the President will characterize as "a brilliant and memorable address":

"You of the younger generation"
"The future is in your hands"
"Liberty"
"Freedom"
"Your place in society"
"Can you hear me?"
"The whole man"
"Leaders of tomorrow"
"Changing values"
"We of our generation will not live to see"
"History teaches us"
"As you go forth"
"You young people"
"That reminds me of the story about"
"Our great country"
"There must be something wrong with the microphone"
"Challenge of our times"
"In conclusion"
"Technological advance"
"The world we live in"
"When I was in college"
"Members of the graduating class"
"Looking ahead"
"To sum up"
"This great institution"

"Your distinguished President"
"God"
"In the words of Thomas Jefferson"
"You will recall Shakespeare's lines"
"If I may take just a few more minutes"

The bright spot of most commencement addresses is when the speaker's notes blow off the lectern.

When the speaker has concluded and there is no further way to prolong the ceremony, the President reluctantly proceeds to confer the degrees. Handing each student a diploma with his right hand and shaking hands with his left until he realizes there is something awkward about this, the President says over and over, "By virtue of the authority vested in me by the Board of Trustees, I confer upon you the degree of Bachelor of Arts." Now and then his tongue gets slightly twisted and it comes out "By virtue of the vest authorized me by the Toard of Bustees. . . ."

At this point one trustee leans over to another and whispers, "Isn't the Prexy getting pretty close to retirement?"

At some colleges the Dean of the Faculty then takes hold of the tassel on the student's mortarboard and moves it from the right side to the left. At other colleges the student is permitted to do this for himself, as a sign of his having reached a level of intellectual maturity and physical coordination when he can do such things on his own. In any case, the tassel which previously had bothered the student by dangling in his right eye, now bothers him by dangling in his left eye.

Some trustees think this shift from the right to the left is part of the Communist conspiracy. "I'm not saying any of the faculty are card-carrying Communists," they mutter open-mindedly, "but altogether too many of them are from Harvard."

Garry Trudeau

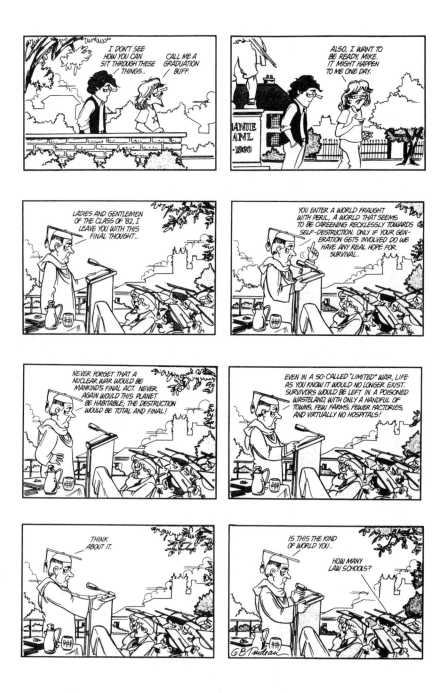

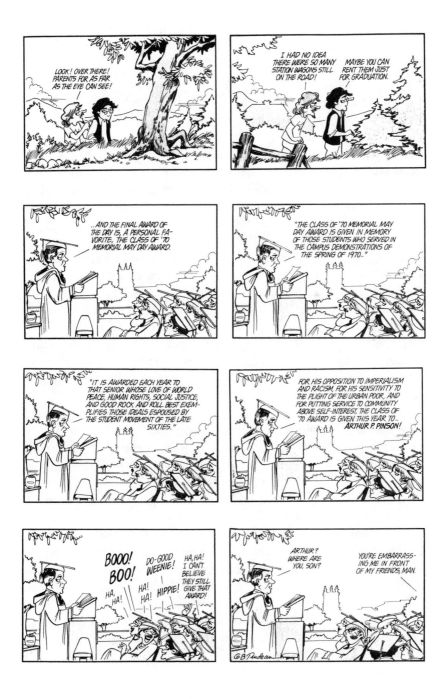

President Robbins of Benton

Randall Jarrell

President Robbins, judge him as you please, was not human. He had not had time to be; besides, his own gift was for seeming human. He had taught sociology only a year, and during the last three months of that year he had already been selected to be Dean of Men at————; two years later he was appointed Dean of the College of Arts and Sciences at————; in six years he was President of Benton. *They* had selected him. But how had *they* known whom to select? Would someone else have done as well? Why had they selected *just him?*

If you ask this, you have never selected or been selected; you would know, then. Such questions are as ridiculous as asking how stigmata know who to select—as asking, "Wouldn't somebody else have done just as well as St. Francis?" A *vocation,* a *calling*—these words apply quite as well in secular affairs as in religious: Luther knew. Have you yourself never known one of these *idiots savants* of success, of Getting Ahead in the World? About other things they may know something or they may not, but about the World they have forgotten—in previous existences for which, perhaps, they are being punished?—far more than you or I will ever learn.

President Robbins was, of course, one of these men. He "did not have his Ph.D."—but had that bothered one administrator upon this earth? All had been as refreshingly unprejudiced about his lack of one as the President of Benton now was about anybody's possession of one. But at Benton all of them were like this: they looked up your degrees so they could tell you that, whatever the things were, they didn't mind. President Robbins had an M.A. from Oxford—he had been a Rhodes Scholar—and an LL.D. granted, in 1947, by Menuire. (It's a college in Florida.) To make the President dislike you for the rest of his life, say to him with a resigned anthropological smile: "I've just been reading that in 1948 Menuire College gave the degree of Doctor of Humor to Milton Berle."

President Robbins had brought seven former Rhodes Scholars to Benton during his first two years there. Benton thought him in most ways an ideal President, but about this they felt as the constituents of a

Republican senator do when he appoints seven former U.N. officials to postmasterships. An ounce of Rhodes Scholars was worth a pound of Rhodes Scholars, in Benton's opinion.

10.

But when the President spoke to them they could have forgiven him a wilderness of Rhodes Scholars. Benton had a day for parents and alumnae which was, or was not, called Founder's Day—I have forgotten. Yet surely it was not: who could have founded Benton? Benton is a Category like Time or Space or Causality.

I have forgotten the name of the day, but I remember its lunch. The day before, a third of our luncheon had been a salad of uncooked spinach, a midnight-green salad with, here and there among the leaves, an eye of beet: a yew-tree's notion of a salad: a salad that was exactly like a still-life by Soutine—had I not been poor I should have had it varnished and framed. But on parents' day we had, among other things, lobster and shrimp in little crumbling shells—no, *big* crumbling shells—of pastry. The girl with whom I used to play tennis was waiting on our table; she mumbled to me, "Gee, what's up?" I flickered my eyes toward the longest table: the President sat there among matrons. Had I been hatted, had I been gowned, had I been shod as were those matrons, I should have sold myself and made my fortune; but alas! they had had the idea before me.

That night we came together to hear President Robbins: the matrons, the girls, the teachers, Constance, Dr. Rosenbaum, Gertrude Johnson, I. "Good God," Gertrude whispered to me when she had looked around her; for once she was wordless. We suffered our way through a long program, and then President Robbins began to speak.

After two sentences one realized once more that President Robbins was an extraordinary speaker, a speaker of a—one says *an almost extinct school*, but how does one say the opposite? *a not-yet-evolved school?* He did something so logical that it is impossible that no one else should have thought of it, and yet no one has. President Robbins *crooned* his speeches.

His voice not only took you into his confidence, it laid a fire for you and put out your slippers by it and then went into the other room to get into something more comfortable. It was a Compromising voice. President Robbins was, in Shaw's phrase, "a man of good character where women are concerned," and he had never touched a Benton girl except in a game of water-polo; yet as you heard him speak something muttered inside you, "To a nunnery, go!"

He would say to you in private in his office, about the teachers of Benton: "We like to feel that we educate [there was a slow, chaste separation between the next two words: they seemed youths and maidens who have become strong and sublimated through remaining apart] each . . . other." If his voice was tender then, consider what it became in public; for that voice did not sell itself to the highest bidder, it just gave itself away to everybody.

President Robbins made a speech that—that—as Gertrude said, you had to hear it not to believe it. When he finished (and not a minute too late; the audience wolfed that speech down the way Afghans ate their horsemeat) he finished by thanking the students, parents, and faculty of Benton for the experience of working with, of learning from, and of growing to . . . love . . . such generous and intelligent, such tolerant and understanding, such—and here he paused quite a long time—such . . . good . . . people. As he said . . . *good* . . . there was in his voice so radiant a freshness, so yearning a transfiguration of all created things— how *chromatic* it was!—that the audience rose from their seats and sang, like Sieglinde: *Thou art the Spring!* No, they didn't actually, insensate things, but they wanted to: you could look at them and see that they were Changed.

Gertrude said softly, "Let's go in and wring the dew out of our stockings; mine are soaked." I thought, "Good old Gertrude"; but as soon as I realized what I was thinking, I stopped.

11.

At our nation's capital, hidden away by legislators, there is a colossal statue of George Washington—seated, antique, naked to the waist; he looks as awful as Ingres' Zeus, but good. I sometimes thought that this statue, rather than the Smith shrike-tree, should have been put at the center of Benton as a representation of President Robbins Being the Spirit of Benton. But the shrike-tree was good too.

People really did think of the President in a costume somewhat similar to the statue's: *Time* and *Life* and *NewsWeek,* just after his appointment, had all carried pictures of him taken in the days when he had not yet thought of becoming an educator, but was only a diver at the Olympic Games. People would say, "Did you see where they appointed this diver a college-president?"—plenty of presidents had been football-players, but a diver was something new. (The picture in *Life* showed him standing between Johnny Weismuller and Eleanor Holm; and I heard a little boy say about it, in the most disgusted voice I've ever heard: "They've made *Tarzan* the president of an old girls' college!") When the President went on money-raising tours among his alumnae and his students' parents and grandparents and guardians—

Poor man! he spent half his time on these, and half making speeches, and half writing articles for magazines and appearing on radio forums and testifying before Congressional committees that it would be unwise, in time of war, to draft the girls of Benton into the Women's Army Auxiliary Corps, and half . . . as you see, he had learned the secret of busy and successful men: that there are thirty-six hours in every day, if you only know where to look for them. If he had known where to find one more, an hour for himself, a kind of Children's Hour for the boy Dwight Robbins, who can say what might have become of him? But he had never known.

His appeals for funds were nowhere more successful than in Hollywood. Several Benton alumnae were stars, socially-conscious scriptwriters, wives or daughters of producers. President Robbins appealed to them sitting in somewhat Hawaiian swimming-shorts at the grassy verge of swimming-pools: as he looked thoughtfully into the thoughtless water he seemed to the alumnae some boyish star who, playing Tom Sawyer, fancies for the moment that he is Narcissus. Not to have given him what he asked, they felt, would have been to mine the bridge that bears the train that carries the supply of this year's Norman Rockwell Boy Scout Calendars. They felt this; it seems far-fetched to me.

He was, in sober truth, in awful truth, a dedicated man (the really damned not only like Hell, they feel loyal to it); and if his dedication was to the things of this world, to this world, should we scorn him for it any more than we scorn some holy *faquir*, some yellow-robed disciple sitting cross-legged among those whom the Buddha addressed as *Bhikkus*? If it were not for men like President Robbins, how could this world go on? *Everything* would be different.

And yet one must admit that such men are in long supply.

My Speech to the Graduates

Woody Allen

More than any other time in history, mankind faces a crossroads. One path leads to despair and utter hopelessness. The other, to total extinction. Let us pray we have the wisdom to choose correctly. I speak, by the way, not with any sense of futility, but with a panicky conviction of the absolute meaninglessness of existence which could easily be misinterpreted as pessimism. It is not. It is merely a healthy concern for the predicament of modern man. (Modern man is here defined as any person born after Nietzsche's edict that "God is dead," but before the hit recording "I Wanna Hold Your Hand.") This "predicament" can be stated one of two ways, though certain linguistic philosophers prefer to reduce it to a mathmatical equation where it can be easily solved and even carried around in the wallet.

Put in its simplest form, the problem is: How is it possible to find meaning in a finite world given my waist and shirt size? This is a very difficult question when we realize that science has failed us. True, it has conquered many diseases, broken the genetic code, and even placed human beings on the moon, and yet when a man of eighty is left in a room with two eighteen-year-old cocktail waitresses nothing happens. Because the real problems never change. After all, can the human soul be glimpsed through a microscope? Maybe—but you'd definitely need one of those very good ones with two eyepieces. We know that the most advanced computer in the world does not have a brain as sophisticated as that of an ant. True, we could say that of many of our relatives but we only have to put up with them at weddings or special occasions. Science is something we depend on all the time. If I develop a pain in the chest I must take an X-ray. But what if the radiation from the X-ray causes me deeper problems? Before I know it, I'm going in for surgery. Naturally, while they're giving me oxygen an intern decides to light up a cigarette. The next thing you know I'm rocketing over the World Trade Center in bed clothes. Is this science? True, science has taught us how to pasteurize cheese. And true, this can be fun in mixed company—but what of the H-bomb? Have you ever seen what happens when one of those things falls off a desk accidentally? And where is science when one ponders the eternal riddles? How did the cosmos originate? How long has it been around? Did matter begin with an explosion or by the word of God? And if by the latter, could He not have begun it just two weeks earlier to take advantage of some of the warmer weather? Exactly what do we mean when we say, man is mortal? Obviously it's not a compliment.

Religion too has unfortunately let us down. Miguel de Unamuno writes blithely of the "eternal persistence of consciousness," but this is no easy feat. Particularly when reading Thackeray. I often think how comforting life must have been for early man because he believed in a powerful, benevolent Creator who looked after all things. Imagine his disappointment when he saw his wife putting on weight. Contemporary man, of course, has no such peace of mind. He finds himself in the midst of a crisis of faith. He is what we fashionably call "alienated." He has seen the ravages of war, he has known natural catastrophes, he has been to singles bars. My good friend Jacques Monod spoke often of the randomness of the cosmos. He believed everything in existence occurred by pure chance with the possible exception of his breakfast, which he felt certain was made by his housekeeper. Naturally belief in a divine intelligence inspires tranquillity. But this does not free us from our human responsibilities. Am I my brother's keeper? Yes. Interestingly, in my case I share that honor with the Prospect Park Zoo. Feeling godless then, what we have done is made technology God. And yet can technology really be the answer when a brand new Buick, driven by my close associate, Nat Zipsky, winds up in the window of Chicken Delight causing hundreds of customers to scatter? My toaster has never once worked properly in four years. I follow the instructions and push two slices of bread down in the slots and seconds later they rifle upward. Once they broke the nose of a woman I loved very dearly. Are we counting on nuts and bolts and electricity to solve our problems? Yes, the telephone is a good thing—and the refrigerator—and the air conditioner. But not every air conditioner. Not my sister Henny's, for instance. Hers makes a loud noise and still doesn't cool. When the man comes over to fix it, it gets worse. Either that or he tells her she needs a new one. When she complains, he says not to bother him. This man is truly alienated. Not only is he alienated but he can't stop smiling.

The trouble is, our leaders have not adequately prepared us for a mechanized society. Unfortunately our politicians are either incompetent or corrupt. Sometimes both on the same day. The Government is unresponsive to the needs of the little man. Under five-seven, it is impossible to get your Congressman on the phone. I am not denying that democracy is still the finest form of government. In a democracy at least, civil liberties are upheld. No citizen can be wantonly tortured, imprisoned, or made to sit through certain Broadway shows. And yet this is a far cry from what goes on in the Soviet Union. Under their form of totalitarianism, a person merely caught whistling is sentenced to thirty years in a labor camp. If, after fifteen years, he still will not stop whistling, they shoot him. Along with this brutal fascism we find its handmaiden, terrorism. At no other time in history has man been so afraid to cut into his veal chop for fear that it will explode. Violence breeds more violence and it is predicted that by 1990 kidnapping will be the dominant mode of social interaction. Overpopulation will exacerbate problems to the breaking point. Figures tell us there are already more people on earth than we need to move even the heaviest piano. If we do not call a halt to breeding, by the year 2000 there will be no room to serve dinner unless one is willing to set the table on the heads of strangers. Then they must not move for an hour while we eat. Of course energy will be in short supply and each car owner will be allowed only enough gasoline to back up a few inches.

Instead of facing these challenges we turn instead to distractions like drugs and sex. We live in far too permissive a society. Never before has pornography been this rampant. And those films are lit so badly! We are a people who lack defined goals. We have never learned to love. We lack leaders and coherent programs. We have no spiritual center. We are adrift alone in the cosmos wreaking monstrous violence on one another out of frustration and pain. Fortunately, we have not lost our sense of proportion. Summing up, it is clear the future holds great opportunities. It also holds pitfalls. The trick will be to avoid the pitfalls, seize the opportunities, and get back home by six o'clock.

Graduationese

Andrew A. Rooney

The headline reads, GRADUATES TO FIND JOBS SCARCE.

How many times have you read that story?

I don't offhand recall any year that wasn't the most difficult there ever was for graduating seniors to find jobs.

Each of us, at one time or another in our lives, has had a tough time finding a job, so we're sympathetic. We want to help. We don't want to give them a job, but we want to help.

The speakers at high school and college graduation ceremonies want to help by giving advice. I've been reading excerpts from some of the speeches.

For some reason, giving a commencement address brings out the worst in a speaker. Otherwise bright, normal, nice people turn themselves into pompous asses for the day. Years ago I spoke to the graduating class at the high school I attended, and I shudder to think what I told them and what my attitude was while I did it.

Pompous speeches are not necessarily the speaker's fault. That's what a commencement speech is supposed to be. The speaker is there to give the ceremony some importance so he or she has to say some important-sounding things.

(I don't know who makes the decision about whether to call it "graduation" or "commencement." There's a big difference in attitude between the two words. "Graduation" suggests students have finished with something and "commencement" suggests they're just starting.)

President A. Bartlett Giamatti of Yale University gave one of the speeches I read. Except for the fact that he uses the "A." that way for his name, Dr. Giamatti is a brilliant, down-to-earth scholar. Normally what I see of his writing is so much smarter than I am that I'm discouraged by it, so naturally I was happy to note that he's only human. When he wrote this, he fell into the rhythm of the traditional graduation speech cliché, proving he's mortal.

There are some easily identifiable clues by which a graduation address can be detected.

First, the speaker starts with some light, often deprecating remark about either himself or commencement speeches in general. Dr. Giamatti did that:

"Commencement speeches are often as difficult to endure as to deliver," he said, "and you are, I trust, relieved that Yale doesn't have one."

That's a good remark for its kind but it is of a kind. And, of course, Yale *does* have a commencement address and he was giving it.

"Commencement speakers who have mastered the genre," he said, "manage to be at once condescending and conspiratorial . . ."

The key cliché there is the phrase "at once." You'll find it several times in most graduation speeches. Dr. Giamatti went for it again a few lines later when he referred to something as "at once satisfying and singular." That's perfect graduation speech language, too, because it's a little obscure and sounds at once important and euphonious.

Look for the word "indeed." This indicates that the speaker has had another idea for padding out his talk.

"Indeed to blend pomp and independence . . ." Dr. Giamatti said.

"Indeed I think a healthy family . . ."

He also told the Yale graduates that "no small challenge lies ahead."

This must mean he thinks there's more of a challenge than if he'd said simply, "A big challenge lies ahead."

No matter how the speaker says it, challenges always lie ahead in graduation addresses.

The meat of Dr. Giamatti's speech, though, came toward the end of it:

"I do not bring you any easy answers," he said.

I was frankly disappointed with that. It costs $50,000 to put a kid through Yale. For that much money, the least their president could do when they graduate is give them a few easy answers.

Henry Martin

*"President Gorman, distinguished faculty, honored guests, members
of the Class of 1980, and impoverished parents . . ."*

• •

*"Congratulations, and please have all bills paid
before leaving the Universitas."*

Grooving with Academe

Russell Baker

For a long time I made commencement speeches. It started with high schools. One had sons, daughters. They went to high school, alas. Hawk-eyed principals desperate for someone—anyone—to harangue their steamy produce spotted me for an easy mark.

How could one resist making sons and daughters proud by a display of public prattling before their assembled schoolmates? More cunning parents resisted it easily. Wiser parents. Parents with no instinct for self-humiliation. Not me. I was easily dragooned. "Go forth, youth of America—." The snickering, I assumed, came from the soreheads, from the types awaiting Juvenile Court action for trafficking in hashish.

Word passed along the principals' grapevine. I was in great demand. "Go forth and light the light of wisdom, youth of America—." I was hooked. A certain college, whose scheduled Demosthenes had seen the light in the nick of time and fled to Samoa, sought me in desperation as a replacement.

It was irresistible. The academic robes, the academic procession, the academic drinking on commencement eve with the academic professors, the academic hangover next morning, the glorious June sunshine filtered through the academic elms—all were immensely satisfying. The young whom I had sent forth from high school four years earlier now sat sprawled before me like a sea of Supreme Court Justices, and I sent them forth again.

"Go forth, youth of America—." They were surlier now. As the 1960's crumbled into the 1970's, they were no longer agreeable about going forth. They were of a mind to stay behind and ignite the physics lab or blow up the commencement podium.

This was the period in which I began receiving honorary degrees. Any sensible person would have re-examined his position as soon as the first honorary degree was offered, but we are talking now about a fevered brain.

Was there something odd about an honorary degree being extended to a person who had been put out of college with a gentleman's C, and granted that release only because the professors feared that, if failed, he might return for one more year?

Was it curious that such a person, whose only notable achievements had been to acquire three cats and make a fool of himself on many public occasions, should be accorded the same recognition as Nobel Prize winners, donors of $25-million bequests and politicians who were, had been or were expected to be Presidents of the United States?

Hoover, who got eighty-nine, received more than anybody else *The Guinness Book of World Records* has been able to discover. If he had my experience afterwards, this means he was plagued by eighty-nine colleges to contribute to their building funds.

A thoughtful person might have said yes—yes, there is something odd, something curious going on. He might have suspected that he was the token nonentity with which the student body was to be pacified. We speak, remember, of a time when the slightest provocation could turn an entire student body into sackers of Byzantium.

In this period, colleges far and wide desperately sought schlemiels who might keep the restless young amused by accepting their honorary degrees between the Nobelist in physics (nuclear, bad) and the politician who refused to support the Vietcong.

There has never been such a shower of honorary degrees upon life's fools. We would meet changing planes at O'Hare Airport and trade notes on honorary-degree conditions around the country and marvel that inconsequentiality was at last receiving its due.

I was oblivious to the reality at that time, of course, and so, when a college of splendid reputation in upstate New York asked me to make the commencement address and accept an honorary degree, I went. On the platform that day sat an unexpected, last minute guest. Ezra Pound. Mentor to T. S. Eliot, companion to Ernest Hemingway, poet extraordinary, a giant of twentieth-century letters. Ezra Pound. I was going to have to make a commencement speech at Ezra Pound.

I did it. "Go forth, Ezra Pound—." Ezra Pound sat through the whole thing. It may have been the most absurd moment in the history of commencements. I wanted to apologize, but Pound had taken a vow of silence and no conversation was possible, though I looked him in the eyes and thought they were saying, "Go forth—and follow my example."

At that moment I took a vow never to let another commencement speech pass my lips. I would have sworn, also, never to let another honorary degree fall upon me, but it wasn't necessary. The offers stopped coming in shortly afterwards, when the young had a change of heart and made peace with society. It was a happy development, not only because it meant that sanity was making a strong comeback, but also because it prevented me from beating Herbert Hoover's record for honorary degrees.

An Old Grad Remembers

Frank Sullivan

(Warning—The following will be incomprehensible to anyone who never went to Cornell University)

WHEN I was a freshman at Ithaca the University was down where the town is now and Ithaca was up on the hill by Bailey Hall. It was toward the close of a particularly frolicsome spring day that the positions were reversed. The Board of Trustees, once the shift had been made, never bothered to remedy it. "Laissez faire!" counselled a trustee who had majored in French.

Hiram Corson, Rym Berry, Goldwin Smith and myself comprised the Varsity crew that year, each man rowing four oars. There were giants in those days. Pearl White was the coxswain of our crew. Pearl White is not to be confused with E. B. (Andy) White, former editor of the *Sun*. Pearl was fuller around here, and here, and Andy wore suspenders. Ah, there were Pearl Whites in those days!

I'm afraid you lads will rue having started an old grad on these memories, but perhaps you will bear with me for a moment, or a week, for the sake of Auld Lang Syne, and the Annex, and Proctor Twesten, and Tar Young, and the short line to Auburn, and those trips up Buffalo hill after missing the jag car. (Buffalo Street ran UP hill in those days.)

I shall never forget the September afternoon I arrived in Ithaca. The seniors were wearing their blazers and the sophomores had just finished Senior Singing over by Goldwin Smith. Ah, there were sophomores in those days! You don't get sophomores like that nowadays. Can't get the stuff.

On a crisp autumn afternoon there was a tang to the air in the gymnasium that somehow made a fellow feel lucky to be alive. The good old Lyceum Theatre was still in existence, and Count Rogalsky and Lew Durland stood then at the northwest corner of State and Aurora. What times we students used to have in the "pit" at the Lyceum; carefree nights in the wonderful world of make-believe, nights which for many of us were our first taste of the drama. It was at the Lyceum I first saw Sothern and Marlowe in "Macbeth," and Sothern and Marlowe in "Floradora," and Marlowe and Sothern in "Juliet and Romeo." You don't see tap dancing like that any more.

I recall, too, those wonderful parties at the Dutch after the theatre, when Lillian Russell, or Lotta Faust, or Helena Modjeska, or some other reigning belle of showdom would come to town. We always drank champagne from the star's slipper, or if we happened to be extra thirsty, from one of the football captain's galoshes.

Where are the golden lads who were regulars at those gay suppers? David Starr Jordan never missed, and neither did dear old Professor Walter Heasley. Leroy P. Ward, Kid Kugler and "Steve" Stevenson were always present, and so was Dr. Hu Shih. Gesundheit! and dear old Professor Bishop, at that time doyen of the Department of Plant Pathology, whom we students, with that unerring instinct of the undergrad for pinning *le nicknom juste* on the faculty, always called "Morris G." But not to his face, you may be sure. Then there was dear old Raymond Howes, curator of the William Hazlitt Upson Numismatic Collection, and William Hazlitt Upson, at that time Raymond Howes Professor of Ornithology.

Will I ever forget the great revolt when the "frosh," as Professor George Lincoln Burr so happily dubbed them, refused to wear the traditional cap? Sure I will.

One of my first and most lasting friendships at Cornell was with a Jacob Gould Schurman who was President of the University. I would meet Dr. Schurman on the campus, tip my hat and say "Good morning, sir" and Dr. Schurman would return my greeting pleasantly. How I used to look forward to those bull sessions with J.G.!

Dear old Sage choir! I always thought it rather a pity that in the middle of a cantata one Sunday, Dr. Henry Ward Beecher suddenly turned a tommy gun on the choir and liquidated the entire mass of nightingales, save for one mezzo-soprano, a lady Vet student who, having heard of the good dominie's unpredictability, had taken the precaution to wear a surplice of chain mail. It was the first machine gun we fellows had ever seen and I recall how we crowded around Dr. Beecher after the massacre, plying him with questions about the new-fangled gadget and entreating him to let us try it out on the Dekes.

I remember those absurd things we used to eat at the Co-op in Morrill Hall between classes. They were called Wilbur Buds and, by Jove, they *looked* like Wilbur Buds, but yum, how good they used to taste. Good old Wilbur Buds. I suppose they have all been eaten.

Final examinations! What larks they were! Much more fun than the prelims, where the instructors served only soft drinks and buns, and never would slip us the answers. Does one ever, one wonders, quite forget the girl one took to one's first prelim?

What a fine body of men there was at Cornell in those days! In my class, for instance, all the men were over seven feet tall with the exceptions of John Wilkes Booth, Benjamin Ide Wheeler and myself. Only the weaklings of the class were allowed to play football. It would not have been fair to the other colleges to use our healthier classmates. Leon Czolgosz was voted Best Dresser of my class. It was Leon who later caused not a few raised eyebrows by shooting President McKinley, though the two had been excellent friends in college.

Percy Field on the afternoon of a big game. The stands are jammed, the October air bracing and the sun is getting low in, if my memory serves, the West. It is the last minute of the last quarter and the bases are full. Dartmouth, on our one-yard line, has taken two of our pawns and a castle. A groan from the crowd! Then, just as all seems lost, a flash of red and white oars in the distance, and we know that Pop Courtney has done it again at Poughkeepsie! What a roar goes up from that crowd! I can hear it now, or is that my blood pressure?

They were wonderful days. *Eheu*, as Bull Durham used to say, *fugaces*. Beer was a nickel a seidel at Hi Henry's. John Paul Jones had just introduced the principle of jet propulsion into the mile run. With Carl Hallock in the White House under the name of Rutherford B. Hayes, the country was happy and prosperous. Little did we dream that two wars and the Alumni Fund were just around the corner.

Ah, well. Those were the days. Excuse my emotion, but I wouldn't exchange the memory of those four wonderful years at Hobart for all the wealth of the Indies.

The Cultured Girl Again

Ben King

She was so esthetic and culchud,
    Just doted on Wagner and Gluck;
And claimed that perfection existed
    In some foreign English bred duke.

She raved over Browning and Huxley,
    And Tyndal, and Darwin, and Taine;
And talked about flora and fauna,
    And many things I can't explain.

Of Madame Blavatski, the occult,
    Theosophy, art, and then she
Spoke of the Cunead Sibyl
    And Venus de Med-i-che.

She spoke of the why and the wherefore,
    But longed for the whither and whence;
And she said yclept, yip, yap and yonder
    Were used in alliterative sense.

Well, I like a fool sat dumfounded,
    And wondered what she did n't know
'T was 10 when I bade her good evening,
    I thought it in season to go.

I passed her house yesterday evening,
    I don't know, but it seems to me,
She was chasing around in the kitchen,
    And getting things ready for tea.

I heard her sweet voice calling: "Mother,"
    It was then that I felt quite abashed,
For she yelled, "How shall I fix the 'taters,
    Fried, lionized, baked, biled, or mashed?"

Richard Cline

"The sun goes up, the sun goes down.
That's as deep as I get."

Alumni News

Andrew Ward

1899

Chester Wheatlock and his wife, **Grace Darling Bayberry** ('03), have been permitted adjoining rooms at the Benign Overlook Extended Care Facility in Dill, North Dakota, following Mr. Wheatlock's retirement from just about everything. "Don't worry about me," pens Chester. "I am fine. Go on and take care of the others, as I am fine."

1920

May Day Frondflusk was removed from her mission in Hua, South Vietnam, where she had labored on behalf of Hua's needy for close to forty years. "Miss Flondfrusk," as she was affectionately known by the natives, had to be forcibly transported by members of the fleeing South Vietnamese army. As head of the Hua Free-Through-Christ Alien Culture Mission, May established the town's first school of palmistry, a home for stray animals, a recording studio, and a chain of short-order restaurants. Miss Frondflusk has accepted an offer to work on behalf of a new Operation Bootstrap project in Shreveport, Louisiana. "But it won't be the same," May laments. "They tax you to death in Shreveport."

1934

Can anyone help **Carter Patapsco?** Carter has moved to his retirement cottage in Bay Ledge, Connecticut, where he has taken up bird-watching. "Before I began to read up on the subject, bird calls were cheerful voices from the wilds, as mysterious and variegated as snowflakes. But now, after a reading of Peterson's *Field Guide*, an afternoon on the terrace is for me like an eternity in the company of lunatics. 'Cheedle cheedle, chee?' Bell's vireo asks, and himself answers, 'Cheedle cheedle, chew!' The cardinal pipes, 'What cheer (cheer, cheer),' while the towhee, in a tone not unlike my late mother's, insists, 'Drink your tea. Drink your tea.' I have always loved it in the country, but have lately contemplated a return to the city, where the noise has at least not been transposed into idiot phrases."

1941

Rip Benson Kidder and his new wife, **Tory** (Brookings, '64), have moved from their Majorca digs to a winter residence in Manhattan. "Rip and I feel *somebody* has to make the urban commitment," writes Tory, who will be teaching wax resist in a storefront school on Fifth Avenue and 64th Street while Rip ghostwrites memoirs. "Tory," Rip P.S.'s, "has opened up whole new areas for me to explore."

1948

D. Stotts Wheelwright, deputy vice president of the International Division of Uncle Ben's Rice, has been named this country's new ambassador to Bechuanaland. "Bechu I don't," Stotts punned in his acceptance letter to the President. "But strictly straight from the shoulder, Marge and I couldn't be prouder, and look forward to representing our nation's interests among the gay, tuneful natives of this burgeoning, nubile young country. To provide our host country with a working model of American free enterprise," Stotts pledges, "my first official act will be to open a commissary."

1954

Dr. Emmett Bowen Friedkin's groundbreaking study, *The Etiology of Induced Toxic Hepatic Necrosis in Unsuspecting Maximum Security Prisoners,* is a runaway paperback best seller under its new title, *It's Your Liver—You Deal With It.* Alert classmates may have caught Emmett's appearance on Merv Griffin's "Salute to the Sick" theme show, where he shared the limelight with Robert Young, Virginia Graham, and an uncharacteristically serious Corbett Monica.

1962

Burl and **Tiffany (Maxim) Swate** write that they've discovered Transcendental Meditation. Tiffany, a children's book illustrator *(The Wonderful Bump* and, with Edwina Holmes Almstead, *Persnickety Two-Shoes Had Three Feet),* writes, "I know it sounds crazy, and it's just the sort of awfully earnest thing you'd never have caught me saying a few weeks ago, but I don't know how I could ever have held up my end of our karma without the Maharishi." "That goes double with me," dittoes attorney Burl.

1968

We better let **Tree Westfall** speak for himself this month: "The bull has wedded the mountain goddess. The thunder bespeaks forgotten truths. I am vapors. In time, I shall transmode my separate biodynamic creed entities into one of binary digital thought cycles. Until then, address all mail care of Hudson Towers, Fort Lee, New Jersey."

1972

Chip Croton and his wife, **Veronica,** have resigned their posts at The Farnham Institute for Pathological Research and have moved to Mill Valley, California. "We were nearing a possible cure for leukemia when we started to feel unfulfilled as persons," writes Chip, who has landed an apprenticeship with a free-form cabinetmaker while Veronica "gets into her head."

1975

Meg (Turley) Bodine and husband, **Tom,** announce the birth of a daughter, Jessica Jennifer. Congratulations may be sent to their home on Pleasant Drive, Darien, Connecticut, where, Meg writes, "We intend to live in bigger and bigger houses, own more and more things, take drives in cars with power everything, have lots of children, make lots of money, wear silly aprons on the patio, do whatever the hell we want."

Twenty-fifth Reunion

Richard Armour

Well, here we are, with husbands and with wives,
Accounting for the passage of our lives,
Remembering the good old good old days
And singing good old Alma Mater's praise
And smiling and exchanging commonplaces
While trying hard to bracket names and faces.
New, unfamiliar buildings frame the Quad,
But these are not so startling, not so odd
As what abrasive years have done to hair
And teeth and such. Oh, no, we mustn't stare,
We mustn't start, or grow the slightest teary
But only slap the stooping back and query
"How many children have you?" "What's your line?"
And always comment on the answer, "Fine!"
The bald wear hats, the ones with dentures hold
Their lips a trifle tight, the fat ones fold
The flesh in so that it won't be apparent. . . .
Be kind, we tell ourselves, and be forbearant,
And afterward let not a moment pass:
Go home and look into the looking glass.

Henry Martin

"Dear Classmate: Old Annual Giving time is here again, so whip out your checkbook and rush off a fat one to us. The sooner you do this the faster we'll get off your neck with repeated mailings and frequent phone calls and that's a promise.

      Sincerely yours,

      Binkey Toddwyler, '48 Fund Chairman"

The Final Final Exam

David Newman and Robert Benton

A SENTIMENTAL EDUCATION

The things you really learn in college have very little to do with academic subjects. You learn to be on your own, how to cope with women, how to grow up, how to stop making a fool of yourself and things like that. The classic cliché is "finding yourself." Whether you have gone or are now going to college, have you found yourself? Or are you still looking? When old alums look back on college days with that sentimental gleam in the eye, they don't remember the dates of the War of the Roses. One doesn't feel that pang in the heart over a Chem. exam once aced. No, what one remembers fondly is college life: learning about girls, getting away from home and testing his wings, being exposed to brilliant teachers for the first time, living with strangers who became friends. And all that good old bushwa. Here is a test on the important aspects of college life, then. Take it and see where you stand. But no cheating, or you'll be expelled from life itself.

Test One: School Spirit

This is a MULTIPLE CHOICE test. Pick the answer that best completes the statement. Think before you answer. Do not trust your first impulse. Anyone who trusts his first impulse hasn't found himself yet.

1. Now that you are President of the student body, you should
   (a) call the Dean of Men by his nickname.
   (b) write the Governor of the state that you will be looking for a job next year.
   (c) ask your daddy for a bigger allowance.
2. Now that you are a cheerleader, you should
   (a) get a haircut.
   (b) stop asking the coach if you can play.
   (c) kill yourself.
3. Now that you are in a fraternity, you should
   (a) stop talking to foreign students.
   (b) learn a trade.
   (c) get out.
4. Now that you are center on the basketball team, you should
   (a) take a bribe.

(b) switch your major from Calculus to Hotel Management.

(c) insist that they give you a red sports car.

Test Two: Teachers

This is a SHORT ANSWER quiz. Answer the questions in one sentence. Do not answer the question if you don't know the answer, jerk. You have five minutes before papers will be collected. Ready, go.

1. If your math instructor says you are a bright kid, but he's afraid you'll have to take a C in the course because that's the way the curve falls, what do you say?
2. There are three discussion sections open in your history lecture. Should you take the good one, meeting at 8:00 in the morning, or the bad ones, meeting at 2:00 in the afternoon?
3. You are a B student in English and your section head says, "I want to see you in my office this afternoon. Bring a copy of the August, 1957, Kenyon Review with you, the one with Richman's article on Henry James. I *know* you happen to have that issue, young man." What's going to

happen to you and how will you explain it to your father?
4. Why does your Psych. professor twitch like that?
5. You fall asleep in the back row of your astronomy lecture. You are awakened by the genial old prof rapping you on the skull with his pointer. Everybody is laughing. What should you say to the genial old prof?
6. What's going on between your Sociology instructor and the secretary in the Sociology Department?
7. Is it ethical to cheat in your Ethics exam?
8. You find that you have filled only four pages of your final exam blue book. What do you write at the end to convince the grader that you deserve an A for being concise?
9. If he's so smart, why is he only making $7,000 a year?
10. At a local beer hall you see your Physics professor completely blotto with a woman who is not his wife. You are failing his course. What is the proper form of greeting?

STUDY GUIDE I

Here are the important rationalizations. They will work for any student.

1. I'm not undermining my education by cheating on this history exam, because history isn't my *major*, for God's sake.
2. It isn't apple-polishing to have coffee with my professor after class. I'll probably learn something.
3. It isn't that I don't want to go on this protest march to the state capital, but I have a lot of studying to do this weekend and I can't neglect my education.
4. So what if I flunk out? I could learn a lot more about what really counts by hitchhiking around the country.
5. Let them laugh at me for being a virgin. I know that sex is probably more beautiful if you're really in *love* with somebody.
6. It would be better to cut the exam than to answer the questions wrong, wouldn't it?
7. It's a good thing no fraternity pledged me. All those guys do is drink beer and party all the time, anyway.
8. Maybe I picked the wrong college, maybe that's the trouble.
9. If I go to the movies now it will refresh my mind so I can study better later.

Test Three: Room-mates

This is a FILL IN THE BLANKS test. Read the statements carefully and supply the missing parts. Avoid slang. Be precise in your wording. If extra paper is needed, you are in trouble, Charlie.

1. Your girl is up at your college apartment. You have just finished dinner. You are necking on the ratty couch. It is fun. Suddenly you hear a key in the front door. In comes your room-mate, who was supposed to be studying at the library that night. "I won't bother you," he says, "but I just couldn't concentrate there. I'll just sit here at my desk and work. Don't pay any attention to me." You say to him, "_____ _____ _____," and your girl locks herself in the bathroom and cries.

2. Your room-mate tells you that some guys in his Chem. 203 class are coming over to seminar before an exam. "Will you

please pick up all your crap, you slob?" he says to you, pointing to old socks, shirts, torn paper and other of your effects strewn casually about the apartment. You tell him if his damn friends don't like it, they can go somewhere else. You tell him *you* never make demands on him when *your* friends come over. But he tells you, and he yells, too, that if your junk isn't cleaned up in an hour, he will throw it all out the window. So you say, "____ _____ _____ _____," and he almost throws *you* out the window.

3. Your room-mate has good study habits, which you of course have not. Every night he studies until precisely 11:00, when he stops, stacks his books and papers neatly on his desk, puts on his pajamas, slippers and Scotch plaid bathrobe, brushes his teeth and gets into bed. Then he reads a bit in his Book-of-the-Month Club selection before retiring. One night you come home from the girls' dormitory where you have just dropped off your date at 11:00. You have an exam the next day, so you begin typing up your notes. It's easier to work with music playing, so you turn on the radio. "Knock it off!" yells your room-mate. "The hell with you!" you cry. "I have an exam tomorrow."

He grabs your radio and ____ _____ _____ _____ _____, so you pick up his neatly stacked papers and ____ _____ _____ _____. The next day you cut the exam.

4. You are looking for your hairbrush and you finally find it at the bottom of your room-mate's shaving kit. You tell him not to use your damn brush. He says, "Why not? Your girl uses it sometimes." You say, "_____ _____ _____ _____," but you don't tell your girl friend you said it.

5. If you have made twice as many phone calls in the last month as your room-mate, but he has drunk most of the milk, and your girl friend jammed the record player which cost $6.38 to fix, but your room-mate's friend spilled grape juice on the couch which will be deducted from the breakage fee by the landlord, then you owe him _____. Or does he owe you?

STUDY GUIDE II

These are the ten *major crises* you will surely face in your college career. If you can master these, you are ready to go out in the world. Memorize them.

1. In the final semester of your senior year the registration office calls you and asks if you realize that you need 4 ½ more hours of Social Science credit in order to graduate.
2. A big athlete in your fraternity is about to whack you on the behind with an oak paddle.
3. You sit down to your first meal at a dormitory and find a strange gelatin mold on a lettuce leaf. You are supposed to eat that.
4. You have a flat tire and consequently get your girl back to her dorm two hours after curfew.
5. At a folk-song hootenanny with all of the sharp kids on campus, you sing the wrong words to *John Henry.*
6. The students, 3000 strong, stage a spring riot and panty raid on campus. During the melee the campus cops grab three students as an example and prepare to prosecute them fully. You are one of the three.
7. You study for weeks for your final exam and when you look at the first question you haven't got the slightest idea what it means.
8. You walk into the office of the literary magazine wearing your fraternity blazer.
9. The girl you used to date in your hometown comes up as a freshman and spreads malicious gossip around the girls' dorm about your past.
10. You wake up after your first big party and find not a hangover as you expected. You find you are still drunk.

Test Four: Parties

This is a MATCH AND MATE test. In the column on the left are listed all the different types of parties that occur in college. In the column on the right are listed all the things that are bound to happen to you when you go to college parties. Match the proper party with the proper event. Be careful. Erasures will be counted against you.

PARTIES	INCIDENTS
Faculty Cocktail Party	You throw up.
President's Tea	You move in on your best friend's girl.
Fraternity Beer Blast	You break up with your fiancée.
Homecoming Weekend Dance	You fall into the punch bowl.
Sorority Party	You lose your virginity.
Spring Mardi Gras	You tell off your Poli. Sci. professor.
All-night Apartment Party	Your best friend moves in on your girl.
Beach House Weekend Party	You propose to a professor's wife. She accepts.
Drama Students Cast Party	You almost drown.
Serenade	You get kicked out of the party.
Artsy-Craftsy Party	You do your James Cagney imitation.
Fraternity Initiation Banquet	You get locked in the bathroom.
Parents Day Dinner	You set fire to four girls' hair.
Post-Football Game Celebration	You get expelled.

STUDY GUIDE III

Here are the things you must learn to say to women. Without them you are nothing.

1. "I used to be just like Holden Caulfield, if you know what I mean."
2. "How do I know you really love me if you won't prove it, huh?"
3. "Oh, I took that class already. I'll lend you all my notes."
4. "Come on, baby, chug-a-lug."
5. "I'm really a very sensitive person, except nobody knows it."
6. "Something about you reminds me of Natalie Wood, kind of."
7. "Actually I had a very moral upbringing."
8. "Next year I'm going to bring my car up. It's a TR4."
9. "I'm not *pawing* you. I'm in love with you."
10. "We've both outgrown Ingmar Bergman. In a sense, we've matured together."

Test Five: Parents

This is a TRUE OR FALSE test. Read the statements carefully. Then answer whether the conclusions are true (correct) or false (incorrect). Do not be afraid your answers will reflect on your personal problems. No one will know. These tests are graded by an I.B.M. machine that knows when to keep its mouth shut.

1. Your parents are visiting you at college for the weekend. You invite them to have breakfast at your place. When they arrive, they find your girl friend busily preparing pancakes and bacon. Your mother says to her, "My, what pretty pajamas you have."

   TRUE   FALSE   (circle one)

2. You are about to go away to college. Your father takes you aside and says, "Son, I was a young man myself once. I know how you young men are. Heh-heh. But remember, son, there are two different kinds of girls. Good girls and bad girls. Don't get a good girl in trouble, son. As for bad girls, you're on your own. Heh-heh."

   TRUE   FALSE   (circle one)

3. You write home and tell your father that you have decided not to go into medical school, but instead are switching your major to Music Theory and Composition. He answers, "I

understand, son. You know what is best for you. As long as it makes you happy, it makes your mother and me happy, too. Do what you want."

   TRUE   FALSE   (CIRCLE ONE)

4. Your father comes up for the weekend. He asks you to come along while he visits his old fraternity house. When you get there, you find your girl friend outside picketing the fraternity because it bars Negroes. Your father says, "Son, I like that girl. She has a lot of spunk."

   TRUE   FALSE   (circle one)

Test Six: Girls

This is the part you'll be most heavily graded on, forever. It is a READING COMPREHENSION test. Read the paragraphs very carefully, very carefully. Do not rush. Then think about them. Then answer the questions below, based on what you have learned from the paragraph. Your answers should be as long as necessary and of the stuff of life and love, throbbing, beating, wonderful. If you have any questions, forget it.

1. You are going with a girl in college. She is cute. She is a little bit chubby, but cute anyway. She is a Voice major in Music School (alto). She comes from a

different part of the country than you do. She is of a different religious faith. All your friends like her and think she has a "terrific personality." They are right. You wonder whether you need a chubby, cute girl of a different faith from another part of the country with a terrific personality, but since she thinks you are so great, you tend to stop thinking about it. One night at a party she gets a little loaded and tells your best friend's girl friend that she thinks you and she will get married. Before the party is over, the word gets back to you. You are terrified. You think maybe she's right and decide to join the Army or the Peace Corps. You take her home and don't even kiss her good night. You never call her up again.

a. Should you ask for your copy of *Lord of the Flies* back?

b. Is it still possible to get a date with her room-mate whom you always secretly liked better?

c. Are you a cad or just a chicken?

d. Can you legitimately call this "an affair" even though you only kissed her on the neck a few times?

e. Is there a comma error in sentence four of the above paragraph?

2. You are going with a beautiful co-ed. She is older than you and in a higher class. She is an Education major and not terribly bright. Mostly you neck with her. She thinks you are "an interesting boy." Her sorority sisters don't like you and convince her that she could do a lot better. One Saturday you take her to the football game. At half time she excuses herself to go get a hot dog. She never returns. You watch the rest of the game in misery. On the way home, you see her walking with one of the guys on the varsity squad.

a. Is your date for the movies still on for tonight?

b. Is there something wrong with the way you neck?

c. Should you ask for your copy of *Lord of the Flies* back?

d. Should you spend the next year getting in shape so you can make the team next time and then she'll be sorry?

e. Can you get a good novel out of this experience?

3. You are a senior in college and you have really fallen in love this time. She is in Nursing School. You plan to get married. She can support you through graduate school, you think. Your family thinks she's great. Her family thinks you are a shiftless bum. They tell

her not to waste her life on you. Her father comes up and warns you to stay away from his daughter or there'll be trouble. You hear that your draft board may be calling you soon. You also learn that your older brother's marriage just broke up. That night your girl calls you and suggests that you elope the next day.

a. Can you cut English 381 tomorrow without getting in trouble?

b. Will you ever be able to call her father "Dad"?

c. Is it not true, in fact, that you are a shiftless bum?

d. If she gets pregnant fast, can you get an Army deferment?

e. Come to think of it, are you sure you want to get married?

Garry Trudeau

Turning Back to the Campus

Russell Baker

Rob Bascomburger is not your ordinary overeducated, overtrained college boy writing sniveling letters to the editor and complaining to Government charity officials because he cannot find a job. Rob is the kind of young man who does something about it, as his letter here illustrates:

I am writing to solicit your support for an entirely new kind of American institution. I propose to call it uncollege. Its tasks will be diseducation and detraining. The need for such an institution is desperate. Its contributions to American life will be immense. Please bear with me while I outline the case.

I have been out of college for more than a year now and am still unemployed. I am informed that my jobless condition results from a miscalculation as to the requirements of the contemporary work force which were made at the time I undertook my education.

At that time, the projections foresaw the need for a much larger force of highly educated, highly trained workers than the economy, in fact, now requires. Having become highly trained and highly educated, I now find myself, along with hundreds of thousands of other young persons, economically superfluous. All of us with our overeducated, overtrained mentalities have become surplus people and, therefore, disposable.

When applying for work which requires little training and less education, I am repeatedly rejected on the ground that overeducation and overtraining disqualify me for the job. Personnel scientists have apparently learned that such people adjust poorly to jobs that do not fulfill their expectations and give them outlets for their skills. One gathers that such persons are potentially dangerous malcontents likely to sow unrest, if not revolution, among the less educated and less highly trained workers.

Whatever the explanation, many of us remain "unemployable." Thus we swell the unemployment figures and place a financial drain on the rest of the work force. The solution should be obvious, but until now no one has undertaken to provide it.

It is to establish the uncollege.

I am persuaded that within months of its opening, the first uncollege could have an enrollment of 30,000 college graduates eagerly seeking to have the defects of their college educations corrected.

At uncollege, these wretched graduates would undergo four years of diseducation. At the end of that period, if they had successfully disachieved down to the high school level, they would be awarded certificates attesting to their fitness to enter the labor force.

Highly trained graduate students, of course, would be required to undergo three additional years of detraining after passing their rigorous four years of diseducation. A certificate of detraining would, of course, be far more difficult to obtain than a simple diseducation diploma. Candidates might, for example, have to be able to demonstrate an inability to do simple sums at a cash register like their working comrades who are already in the labor force.

How, you will ask, can such an ambitious undertaking be established? At first blush, the costs would seem prohibitive. We shall need a large faculty highly trained in detraining and diseducating. These would not be called professors, but "stupidifiers." We would need extensive plans to give the destudent body every opportunity to master woolgathering, repetitive error, clockwatching, time killing, indifference, incompetence, passivity and the hundreds of other valuable nonskills essential to rescue them from the ranks of the unemployable.

Can you doubt that the parents of America, who have already shown their eagerness to mortgage their lives to put their children through college so that they might become employable, will gladly accept more financial chains if they can save their young from the unemployability which college has inflicted upon them?

If parents balk at making a second trip to bankruptcy, we can bring the powerful force of guilt to bear on their bank accounts. Was it not the parents' sin of pride which led them to render their children unemployable by lavishing expensive college educations upon them? Do these parents not now owe it to their children to atone for their sins by shelling out?

Frankly, I believe we can get in on the ground floor of the mint if we move quickly. This is why I am offering you this splendid opportunity to invest now in the American bonanza of the future—uncollege. Remember, a little learning may be a dangerous thing, but a lot of learning ain't what makes the world go round no more.

Yours for enterprise,
Rob Bascomburger

Improbable Epitaph

Don Marquis

A REMARKABLE MAN
WAS SOLOMON GAY
WHO IS PLANTED
HERE
TILL THE JUDGMENT DAY.
WHEN HE FOUND
HE HAD NOTHING
IMPORTANT TO SAY
HE WOULD KEEP HIS MOUTH
SHUT
AND GO ON HIS WAY.

Acknowledgments

The editors and Fordham University Press herewith render thanks to the following artists, publishers, agents, and individuals whose interest, cooperation, and permission to reprint have made possible the preparation of *Hail to Thee, Okoboji U! A Humor Anthology on Higher Education*. All possible care has been taken to trace the ownership of every selection included and to make full acknowledgment for its use.

"My Philosophy." From *Getting Even* by Woody Allen. Copyright © 1969 by Woody Allen; Reprinted by permission of Random House, Inc.

"My Speech to the Graduates." From *Side Effects* by Woody Allen. Copyright © 1980 by Woody Allen. Reprinted by permission of Random House, Inc.

"The Curriculum," in *Going Around in Academic Circles.* McGraw-Hill. Copyright © 1965 by Richard Armour. Reprinted by permission of Kathleen S. Armour.

"The Degree," in *Going Around in Academic Circles.* McGraw-Hill. Copyright © 1965 by Richard Armour. Reprinted by permission of Kathleen S. Armour.

"Great Poets," in *It All Started with Freshman English.* McGraw-Hill. Copyright © 1973 by Richard Armour. Reprinted by permission of Kathleen S. Armour.

"How to Get In," in *Going Around in Academic Circles.* McGraw-Hill. Copyright © 1965 by Richard Armour. Reprinted by permission of Kathleen S. Armour.

"Lines Long after Pope, by a Reader of Freshman Themes," in *Light Armour: Playful Poems on Practically Everything.* McGraw Hill. Copyright © 1954 by Richard Armour. Reprinted by permission of Kathleen S. Armour.

"A Short History of Higher Education," in *Going Around in Academic Circles.* McGraw-Hill. Copyright © 1965 by Richard Armour. Reprinted by permission of Kathleen S. Armour.

"Twenty-Fifth Reunion," in *Light Armour: Playful Poems on Practically Everything.* McGraw-Hill. Copyright © 1965 by Richard Armour. Reprinted by permission of Kathleen S. Armour.

"Graffiti on a Washroom at M.I.T." by Mrs. Gene Arthur. Reprinted with permission from the May 1969 *Reader's Digest.* Copyright © 1969 by The Reader's Digest Assn., Inc.

"Theoretical Theories" by John Bailey. Reprinted from *The Saturday Evening Post* © 1952.

"Grooving with Academe" (June 4, 1978) by Russell Baker. Copyright © 1978 by The New York Times Company. Reprinted by permission.

"One Very Smart Tomato" (May 3, 1977) by Russell Baker. Copyright © 1977 by The New York Times Company. Reprinted by permission.

"Turning Back to the Campus" (December 18, 1976) by Russell Baker. Copyright © 1976 by The New York Times Company. Reprinted by permission.

"Marshyhope State University" by John Barth is retitled in this collection. The original title is "A: Lady Amherst to the Author." and "N: The Author to Lady Amherst." Reprinted by permission of The Putnam Publishing Group from *Letters* by John Barth. Copyright © 1979 by John Barth.

"How to Understand Music" from *The Benchley Roundup* by Robert Benchley. Copyright 1954 by Nathaniel Benchley. Reprinted by permission of HarperCollins Publishers.

"Shakespeare Explained" from *The Benchley Roundup* by Robert Benchley. Copyright 1954 by Nathaniel Benchley. Reprinted by permission of HarperCollins Publishers.

"The Faculty Meeting," in *The New Yorker*, August 16, 1982. Reprinted by permission © 1982 Jeremy Bernstein. Originally in *The New Yorker*.

"Professor Gulliver Grebe's Adventures among the Snarfs." From *My War with the Twentieth Century* by Pierre Berton. Copyright © 1965 Pierre Berton. Used by permission of Doubleday, a division of Bantam Doubleday Dell Publishing Group, Inc.

"Letters," in *Up the Family Tree* by Teresa Bloomingdale. Doubleday, 1981. Reprinted by permission of the author.

"Off to College," in *Up the Family Tree* by Teresa Bloomingdale. Doubleday, 1981. Reprinted by permission of the author.

"The Rich Scholar," in *Up the Family Tree* by Teresa Bloomingdale. Doubleday, 1981. Reprinted by permission of the author.

"Gather Round, Collegians." From *Now, Where Were We* by Roy Blount, Jr. Copyright © 1978, 1984, 1985, 1986, 1987, 1988, 1989 by Roy Blount, Jr. Reprinted by permission of Villard Books, a division of Random House, Inc.

"Thinking Black Holes Through" by Roy Blount, Jr. From *One Fell Soup* by Roy Blount, Jr. Copyright © 1980 by Roy Blount, Jr. First appeared in *New West*. By permission of Little, Brown and Company.

"The Truth about History" by Roy Blount, Jr. From *What Men Don't Tell Women* by Roy Blount, Jr. Copyright © 1984 by Roy Blount, Jr. By permission of Little, Brown and Company.

First published as "1976 and All That: The First Memorable History of America" by Caryl Brahms and Ned Sherrin in *Esquire*, September, 1975. Reprinted courtesy of the Hearst Corporation.

"The Shakespeare Interview" by Brock Brower in *Esquire's World of Humor*. Copyright 1964. Reprinted courtesy of the Hearst Corporation.

"There once lived a teacher named Dodd . . ." and "There once was a scholar named Fessor . . ." in *The Life of the Party* by Bennett Cerf. Garden City Books, 1956. Reprinted by permission of Phyllis Cerf Wagner.

"Parlez-vous Presidentialese?" by Richard Chait and Madeleine Green. Reprinted with permission from *Educational Record*, Vol. 71, No. 1 (1990), American Council on Education, Washington, DC.

"Faculties at Large" by John R. Clark in *College English* (February 1972). Copyright 1972 by the National Council of Teachers of English. Reprinted with permission.

"The sun goes up, the sun goes down. That's as deep as I get" by Richard Cline, in *The New Yorker* (February 25, 1991). Drawing by Cline; Copyright © 1991 The New Yorker Magazine, Inc.

"Professor Tattersall" by Peter De Vries. From *The Cats Pajamas & Witches Milk* by Peter De Vries. Copyright © 1968 by Peter De Vries. By permission of Little, Brown and Company.

"A Taste of Princeton" by Max Eastman in *From Humor to Harpers*, eds. John Fischer and Lucy Donaldson. Harpers, 1961. Reprinted by permission of Yvette Eastman.

"The Secret Life of Henry Harting" by Mark C. Ebersole in *The Chronicle of Higher Education* (April 9, 1973). Reprinted by permission of the author.

"Mr. Science." From *Write If You Get Work: The Best of Bob and Ray* by Bob Elliott & Ray Goulding. Copyright © 1975 by Robert B. Elliott and Raymond W. Goulding. Reprinted by permission of Random House, Inc.

"Webley I. Webster." From *Write If You Get Work: The Best of Bob and Ray* by Bob Elliott & Ray Goulding. Copyright © 1975 by Robert B. Elliott and Raymond W. Goulding. Reprinted by permission of Random House, Inc.

"The Groves of Academe: Deep, Deep Words," in *O Thou Improper, Thou Uncommon Noun* by Willard R. Espy. Potter, 1978. Reprinted by permission of the author.

"I'm intelligent and get nowhere." From *Feiffer: Jules Feiffer's America from Eisenhower to Reagan* by J. Feiffer, edit., S. Heller. Copyright © 1982 by Jules Feiffer. Reprinted by permission of Alfred A. Knopf, Inc.

"The professors discuss nuclear war." From *Feiffer: Jules Feiffer's America from Eisenhower to Reagan* by J. Feiffer, edit., S. Heller. Copyright © 1982 by Jules Feiffer. Reprinted by permission of Alfred A. Knopf, Inc.

"Students of the class of '58 . . ." From *Feiffer: Jules Feiffer's America from Eisenhower to Reagan* by J. Feiffer, edit., S. Heller. Copyright © 1982 by Jules Feiffer. Reprinted by permission of Alfred A. Knopf, Inc.

"Today's book is a rather bulky but promising . . ." From *Feiffer: Jules Feiffer's America from Eisenhower to Reagan* by Jules Feiffer, edit., S. Heller. Copyright © 1982 by Jules Feiffer. Reprinted by permission of Alfred A. Knopf, Inc.

"A Philosopher" by Sam Walter Foss in *The Oxford Book of American Light Verse,* ed. William Harmon. Oxford University Press, 1979.

"Sexual Harassment at Harvard: Three Letters." From *A View from the Stands* by John Kenneth Galbraith. Copyright © 1986 by John Kenneth Galbraith. Reprinted by permission of Houghton Mifflin Company. All rights reserved.

"Solemnity, Gloom and the Academic Style: A Reflection." From *A View from the Stands* by John Kenneth Galbraith. Copyright © 1986 by John Kenneth Galbraith. Reprinted by permission of Houghton Mifflin Company. All rights reserved.

"A Pure Mathematician" by Arthur Guiterman in *The Laughing Muse.* Harper & Brothers, 1915.

"Professor Gratt" by Donald Hall, in *Jiggery-Pokery: A Compendium of Double Dactyls.* Eds. Anthony Hecht and John Hollander. Atheneum, 1983. Reprinted by permission of the author.

"I know, but all promises are off when Daddy's writing his grant proposals," in *The New Yorker* (January 14, 1991). Drawing by Wm. Hamilton; Copyright © 1991 The New Yorker Magazine, Inc.

"President Robbins of Benton" by Randall Jarrell. From *Pictures from an Institution.* Farrar, Straus and Giroux, 1954. Used with permission of Mary Jarrell.

"The Cultured Girl Again" by Ben King, in *The Oxford Book of American Light Verse,* ed. William Harmon. Oxford University Press, New York, 1979.

"Catalog of Courses: Aquarius U. Non Campus Mentis" by John D. Kirwan in *National Review* (January 21, 1972) © 1972 by National Review, Inc., 150 East 35th Street, New York, NY 10016. Reprinted by permission.

"The Easy Road to Culture, Sort of" by Eric Larrabee, in *From Humor to Harpers,* eds. John Fischer and Lucy Donaldson. Harpers, 1961. Reprinted with permission of Eleanor Doermann Larrabee.

"Nonsense Botany" by Edward Lear, in *The Complete Nonsense of Edward Lear,* ed. Holbrook Jackson. Dover, 1951.

"Science" in *Metropolitan Life* by Fran Lebowitz. Copyright © 1974, 1975, 1976, 1977, 1978 by Fran Lebowitz. Used by permission of the publisher, Dutton, an imprint of New American Library, a division of Penguin Books USA Inc.

"Congratulations, and please have all bills paid before leaving . . ." by Henry Martin, in *The New Yorker* (June 12, 1971). Drawing by H. Martin; Copyright © 1971 The New Yorker Magazine, Inc.

"Dear Classmate: Old Annual Giving time is here again . . ." by Henry Martin, in *Good News Bad News*. Scribner's. © 1978 Henry R. Martin.

"President Gorman, distinguished faculty . . . impoverished parents . . . ," in *The New Yorker* (May 26, 1980). Drawing by H. Martin; Copyright © 1980 The New Yorker Magazine, Inc.

"So this is the hundred-thousand-dollar Wilson P. Donovan Chair . . . ," in *The New Yorker* (May 31, 1969). Drawing by H. Martin. Copyright © 1969 The New Yorker Magazine, Inc.

"Well, today I begin my wonderfully perceptive and cogent book . . . ," in *The New Yorker* (August 2, 1969). Drawing by H. Martin; Copyright © 1969 The New Yorker Magazine, Inc.

"The Boring Leading the Bored" by Steve Martin. Reprinted by permission of The Putnam Publishing Group from *Cruel Shoes* by Steve Martin. Copyright © 1979 by Steve Martin.

"Improbable Epitaph" by Don Marquis. Copyright 1946 by Doubleday, a division of Bantam Doubleday Dell Publishing Group, Inc. From *The Best of Don Marquis* by Don Marquis. Used by permission of Doubleday, a division of Bantam Doubleday Dell Publishing Group, Inc.

"The Rivercliff Golf Killings," copyright 1921, 1928, 1929, 1930, 1934, 1935, 1936 by Don Marquis. From *The Best of Don Marquis* by Don Marquis. Used by permission of Doubleday, a division of Bantam Doubleday Dell Publishing Group, Inc.

"The Universe and the Philosopher." From *Noah an' Jonah an' Cap'n John Smith* by Don Marquis. Copyright 1921 by D. Appleton & Co. Used by permission of the publisher, Dutton, an imprint of New American Library, a division of Penguin Books USA Inc.

"Jocelyn College" (retitled in the present collection) by Mary McCarthy, excerpt from "Ancient History," in *The Groves of Academe*, copyright 1952 and renewed 1980 by Mary McCarthy, reprinted by permission of Harcourt Brace Jovanovich, Inc.

"How Newton Discovered the Law of Gravitation," by James E. Miller. Reprinted from *A Stress Analysis of a Strapless Evening Gown*, ed. Robert A. Baker. Prentice-Hall, 1963. Used by permission of American Scientist.

"From the cyclotron of Berkeley to the labs of M.I.T. . . . ." by Frank Modell, in *The New Yorker Album of Drawings 1925–1975*. Viking Press, 1975. Drawing of Modell; © 1958, 1986 The New Yorker Magazine, Inc.

"Soby" by Wright Morris. From *What a Way to Go*. Atheneum, 1962. Reprinted by permission of Josephine Morris.

"Professor Pnin." From *Pnin* by Vladimir Nabokov. Copyright © 1989 by the Estate of Vladimir Nabokov. Reprinted by permission of Vintage Books, a Division of Random House Inc.

"Botanist, Aroint Thee." From *There's Always Another Windmill* by Odgen Nash. Copyright © 1968 by Ogden Nash. By permission of Little, Brown and Company.

"If He Scholars, Let Him Go," and "The Mind of Professor Primrose". From *Verses From 1929 On* by Ogden Nash. Copyright 1935, 1945 by Ogden Nash. Copyright © renewed 1973 by Frances Nash, Isabel Nash Eberstadt, and Linell Nash Smith. First appeared in *The New Yorker*. By permission of Little, Brown and Company.

For "Hell Only Breaks Loose Once" & "If Grant Had Been Drinking at Appomattox." Copr. © 1935 James Thurber. Copr. © 1963 Helen Thurber and Rosemary A. Thurber. From *The Middle-Aged Man on the Flying Trapeze*, published by Harper & Row.

For four drawings; "She's all I know about Bryn Mawr . . . ," "He doesn't know anything except the facts," "Capture of three physics professors" and "He knows all about art . . ." Copr. © 1943 James Thurber. Copr. © 1971 Helen Thurber and Rosemary A. Thurber. From *Men, Women and Dogs*, published by Harcourt Brace Jovanovich, Inc.

For "Prehistoric Animals of the Middle West." Copr. © 1948 James Thurber. Copr. © 1976 Helen Thurber and Rosemary A. Thurber. From *The Beast in Me* and *Other Animals*, published by Harcourt Brace Jovanovich, Inc.

For "The Philosopher and the Oyster." Copr. © 1956 James Thurber. Copr. © 1984 Helen Thurber. From *Further Fables for Our Time*, published by Simon & Shuster.

"Wherefore Art Thou Nittany?" by Calvin Trillin. From *If You Can't Say Something Nice*, published by Ticknor and Fields. Copyright © 1987 by Calvin Trillin.

"Holy Moses, will you look at these insipid faces?!" by G. B. Trudeau (1973); Doonesbury copyright 1973 G. B. Trudeau. Reprinted with permission of Universal Press Syndicate. All rights reserved.

"Interview of Professor Cavendish" by G. B. Trudeau, in *The Doonesbury Dossier: The Reagan Years*. Holt, Rinehart and Winston, 1984. Doonesbury copyright 1984 G. B. Trudeau. Reprinted with permission of Universal Press Syndicate. All rights reserved.

"More of President King" by G. B. Trudeau, in *The Doonesbury Dossier: The Reagan Years*. Holt, Rinehart and Winston, 1984. Doonesbury copyright 1984 G. B. Trudeau. Reprinted with permission of Universal Press Syndicate. All rights reserved.

"President King" by G. B. Trudeau, in *The Doonesbury Dossier: The Reagan Years*. Holt, Rinehart and Winston, 1984. Doonesbury copyright 1984 G. B. Trudeau. Reprinted with permission of Universal Press Syndicate. All rights reserved.

"President King at Commencement" by G. B. Trudeau, in *The Doonesbury Dossier: The Reagan Years*. Holt, Rinehart and Winston, 1984. Doonesbury copyright 1984 G. B. Trudeau. Reprinted with permission of Universal Press Syndicate. All rights reserved.

"Report on the Barnhouse Effect," from *Welcome to the Monkey House* by Kurt Vonnegut, Jr. Copyright © 1961 by Kurt Vonnegut, Jr. Used by permission of Dell Books, a division of Bantam Doubleday Dell Publishing Group, Inc.

"The Immortal Hair Trunk" by Mark Twain in *A Tramp Abroad*. Harper, 1903.

"Reforming Yale" by Mark Twain, in *Plymouth Rock and The Pilgrims*, ed. Charles Neider. Harper & Row, 1984.

"Alumni News" by Andrew Ward, in *The Atlantic* 237 (June 1976), pp. 92–93. Reprinted by permission of The Atlantic.

"Book Learning," from *One Man's Meat* by E. B. White. Copyright 1942 by E. B. White. Reprinted by permission of HarperCollins Publishers.

"Professor Piccard–After," from *The Second Tree from the Corner* by E. B. White. Copyright 1937 by E. B. White. Reprinted by permission of HarperCollins Publishers.

"Professor Piccard–Before," from *The Second Tree from the Corner* by E. B. White. Copyright 1937 by E. B. White. Reprinted by permission of HarperCollins Publishers.

"Memo from Osiris" by Gary Jay Williams, in *National Review* (September 28, 1973); © 1973 by National Review, Inc., 150 East 35th Street, New York, NY 10016. Reprinted by permission.